Praise for
Chains of Freedom

"I wrote the intro for *Chains*. In one of those crazy last-minute bits of confusion that sometimes strike when covers and books are in production, that useful information slipped from the cover—but I recommended this book in that intro, and I still recommend it. Rosen spent fifteen years working on this one: it's got a lot of action, and a great deal of an author's heart and soul. For those of you who read _Queen of Denial_, Rosen's last book, this is very different—different in everything but quality—proving that she's no one-trick pony. For those of you who like an author who can write different sorts of books—try this one.

"Does honesty and the fact she writes really good, wise, funny and serious books mean immediate, widely reputed success in the writing business? No. It's easier to sell something "just like" the last thing, and Rosen's just-like nothing else. Does it mean the books get distributed with grand advertising fanfare? No. So here we are. *I'm* putting out the word, because I believe in her. Buy this woman's books!"—C J Cherryh

"*Chains of Freedom* is the latest work from one of my favorite authors, Selina Rosen. From the first sentence I knew it would be a wild ride, and it kept me up way past my bedtime. Finally, a kick-ass character who isn't afraid to keep a rocket launcher by her bed at night. Besides being a top-notch thriller, the intimacy between the main characters far exceeds the standard fare of action-adventure. Not for wimps."—Mark Shepard

Praise for *Queen of Denial*

"*Queen* is funny and pointed. Ms. Rosen takes a Star-Trek-like plot, introducing the social ills of a world that could be our own, and attacks them with ruthless humor. Drewcila Qwah isn't your everyday heroine, with a foul mouth and almost every other bad habit known to civilization, but she's likeable and honest. *Queen* is a fast read with a satisfying conclusion."—Jody Lynn Nye

"Should appeal to anyone who loves a riotous, wickedly funny read."—Jane Fancher

"A rip-snorting space adventure the likes of which we don't see often enough these days!"—Lawrence Watt-Evans

"*Queen of Denial* is a freewheeling, fun and frantic space opera. It takes the usual conventions of pulp action Science Fiction and stands them on their head by featuring a female lead character as tough as any man in the book, and twice as smart."—Robert Weinberg, author of *The Termination Novel*

"Down-home science fiction? Redneck interstellar adventure? A full-throttle journey through the rural spaceways? Hey, it can happen and happen convincingly when the writer is damned authentic and has lived the tone she's writing about. That's Selina Rosen to a T. *Queen of Denial* cooks-not just with high energy and in-your-face attitude, but with the metaphorical flavors of grits, red beans and rice, and sweet potato pie. When MIR morphs into a cut-rate orbital truck stop for space jockeys who can't afford the International Space Station, Selina Rosen's debut novel is the sort of book that'll feature prominently in the spinner rack right between the displays of alien fuzzy dice and zero-gee mud flaps."—Ed Bryant

"*Queen of Denial* is a rollicking, high-spirited romp through space that grabs you by the shirt with the very first page and never lets go. The pace is breakneck, the humor bawdy, and the heroine one of the most original I've seen in years!"—K. D. Wentworth

CHAINS OF DESTRUCTION

(The second book in the Chains Trilogy)

by

Selina Rosen

Introduction by Claudia Christian,
Babylon 5 ®s Ivanova

For Doug & Helen,
It's all about
the body count!
Selina R.
2004

Meisha Merlin Publishing, Inc
Atlanta, GA

Chains of Destruction Copyright © 2002 by Selina Rosen

CHAINS OF DESTRUCTION

Published by Meisha Merlin Publishing, Inc.
PO Box 7
Decatur, GA   30031

Editing & interior layout by Stephen Pagel
Copyediting & proofreading by Josh Mitchell
Cover art by Charles Keegan
Cover design by Kevin Murphy

ISBN: 1-892065-69-X

http//www.MeishaMerlin.com

First MM Publishing edition: June 2002

Printed in the United States of America
0 9 8 7 6 5 4 3 2 1

For Meyer and Nick –
my kids whether they like it or not.

and

In memory of Chance Tyler Rosenzweig –
I never got to hold him, but I'll never let him go.

A personal introduction to Selina Rosen

So I'm sitting in a bar in some no name convention type hotel innocently playing trivial pursuit, when all of a sudden I hear this ear splitting, unbelievably loud and somewhat animated voice booming from another table. *My God*, I thought, *this woman is in her cups! AND she is having a bloody grand time!...I MUST meet this freak!* Well, a few thousand drinks and a couple hundred jokes later, I must say that I had found a new friend.

Selina is an amazing spirit, a woman who literally can suck the air, energy and life out of the best of us. She has left me aching from laughter and cursing her in the morning for keeping me up past my bed time.

I know she can write, and so do you, or else you wouldn't be reading this right now after having purchased the book...***correct?***

So read and enjoy *Chains of Destruction,* and remember as you are lost in the brilliant action scenes and caught up in the trials and tribulations of the memorable characters, that this was written by a woman who I out drank in a cheesy hotel in Houston Texas.

......Hey, Selina, wanna fight?!

Claudia Christian
California, Earth
January, 2002

Chains of Freedom in 900 Words or Less

The world went to hell in a hand basket and was taken over by an evil empire known as the Reliance. The Reliance has turned the Earth into a planet of agricultural slaves and gone off in search of better, more mineral- and resource-rich planets where they ran into a bipedal hominoid race known as Argies who were doing the same thing. The Reliance instantly decides not to share the universe and goes to war.

David Grant, a disgruntled farm work unit, gets incarcerated in a prison work camp for trying to talk the inhabitants of his village into rebelling. He escapes and, while fleeing, runs into RJ, a female ex-elite and the secret experiment of a man named Stewart who created her as part of a batch of genetically superior humanoids(GSHs). RJ has been confounding the Reliance, and in paticular one sector leader, Jago, by screwing with their supply lines. Her favorite weapon is a long length of chain she keeps wrapped around her body. David and RJ join forces and go to Alsterace, a city where all social, political and deformed citizens eventually wind up if they can actually escape the system, and here our two comrades start to build an army.

They assassinate a key government official who happens to have been the lover of Jessica Kirk, who, it turns out, is also one of Stewart's experimental batch. She goes after RJ and David with a vengeance, but they stay a step ahead of her while stealing the supplies they will need for an army.

Stewart kills himself to keep Jessica from finding out what he knows about RJ and Stewart's robot son Poley goes to be with his genetically superior "sister," RJ.

They start to assemble a ragtag band of followers and find Topaz, a 500-and-some-year-old man living in an old fortress with a supercomputer that he has made named Marge.

RJ falls in love with David, who rejects her, and she winds up falling in love with a half-Argy giant named Whitey Baldor.

With the help of Topaz, Marge and their newly formed army our heros do a huge simultaneous prison break across zone 2-A (formerly known as America), further angering Kirk, who decides to make a GSH of her very own, one capable of killing RJ.

David, who is proving that power corrupts, has also fallen in love with a half-Argy, a woman named Kirsty whose motives are anything but pure. She starts to twist David's mind against RJ and forms an evil alliance with Kirk.

At Jessica's orders, Kirsty talks David into taking half the population of Alsterace and going to fight an uprising in another city, a battle that RJ refuses to get into. When David and half the population leave, Jessica's GSH and the Reliance army descend on Alsterace, Whitey is killed as is over half the remaining population. Poley is decapitated and his head stolen, and RJ is badly wounded. The GSH takes her chain and departs. RJ is saved by an unlikely member of her entourage named Levits, a man who up till then has seemed to be mostly a self-serving coward.

David runs into a trap in which most of his people are killed, and he barely escapes with his life. When he gets back to where he left Kirsty, she's gone, and he realizes that she has duped him. He runs into her by accident and kills her. He starts back for Alsterace, where death and destruction meet him. He finds the remnants of the population at Topaz's fort, where RJ is only about half alive and completely despondent, and everyone hates him. To win redemption and bring RJ back he makes a trip to Capital—the lair of the triumphant Jessica Kirk—and steals back both RJ's Chain and Poley's head. Topaz reassembles the robot, RJ recovers and they make an assault on Capital, killing Jessica's GSH, destroying the city, and taking out one of Jessica's eyes.

However, Jessica survives…

CHAINS OF DESTRUCTION

Prologue

Jago stared at his two subordinates with utter contempt. They were beaten, battered and dripping filth all over his throne room. If he had been angry when he summoned them, he was furious upon seeing them. Especially Kirk. She stood there with an infuriating look of arrogance, as if she had done nothing wrong and dared him to say otherwise.

"You incompetent idiots!" Jago screamed, his blubber shaking in rage. "You utter fools! How could you let this happen?"

"We thought...We thought she was dead. We thought the rebellion had been utterly obliterated. We couldn't have foreseen this. How could we have prepared for something no one could have seen coming?" Governor-General Right tried to explain their actions, or lack thereof. He had spent a lifetime cultivating the fine art of appeasing those above him in rank, and considered himself quite good at it. Good enough, in fact, to talk his way out of even this most recent disaster. He had one problem, however, and Jago was looking right at her.

"What about you, Kirk? Enlighten me. This was *your* zone; ultimately *you're* responsible for what has happened there. What do you have to say for yourself? Anything? Anything at all!"

Jessica had been staring at a spot on the floor with the eye she had left after her encounter with RJ. She was focusing intently on a place where the dried blood had flaked off her hand and formed a small pile at her feet. Slowly she looked up at Jago with more contempt than even he could muster. She smiled, not at all a pleasant sight, and much to Right's dismay she began to speak.

"You giant, ugly, malignant toad! You asked us to accomplish the impossible, and we tried. We all tried. We bent and

broke laws; we did everything in our power. We went above
and beyond. Do you truly believe I would have let my guard
down for even a minute if I hadn't been sure she was dead? If
I had known RJ was alive I couldn't have slept; I couldn't have
eaten. RJ, self-righteous and indignant, confounded us for
years; an angry RJ will totally annihilate us.

"Look at me! Do I *look* like I didn't try? You can't beat RJ!
It can't be done!" Jessica's eye grew large and wild. "She's
like cockroaches. You think that you've killed her, but she
just comes back mutated and does bigger and badder things.
Hell, she robbed the bank at Satis and blew up Capital *after*
she was supposed to be dead."

Jago started to speak, but Jessica fixed him with a cold
stare that seemed to suck all the air out of him. "No! You
shut up. Just shut the hell up! I know what you plan to do to
us. You'll do what you always do to cover up your own in-
competence; you'll have us executed. Well, kill me if you
want. Kill me because I have failed. I only cared about one
thing, and I can't do it! She's always going to win." Jessica
started to laugh hysterically, and the guards moved closer to
her. She stopped laughing abruptly and fixed Jago with a stare.

"On second thought, I'm not ready to die." Suddenly she
leapt through the air, landing with her feet planted on Jago's
lap. Without stopping she knelt down, grabbed his head in a
headlock and gave it a cruel twist. She jumped back to the
floor as a gurgling sound left Jago's lips. The guards watched
in horror as he fell from his chair face first onto the floor. His
fat hadn't quite stopped rippling when Jessica put a hand to
her mouth in mock horror. "Oops!"

While the two rattled guards were trying to figure out what
had just happened and how, Jessica leapt at one, delivering a
killing kick to the bridge of his nose. Grabbing his weapon,
she turned and fired on the second guard as she ducked away
from the laser bolt he had just fired at her. Then she ran over
and grabbed his weapon as well. As she stood to her full height
she turned to look at Right.

"Are you coming?" she asked.

Right looked from her to the fallen body of Sector Leader Jago. "My God, Jessy...What the hell have you done?"

"I killed him. They were going to kill us anyway, Right. They can only kill me once, and I'm damned if I'm going to make it easy for them. The only question you should be asking yourself now is do you stand a better chance *with* me, or with*out* me?"

She offered him one of the lasers, and he took it, nodding. "I'm with you."

The two guards that had been stationed outside the chamber door chose that moment to rush in and die, but they had already sounded the general alarm.

As Kirk and Right ran through the halls of the palace, Right realized that this was what Jessica Kirk had been created for. She was a GSH, a genetically superior humanoid, created for battle. Putting her behind a desk had been a waste. She sensed would-be ambushes before they appeared and killed trained soldiers before they could fire a single shot. Perhaps if Jessica had been physically leading her troops instead of just giving orders she might have beaten RJ.

Maybe, but Right somehow doubted it. RJ and Jessica might have been made from the same genetic stuff, but RJ was superior even to Jessica. And RJ's troops were motivated by something the Reliance couldn't hope to understand, much less duplicate.

It was rather late in the game to think about any of that now—way too late. In a split second Jessica had turned them into the enemies of not just the rebellion but of the very Reliance they had spent their lives serving.

The Reliance was the single strongest power in the universe. He'd been taught this since birth. He didn't even know why they were running. Where the hell they were going? Was there any place in the universe remote enough that one of their enemies couldn't root them out? What sort of life could they possibly have? What sort of an existence could they hope to eke out when every hand was turned against them? He'd probably be better off dead, yet he didn't lower his weapon, and he never stopped fighting. There was something in him stronger than logic something that wanted to live.

The helicopter port was adequately manned and guarded for a normal attack, but this was no normal attack. This was an attack by a crazed madwoman with the strength and armor of a small tank. In seconds the way to the copter had been cleared, and Right found himself being dragged along behind her. She practically slung him into the copter before getting in herself and punching the ignition. They took off under a hail of laser fire, and Jessica started laughing. In moments they were out of range of even the laser cannons, and she just kept laughing. For one horrible moment Right was sure she was never going to stop.

"We've lost everything, Jessica, everything! We have nowhere to go and no one to turn to. We are fugitives with no real options. What's so damn funny about that?"

"I just realized something. Something so awful I don't even want to think it, but I can't help myself." She quit laughing. "It came to me when I was looking at fat, pompous, worthless Jago—just before I killed him—and I knew what people mean when they say *My blood ran cold,* because it did. Suddenly I knew something so true and so horrible that I was consumed by it for a moment." She started laughing again. In fact she laughed harder than she had before.

"What?! What do you know, Jessica?" Right demanded, losing his patience.

"We were on the wrong side," Jessica said, turning to look at him with no sign of laughter in her voice or in her features. "You, me, Jack. All on the wrong side. Worse still, I know this only now when I have made an enemy of the only person in the universe who is likely to be able to kill me, and I went after her not because she killed the man I loved. I never really loved Jack. I went after her with such a vengeance because she broke something I wasn't done playing with yet, and because she was *better* than I was. We're free, Right. Don't you get it? For the first time in our lives we have no one but ourselves to answer to."

"We probably won't live a week," Right mumbled.

"So? We'll live one week free. A whole week with no one to answer to and no orders to follow, and it will be the most wonderful week of our lives. This is it. This is what RJ and her goons were fighting for." Much to his dismay she started laughing again. "We were on the wrong side, Right. We were on the wrong side all the time."

Right cringed at the manic sound of her laughter as it echoed around the tiny cockpit. He took a deep breath and released it slowly, fighting panic. There was no doubt that she was now completely mad, so Right took no comfort in the knowledge that she was probably right.

Chapter One

When Governor General Right and Senator Jessica Kirk as-
sassinated Sector Leader Jago, they left Zone 2-A completely
without leadership. The Reliance quickly filled the empty positions with officers who were even more incompetent. Officers who didn't know or understand the Zone, and personnel
who had no idea how the rebels worked.

Taking immediate advantage of this total lack of compe-
tent leadership, RJ led her troops in one successful attack after
another. Like dominos, Reliance installations inside the Zone
fell before them. Within months, the Reliance pulled out of
zone 2-A altogether.

The Reliance never called it a defeat. Officially they simply decided that Zone 2-A had become an unprofitable ven-
ture, a liability. That it would cost more to make the zone
functional for the Reliance than it was worth.

They offered the New Alliance a treaty that neither side
ever signed. There was never a summit; the two sides never
met. Instead there was a silent agreement. The Reliance would
stay out of Zone 2-A as long as the New Alliance didn't attack Reliance installations outside the Zone. It was an agreement neither group trusted the other side to keep, so there was
at best a guarded truce, with both sides just waiting for the
other to step even one foot over the border.

To make sure the work units outside the zone understood
that the Reliance had actually won, the Reliance imposed harsh
economic sanctions against the Zone. When it was obvious
that the Zone didn't need them to survive, the Reliance built
a huge studio housing a fake Zone 2-A and broadcast daily
reports about how badly the free state was faring. According
to the Reliance, people in Zone 2-A were starving, and disease was rampant.

The Reliance turned a liability into an asset. The unrest that had started to erupt throughout the work units around the world came to an abrupt halt when they believed they would pay for their freedom with starvation and disease. They put down their weapons and went back to work when they saw the horrible "realities" of freedom.

Of course the Reliance reports were far from the truth. Life had never been any better in the land the New Alliance called New Freedom. There was plenty of food, plenty of clean water, and the people were free to do as they wanted.

In fact, that seemed to be their only real problem.

"I said," RJ repeated through tightly clenched teeth. "I abstain. As in I'm not voting."

"Why not?" Mickey asked. "We are all in agreement. If we do not set up a system of government soon, New Freedom will fall without the help of the Reliance. In the beginning, the people ran around like they were crazy engaging in every form of debauchery and pleasure. Just when we were all sure that they would kill each other they got tired of playing, and now they just sit all day waiting to be told what to do. They are so used to being ordered around they don't know how to act. They need some guidance, some rules and a purpose."

"He's right, RJ," Topaz started. "These people don't know what to do with their freedom. The zone is in ruins; institutions must be rebuilt. We need schools and hospitals, and we need people to be trained as doctors, nurses, and teachers. Even you must agree that we need a military of some kind to protect what we have won, or we have no chance of keeping it."

"I know all that, but I don't have to like it. You don't need my vote for it to pass, and I don't want to vote on this." She stood up. "In fact, I don't want to vote on anything. I'm not cut out for any of this rule-making crap! You guys do it, and call me when we have a war to fight."

She walked out. Both Levits and David started to follow her. When they came up even with each other they stopped and glared at one another, each challenging the other's right to go after RJ.

It was a power struggle that Topaz was tired of and not in the mood to deal with.

"We don't have time for any chest-pounding, gentlemen. We have decisions to make," Topaz said. "RJ has made hers, and we all know that no amount of coaxing is going to get her to change her mind."

Both men nodded and sat down.

The meeting went on for hours. In the end they decided that, since general voting was impossible to implement in a largely illiterate, mostly non-technological society, the inner circle would choose six people from each community to govern. Mickey was made President of New Freedom. He would solve problems that couldn't be solved at a community level with the help of the rest of the members of the inner circle and the supercomputer Marge.

Their first priority was civil defense. All citizens over the age of sixteen would be enlisted and armed. Once a week they would meet in the town squares across the country and drill to make sure that they were always combat-ready. The six governors of each community would double as drill Sergeants.

Each citizen would be required to give three days a month to community service in an effort to rebuild necessary military installations and power plants destroyed in the war. They would also build hospitals and schools. The first order of business would be to repair the viewing screens in each town. Then the viewing screens could be used to warn people of bad weather and other troubles and teach them necessary skills. Everything from reading to surgical techniques could be taught this way.

"I'll go tell RJ," David said as the meeting ended.

"I'll tell her," Levits hissed. "Why don't you go do what you're best at, turning good things into shit."

Topaz cleared his throat. "I'll tell RJ." For whatever reason they didn't argue with him.

Topaz took a deep breath and let it out. He thought he knew where to find her. He walked out of the ancient prison and out onto the wall that surrounded the old exercise yard. As expected RJ was standing at the very end, looking out across the water at the site that had once been a great city.

Topaz often thought of RJ as a ghost that haunted this place. Right now as she stood staring at something he knew was gone, her expression unreadable and her white hair blowing in the slight breeze, she looked the part.

He walked up to her, and, without waiting for her to acknowledge his presence, he told her all that had been decided in the meeting.

"It sounds feasible," RJ said in a noncommittal tone.

"You want to tell me what's wrong?" Topaz asked, gently putting a hand on her shoulder.

"Everything is futile." She sighed. "I have just realized that in civilization there is no true freedom, only degrees of enslavement. That eventually, try as you might to set it up so that it can't happen, governments take away most, if not all, rights. It is a natural progression over which the masses have very little control because you have taken control away from them for their own good. Anarchy doesn't work, therefore you have to build a government. People run a government. People in power become aware of their power, and if they don't, it's a sure bet that the ones who take over from them will.

"People have different likes and dislikes and different things that annoy them. They start out with obvious rules about not killing one another or stealing from each other, but before you know what has happened there will be rules about how fast people can drive, who they can drive with, what they can wear, eat, drink, watch. Who they can have sex with, who can reproduce and who can't...It's all just a matter of time. Governments start out doing just what's right, but "right" is subjective, and humanoids are easily swayed. Eventually, the New Alliance will turn into the Reliance, for no other reason than that each new group that comes to power would be annoyed by different things.

"Most type-E planets develop many different races through natural selection, and those races develop even more diverse cultures, religions and governments. But sooner or later the more plentiful or more progressive races take over the planet. One by one they kill off the less-powerful races until the planet is one race, one government. It happened on Argy, it happened here, and because of the Reliance and the Argy it is currently happening at an accelerated rate on dozens of worlds. They are killing off entire races and cultures, just as we killed off the different races and cultures on our own planet. We can slow them down, but we won't stop them because eventually our own people—the government that we are starting today—will finish the Reliance cause. They will, that is, if the Argies don't win. In the end, not even the entire universe is big enough for more than one race.

"Knowing the inevitability of history repeating itself, knowing that ultimately nothing I do will change anything in the long scheme of things, how can I go on doing, *anything?*"

Topaz sighed, mostly because, having lived as long as he had, he knew that all she said was true. "Because we have to try, RJ. That's what intelligent beings do. They try to make things better, make them different. They try to change the ultimate outcome."

"But they won't. No one can…"

"You can't know that, RJ. Perhaps no corrupt man will ever come to power in the New Alliance, we will utterly defeat the Reliance, and we will change the course of history," Topaz said.

RJ laughed then, though obviously not amused. "You forget what I am, old man. I know you don't believe what you just said any more than I do."

"True enough. But I do believe it's our duty to confound destiny, and if you and I can't do that, RJ, who the hell can?" Topaz challenged with very real determination. "Governments get huge, the people rebel and knock them down and the process starts all over again. We are doing our part by knocking down the Reliance. It's our part in history to be the ones to temporarily knock down the oppressors so that our descendents can become the oppressors. We are important, and what we're doing is important. We have to think about the *here and now*, we can't think about the distant future."

"How can you and I not think about the distant future? In all likelihood, barring some unbelievable disaster, we will still be around," RJ said looking at him for the first time.

Topaz smiled at her and had no problem at all holding her gaze, although most people quickly looked away. He rested his hands on her shoulders. "Then you and I may be able to make sure that it doesn't all go to hell in a hand basket. So what are you brooding about?"

RJ shrugged as Topaz removed his hands from her shoulders. "I...I don't know what's wrong with me, Topaz. I don't feel the way I used to feel about anything. I get confused; I never used to get confused. I find myself asking myself questions with no real answers. Some mornings when I wake up I don't want to get out of bed; I just want to lie there. I want time to stop and for me to be nowhere. I have no ambition to do anything. I've even gotten tired of looking for J-6. There was a time when I was consumed with revenge. When I wanted to see Jessica dead more than I wanted to live. Now, I think she's made a better hell for herself than I could ever make for her, and even if she hasn't, I just don't care anymore. I know she's left the planet, and there is a good chance she and Right are on some third-class planet right now drinking tea, ecstatically happy. And I just don't care. I want to. I want to be mad as hell. But I'm just not. Does any of that make any sense?"

Topaz took a deep breath and held it a moment before he let it out. It made perfect sense to him, but how did you explain to a genetically superior humanoid, who was capable of not only great feats of physical strength but was also an empath with an IQ that was so far off the charts it wasn't measurable, that she had suffered a nervous breakdown? That she was probably never going to feel like her old self again. He took the easy way out. "I think you're just still mourning your loss, RJ. It hasn't been that long since Whitey and the others died. I think you finally realized that killing Jessica Kirk isn't going to bring them back, and like you said, she's made her own hell."

RJ looked back across the water at the bare land on the other side. "I hope you're right, Topaz. I don't know how much longer I can go on feeling nothing. Nothing at all."

New Freedom had been free for two years. Its government was firmly established and was well on its way to running like a well-oiled machine. A machine that didn't need their constant attention and pampering.

The inner circle was quickly becoming unnecessary.

New Freedom had new leaders now, leaders that ran the country in as democratic a fashion as possible. It didn't need generals to run a war. They weren't at war. RJ was completely without direction and at least part of the reason was that there was really nothing that needed her personal attention. RJ was restless, and she was bored.

The others were perfectly happy to wallow in their success and freedom. They relished the notion of living out their lives here in the free zone, but then most of them weren't going to live as long as she was, and therefore didn't become bored as easily.

They also didn't seem to be worried about a simple truth that RJ was all too aware of. As long as the Reliance existed anywhere, in any form, it was only a matter of time till they came to reclaim Zone 2-A. The Reliance was the embodiment of greed. They would never be happy with some; they had to have all. It was the reason they were constantly locking horns with the Argies; they didn't want to share.

Of course, neither did the Argies.

RJ walked the wall of the ancient prison that now served as Capital for New Freedom. She looked out at where the city had once stood. Crews had bulldozed, burned and buried the debris. Now it was nothing but grass with a memorial to their fallen comrades where the building she had called home once stood. There were plans to start building businesses within the year, but for now there was nothing but plants and ghosts.

It had once been one of the most flamboyant cities in a free empire. It had once been the golden city by the bay, San Francisco. RJ had never seen the city in its heyday; by the time RJ had first seen it, it had already fallen into decay and become known as Alsterace. It had become a hole for Reliance outcasts to hide in. Everyone from the deformed and the discontented to the criminal had found a home in Alsterace—the last freehold in a repressive society.

It was here that they had started to build their army, and here that so many of their people had been killed. She'd almost died there, her lover had. The scars on the outside of her body had healed, but the scars on the inside were still fresh and raw.

Looking at the place where she had once been happy made her heart ache. Thinking of her loss made her hatred fester. It was a self-inflicted torture that she endured on a regular basis because it pleased her to feed her hate. Feeling the righteous anger burning inside her was sometimes the only way that she knew she was still alive. It seemed to be the only emotion she was capable of sustaining for more than a few moments.

She could hear the roar coming from inside the building. No doubt yet another toast. Inside they celebrated two years of New Freedom. Out here she grieved for all that she had lost and wondered if she would ever feel like celebrating again.

It was hard to feel like cheering when your heart felt empty and cold. When you longed to talk to a friend who wasn't there, or hold a lover who was long dead.

She reached into her pocket and drew out a small resin cube. Embedded in the cube was Jessica Kirk's eye. The one RJ had knocked out with her chain when they had fought. She looked at the cube, and it looked back, and she felt strangely comforted.

It was high time that she tried to get back to her old self, quit moping around and letting one day follow the last. It was time for her to do something even if it was wrong

The party roared all around him, and it was pretty clear that it wasn't going to wrap up any time in the near future. The "President" was stoned out of his gourd.

He slapped David on the ass, which was as high as he could reach, and screamed, "Come on, David, join the party!"

David just glared at him. Mickey shrugged as if to say that was as much effort as he was going to waste on David, and then he stumbled back into the middle of the party.

David wasn't in a party mood; of course he could scarcely remember the last time he was. There had been a time when he had been the life of the party, with a new girl every day.

Those times were long gone, and these days even smiling was an effort for him. His guilt wouldn't allow him any happiness, and it didn't help that most of the people who surrounded him didn't think he deserved any, either.

RJ had once told him that remembering everything was more a curse than a blessing. At the time he hadn't understood what she'd meant. Now he remembered things he couldn't forget no matter how hard he tried. How could he forget that it was through no small effort of his own that so many of his friends and comrades had died? He had trusted the wrong person and turned his back on RJ. They had all paid for his acts of ignorance and disloyalty. His sin of self-importance had been redeemed in the blood of the brave and the innocent.

He had lived.

Lived to feel the stares of his former friends boring into him like daggers filled with hate and loathing. Lived to see Alsterace on fire and RJ broken, battered and barely alive. She had healed, but there was something missing. The spark of humanity she had carefully cultivated had withered and died, and RJ had returned to the cold, calculating military bitch she had been when he first ran into her in the forest on the day of their fateful meeting. All business, all drive, with little patience or time for things she considered frivolous.

The only difference, in fact, seemed to be that RJ no longer possessed any sense of self-preservation. She would jump into a situation without being sure she could jump back out again. She just didn't seem to care what happened to her, or anyone else for that matter. She had become self-destructive, and God pity the fool that got caught in the fallout.

How could he forget what he had done when seeing her and what she had become was a constant reminder of the biggest mistake he had ever made? When he knew that she had neither forgotten nor forgiven. RJ tolerated him; he had no delusions that she now harbored any warm feelings for him whatsoever. Levits was now clearly her right-hand man, and while they fought and argued constantly, it was clear that if it could be said that she actually felt real affection for anyone *living*, it was for Levits. Topaz had become her confidante, the only one she ever really talked to, and they shared something the rest of them couldn't really understand—immortality. Her "brother" Poley took care of whatever other emotional attachments she needed.

There was no room for him in her life, and nowhere else for him to go.

David noticed that RJ was conspicuously, but not surprisingly, absent from the festivities. He knew where to find her. He tried to sneak out without being noticed. Unfortunately the drunken "President" noticed him moving towards the door.

"Where you going, David?" he asked in a slurred voice as David walked past him.

David looked down at him. "I'm not really in a party mood, Mickey. I thought I'd go find RJ," David explained.

Mickey looked around. Apparently he hadn't noticed that RJ was missing till David pointed it out.

"Maybe it's better to let sleeping dogs lie, David," Mickey said in a moment of sobriety.

"Maybe," David shrugged and kept going.

Mickey watched David go with a frown.

"Where's David off to?" Topaz asked. Mickey jumped a little. "Sorry, Mr. President," Topaz said, a hint of laughter in his voice.

"It's all right; I was just thinking," Mickey said. "David went to find RJ. He said he wasn't in a party mood. I guess she wasn't, either," Mickey said sadly.

"They'll find their way back, Mickey," Topaz said in a comforting tone.

"How, Topaz? When? It's been years. RJ takes no joy in anything, and David can't forgive himself until RJ's happy. I used to believe that time healed all wounds, but I'm beginning to think that not even RJ has that much time," Mickey said.

Topaz thought he was awfully insightful for a drunken midget. "Enough already! No need for us all to be maudlin. It's a party, back to the celebration." Topaz shoved Mickey in the direction of the party and then went off in search of a woman who was easy. He didn't have to look very hard.

David walked out on the wall and joined RJ in looking at the mainland. If she had been pacing it wouldn't have been so bad. Pacing meant she was thinking. The fact that she was just standing and staring meant she was wallowing in her grief, and his guilt was immediately intensified.

He had been standing there quite a while when she said without looking at him, "I've made up my mind about something."

David held his breath. He wasn't sure he wanted to hear. Finally he asked, "About what?"

"I can't stay here anymore. It's time I make my next move."

"You have searched the entire planet looking for Jessica…" David started.

"I've given up on that…At least for the moment. I have another plan in mind," RJ said thoughtfully, almost as if she was talking to herself more than him.

"What would that be?" David asked hardly daring to breathe.

"Well, first I have to get up there," she said pointing upwards.

"The moon?" David asked following the direction her finger indicated.

"Yes," RJ said nodding her head. "It's really not all that hard. All I have to do is break into a Reliance shipping base and hijack their trans-mat station for a couple of minutes." She had that look in her eyes that she got just before she went into battle. She was almost happy, and this made David smile. "It's all so easy I don't know why I didn't think of it before."

David was sure that there was nothing *easy* about *it* whatever *it* might be. He was just as sure that she could do it. But she wasn't going to do it alone. She wasn't the only one who was tired of sitting around and doing nothing.

Chapter Two

Janad looked around the ship at her fellow passengers. *Passengers, ha!* They were prisoners; that's what they were. These idiots may have bought the bill of goods the priests sold them, but Janad wasn't about to. She might not be all that bright, but she most certainly knew the difference between when she wanted to do something and when she was forced to do it.

The priests crawled out of their temples and gave long speeches about civic duty and everyone doing their part. A few days later armed aliens marched into the village bearing gifts and started picking and choosing all the best warriors. They loaded the warriors into a box from which they vanished, and when they reappeared they were on a man-made space station where they were poked, prodded, injected and herded into starships like common livestock. The aliens explained that they were being transferred to another planet to fight and die in another people's war—whether they liked it or not. It didn't take a genius to figure out that they weren't making an informed decision; they were slaves.

The Reliance had traded goods with her planet for generations, and now they were trading for slaves. She hoped the priests had at least traded them for something that would help the people of her village and not just more baubles for them to horde in their temples

Janad didn't want to be a slave. She didn't care that they called it civic duty or promised financial gain for her clan members back on her home planet; she'd wanted no part of it. She was a hunter, a warrior, and she wasn't used to confined places. She wasn't even really used to walls.

The aliens hadn't left them much choice. The aliens chose you, the priests blessed you, and you got into the box or they shot you with a weapon that spit light and bored right through your body. There was no escape, at least not realistically.

They were the chosen, promised by the priests a destiny of greatness, and so they sat here in this ship waiting to land on a world they knew nothing about. About to be forced to fight a battle that wasn't theirs. To die on a strange world for the glory of an alien power.

Look at the fools smiling and laughing. They're too stupid to realize the implications. So what if our planet isn't the most happening place in the galaxy? Who cares if we're always fighting amongst ourselves and we spend all the time we aren't fighting working? At least it's home. You just don't leave home without a fight.

Of course her attitude had done nothing except get her shackled to the wall of the ship while the rest of the "passengers" were left to roam freely.

Here he came again—the man she had taken to calling Shit-Head. She wished now that her mother hadn't forced her to learn the Reliance tongue in school. She was sure that it was one of the reasons she had been chosen as a slave. Besides, it meant that she could tell what the drooling bastard was saying.

He walked over smiling and showing a mouth full of jagged teeth in his yellow head.

"So, how's it going my little firebrand?"

"I'm just fine, Shit-Head," she spat back.

He laughed at her accent and the way she pronounced Reliance words. "You're a wild lot on Beta 4. Just what the Reliance needs to fight RJ and her band of rabble-rousers. Put them back in their place. You should relax a little. Don't you realize what you're being offered? You'll be a Reliance soldier with all the privileges that has to offer, and you don't even have to go through the ranks. It's quite an honor."

"Go use your breath on some of those idiots. Don't waste your speech on me, Shit-Head. I know what we are to you, and I know what our reward will be," Janad said. "If you get in my face again, I'll bite your nose off."

He frowned and then laughed hatefully. He ran his finger carefully down her face as if daring her to bite him. She tried and he jerked his hand quickly away.

"If you don't start singing a different tune before we get to Earth, you will be terminated," he informed her. "And it would be a terrible shame if I didn't get to fuck you at least once while you were still alive."

He thrust his hips in such a manner that she understood what "fuck" meant. It didn't take a genius to figure out what "terminated" meant, either.

"And if I'm not killed as soon as we land, I'll be sent to the front lines of your war zone, where I'll be killed. We're expendable bodies. I am a warrior; I know what you will do with us. You will send us in first to knock down their numbers before you send in your own people," Janad said. He gave her a startled look. "We're not *all* stupid. So save your lies for those of my people who believe the priests, and kill me now if it pleases you. If you don't kill me now, I shall surely kill you first chance I get, and my people...You may think we are all just stupid animals, but we are not stupid animals. It is only a matter of time till they figure out what I already know. We do not like to be tricked. Turn your backs on us, and you will find that you have two enemies instead of one."

His superior called for him, and he gave her an angry look and walked away.

She felt smug for a few seconds, but her triumphant feeling didn't last long. Shackled to the ship wall with no prospects for escape, her words sounded hollow even to herself. She was doomed; they only took the shackles off to let her go to the bathroom, and even then two armed guards accompanied her. She knew she was being made an example of, and as such any attempt on her part to escape would be met with immediate weapon fire. Their treatment of her made the others sure that they wanted to behave themselves, and if they killed her so much the better. She was nothing more than product to the Reliance, and expendable product at that.

Suddenly Janad grew impatient with herself. She was giving up too easily. She was a hunter, a warrior of the clan of Nond, village of Ducont, and nothing was impossible. Except...

If she got away, where would she go? The ship was huge; surely she could find somewhere to hide. She relaxed and started to form a plan.

She hollered till Shit-Head and another man came to take her to the bathroom. As the shackles came off she hit Shit-Head in the face with her fist. Then she spun, hitting his friend with a roundhouse kick in the knee joint that took him down. She took off at a dead run for the door. As laser fire struck all around her she ducked under the two guards who had run into the doorway, rolled across the floor and rose into a crouch. Quickly she checked the hall in both directions before she jumped to her feet and started running. A stray shot hit one of the guards who had run into the door-way, and they were all screaming at each other over whose fault it was, giving her a few seconds when their attention was everywhere but on her. She used the opportunity to run down the hallway she had entered. She had no idea where the hall went, but at least it was away from the angry guards who were now chasing her.

Somewhere someone turned on a siren; she had never heard anything like it before, but she knew it meant trouble for her. Knew that the sound was alerting more guards that she had escaped. She had to find a place to hide, and she had to find it quick. But the ship was not like the forest around her home, and hiding places were few and far between. She saw an open door and ran into a room filled with bunks. The ceiling was made of tiles, and Janad realized on examination that some of these opened. She saw one that looked loose and jumped up, shoving it through easily. She hung onto the edge only a moment before she pulled herself up into the space and closed the tile. Just in time—a troop of guards ran past below her.

The space was small, only about two feet tall and four feet wide. The length of it was filled with service cables and junction boxes, and was so long she couldn't make out the end. To make matter worse, the tiles were made of some flimsy material that wouldn't support her weight, so she was forced to straddle the tiles and crouch on the thin metal braces the tiles were set in to keep from falling through the ceiling. It certainly wasn't the most comfortable hiding place she had ever found. It was small, and the dust made her head hurt, but it would have to do till she could find something bigger.

She smiled as she looked at her surroundings. It wasn't the forests she was used to, but it was a forest of sorts. As long as she kept her wits about her she could stay alive. Maybe she could even get back to her planet and try to tell the others what was really happening. Of course she wasn't sure how *they* were going to stop the Reliance.

Within a few days she knew the guards' patterns, and she could get around the ship with little or no problem. She couldn't read their language, but there were pictures beside the words that were easily read. Not too hard to figure out which areas were restricted or dangerous. No problem finding bathrooms or the kitchen. She sneaked food, went to the bathroom whenever she needed, and she was only nearly caught once. Janad was actually enjoying herself; in a strange way this was the most exciting time of her life.

Then one day there was a lot of noise followed by some jerking that almost knocked her off her perch in the service area. Then the ship was still. She didn't know how she knew, but she knew they had stopped.

She watched from a hole she had drilled in a tile with a piece of wire as first her people and then the Reliance personnel left the ship. Hours later, having heard no further signs of life, she was sure that she was alone. She came out of hiding slowly and carefully and started to check out the ship, fearing a trap. With any luck they'd take this ship back to her planet with her stowed away on board. She'd sneak off the ship into the vanishing box, and once on the surface of her planet she would warn her people of the Reliance's plan.

Of course the real problem was that her people already knew about the Reliance's plans and were more than willing to go along with them because the priests had convinced them that they were performing the will of their God. Which of course they were because this is what he had said he wanted them to do. Janad wasn't at all sure that their God was really any sort of god at all. Of course she couldn't tell her people this, or they'd rise up and kill her as a blasphemer. Perhaps she was naive to think she could save her people. Perhaps she had better worry only about getting off this damn ship and back on her own planet. Perhaps she had better make saving her *own* ass the priority.

She found food and water, and had an entire ship to explore. It truly seemed that all she had to do was play the waiting game, and then the metal rolling things appeared. She saw one coming from the end of the hall and ducked into cover just in the nick of time.

She wasn't really sure what it was, but she gathered from its movements that it was, like herself, a hunter. It was box shaped and rolled on wheels. It also had metal arms and hands that looked more like claws. She had no doubt it could do some real damage if it got ahold of you.

Her village, in fact her whole planet, was primitive in many respects, but they'd all seen the space ships, and they'd seen the Reliance equipment. She knew what a machine was. She didn't know how it worked, but she knew what it was.

This one was a hunter that didn't need to sleep or eat. It was much harder to get around the metal rolling things than it had been to sneak around the Reliance soldiers.

The soldiers had given up even looking for her after a few hours, apparently deciding that as long as she wasn't doing any harm, hunting for her was simply more trouble than it was worth.

Not so the metal rolling things. They were hateful and relentless. She became convinced that they somehow knew she was on the ship and looked for her constantly.

It had ceased to be fun.

She lost track of time because she got very little sleep. What sleep she did get was filled with horrible nightmares. She was fortunate that the clumsy metal boxes, like most machines, made noise when they moved. It was the only warning she got. In her efforts to stay out of the claws of her metal demons she went all over the ship. She even tried to get off, but the doors would not open, and when she punched the buttons the metal things immediately came to where she was, and she was running for her life yet again.

She began to believe that she would never leave the ship. At least not alive.

Chapter Three

"Have you gone completely apeshit?!" Levits screamed at
RJ. "We have everything we need right here. We are living in
a free land. The country is just now getting on its feet. Things
have just started to calm down, to be normal, relaxing. Now
you want to go gallivanting across the universe on some freaking suicide mission!"

"It's not a suicide mission, and I'm not asking any of
you to go with me," RJ said as she calmly looked at her
immaculately groomed fingernails for any sign of dirt. She
was apparently indifferent to Levits' screaming. Of course
Levits talked in a scream most of the time, so it made a
certain sense that she had become anesthetized to it. "In
fact, it's an in-and-out sort of thing. After all, we have a
common enemy."

"Going to the Argies and asking for their help in over-
throwing the Reliance is complete and utter lunacy. These
aliens hate humans. They kill humans with wanton abandon. You can't trust the Argy." Levits punctuated his words
by pounding his fist into his palm.

RJ coughed loudly.

Levits gave her a curious look and then blushed. "I wasn't
talking about you, RJ. You're not one of them."

"Technically, I'm as much one of *them* as I am one of *you*,"
RJ said.

"Damn it, RJ, you know what I mean," Levits said hotly.

"Say whatever you like about the Argy, but they hate the
Reliance as much if not more than we do. That makes us
logical allies," RJ said.

"What if they don't see it that way?" Mickey asked.

"Then I'll persuade them," RJ said with a crooked grin.

"Wait a minute!" Something she had just said dawned on Levits. "You're planning to do this alone? Without us?"

"Well, dud! I thought I'd made that clear. However I won't be entirely alone; I'm taking Poley," RJ said.

"No!" Levits jumped to his feet and glared down at her. "Absolutely freaking NOT." He threw his arms around in wide arcs as if warding off her inconceivably stupid idea. "Your plan has just gone from stupid to bat-shit crazy."

RJ looked at him with raised eyebrows. "Strange, I don't remember asking your permission," she said coolly.

"Because you're a bitch!" Levits exclaimed.

"That's so mature. Isn't that mature?" RJ asked Topaz.

Topaz just shrugged. He certainly wasn't going to argue with her, but he for one had no intention of staying here if RJ and Poley were leaving.

Topaz knew it wasn't easy to be RJ. He also knew that at least part of her reason for wanting to take this particular course of action had very little to do with strategy and everything to do with getting away from the place which harbored so many painful memories for her. RJ didn't do anything small. A normal person might have moved to the next town; RJ wanted to go to another galaxy.

Levits was the most vocal of the group, not that RJ listened to him any better. Because Levits knew RJ was mostly ignoring him, he had reverted to screaming at the top of his lungs, as was his habit.

"Damn it, RJ! Would you listen to reason? You can't leave the planet right now; it's too soon. You can't do this with just Tin Pants, and none of the rest of us want to go."

"I want to go," Topaz said. "I think it'd be great fun."

Levits glared at him. "Shut the fuck up, old man!" he snarled out. Then he turned back to RJ. "This is just freaking insane! Ever since Whitey died and you damn near did, you don't seem to give a shit whether you live or die. This is just freaking bullshit! God damn it, RJ! Are you listening to me?" His face was now as red as the shirt he was wearing.

For answer RJ looked with great interest at the carving Poley had just handed her. Poley had taken to finding pieces of driftwood along the shore and carving them into geometric shapes. It wasn't very artistic, but considering what he was, it was quite an accomplishment.

"Now that is an excellent job. Would you look at that, boys? A perfect cube!" RJ said admiringly.

Poley grinned as broadly as his genetically engineered sister, at least as pleased with her as she was with her robotic brother.

Levits' anger hit the boiling point. "God damn you, RJ, you bitch freak!"

The silence that followed was almost tangible with everyone holding their breath waiting to see what RJ would do. RJ didn't really mind being called a bitch, but everyone knew she didn't like to be called a freak, which was a derogatory term for a GSH. This was of course exactly why Levits had said it. Although it was clear by the look on his face that he wished he hadn't said it now.

"You know what I think you need?" RJ asked.

"No what?" Levits asked with a lump in his throat.

"I big wet kiss." RJ stood up and moved towards him.

He backed away from her. "Now damn it, RJ…Damn it, I'm trying to have a serious discussion with you, and…"

"Shut up and kiss me," RJ said.

"Leaving our base, going across the universe on a suicide mission…I can't let you do that alone, RJ! It's just crazy…"

RJ pinned him against the wall and kissed him. He tried to push her away, which of course he couldn't do till she wanted him to. Everyone was laughing.

"Now, damn it, RJ, this isn't funny."

"Everyone else seems to think it is. If you're going to call me a bitch freak, you had better by God give me one hell of a kiss," RJ ordered.

Levits smiled in spite of himself. "You really are a bitch," he laughed.

"And you're really a bastard; so kiss me," RJ said. She moved her hips against him seductively.

He kissed her. They kissed long enough to make everyone else uncomfortable before they parted.

Topaz saw the look in Levits' eyes and the bulge in his pants, and knew at least one of them hadn't been playing.

"So, since we're all in agreement, I see no need to postpone my little trip. I say Poley and I leave a week from tomorrow." She turned and left.

Levits turned to look at the others. "Damn it all. Do you realize what she wants to do? She's talking about leaving Mickey in charge here, taking Poley and riding off to Argy to try to con the aliens into helping us kick the Reliance's ass. She's not happy to rid the zone of the Reliance, she's not even happy to kick them off the planet. She wants to kick them out of the universe and that...It's crazy; it can't be done."

"Well, she's not leaving me here. I can tell you that right now. But RJ's never wrong. If she thinks we should try to get the Argy on our side, I say that's what we do," David said.

"David...if she told us we should launch torpedoes from our butts you'd agree with her. If she just has to fight, then let us pick the next zone and take it on," Levits said. "Going into space...It's just crazy."

"I agree...I say no," Mickey said authoritatively. "RJ can't leave. Not now, not ever."

"My sister will do what she wants," Poley said, not looking up from the new carving he was working on. "None of you will be able to stop her."

"He's freaking right." Levits started pacing the room like a caged animal. "If she wants to go, then she's going, and there's no stopping her. Shit!"

"I understand why Mickey is so against RJ's plan," Topaz said. "Because of Mickey's position here he doesn't have the option of leaving. He doesn't want to lose his friends." Topaz fixed Levits with a stare. "I don't understand you, Levits...What's really bothering you?"

Levits stared daggers back at Topaz. "Don't try your pop psychology shit on me, old man. She wants to go, I say let her go. I'm staying right here. Rest of you saps hell-bent on joining her on her suicide mission go right ahead." His words sounded every bit like the crap that they were. They all knew that he'd swear he wasn't going right up till the last minute, and then, bitching all the way, he'd be the first to follow RJ where ever RJ was going, and the fact that they all knew he was just blowing pissed him off royally. He turned and stomped out of the room.

"Who shit in his cereal?" Poley asked. They all turned and stared at the robot. "What?" he asked with a shrug.

Exhaustion was starting to take its toll on Janad. The metal rolling thing had been almost upon her before she woke up, and she'd barely gotten away. She couldn't remember the last time she'd managed more than a few minutes sleep in a row, got to eat a whole protein bar at one sitting, or even gone to the bathroom without having to jump up and run to stay ahead of the relentless metal bastards.

She'd learned the hard way what would happen if they caught her. She hadn't moved fast enough, and one had shot a beam of light like the weapons she'd seen the Reliance soldiers use. It hit her arm, leaving a bad burn. Left untreated, it caused an equally bad fever.

She didn't know how much longer she could hold up.

"Because I don't want them to go, that's why!" RJ said insistently. "I don't want them with me."

"You said *them*. I'm assuming that means you're all right with me going, then," Topaz said.

"I understand your reasons for wanting to go…"

"You forget who the hell you're talking to!" Topaz said losing patience with her for the first time during their conversation. "I know *exactly* why you don't want them with you. *Because they're going to die.* You, me, Poley, we're not likely to die. But David and Levits will. You think if you remove them from your life now you won't have to live through losing them. But the truth is you'll just lose them sooner. Normal people die, RJ, and people like you and I have to learn to live with that. They want to go with you…"

"They don't want to go. David insists on going because he thinks he has to pay for his crime by suffering as much as I do, and Levits…" she laughed. "He doesn't want anything to do with any part of this mission. He is only now insisting on going for what you and I know is the most stupid of reasons…"

"Because he loves you," Topaz said with a gentle smile, "that's not such a stupid reason."

"That's not what I was going to say," RJ said nervously.

"But it's the truth. I'm not an empath, and I know it, so I know that you know," Topaz said gently.

RJ sighed. "The mission has a lot more chance of succeeding without them getting in the way."

"I disagree; I think it has a better chance of success with them," Topaz said.

"How so? Levits hates David, and he never wants to go into space again. David hates Levits, and he knows nothing about space or space travel. In a lot of ways he's still just a green work unit."

"Levits is a starship pilot…"

"Who's terrified of space and flying…"

"But he knows what he's doing, RJ. You're a quick study, but you've never actually flown a starship; he has. David thinks on his feet when his dick doesn't get in the way, and whether you want to believe it or not, you need them. Look at what you have accomplished together. True, there were setbacks. But together you freed a country," Topaz said.

RJ seemed to accept what he was saying. She sat down and ran her fingers through her hair before looking at him again. "But, Topaz…Don't you see? If they go with me there is a very good chance that they will never see Earth again. That they will never have normal lives. They could have that here, but only if I leave. I want them to be happy."

"Levits has already lost one woman that he loved. Do you really think he could survive losing another? As for David, I think he only lives for the chance of redeeming himself in your eyes. If you can look me in the eye and tell me that either of them will be happy if you leave them here, then I'll quit arguing with you right now."

RJ looked at Mickey, and Mickey looked at her. "You're leaving me here. Can't you see how that makes me feel? You're all going away, and I'm staying here."

"I will miss you, too, Mickey, but it's the only way. You're too important here...Besides, you have a life here. None of the rest of us really do. You have to stay here and have a normal life for all of us. You have to stay and be our eyes and ears here on Earth. Someone has to stay with Marge; someone has to maintain her."

"If you go..." he shook his head and tried not to cry. "I'll never see you again. I know that, RJ. I know when you leave that you'll never come back."

She knew he was probably right. "I may come back."

"No you won't. I know you won't." His tears fell then. "I know I have to stay, but I don't think you *have* to go. I think you *want* to go. That even Levits who is bitching and moaning *wants* to go. But you can't run from your pain, RJ. It won't stay here; it will follow you."

She nodded. "What can I say? You're right. I know you're right." She turned to look at the mainland. "But there is nothing for me here but pain, Mickey. I don't want to leave you behind, but I do *want* to go. I can't stay here. Something has happened to me, and I have to try and fix it because I don't like the way I feel."

"Why...Why did you make me President?" Mickey asked. "Surely I was not the best choice! Topaz, or David, or Levits...*you*."

"Me!" She laughed. "No, not me, Mickey, and not David. Never David. No one trusts David anymore. Topaz? We all know Topaz isn't playing with a full deck. Besides, he belongs to another time. And Levits? Levits has been in a leadership position before. Something went wrong, and he never wants to be in that position again. Don't you get it, Mickey? We're all crazies in one way or another. You're the only one of the inner circle that's sane—normal."

The little man laughed. "Me, normal! Look at me. I'm not even three feet tall."

"But your head is normal, Mickey. Your wants, needs and desires are normal. You're not filled with hate or fear of failure. You aren't consumed by grief or looking for things you haven't lost yet. When the chips were down, you came through. Under pressure you kept things going. The people know they can trust you if there is a crisis. They also know you're one of them; that they can trust you to do what's right."

Mickey dried his face. "I've never had to do any of it alone before."

"You're doing it alone now, Mickey," RJ said. "When is the last time the inner circle made a decision on policy? Besides, you won't be alone. You have a wonderful mate in Diana, you have surrounded yourself with capable people, and don't forget you'll have Marge. We'll be able to communicate over com-link most of the time."

Mickey nodded and swallowed hard. He couldn't make her feel bad about leaving because he realized she had to go, and the others had to go with her or *she* would be alone.

He mustered a smile. "At least say you'll try to come back to visit."

She nodded, her own tears spilling onto her cheeks. "I'll try." She hugged him tightly.

"Careful, RJ. You'll break me."

They both laughed and talked about something less serious—matters of state.

Topaz saw her walking on the wall and went to join her. She was brooding again.

"You know leaving won't change things," he said at her shoulder. She didn't jump; she'd known he was there. He wished just once he could sneak up on the bitch and scare her silly. "You can leave all that behind, but you can't run from what's inside you."

"So I've been told. But I can sure as hell give it a try," RJ said.

"You have to let go of your grief, RJ," he said quietly. "It's consuming you, stealing any happiness you might have. They wouldn't have wanted that. Not Sandy, and certainly not Whitey."

"I can't help the way I feel, Topaz. I can't just turn it off," RJ said.

"How do you know? You haven't even tried. I'm not asking you to turn it off, just turn something else on. Open yourself back up." Topaz drew a deep breath and released it slowly. "Listen to me. I know how you feel. Don't you think I've had grief? Here's a simple, inescapable fact—they're all mortal; you and I and your metal brother are not. Unless a meteor drops on us we will probably go on living forever. I've been doing it longer than you have; I know what it's like to watch everyone you love die. Realize this, you would have lost him eventually anyway. Best-case scenario, you would have watched him grow old and sick and die. Let them go. Start to live again. You can't grieve forever."

"Have you ever had your beating heart ripped from your chest?" RJ turned to face him, her expression a mask of rage. "No, you haven't. So don't tell me you know how I feel, because you don't. No two people feel things in quite the same way, and as you have just so carefully reminded me, I am very capable of grieving forever." She turned on her heel and stomped towards the building.

"That doesn't mean you should!" Topaz yelled after her. He looked out at the mainland and mumbled. "Damn hard-headed girl. Sometimes she reminds me of myself."

It was a Reliance trans-mat station located deep within the bounds of Reliance-held territory, far away from the rebels in their starving, disease-riddled state. It was run by the military, as were most things Reliance, but it was not a military installation, and most of the personnel were common class-two labor units.

They did a valuable service for the Reliance. They transported items from the planet's surface to the moon to be shipped to the outer worlds. They also received from the moon goods that had been transported from the outer planets.

Lately they'd mostly been shipping crates of cotton and wool fabrics, simple metal farm equipment, and cooking utensils. They'd been receiving hundreds of brown-colored humanoids from the planet Beta 4. These humanoids were to be trained briefly and used as shock troops in the event of any new attacks by the rebels.

The new free state was a total failure. All military personnel had been warned and placed on alert. The Reliance felt that it was only a matter of time till the rebels, driven by hunger and out of hope, would attack other Reliance-held zones in the hope of securing much needed food and medical supplies.

But this far from the front Jake wasn't worried about the rebels. Jake wasn't worried about anything. He watched as the truck backed in and the forklift took the crate off the back and brought it towards the trans-mat loading area. He knew what was in the crate before he even looked at the manifest the truck driver handed him. More cotton. All morning it had been cotton. He nodded his head, and the forklift put the box down in the trans-mat loading area. He pushed a button and watched as it disappeared before his eyes. As many times as he did this in a day you would have thought it would have become routine, but he still marveled at the process. Something that big and that heavy just vanishing only to reappear thousands of kilometers away on the moon! Several people had tried to explain to him how it worked, but he still didn't have a clue. So for him, the moment when something disappeared or appeared was still magical. He signed the trucker's manifest and handed it back to him.

Just when Janad was sure she couldn't make it one more day, the soldiers came back, and the metal rolling things went away. Relieved, she found a locker she had used to hide in before and crawled in. Her arm throbbed in pain, and her head pounded. She was fevered, so sleep was a long time coming. Finally exhaustion took over, and she fell into a fitful sleep.

"Hey!" Thomas said. "Look at this data from the robot."

"Looks like we have a stowaway," Michael said rubbing his chin. "You suppose it's the same girl we were chasing around on the way in?"

"If it is, she's a hell of a lot smarter and quicker than I would have thought these primitives would be," Thomas said. "We better hunt her up before we go. Shoot to kill."

Janad didn't get much sleep. She awoke to the sounds of the crew pounding on the walls and screaming, and she didn't have to wonder what they were looking for—she knew. They had apparently turned the metal things back on, because she could hear the all-too-familiar clicking sound they made when they moved. Resigned to the inevitable, she sunk down in the locker. She was too tired to keep fighting and in too much pain. She didn't have the energy she needed to escape them. Maybe if she stayed put they wouldn't find her. It was unlikely, but if she came out now they'd find her for sure.

RJ stood on one side of the crate and Poley on the other. With one kick, they sent the door flying across the cargo hold. Topaz, Levits and David jumped out with lasers at the ready. They were sort of disappointed when no one was there to greet them. Just crate after crate of cotton cloth.

Levits walked up to RJ and whispered in her ear, "All right; it worked, but it still sucked." Levits hadn't appreciated being nailed into a crate and basically delivered into the hands of the Reliance.

"It wasn't my idea; it was Topaz's," RJ whispered back.

"Actually, I stole it from some old Greek dudes," Topaz said.

RJ nodded her head towards the door leading to the rest of the ship, and Poley walked over to it. He pried the cover off the control panel with his fingertips and shorted the wiring out so that the door opened with a shower of sparks. He looked back at RJ and smiled.

"Let's move. The party isn't over yet, boys." RJ took point, and Poley brought up the rear. As they rounded a corner they ran into a troop of armed soldiers following a security droid. RJ hit the droid with her chain, making it fly into a hundred pieces. With the laser in her other hand, she killed one of the soldiers.

"Geee-od, it's RJ!" One of the soldiers screamed. The troop turned and ran in the opposite direction, firing over their shoulders.

The rebels gave chase.

Michael closed the door to the flight deck. He was out of breath, and his leg was smoking. He slapped at his pants, putting out the fire there. He was so scared his limbs were trembling, and he felt like he was going to vomit. He punched the buttons and opened a channel to the moon base.

"We are under attack! Repeat. We are under attack. The rebel RJ is on our ship! Repeat. The rebel RJ is on our ship, and we are under fire. Please open hatches and send reinforcements immediately!" Michael screamed into the receiver.

Laughter was his answer.

"I'm not fucking kidding!" Michael said in disbelief.

"No, but you are fucking screwed," a voice answered back.

"Who the hell is this?" Michael screamed.

"It's me."

The door behind him crashed in with a shower of sparks. The woman stepped up on the fallen door, her wrist communicator held to her smiling mouth.

"Over and out," she said as she snapped the chain into his head.

Janad could hear them right outside the closet door. It wouldn't be long now. She could pretend to be dead. Or maybe, if she didn't put up a fight, they would just chain her up again, and she could live to fight another day.

She heard someone's hand on the locker handle and froze, still not sure of her course of action.

RJ and Levits had headed for the flight deck. David, Topaz and Poley had headed for the mess hall where Poley detected a second security droid and, they presumed, more men.

They weren't disappointed.

David had assumed that the soldiers were looking for them, but it was pretty obvious by their shocked looks that they had no idea that they had been boarded. There were six of them and the droid. The combat-ready rebels took them down as fast as they could fire their lasers.

Topaz looked at the size of the mess hall. It was huge, and that just didn't seem right for a cargo ship.

"This can't be a cargo ship," Topaz said. "Why would they need a mess hall this big, and why are there so many soldiers on board? A cargo ship only needs about six people to run the whole show, and we've already killed more than twelve ourselves."

"This isn't a cargo ship," Poley said matter-of-factly. "It's a military troop carrier."

"What the fuck is going on?" David asked.

Topaz shrugged.

"Come on. Let's find RJ," David said.

They left the room at a run.

Janad poked her head out of the closet. The metal rolling thing was smoking, obviously broken, and all of the soldiers lay dead. Whoever those people had been, they didn't like the Reliance any better than she did. But she wasn't about to come out until she knew a lot more than she did now. She closed the door, curled up in a ball and went back to sleep. She knew instinctively that these people were not going to be interested in hunting for her.

On the bridge, RJ checked out the ship's log. "Did we kill twenty-five men?" RJ asked.

"Yes," Poley answered.

"We're being hailed from the freaking base," Levits said. "We have to answer them. We are still tethered, and we have to have them un-tether us. If we say the wrong thing...we are so freaking screwed."

"Then talk to them, and don't screw up," RJ said.

Levits gave her an angry look. RJ took more chances these days. She didn't care what happened. She wasn't afraid of dying. In fact, Levits got the idea that she would welcome death. What she seemed to forget on a regular basis was that *they* would die a lot easier than *she* would, and he, for one, didn't want to die. Not yet. Hell, he didn't feel like he'd even had a chance to live.

It had been a long time since he'd piloted a starship. The last time he'd done it everything had gone horribly wrong. He wasn't as sure as RJ was that he even knew the right thing to say to moon-base control. He sure as hell wasn't as sure as she was that he was up to flying this thing.

Levits looked at Topaz who nodded his understanding and raised his wrist-com to his mouth, "Marge, clear the channel."

"Done," the mock female voice squawked over his transmitter.

"What the hell's going on over there, Michael?" the space traffic controller's voice screamed.

"Had some trouble with the communication system, but we've got it fixed now, and we're prepared for takeoff."

"I was beginning to think you guys had been attacked by rebels or something," the guy said in a joking tone.

"No, everything's fine here. We're prepared for un-tether."

"Roger. Un-tether in five…four…three…two…one…"

They felt the ship jerk as the tube that tethered the ship to moon base and allowed the ship to be loaded and unloaded was detached.

"Commence undocking," the space trafficker said.

"Powering up front thrusters and undocking…now," Levits began backing the ship out of the dock. It wasn't easy; it wasn't a procedure the computer could do. You had a readout with a picture of your ship between two lines, and you had to stay in just the right spot. Jerk even one centimeter one way or the other, and you could strike the docking bay, tearing a hole in your ship and ripping the bay apart. Not exactly the stealth approach one wanted to take when you were stealing a Reliance ship. When they had backed out of the dock without incident, he breathed a sigh of relief.

"Moving toward the jump gates now."

"You're all clear. Take off when ready. Safe flight," the tower informed them.

"Thanks," Levits answered.

Levits powered the ship up and started to move slowly away from moon station and toward the jump gate. When he got a good look at the gate, Levits relaxed a little. The jump gate was big enough to hold three battleships at once. If he couldn't hit that hole, then they all deserved to die in the cold vacuum of space.

RJ sat next to him accessing the ship's database. "Twenty-five men to man a freighter; that makes no freaking sense at all," she said.

"This isn't a freighter. It's a military troop carrier," Poley and Levits said in unison.

"Then why the hell are they using it to haul cotton fabrics to a third class planet like Beta 4? Hell, Beta 4 is a planet that both the Reliance and the Argy's consider to be too useless to conquer. What are they getting from the planet that they find it necessary to use a military ship with full armaments, manned by twenty-five armed soldiers?" RJ asked absently of no one in particular as she continued trying to find the part of the manifest which would tell what the ship was picking up on Beta 4.

"Maybe the Argy have been trying to cut off supply routes," David suggested.

RJ nodded. "Yeah, that's a good answer. But it's too easy, and for some strange reason, the older I get the more I distrust easy answers." She scrolled back a page. "'Livestock.' The manifest says that they just delivered a shipment of 'livestock.' We're supposed to pick up another shipment of 'livestock' this time round."

"Well that explains the extra manpower, anyway," Topaz said thoughtfully.

"But it doesn't explain why they're using a military transport," RJ said. "And it doesn't say what sort of 'livestock' they are taking from Beta 4. Besides, we were in the ship's hold; it didn't smell like shit to me."

Levits didn't want to deal with something as trivial as missing shit. He had enough to worry about, like hitting the gate and slinging this thing into hyperspace in less than five minutes. "They sterilize every ship that comes in as soon as it's unloaded. When a cleanup crew gets done on a ship like this…"

"There would still be some trace of shit," RJ said getting out of her seat. "Then there's the problem of the livestock itself."

"What do you mean?" Topaz asked.

"Well, the way I understand it, the only animals that populate Beta 4 are lizards and a few small mammals. Nothing worth transporting across the vastness of space," RJ said thoughtfully. "Poley and I are going to go down to the hold and see what we can find."

"RJ, I'm getting ready to make the jump to hyperspace in less than five minutes, and just between you and me, I'm not at all sure that I remember how to do this," Levits said. "I thought I would be piloting a freighter. I had Marge give me a crash course on freighters, and now I'm flying a freaking troop carrier. They aren't the same."

"I have faith in you," RJ said, turning to smile at him. "If you can't hit a jump gate that big, we deserve to die in the cold vacuum of space."

Levits mumbled obscenities under his breath as RJ and Poley left the flight deck.

David and Topaz stood at a view port looking out at the planet Earth. Both men were transfixed, momentarily forgetting everything except the fact that they had traveled through space and were now looking down at the planet of their birth. It seemed surreal.

Topaz who had spent hundreds of years on the surface of the planet, looked at Earth set in space and thought about the beauty of it. To think that when he was a child few men had ever seen this view firsthand, and interstellar travel was only a dream. As a child he had dreamt of going to the stars and conquering new worlds, but by the time interstellar travel had become a fact, he was already in hiding from the Reliance. Now he was finally going on a real adventure. He was finally in the heavens, leaving the Earth behind, seeing truly different things, and having completely different experiences. He couldn't wait till the Earth disappeared from view.

David, on the other hand, looked at the Earth with longing. Something told him he had better take a good long look because he was never going to see Earth again. In a few minutes the ship would take off, and the Earth would vanish from view. He was never going home. He really didn't know where they were going or why. He was leaving behind everything that was familiar, including the free country he had dreamt of and fought for. He was going off into space on a mission that he didn't understand and that was probably impossible to execute. There was nothing under his feet but several metal floors and empty endless space. It felt to him like he was standing on a string over a bottomless pit. Thinking about it left a weird, over-empty feeling in his stomach. Of course that just might be the residual effects of the terror the trans-mat had thrown him into.

David hadn't understood the way the trans-mat worked. He assumed that the box simply moved through space somehow. He certainly hadn't been prepared at all to have his body completely disassembled and its particles flung through space to be reassembled. It was over in a matter of seconds, but he didn't think he was ever going to get over the filthy feeling it left him with. It was as close to being dead as he could imagine being. Levits and RJ seemed to take it in stride, and he hadn't expected the robot to react. Topaz' reaction was one of pure adulation. In fact, upon completion of the reconstruction of his body's atoms, he had yelled *Cool!* so loud that RJ had immediately clamped a hand over his mouth, and they had all prayed that they hadn't been detected.

David didn't want to leave Earth. He knew he wasn't important to this mission that he didn't understand, and he would have preferred staying on Earth. But he was damned if he was going to be left behind, and he didn't want to stay in Alsterace alone. Couldn't, in fact, have stayed there without the others if he had wanted to, because someone would have killed him.

RJ was leaving, and he was sure RJ had no intention of returning to Earth. David could barely remember his life before RJ, and although the closeness they had once shared had been shattered, he still couldn't imagine being separated from her now.

The ship jumped into hyperspace with a jerk that almost knocked David down, and the Earth was gone from view. He took a deep breath and quickly wiped the tears from his eyes. It was way too late to change his mind now even if he had wanted to.

David wondered if he would ever get over this horrible feeling that there was nothing substantial under him. He wondered if he was ever going to get used to the fact that he was basically nowhere. Wondered what he was expected to use as a point of reference for his existence. Was he here? No, he had moved and now he was here. No, moved again! The whole thing was weirding him out.

RJ fingered one of four sets of manacles affixed to the walls of the hold. "Now what do you suppose these are for? I can't think of any 'livestock' that has hands."

Poley shrugged his shoulders. "Nor can I. Perhaps it is used as punishment for unruly soldiers."

"Every ship has a brig for that," RJ said moving away from them. "Of course they might have changed policy. Those are a lot cheaper than a cell, and a lot more irritating."

RJ took a pocketknife and scraped the crevices in the hold's floor. She handed what she found to Poley who quickly examined the findings.

"No animal waste," Poley informed her.

"Don't tell me what there isn't, Tin Pants," RJ said in an exasperated tone. "Tell me what there is."

"A few cotton and wool fibers. Dirt, I'm assuming from both planets, human skin fragments, DNA, and what I have to assume are the skin fragments of a Beta 4 humanoid. More of the latter in fact than the former."

"Now...I wonder why that is?" RJ asked rubbing her chin.

"Maybe it fell off the crates that were loaded in here from the planet, and maybe..."

"Maybe we have no idea. I don't like it, Poley. I don't like it at all."

"Avonlea, Avonlea! You're off course. Repeat you're off course." The moon base operator was screaming at him over the communications port.

Levits decided to have a little fun. He linked in. "Yeah, well, how's this? I'm stealing your freaking ship, so I don't give a shit!"

RJ skidded to a stop beside him. "Change course for Beta 4."

"What?" Levits screamed at her.

"Change course; we're going to Beta 4," RJ said.

"For shits sake, RJ, I just told moon base…"

"What the hell did you say?" the moon base operator asked.

Levits cleared his throat. "Ah, we ah…Just a little ship humor, sir." He shrugged silently in answer to the look that Topaz gave him. "I'm making that course correction now. Thanks. I sure wouldn't want to get lost out here in hyperspace."

"You OK, Michael?" the operator asked.

"Yeah, just a little constipation. Happens every time I spend any time in a space station. Over." Levits cut the transmission and turned to face RJ.

"You want to tell me what the hell's going on?" he asked.

RJ smiled at him and bent down to kiss his check. "Now if I knew that, we wouldn't have to go to Beta 4, would we?" She straightened, turned on her heel and started out of the room.

"Damn it, RJ, would you give me a straight answer? What happened to your big *win the Argies over* plan, and why in hell's name are we going to a hole like Beta 4?"

She was gone and obviously wasn't going to answer him.

Levits turned to Topaz. "OK then, answer this one for me. Why does she keep kissing me when I'm screaming at her?" Levits asked.

Topaz and David both laughed.

"She does it because you find it unsettling," Topaz said.

"I think she does it because she likes him," Poley tossed out and then left, obviously to go look for his sister.

They all laughed now. "Better take your vitamins, Levits," David teased. "Think you're up for it?"

"I'd certainly find *that* unsettling," Levits laughed.

Chapter Four

Taheed looked out the huge window at the bright red-and-gold-striped sunset and smiled. "Exquisite!" he exclaimed, waving his handless arms around in circles. "Don't you think so, son?"

"Oh, yeah, great," Taleed said with no enthusiasm. He sat staring not at the sunset, but at a spot on the floor.

"Can't you enjoy anything?" Taheed turned an annoyed face to his son. "Must you continue to walk around the palace with your chin dragging on the ground? Haven't you punished me enough?"

"I have a right to disagree with your policies, Father, and I very heartily disagree with this latest trend."

"Oh, yes, how terrible! The kingdom grows richer each day..."

"It's the *way* we grow richer that bothers me. Father, you are selling our people into slavery. I do not trust the motives of this Reliance. I do not think they are dealing with us in good faith," Taleed said. "For generations the priests warned us against trade with the Reliance. Slowly, reluctantly, they agreed to trade lizard skins, beads, other hand-made items to the Reliance for farm implements, utensils, and light bulbs. Now, however, they push us to trade our people for this gold metal. How does this serve the people? How does it serve us? We are taught that The Ancestor wanted nothing to do with the Reliance. There had to be a reason for it, and a reason for the priests to be reluctant to trade with them."

"And there is a reason for us to trade with them now," Taheed said in an exasperated voice.

"Father...They are taking all our best warriors. What's to stop them from waiting till most of our good fighters are gone and descending on us in droves? Conquering and enslaving us all as they have done to countless other worlds," Taleed said.

"Son...Someday you will be King. You must learn to make the tough decisions. I think you are losing sight of the big picture. We have an overpopulation problem. A problem so big that not even constant war can keep the numbers of the peasants down. The Reliance has gold metal. They have fabrics that we need and also metal and electrical utensils that will help our people. Perhaps the priests will have no need to order wars if there are fewer of us to feed. Surely it is much more profitable to our people to make war on some other planet. The outcome is ultimately the same—a lower population."

"Surely some form of birth control is preferable to enslavement or war!" Taleed argued. "There are several ways to keep from reproducing. If we know when a woman is fertile, we also know when she is not. A man could remove his member before..."

"Blasphemy!" Taheed screamed holding his stumps over his ears. "We are here because we were chosen by the gods to be gods. The priests know what is good and what is true. They speak the will of the gods. Birth control is an abomination..."

"Do you even listen to yourself, Father? Birth control is an abomination, but making our people fight wars to keep from starving and selling them to the Reliance to die at alien hands, fighting a battle which isn't ours...these things are blessed in the eyes of the gods?"

"How dare you question me? I am a god!" his father screamed back.

"You are no more a god than the things that belch smoke in the mountain. There are no gods. There is no magic. These beliefs have stuck us in a rut and kept us from progressing to a position which would allow us to fight the Reliance on their own terms if they decided to try to take us over," he said with passion. "The priests decided it was all right to deal with the

Reliance after generations of saying they were evil. They made this decision for one reason and for one reason only—they were afraid not to. Now they trade our people for gold metal, not because of what the gods have told them, but because they like gold metal! They have forgotten the reasons why we did not trade with the Reliance; they have forgotten the reason that The Ancestor hated them. The truth…The truth that you all hide is that there are no gods. Just the greed of priests and kings playing on the superstitious nature of a people they have purposefully kept ignorant of technology."

The King still held the ends of his stumps over his ears. "Blasphemy! I will not hear it from one whom the gods themselves have chosen to rule…"

"*Chosen*, Father? Don't you mean *maimed*? Don't talk to me of being chosen, or tell me how blessed I am to have servants who do everything from feeding me to wiping the dung from my bottom. I grow tired of hearing the lies."

"Enough!" the King screamed finally taking his stumps from his ears. "Why must you grieve me so? Why do you hate your life? You have everything a man could need. Everything a man could ask for…"

"I don't have hands!" Taleed screamed then turned on his heel and headed for the door. The mute, illiterate servant standing there opened the door for him, and when he went through closed it behind him. Taleed stomped all the way down the hall to his room. At his door another mute, illiterate servant opened the door, followed him in, and closed it behind them. The servant stood at the door, silently awaiting his next order—either spoken or implied.

Taleed was in a rage; he kicked a chair across the room then jumped around on one foot. Finally he flopped onto his bed.

"Everything I want! Everything I want!" Taleed screamed at the ceiling his nostrils flaring. He held up his handless arms and glared at them. Then he turned to talk to the servant. "Chosen! Chosen! What a royal joke! Some sick priest comes on the day of the birth of the King's children. If the sacramental knife feels heavy, then *Chop!* they cut off the child's hands to show that he is chosen and therefore never has to work. I was chosen to be handless just as you, my friend, were chosen to be mute. Some sick priest saw a different sparkle in our eyes than he had in the siblings that were born before us, and so whack! They deform you and ruin you for anything but what they wanted you to do. Which, in essence, is to help them make the people into puppets."

"They cut out your tongue before you had a chance to know if you could sing, and they cut off my hands before I knew what it was like to pick fruit from a bush, hold a friend's hand or throw a rock. They say the procedure causes little pain, but what do they know of my pain? The pain I feel when I see lovers holding each other, gladiators in mock warfare, or even the simple act of a child throwing a ball. All of these things were stolen from me as your ability to speak was stolen from you."

The man nodded his head and made hand signals that only the two of them could read. Haldeed had been with him as long as Taleed could remember; he was his personal servant and his best friend. Haldeed was his hands, and he was Haldeed's voice. They'd had this talk many times before because both were unhappy with their lots in life. Haldeed said what he often did, that someday Taleed would be King, and when he was in charge he could change all the rules.

"But my father is not an old man, and he is in good health. I may be old and gray before I come to power, and then what life is left to either of us? No! We must leave here and go out on our own. Start anew someplace far from the palace where no one knows us," Taleed said. "We must have an adventure."

Haldeed took a deep breath and tried to talk sense to his old friend. He reminded him that they had run away six times before and had been caught every single time in no more than a few hours. It hardly seemed worth the effort to him. He reminded Taleed how hard it was to hide a handless man and a mute.

"Ah, but last time we did hide longer than ever before, and I think we grow wiser with age. Let us at least try again. If nothing else it will give us a break from palace boredom."

Once again Haldeed found himself digging through his wardrobe and dressing himself and the Prince in the simple sleeveless tunics made of rough linen that were worn by the peasants.

"Oh, and I need a pair of gloves," Taleed said.

Haldeed shot him a strange look and then laughed making the one sound he could make that sounded close to normal.

"I'm not kidding," Taleed said. "I've got an idea."

Haldeed found a pair of old gloves and held them out to Taleed with a questioning look on his face.

"Stuff them full of cotton or something. We'll glue them to the ends of my stumps, and then it will look like I have hands," Taleed said.

Haldeed nodded his head in excitement. They would probably only be caught again, but at the very least they might have a few hours of adventure. While looking for cotton and glue he found some old wire. He rushed back to Taleed in excitement. He put a piece of wire into one to the fingers of the glove and bent it. He looked at Taleed's face to see what he thought, and Taleed smiled.

"Great idea, Haldeed. We can pose my hands—make them look more real. We can even change them every once in awhile."

It took a while for Haldeed to construct the 'hands,' but when he had glued them onto the Prince's arms they looked real enough.

Taleed was silent for a moment as he looked down his arms at the fake hands. He found himself filled with emotion. "I...I look like a whole person."

Haldeed made hand signals.

"Yes, we just might make it this time. Come on. Let's go."

RJ walked through the ship with Poley at her side. "I should have known looking at the size of the hold that this was no cargo ship," RJ said thoughtfully as they looked into yet another long, narrow bunk hall.

"I knew," Poley said matter-of-factly.

"Then why didn't you say something, Tin Pants?" RJ asked harshly.

"You didn't ask," Poley said, shrugging.

RJ sighed and popped herself in the head with the palm of her hand.

"Why do you do that?" Poley asked curiously.

"Because it feels so good when I quit," RJ explained with a grin.

"Hum...disposable plastic wrapping on all the beds," RJ said under her breath. "Probably no chance of getting any decent samples in here."

"I can hardly hear you," Poley said. "Why are you whispering?"

"I'm not whispering, and I'm not talking to you," RJ snapped back. She usually had more patience with Poley. She didn't know why she felt so edgy. It was true she didn't like to be surprised, and she sure as hell didn't like changing her plans at the last minute, but it wasn't like she wasn't used to having odd pieces thrown in where they didn't belong. On the contrary, if everything had gone perfectly according to plan then she would have been *really* worried.

She started looking under mattresses to see if perhaps something had been missed in the cleaning.

"Who are you talking to then?" Poley asked as he followed her, looking under the bottom mattresses as she looked under the top.

"Huh?" RJ asked.

"If you aren't talking to me, then who are you talking to?" Poley asked again.

RJ sighed, knowing what her answer would do to his circuits. "I was talking to myself, Poley."

"That doesn't make any sense, RJ. Talking to yourself is a sign of mental instability," he said with as much concern as he was able to convey.

"I never claimed to be mentally stable, Poley. In fact I've taken being crazy to its highest possible level!" RJ shrieked, coming to the end of her patience.

"Oh," Poley said simply.

"What is that supposed to mean?" RJ snapped at him.

"Nothing," Poley said quickly.

"Don't you 'nothing' me, metal head. What did you mean by, 'Oh?'"

"You're acting irrationally, you're irritated and nervous, obviously you're cycling," Poley said.

"Poley…" RJ laughed, stopped what she was doing and moved to put an arm across his shoulders. "Poley, I don't have periods, you know that."

"You don't bleed from your sexual organs, that's true, but you do have hormonal cycles. I've noted them; would you like to see a chart?" Poley asked helpfully.

RJ pulled away from him, stiffening. "So basically what you're saying is that while Stewart made me incapable of re-producing, he didn't do away with my PMS. Now isn't that just fucking beautiful? Doesn't that just figure in?"

She stomped out of the bunkroom, and Poley followed. "Do you *want* to have babies, RJ?" Poley asked curiously.

"It doesn't really matter what I want," RJ hissed. "Just like everything else, it was decided for me before I was born, from the way I look to what I'd do. There was never any chance that I'd be anything but a soldier; it was built into my biologi-cal make up. I'd have PMS, but I wouldn't have any babies. I'd be damn near indestructible. I'd outlive everyone…"

"Except me," Poley said with a smile.

"Talking to myself or talking to a robot—what's the dif-ference!" she screamed at him.

He stopped in his tracks and glanced down at his feet, looking genuinely rejected.

"I'm...I'm sorry, Poley. God, I don't know what's gotten into me today." She moved to hug him.

"It's just the PMS," Poley said. He even patted her on the back.

"I think it has a lot to do with leaving Earth. It makes it all seem so final." She shrugged and moved away from him.

"We will miss Mickey," Poley said.

"Yes," RJ said. "We will miss Mickey. And, as stupid as it may sound, I think I am going to miss staring out at what used to be Alsterace and remembering all that I have lost."

"Maybe remembering what you have lost reminds you of what you had, and what you had was good," Poley said.

RJ realized that he was right and felt doubly guilty for having screamed at him. In many ways, he often acted more human than she did.

Janad awoke to the sound of movement in the mess hall. She looked out the crack in the door and saw a white-headed woman and a stiff, dark-headed man removing the bodies. They left and then came back for another load. Janad took a long look at the female; she was not like any being Janad had ever seen before. Not like them and not like the Reliance people, and neither was the male. She remembered talk of the other aliens, the ones the Reliance fought with, and deduced that these must be those aliens. Except that they spoke the Reliance tongue, and that didn't seem to make any sense. Besides the others had looked like Reliance. In fact this man *looked* Reliance; it was the way he moved that was all wrong. He was quick but stiff, and strong, but his muscles didn't expand or contract with movement. She couldn't quite put her finger on it, but there was something peculiar about him.

The woman turned then, and Janad was sure that the woman had found her. She was a beautiful creature, tall and well muscled. Obviously she was no stranger to combat. She moved with the grace of an animal stalking prey. Her hair was as white as anything Janad had ever seen, her eyes as blue, and her skin was a beautiful bronze. She wore a sleeveless black jumpsuit and black boots. There was a chain wrapped around her waist, and in the coils of the chain was a weapon similar to what the Reliance men carried—only much bigger.

The male was still moving, and the woman put a hand on his chest. "Listen," she ordered, and he stopped.

"There is someone in the room with us," he said matter-of-factly.

Janad froze. How could they know? She hadn't moved a muscle, hadn't made a sound except for her breath and the beating of her heart. She held her breath and watched through the crack as they moved closer. They knew right where she was. She had to take action, and it had to be quick.

When they were almost to the locker she kicked the door open and jumped, springing like a cat from her perch on the locker floor. She started to jump at two feet above the deck and sailed through the air and over their heads. She landed clean and took off running. They followed.

"Boys we've got company, and she's heading your way. Catch her alive," RJ ordered over her wrist communicator.

"I'm trying to pilot a ship here, RJ!" Levits replied angrily.

"Then I wasn't talking to you, was I," RJ spat back. "She's heading for the hold. You can cut her off if you move now."

Janad would have made a jump for the tiles and the relative safety of the service grid, but the woman was right behind her and gaining ground fast. She rounded a corner, and an older man grabbed her. She elbowed him in the ribs and escaped, but the second man was younger and stronger, and he grabbed hold of her wounded arm. She slung her fist into his face.

"You fucking little bitch!" he screamed, doubling over with pain as the blood poured from his nose.

The woman was almost upon her; Janad jumped up and through one of the tiles, heading for the safety of the service grid. But before she had time to know what was happening, the woman was in the small space with her. She jumped on Janad, and they both went crashing through the ceiling onto the floor. The white-haired woman landed on the bottom, and Janad expected the woman's grip on her shoulders to at least relax a little, but it didn't. When she looked into the face of her opponent, the woman was smiling as if she had won some great victory. If she had been hurt at all in the fall, she wasn't showing it. These two things together really made Janad angry, and while she knew there was no escape she kicked the woman in the shins hard anyway.

To Janad's added frustration and astonishment the woman just laughed at her, then, in one motion, she jumped to her feet, hauling Janad with her.

Even this show of strength didn't stop Janad from fighting to get free. She kicked at her opponent and squirmed in her arms.

"It's a GSH!" David screamed, pulling his weapon.

"It's not a GSH," RJ laughed. "Put your weapon away." She looked the girl over. Her hair was short and curly. She was well muscled, and her brown skin shone with the sweat from her exertion. She was only five-six, obviously wounded and probably sick, yet she was still stronger than any of the men RJ had with her. She wore a simple loincloth made of red cotton fabric and a short vest made of reptile skin that was laced up the front with a piece of leather thong. There were three strings of large glass beads around her throat. Her hands were callused, her vision quick and challenging, and her stance that of a battle veteran. RJ was sure that the girl had seen combat or had, at the very least, been combat trained.

"She's an attractive creature," RJ said conversationally.

"What the hell is she?" David asked wiping the blood from his nose and face.

"She's a Beta 4 humanoid," Poley said. He put one hand on David's forehead, grabbed his nose with his other hand and gave a sharp tug, putting David's nose back where it belonged.

"God damn it, Poley!" David hollered, taking the hand-kerchief Poley offered and holding it to his nose.

"It was busted," Poley defended himself.

"You might have said something before you did it," David whined. His vision was still blurred, and he felt like the bleed-ing would never stop. He leaned his head back. "She's an alien, then?"

"Yes," RJ said matter-of-factly.

Topaz was still doubled over, trying to catch his breath. He glanced up at the girl and did a double take. "That's no alien," Topaz said, forcing himself to straighten. His cracked ribs were already starting to heal. "That, boys and girls, is a black woman."

"Well, duh," David said. "We can tell that she's female and that she's black."

"She's brown," Poley corrected.

"I know what you mean," RJ said looking at Topaz curi-ously. "Like those people in some of the old pictures that Marge showed us. You said there used to be lots of them."

"That's right," Topaz said. "Among their many faults, the Reliance are also white supremacists. They were white, and so they wanted an all-white race. They gave fewer breeding permits to the blacks, Orientals, and Hispanics. Then they very carefully crossbred everyone so that we eventually wound up being basically the same color. If they have their way, in another hundred years everyone will basically be the color of our good friend Levits."

"But Topaz…how would a black human wind up on Beta 4?" RJ asked. Not even seeming to notice the squirming girl in her arms.

"I'm sure I don't know. Perhaps like you, RJ, she is a hybrid, taking all her external makeup from the one race." Topaz drew nearer and looked at the girl closely. "I'm tell-ing you, RJ, I'm sure that this creature is no more alien than you are. Maybe a hybrid, but at least part of her heritage is human."

"She is hurt," Poley said as he moved forward and touched the wound, taking a good look. The girl howled in pain.

"See? She doesn't like it any better than I did," David said, glaring at Poley.

"It's infected," Poley informed them.

Topaz looked at the wound and nodded. "We may have to sedate her happy ass in order to take care of it."

"Topaz, if she isn't human—and you can't be sure that she is—something that sedates us might very well kill her," RJ said.

"That is correct," Poley agreed.

"Like the Pronuses you take," David said showing his understanding.

"I ran a quick scan on the tissue sample I found in the hold. Their DNA is different than human DNA," Poley said.

"Every living creature's DNA is different, Tin Pants," Topaz said. "A black human's DNA is going to be different than the homogenized DNA of Reliance-bred humans, but we're all still human. Except you."

Janad listened to them talk. She couldn't understand everything they said. They talked faster than the Reliance people had, and they used what she assumed were slang words, but she did understand that they wanted to take care of her wounded arm. Obviously at least for the moment they meant her no harm. She quit squirming.

"Finally give up, huh?" the woman said with a laugh.

"Yes. You are stronger than I am."

They all stared at her.

"She speaks Reliance," the older man said, sounding more than a little shocked.

"If they've been trading with the Reliance it makes sense that some of them would," the woman said thoughtfully. "So, girl, why did you run?"

"Why wouldn't I?" Janad answered. "I no longer know who the enemy is."

The woman released her. "As long as you don't try anything, we aren't your enemy. Try anything stupid, and we'll kill you on the spot. Topaz, Poley, take our little friend down to the sickbay and see what you can do to fix her arm, and..."

"Run some tests while we're at it," the older man finished for her,

"Maybe David better go with you and at least get a shot for the pain. It wouldn't hurt him to get cleaned up, either," the woman said.

The stiff man took hold of her good arm and started to guide her down the hall. The older man and the man whose nose she'd broken followed them.

"So," the older man started, "my name is Topaz, this young man is Poley, and the man whose nose you just 'fixed' is David. Who may I ask are you?"

"Janad," she answered.

"That's a nice name," Topaz said. He smiled at her, and she realized she had nothing to fear from him. On the other hand the man who held her by her arm made her more uncomfortable by the minute. She tried to jerk out of his grip and found that she couldn't. What was more, he seemed not to notice at all. Every time she looked at the one they called David he shot daggers at her from his eyes. She couldn't really blame him; if someone had busted her nose, she wouldn't have been too quick to get chummy with them either.

"Poley, let the girl go," Topaz said. "She's not going to try to get away again." He looked at her then. "You aren't going to try to get away, are you?"

"No." She was glad when the strange man released her. She leaned close to Topaz and whispered, "What's wrong with him?"

Topaz laughed. "There's nothing wrong with him. Much to the contrary, everything is right with him. In fact, he just heard everything you said. He's a robot."

It must have been obvious by the look on her face that she didn't understand, because Topaz said, "He's made of metal and plastic and circuits. He's a machine that can think."

Janad looked at Poley again. Now that was the most absurd thing she had ever heard. He couldn't be a machine. Machines didn't look like people, and they most definitely did not think.

"Don't talk about him like he's not here," David said in a scolding tone.

"Thanks, David," Poley said, looking at his feet.

"I'm sorry, Poley," Topaz said.

Janad looked at Poley; he looked sad. That was another thing machines didn't do; they didn't feel.

In the sickbay Topaz helped her to sit on one of the examining tables as Poley started to clean up and care for David's broken nose.

"Now this is going to sting a bit," Topaz said. He held a machine to her arm. It was the same as the thing the Reliance had used on her before taking her from the planet. She steeled herself for the pain, but found that it didn't hurt as badly when you weren't putting up a fight. Topaz looked at the data with a curious look on his face.

"Poley, could you come look at this?" Topaz asked.

Poley finished up what he was doing with David and walked over. David got up and wandered over to look out the porthole at space.

Poley looked at the data Topaz handed him.

"Beta 4 humanoid DNA," Poley said.

"Doesn't it look awfully familiar?"

"Yes, but..."

"Sometimes you can be such a computer, Poley," Topaz said in an exasperated tone.

David let out a sound that was almost a scream and jumped back from the porthole. Janad saw why as a naked body floated by. "What the hell!" he screamed.

"RJ must have opened the airlock to dump the dead bodies," Poley said matter-of-factly.

David shuddered and walked quickly away from the porthole. "Why did she strip them?"

"You know RJ. She hates to throw away anything she might need later," Topaz said.

"Why does she have to use that damn plasma blaster instead of a laser? It makes such a mess," David observed almost conversationally.

"I imagine that would be why," Topaz said with a laugh. "Come here, David, I need a blood sample."

"I think I've bled enough today. Couldn't you just take a piece of my hair if all you need is DNA?" David protested.

"Come on, Dave, humor an old man," Topaz said.

David held out his arm, and Topaz got the sample.

"See, Poley?" Topaz tapped on the screen as it showed a comparison of the two DNA samples.

"They aren't even close," Poley said.

Topaz sighed. "Oh, yes, they are. This girl is at least half human. Look more closely at the data. I can't put my finger on it, but there is something very familiar about her DNA."

"Wow," David groaned. "That has got to be the worst come-on line I have ever heard! I'm outta here. Think I'll go lie down for awhile."

Poley nodded. "I do see many similarities and would have to agree that, yes, the subject is at least half human."

"Then I'm going to assume that it will be safe to treat her with the same medicine we would use on humans," Topaz said.

Janad watched as they cleaned the wound. They applied a salve, dressed it, and then Topaz put the thing back on her arm and she felt a slight sting. She trusted him. She didn't know why, but she did.

"I suggest you find a bunk and get some rest. RJ's going to have a lot of questions for you," Topaz said.

Janad nodded.

"Poley, put Janad in a convenient spot," Topaz ordered.

Poley nodded and started to walk away. Janad followed him reluctantly. She already felt better. He took her to a room close to the flight deck. Obviously it had been some big shot's quarters, as it held only one bed instead of sixty. She lay down.

To her surprise, Poley covered her up before he left. She closed her eyes and was almost instantly asleep.

RJ joined Levits on the flight deck.

"Is everything alright?" she asked as she sat beside him.

"Why don't you tell me?" Levits asked. "You've changed dicks right in the middle of a screw, and I really have no idea why."

"The Reliance is up to something on Beta 4. They're hauling something back from there, and it sure as hell isn't any livestock we're familiar with. We just caught a wounded Beta 4 humanoid on this ship, and it looks like she's been hiding here for a while. Now here's a good question. Did she hide to ride on the ship, or is she hiding to go back?"

"That doesn't make any sense," Levits said. "What would a Beta 4 humanoid be doing on Earth?"

"I think they're the 'livestock' the Reliance has been shipping in from Beta 4," RJ said.

"But why?" Levits asked. "Why would they do that? They have enough trouble feeding their own people on Earth right now. Why bring in more mouths to feed?"

"Levits, sometimes you think like a farm unit," RJ said in exasperation.

Levits shrugged. There was so much crap swimming through his brain right now that he would have gladly settled for half the brain of a common farm worker with which to work.

"How many Reliance troops did the New Alliance kill on Earth? Thousands? Hundreds of thousands? A large part of the reason they surrendered Zone 2-A to us was because their war with the Argies has escalated on two fronts and they can't afford to divert troops from space back to the home front. If they want to keep us from running over the rest of the planet, or if they want to take back what ground they have lost, they are going to have to have troops from somewhere," RJ explained. "There was a girl out there about

Sandra's size, five-six, maybe weighs one-forty soaking wet. In a matter of seconds she had cracked Topaz' ribs and broken David's nose. I had to jump up in the service grid to catch her, and she was far from easy to hold. And get this, Levits, the girl was wounded and fevered. She'd probably been sick for a while from the looks of the wound and the extent of the infection. Looked like she'd been shot in the shoulder—probably by one of the security droids."

"Damn!" Levits said as realization dawned. "We'd better tell Mickey."

"Let's wait till we know for sure what's going on," RJ said. "No sense in causing panic if I'm wrong."

Levits nodded. "Well, at least that explains the course change...Now, was that so hard?"

RJ smiled and stood up. She moved to rub his shoulders, and he stiffened instead of relaxing. "Relax, Levits, you ought to know by now that you can trust me." He relaxed slowly under her hands, and she continued to massage his neck and shoulders.

"It's hard to relax when I know you could snap my neck if you wanted to, and I have no idea where your head is any more, RJ. I didn't always want to go along with all your schemes, but at least there was some pattern to them. Some logic, now..."—He pushed her hands gently away and swiveled his chair to face her.—"...you royally piss me off."

"What?!" RJ exclaimed. "What?"

"You heard me. You piss me off! Look at you. Your life isn't over; hell, it hasn't even begun. But you've got a death wish, and you're hell-bent on taking the rest of us with you."

"Excuse me! I didn't want you to come. I didn't want *any* of you to come, you insisted..."

"Give me a big freaking break. You knew damn good and well that we were never going to let you go off on this crazy-assed mission half-cocked, alone...Do you think I don't hurt? Do you think I don't have pain? I, however, am growing older. I don't have time to wallow for forty years in my grief, because I'm just not going to live that long. In fact, working with you,

I'll be lucky to live out the week. I want to have a life; is that some crime? But instead of finding some nice girl, settling down in the free zone and maybe having a couple of kids. I'm out here in freaking space, where I never wanted to go again. I'm piloting a crappy ship, which is something I never wanted to do again. Why? I don't freaking know why!" He had wanted to say these things for a long time, so while he was trying not to scream, he just wasn't making it.

RJ was more than a little taken aback, and she didn't really know what to say. "I'm sorry, Levits, I didn't know you felt this way."

"You know what, RJ? Maybe that wouldn't sound like such bullshit if you weren't a freaking empath! I'd ask if you remembered what happened between us six months ago because you've never brought it up, except I know you have total recall, so I know damn good and well that you do."

RJ turned away from him to hide her anger. She couldn't believe he was bringing it up at all, much less now.

"We almost had sex, RJ. But we didn't, because you put the brakes on and ran off. I didn't understand why you stopped it. It didn't make any sense to me at the time. I went and took a cold shower and tried to forget about it. But I know why you ran off now—because you might have enjoyed it. God forbid that anything should get in the way of your grieving off into infinity. God forbid that you might actually *feel* something for me—or anyone else for that matter. If you want to suffer forever that's fine, do it. But quit making the rest of us suffer with you." Levits got out of his chair. "You watch the bridge. I know damn good and well that you can fly this thing as well as I can. So you sit here and watch it while I get something to eat and find a nice quiet place to beat off, because I am sick to death of taking orders from you. I'm sick to death of taking orders from *anyone*." He stomped off the bridge as Poley walked in.

RJ took a deep breath as she looked at her brother. "And you thought *I* had PMS."

Chapter Five

They left the palace under cover of darkness, long after everyone else had gone to sleep. Even the guards at the back entrance were leaning against the wall at their posts, snoring loudly. How they did that always amazed Taleed.

This time, they didn't steal the holy vehicle. In the past all that had done was make them easier to track and totally annoy the priests. They walked through the streets on foot, sneaking between the dwellings of carved stone down to the river. There were many woven-reed boats there, but they would not take one here. They would not take anything that might be missed and give them away. Instead they would walk a good ways down the river, and, using the tools they both carried in their backpacks, Haldeed would make one of the reed boats. They walked through the night before stopping in the middle of a patch of reeds to make camp just as day broke.

Haldeed made a small fire, put up their tent and cooked their meal. Taleed took off his shoes and helped as much as he could. Over the years he had gotten quite good at doing certain things with his feet. However he wasn't supposed to use his feet for anything but walking, and so he hadn't managed to get all the practice he needed to be really good at it.

"I'm sorry that I can't help more, Haldeed. I'm sure that, with more practice, I will get quite good at doing things with my feet."

I don't mind, Haldeed signed.

"I know you don't mind, my brother, but it isn't fair that you should have to do all the work." He shoved a piece of wood into the fire with his foot and didn't burn himself. He smiled at Haldeed. "See? I'm already getting better at it."

Haldeed looked worried and signed at Taleed. *I don't know how to make a boat.*

"Nonsense! I'm sure you can make a boat, Haldeed. You can do anything you set your mind to," Taleed insisted.

Haldeed signed more frantically, *We don't know how to sail a boat, Taleed, or navigate a river. I don't think this is a very good plan.*

"It's a great plan, my best ever. How hard could it be to travel the river on a boat? You get in, the river flows, it carries you along; it's really quite simple."

But you don't know how to swim, Haldeed signed even more frantically.

Taleed laughed. "You worry too much, brother. If I fall in, then I shall have to learn to swim, won't I? Isn't that what they always say is the best way to learn? Just jump in! We'd better get some sleep. I for one am dead tried."

By the time they woke up, it was getting dark. Well rested, a slightly more confident Haldeed started to make the boat. Taleed helped him as much as possible by holding things down with his feet. He found that his stumps, which he had always deemed useless, were actually of more use than he had thought. He hadn't realized how much he used them until he covered them up and made them truly useless. He would have pulled his fake hands off except they had brought no glue to reattach them, and besides, he sort of liked the way they looked. By daybreak on the fourth day the boat was finished. They ate in silence, both totally exhausted. Neither wanted to admit that it was because they weren't used to hard physical labor or sleeping on anything but the very best fur-filled mattresses. They lay down for sleep in the small, cramped tent with the reeds they had stomped down to make their camp poking at them through their bedrolls.

Taleed rolled, trying to get comfortable, and finally said to Haldeed, "I'm very uncomfortable and very tired."

Haldeed tapped him- his in-the-dark sign for *me, too.*

"I'd still rather be here than in the palace."

Haldeed hit him again.

Finally, too tired to worry about the reeds poking them, they went to sleep.

When evening fell the next day, they ate quickly, packed their gear, loaded it in their boat and set off down the river. With six moons, there was always some light to shine on *Balancer*, but they were still less likely to be seen during the night.

The river was slow here, and Haldeed helped them along with the paddle he had woven around a stick. The boat and the oar looked just like the ones the local fishermen used.

"You did a very good job, Haldeed," Taleed said when they had been on the river about an hour and still hadn't taken on any water. They sat facing each other in the boat.

Haldeed put down the oar temporarily and signed, *Don't say anything till we get where we are going, wherever that is.* He picked the oar up and started rowing again.

"No one has found us yet. We will travel as far on the river as we can and then we will go inland. We will find some remote village. One that has no temple, where no one knows us, and we will live out our years as teachers...or beggars. I don't care what we do as long as I never have to go back to the palace. As long as I never have to see another priest."

RJ stood in front of the viewing port in the room she had taken, rolling the object in her hand back and forth across her fingers. She looked out at the vast emptiness of hyperspace and realized she was still seeing the ruins of Alsterace. Her lips curled into a snarl. Topaz and Mickey had been right. She couldn't leave it behind because it was right here with her. Standing here looking at space was the same as standing on the wall looking at the bare land where the city had once stood. Her demons were following her.

Levits was right, too, although she was far more reluctant to admit it. She didn't let go of the past because then she would have to live in the present. She might actually be happy again, and when you were happy, you had everything to lose and losing hurt. It was way too easy to fall into the pattern. In order to be happy you had to care about people and they about you. Eventually they died, one way or another, and when they did it hurt.

They'll all die, David, Levits, Mickey. Well, at least I won't be there to see Mickey die, but I miss him. Damn Topaz! Why does he always have to be right? Crazier than a bug in a box and yet he knows more than anyone I've ever known.

She didn't want to think about it, any of it. She put the eye back into her pocket and pulled a coin out. She put it around a link of the chain and smashed it closed.

That's it, RJ, concentrate on the victories. Think about the battle. Be happy with the war. After all it's a sure bet that war will always be there. Don't think about the battles lost. Don't think about Alsterace in flames. Don't think about the guy who used to run the Golden Arches or the fat bastard who was always so worried we were going to let a corpse rot in his fucking hotel. Don't think about Sandy or how just talking to her could make you feel better. And whatever you do don't think about Whitey Baldor. God, please don't let me think about him, because when I do I cry, and I just don't think I have any tears left.

She was wrong. A tear spilled out of her eye and ran down her check. She dried it quickly away.

Damn it I'm talking to myself again. I'm really fucking losing it. At least I'm not talking out loud.

"What?" David asked from the doorway.

"Damn!" RJ cursed under her breath. "What do you want? Can't you see I'm busy being morbidly depressed?" She turned to face him and forced a smile. He smiled back.

"The girl's awake now," David said as he walked in the open door. Since the attack on Alsterace, RJ had developed a phobia about sleeping in a room with the door closed and now couldn't sleep unless the door was open. Although it was pretty obvious from the look of the bed that RJ hadn't done any sleeping. It was just as obvious from the look on her face that she had only been about half-kidding about her mood. "You all right, RJ?"

"PMS," RJ explained as she walked across the room, pushed around him and started down the hall towards the bridge. "Get the girl and meet me on the bridge."

"All right." David hurried to catch up with her. He didn't say anything. He just raced along beside her till he reached the girl's door. David knocked before walking in. The girl was sitting on the bed. She gave him a curious look. "RJ wants to talk to you now."

"Is she your leader?" Janad asked standing up.

"Yes," David said without hesitation.

"She's very strong. What is she?" Janad asked.

David laughed. "That's a good question. I'm not sure how to explain what RJ is. For one thing, she's a GSH. Do you know what that is?"

"No," Janad answered as she followed him down the hall towards the bridge.

"It's a genetically superior humanoid…" It was obvious by the look on her face that she still didn't have a clue. They turned a corner and walked onto the bridge.

"David…this girl broke your nose. The jury's still out on whether she's a hostile or not," RJ said, then added abruptly, "She doesn't need to know what I am. I just need to know what she is."

Janad looked around the room. There was another man with them this time, a tall thin black-haired man with dark brown eyes and a scruff of beard. He wore black pants and a short-sleeved black shirt. There was a weapon hanging at his hip in a holster, the end of which was tied to his leg. In his eyes she saw pain and anger, much the same as in the eyes of the one they called RJ. He stood behind the chair RJ sat in, and the strange stiff man stood at her right side. Janad almost smiled. The woman looked every bit like royalty surrounded by her court.

Janad didn't think she had ever seen five stranger people in her life.

"You'll get more flies with honey than you will with shit, RJ," Topaz said in a near whisper.

"Who said I wanted any flies?" RJ frowned deeply, and Janad got the impression that the only time she smiled was when she was beating someone senseless or killing them.

David stood behind Janad as if to block her exit, which did nothing to put her at ease. However, she didn't fear him. He seemed to her like a man who had been broken and was devoid of spirit. He moved like a child who had broken the rules and been spanked, with his shoulders pointed down and forward, his head low, hardly ever making eye contact. He was someone who needed protection, not someone you needed protection from.

Topaz was leaning against the wall looking out at the stars. He seemed to be the only one of them who was normal.

"So, let's start this with a simple question," RJ said. "What are you doing on this ship?"

Janad saw no reason to lie. On the contrary she had the feeling that they were more likely to help her in her quest if they knew just what was going on.

"The Reliance is buying my people from our greedy King to use as shock troops to fight something they call the Rebellion on a planet called Earth."

"That's what I thought," RJ said looking troubled and triumphant at the same time, if that was possible or made any sense at all.

"One of the guards mentioned you by name," Janad said.

RJ seemed to ignore this information. "So how come you didn't get offloaded?"

"I didn't want to go. I caused trouble so they chained me to the wall. I got them to let me go to use the bathroom and then I got away. I hid mostly up there." She pointed at the ceiling. "I hoped to get back to my planet to try to tell my people what the Reliance is doing. Not that it will help. My people do whatever the priests tell them to do."

RJ rubbed her chin thoughtfully.

"Do we call Mickey now?" the tall man standing behind RJ asked.

"Wait a minute," RJ said impatiently. She looked back at Janad. "Do you know how many of your people have been sent to Earth?"

"Most of the warriors in our village except the old and the young. Many villages have been completely emptied in the same way. Thousands of my people have already been moved to your planet."

"Can they all fight like you?" RJ asked.

"I told you they took all the warriors."

"Just because a man is a soldier doesn't mean he can fight. Have they seen action?"

"Action?" Janad knew the word but didn't now what RJ was asking.

"Have they fought?" Topaz asked.

Janad nodded excitedly. "Yes, because of the wars," Janad answered.

"The wars? Wars with who?" RJ asked.

"The other villages. The Priests say that the gods want us to fight because blood cleanses the land. So one village fights another, and at the end of thirty days, whoever has the most people wins and they get new clothes," Janad explained.

RJ sighed and rubbed her hands down her face.

"What?" Topaz asked of the look on RJ's face.

"Don't you see, Topaz? It's nothing more than a fancy way to do a cleaning assignment. Obviously they have a population problem. The priests find the areas that have the worst problem—a drought in a certain area causes a crop failure, bugs eat the crop, not enough vegetation causes a lack of animals to hunt—etcetera. The gods' call a war, many people are killed so there is no famine, and the people think that the gods have saved them because they fought. It's the same damn thing the Reliance does, only, unfortunately for us, this little cleansing exercise helps survival of the fittest. Whoever is stronger and smarter in battle lives to reproduce, and everyone else dies. So what they have just shipped to our planet to be trained to fight us are a people who are genetically superior and experienced in battle."

"So do I call Mickey now?" the one they called Levits asked again.

"Yes, and tell him I'll tell him what to do when I know more," RJ said.

Levits turned and started punching buttons on the console.

RJ turned to Janad. "So, Janad, tell me—what do your gods look like?"

By the end of the first day the boat was taking on water. Haldeed rowed it over to the shore and they unpacked feeling wet, tired and more than a little sunburned.

Haldeed pulled the boat into the reeds with them and worked on fixing it while Taleed stomped down a big enough area to set up camp. "We should have brought hats."

Haldeed nodded in agreement as he wove new reeds into the leaks.

"And more food," Taleed said. Again Haldeed nodded. "On the upside, we've been gone six times as long as ever before."

Haldeed signed, *It is hard to get excited when your belly is empty and the sun has baked your skin into blisters.*

Taleed sighed. "I suppose you're right. I'm kind of use-less, aren't I? You do all the work—all the rowing. I'm no good for anything."

Haldeed signed, *You're good at thinking, why don't you think of something?*

"You're right, I will." Taleed started to pace back and forth. After a few minutes he jumped up and down startling Haldeed. "Sorry…But I've got it, Haldeed! You can weave us hats like you did the paddle, only leave a hole in the middle for our heads to go through. Then our faces will be blocked from the sun."

Fine for my face but what about my belly? Haldeed signed.

Taleed paced some more then started jumping up and down again, this time Haldeed was prepared for it. "I've got it! We could trap some *colimaçon*; the river is filthy with them. We just make a cone out of reeds, put a worm in the bottom of it, have a string on the cone, and when a *colimaçon* gets inside we pull it out. Maybe I can think of a way to watch the trap while you make hats. That would be useful!"

Haldeed nodded. As soon as he finished the repair on the boat, he went to work on the *colimaçon* trap. He tied the string from the trap to Taleed's big toe as instructed.

A few minutes later Taleed pulled the trap out of the water. Inside was a five-inch round snail. Haldeed dumped it on the ground and killed it by breaking its shell with a rock. Taleed caught six before they quit. Haldeed made a fire and cleaned the *colimaçon*, cutting its, guts out and scraping the shell away. They weren't very complicated animals, and were mostly flesh, so they roasted them on sticks and had quite a feast. As they roasted their feast, they caught some of the oil off the *colimaçon* in a small jar. When it cooled to a gel-like consistency, they rubbed it on their sunburned skin.

They fell asleep that night with their sunburn eased and their bellies full. They were getting used to life on the river.

At the palace, Taheed stormed around in a foul mood. "What do you mean you have not found him?" he screamed at Toulan, Captain of the King's royal Army. "How far could they have gotten? You've been looking for them for days. Are you telling me that the whole of the King's army is unable to find a missing handless youth and his mute servant? They are young and inexperienced, and this time they did not even take the royal vehicle; they are on foot! You find him. Find Taleed before the priests realize that he's missing. Find him before the people find out and we all lose face."

"Sire…he was not abducted. He has run away again, and no one would dare to find you at fault. Not even the priests, for you are infallible," Toulan said.

Taheed launched himself onto his throne and turned to glare at the big man. "Then you shouldn't think me harsh when I tell you that if you do not bring the prince home safely, and soon, I shall have your head removed from your shoulders by way of pulling. Now get out of my sight!"

They had been talking, and so neither of them had noticed that the water was moving faster. By the time they did, it was too late; they were caught up in the current. Taleed quickly turned around so that he could see where they were going. He didn't like what he saw; it looked like...Yes, it was! They were about to go over some falls.

"Jump, Haldeed, jump!" Taleed screamed and turned the boat over in his hurry to get out.

"Haldeed! Haldeed!" Taleed screamed. He went down but quickly kicked his way to the surface. Before he had a chance to remember that he couldn't swim, he was doing it. He realized that at least in this instance the fake hands were actually of use. Cupped as they were with the wires inside they actually helped him to pull through the water. He made it to shore with less effort than he would have thought and hauled himself out of the water. There was no time for him to celebrate his newfound skill, though. Haldeed was missing.

"Haldeed! Haldeed!" Taleed screamed into the waves. But he saw nothing. No trace of his lifelong friend. He scurried down the hill to the bottom of the falls. They weren't that tall; maybe only a ten-foot drop. "Haldeed! Haldeed!" Then he saw the body bobbing on the water. He dove in without delay, and with his new found ability swam over to Haldeed. He rolled him onto his back and took hold of his shirt collar with his teeth. Then he started kicking and splashing his way to the shore. When he reached shallow water, he hooked his arms under Haldeed's and pulled him out. It was then that he realized to his horror that Haldeed wasn't breathing. He thought quick; perhaps if he breathed his own air into Haldeed it would help. He knelt beside his friend and breathed into his mouth once, twice, three times. On the third time Haldeed spit out water, coughed and started to breathe.

Haldeed sat up slowly and looked at Taleed. *What happened?*

"I learned to swim!" Taleed said excitedly.

"You want me to do *what?*" Mickey asked. He looked at Diana to see if she understood, but she shrugged—just as confused as he was.

"I want you to get John Henry, take his prostheses off of him and paint him brown," RJ repeated with obvious impatience.

Mickey shrugged and wrote it down. "All right, go on," Mickey said.

"After he's brown all over, fit him with a silver jumpsuit. Meanwhile, I want you to find where they're training the Beta 4 humanoids. This shouldn't be too hard for Marge. Tell her they're calling them 'livestock.' No doubt they realize that we can tap into any of their communications and have made sure that no red flags would pop up.

"Next, I want you to have our people sneak John Henry into the Beta 4 training facility. If he's painted brown and wearing his prostheses, it shouldn't be too hard to make the guards think he's one of the Beta 4 humanoids. He'll have the silver jumpsuit under his clothes, and when night comes and the guards aren't in sight, he's to take off his prostheses and his outer clothing, leaving him clothed only in the jumpsuit. Make sure he knows not to let the Beta 4 humanoids see him do this. Then he should go to the Beta 4's, being careful not to be caught by the guards, and he should say this to them, *My children, the time has come to fight. You must cleanse the Earth with the blood of the Reliance people. Rise up and smite your oppressor.* If he says this exactly—or at least close enough, they will listen to him and do exactly as he says, so you have to make sure that nothing happens to him until they have successfully joined with our people in Zone 2-A."

"Are you alright, RJ?" Mickey asked looking at the list he held in his hands.

"It sounds crazy, but it's a good, sound plan, Mickey. So just do it," RJ ordered.

"Okay, RJ," Mickey said. "If you say so."

"Alright, tell me what you're supposed to do."

"Take a handless man, paint him brown, put him in a silver jump suit. Sneak him into the camp where they are training the Beta 4 humanoids, and have him tell them that they have to cleanse the earth with the blood of the Reliance. Don't worry; I wrote it all down," Mickey said.

"You have a supercomputer, and you wrote it down!" RJ laughed.

Mickey looked at Diana and shrugged, then said more to her than to RJ, "It helps me remember."

"And a supercomputer can't?" RJ asked.

Mickey smiled in spite of himself. "Is that all, RJ?"

"No. One more thing," RJ said. "Tell John Henry to try to sound like a god."

"Is this a joke, RJ?" Mickey asked.

"Would I call you across the vastness of space to play a joke on you?" RJ replied.

Mickey thought about it for a moment. "Yes, I think you would."

"Well, I'm not. Now just do it. Believe me, you *want* these people on your side."

Chapter Six

Smoke and flames and screams. Levits found himself on the bridge of the ship screaming into the com-link. "Abandon ship! Abandon ship!"

What the hell had happened? He had been farting around when he should have been on the bridge. He had thought they were safe; he hadn't realized they were in any danger until they'd been hit. They'd spit back a long stream of return fire on the alien ship, but it was too little, too late. One of the hits had caused a fire, and that fire was running through the ship unchecked because for some reason the extinguishing system wasn't working. He got hit full in the face with the smell of burning flesh and when he rounded the corner he stepped on the corpse of one of his friends.

It was all over now, they were all going to die, and it was his fault. His fault, because he had been lax. His fault, because he hadn't given the order to evacuate till it was too late, and his fault that he didn't go down with the ship.

Levits woke up screaming and was glad to see RJ sitting on the bed beside him. She must have shaken him awake. He drew a deep, shuddering breath and let it out. "What are you doing here?" he asked when his mind cleared. "Is something wrong with the ship? Who's at the helm?"

"Relax. Nothing's wrong with the ship, and Poley is at the helm," RJ said. She rubbed a hand down his shoulder. "Everyone's asleep. I felt your distress. Must have been one hell of a dream."

"You wouldn't understand," Levits said.

"No, of course not. That's why I was awake when everyone else was asleep. I have my own horrors, Levits."

"Yes, but nothing that has ever happened…None of it has been your fault," Levits said as he sat up in bed.

RJ laughed, although definitely not amused. "I wish I could convince *myself* of that. Everyone has their *what ifs*, Levits. What if I'd done that instead of this, or this instead of that? If only I'd paid more attention, if only I'd gone forward instead of backwards. If I'd been faster, smarter, more alert. If only the fucking bedroom door hadn't been closed. If only I hadn't let David leave," RJ said. "I'm sure whatever you think you have done was no more your fault."

He nodded. She really did understand.

She smiled at him then. "So, I've been thinking about what you said…"

"I'm sorry, RJ. Really sorry," Levits said.

"No, you were right. The only ironic part is that you're no better than I am. I wasn't the only one who pulled back that night, you know, and I'm not the only one who spends the day sitting around mentally licking my wounds."

"All right, I'll accept that. So I guess the question is what are we going to do about it?"

"Poley seems to think I'm moody because of PMS. I personally think it has a hell of a lot more to do with sexual tension," she said.

"I've only had sex—besides with myself—six times in the last three years," Levits announced.

"Well that would give you about six up on me," RJ said.

"Are you serious?" Levits asked in disbelief.

"Would anyone joke about a thing like that?" RJ took a deep breath and looked around. "You know that we have chemistry."

"Yes, of course we do, that's why we spend so much time biting each other's heads off," Levits said. "Do we have to analyze it, RJ?"

"No." RJ pushed him back onto the bed and moved to lie on top of him. Her lips came down on his, and passion flared. Before he knew what had happened they were naked

and engaging in the most satisfying and amazing sex of his
life. Then she had an orgasm, and he felt his limbs being
pulled apart. He looked down at his ultimate pain, and his
dick was gone.

Levits woke up screaming. His door opened, and RJ stuck
her head in. "You OK, Levits?"

"Stay away from me! Just stay away!"

RJ shrugged and walked away. Levits looked at the clock;
it was time for his shift. He remembered that was another
thing he hated about space flight—no concept of day or night.

"Levits, get in here!" RJ ordered abruptly. Obviously something was terribly wrong.

Levits pulled on his pants and ran down the hall without
his shirt and shoes. He found RJ in David's room. David was
curled up in the middle of his bed crying.

"What's wrong with him?" Levits asked.

"We're all going to fall!" David cried. "We're all going to
fall, and there's nothing to land on. You just float out there,
forever, like the living dead!"

"Shit!" Levits exclaimed.

He looked at RJ, and together they said, "Space sickness."

RJ sent Levits to get Topaz and a sedative. She sat down
beside David and stroked his back.

"It's all right, David. No one's going to fall. You just have
to calm down. This sometimes happens to first-time spacers.
You should have told someone how you felt; we could have
given you something that would help."

"My stomach. No matter how much I eat, it feels empty,"
David cried.

Topaz ran with the pocket medic, struck a pose, and yelled,
"Oh, no! It's space madness!'

"Don't flake out on me now, Old Man, I need your help,"
RJ said in an agitated tone.

"I was just trying to add a little levity to the situation.
Besides, do you know how long I have waited to say…'Oh no
it's space madness!'" Seeing that no one was laughing, Topaz

held the pocket medic over David's arm, and it gave him a shot of sedative. A few minutes later David was asleep.

"I'm sorry, RJ, I should have seen this coming. He's been acting strangely for a couple of days now," Topaz said.

"He always acts like that. How was anyone supposed to know?" Levits asked. RJ gave him a dirty look and he shrugged. "What?"

RJ ignored him. "He's too far gone now for a space sickness shot to work."

"It would probably do more harm than good at this point," Topaz agreed.

"Yeah, but you won't know unless you try it," Levits said with a crooked grin. When both RJ and Topaz glared at him he just shrugged and smiled broader. "Just trying to help."

"We're going to have to keep him sedated for the rest of the trip," RJ said.

"That's three *days*, RJ," Topaz said in disbelief. "It's not healthy to keep someone sedated for three days. Even with the new drugs with the stabilizing feature and IV fluids there is still some dehydration, and after being completely shut down for that long there is a risk of bladder infection, not to mention an impaction. I'm telling you right now I'm not doing any turd spelunking when he can't take a dump."

"Topaz," Levits started. "Have you ever seen what happens to someone with space sickness?"

"You know I haven't, smart-ass," Topaz said. "But I've read about it."

"I've seen it," RJ said. "We don't have a choice."

Janad didn't think she could answer even one more question about her planet. RJ and her weird brother were relentless. How much does it rain? What is the plant life like? What kind of animals? Questions about their government. Questions about their religion. How much did they sleep? What did they eat? Where did the Reliance ships land, when and if they landed? Did they have a spaceport on the planet's surface?

Did they have a satellite docking station, or one on a moon, or did the ships always land on the planet?

Some of the things they asked her she flat didn't have an answer for. In fact, she didn't even know what they were talking about half of the time. While RJ and Poley kept asking questions about her planet and the way they lived, weapons, fighting styles and such, Topaz bombarded her with questions about her family tree. What color were her ancestors? Was everyone the same color? What were the traditions about their ancestry?

At one point, tired of all the questions, she snapped at them, "How would I know? I'm not a priest!"

"The priests know the origins of your race?"

"They know everything; they talk to the gods," she said.

"Your King?"

"And the others—those that breathe the clouds into the sky," Janad said. "The ones who give us light and water."

Topaz looked confused.

For her, things were much easier than things were for these people. They never seemed to be happy with her answers; they always wanted to know why and how. No answer ever seemed to be good enough for them. A simple answer didn't seem to satisfy them at all. She didn't understand them completely, however she did know that they took the same information she had and came to conclusions she had never even thought of before.

She was purposely avoiding them now. She walked down the hall away from their voices, walking as lightly as she could and munching on a protein bar.

Stupid questions all the time. I feel like my brain will explode. I have to stay away from them; they aren't leaving anything in my brain. They are taking everything out.

She walked past David's room. The door was open, and she looked in. He was asleep; no, wait a minute—he looked...dead! She crept in the room, walked up to him and watched him closely. She could see his chest moving with his breathing, and she started to breathe again herself. He didn't move, though. It was the way he was lying; he just didn't look right. She sat on the bed and poked at his shoulder lightly. He didn't move, so she poked him a little harder. He still didn't move, so she punched at his shoulder. When he still didn't wake up, she drew back her fist to hit him hard.

"What the hell are you doing?" RJ said as she grabbed Janad's fist in mid-swing.

Janad was scared; no one had ever snuck up on her before. She was a hunter, a warrior; no one should have been able to do what RJ had just done. RJ jerked her up off the bed with a single motion. Janad's natural instinct overrode her good sense, and she punched RJ in the face with her other hand. RJ easily grabbed hold of her other wrist and held it, too.

"Well, you're fast. I'll give you that," RJ said. "I asked you a question."

Janad worked at not looking as scared as she felt. RJ's face seemed none the worse for wear; meanwhile Janad's hand hurt like hell. Punching her was like punching a rock. She made Janad almost as uneasy as her creepy brother Poley did. They weren't right—either of them.

"I was the hell checking him to see if he was all right. He's in a coma or something," Janad said.

RJ let Janad go giving her a look that let her know she'd better not try anything. She turned her back on Janad, which really pissed Janad off. Obviously RJ saw her as no threat at all. She, who had lived through two wars and brought home much game, didn't frighten this abomination of flesh in the slightest.

RJ sat down on the bed beside David and started to pat his head, moving the hair away from his face. "He's sick," RJ said by way of explanation.

"What's wrong with him?" Janad asked. After all the questions they had asked her, she wasn't really satisfied anymore with such a simple answer.

RJ was silent and for a minute. Janad thought RJ was just going to ignore her question. Finally she spoke. "He has the space sickness. We should have medicated him for it before we left Earth. At the very least we should have noticed and medicated him before he got really sick. Now we have to give him something to keep him asleep until we get to the surface of your planet. A few days on solid ground and he should be fine," RJ said.

"How will we get to the surface of my planet?" Janad asked.

"It just so happens that we're still fighting about that," RJ said. She turned to Janad and smiled, the first smile Janad had seen on her face since they had crashed through the ceiling onto the floor. When she smiled Janad didn't find her nearly as terrifying. "Come on; Topaz has decided to cook. It should be interesting if nothing else." RJ got up and started for the door. Janad followed reluctantly.

"Are you going to ask me more questions?" Janad asked wearily, and she heard RJ laugh for the first time.

"I guess we have sort of bombarded you, but you have to see where we're coming from. We don't know anything about you, your people or your planet. There are only a few of us. If we are going to succeed we are going to have to know as much as possible. Knowledge is power and our most important weapon. But I'll tell you what, while we're eating dinner we'll try not to ask you any questions."

"Then I'll come," they started down the hall. "What's wrong with your arm?" Janad asked.

RJ looked down at her right arm, which was jerking a little bit more than usual. Most of the time she didn't even notice it. If she was using it for a specific purpose it stopped; it was only when she relaxed that it started ticking. "It's nerve damage."

"Doesn't it bother you?" Janad asked.

"Not really. I've been this way all my life. My father made a mistake when he was making me, and this happened," RJ answered.

"What do you mean when your father made you?" Janad asked with a confused look on her face.

RJ laughed. "Now who's asking too many questions?"

Topaz had made some sort of soup from what he had found in the galley. It looked funny but was surprisingly good.

"I'm used to cooking with fresh vegetables from my garden, but when in space…" He laughed and shrugged.

Janad noticed that Poley was not present and presumed that he was flying the ship.

"So…how do you propose that we get to the surface of the planet?" Levits asked.

"The same way we got from Earth to the moon," Topaz said. "The girl said they transported them up to this ship. So we simply dock at whatever temporary station they've set in space…"

"More," Janad said holding out her bowl.

"All right, Oliver," Topaz said with a laugh as he ladled soup into her bowl. "Any way, as I was saying. We get back in the crate, let them unload us, and they teleport us down to the surface of the planet."

"And of course the Reliance is so stupid that they're not going to even notice that there is no crew!" Levits shook his head in disbelief. "They won't even wonder where the twenty-five men who are supposed to be on this ship are."

"Oops!" Topaz said with a laugh. "I hadn't thought of that."

"More," Janad said, holding out her empty bowl again.

Topaz looked into the empty bowl and then filled it with soup again. "Do you have a hollow leg?"

"I don't know," Janad answered, shoveling the food in her mouth again.

"We have to find a decent spot to land the ship away from everything. This ship's not really meant for landing on a planet, so it has to be someplace nice and clear with lots of room for error. From what I've learned about the ship it seems that it only has emergency landing gear, and that doesn't look like it's ever been tested outside the docking station. We don't want to be stuck on that planet with a crippled ship and no way to get off," Levits said thoughtfully.

"That planet is denser than Earth," RJ said matter-of-factly.

"So?" Levits asked with a shrug.

"It's mass is about one-and-a-half times Earths," RJ said. "If no large crafts land on Earth because of the fuel necessary to reach escape velocity…"

Levits understood now. "If we land on the planet's surface, we might not have enough fuel to even make escape velocity much less go anywhere else. We'd definitely be stuck on the planet. OK, so what's your big plan? Kill every Reliance man on the docking satellite and take over with one of our men in a coma and a primitive girl with a bag full of rocks?"

"I don't have any rocks," Janad said in a confused tone.

"Actually, I was thinking we could take one of the skiffs," RJ said. "There are actually two on the ship."

Topaz laughed at the look on Levits' face, and even Levits started to smile.

He shrugged. "I guess if I had checked things out a little more thoroughly I would have known we were carrying skiffs. It's not standard equipment for this vessel."

"I'm assuming they were taking them to the satellite. They probably use them to shuffle the transport stations and personnel around the planet," RJ said.

Levits nodded; that made sense.

"But what do we do with this ship, RJ?" Topaz asked. "When it doesn't make its delivery, the Reliance is going to know it's missing. They're going to look for it."

"Especially with all that gold metal," Janad said shaking her head.

"Gold!" the other three exclaimed.

"Yeah, there's a bunch of it. I saw them put it in a room with a thick door that wouldn't open," Janad informed them as she finished off her bowl of soup.

Janad wished she hadn't said anything. They didn't even let her finish eating. They immediately made her take them to where the gold metal was hidden in a supply closet behind a fake wall.

"Did you see what the combination was?" RJ asked.

Janad shook her head no.

"Screw it." Levits pulled his sidearm.

"No!" RJ screamed as he fired. "Hit the deck!"

Janad didn't have to be told twice. She hit the floor beside RJ and watched Levits dance around as the laser blast hit the safe and started to bounce around the room before dying in Topaz's left side.

"Ouch!" Topaz screamed. He gave Levits a heated look.

"Sorry, old man," Levits said with a shrug.

Janad jumped up at the same time RJ did. She went to Topaz to help him while RJ, ignoring the older man's pain, started yelling at Levits.

"Levits! You idiot! Do you really think they would go to all this trouble to hide their shipment from potential pirates and then not put a laser reflecting force field over it?" RJ shoved him in the shoulder, and he stumbled back a step. Levits righted himself and shoved her back, which caused no reaction in her what so ever.

"Are you all right?" Janad asked Topaz. She was worried about him. The ray seemed to have gone right through him and the wound was smoking on both sides. His "comrades" seemed to be completely unconcerned.

"I'll be fine. However it could use a cleaning," he said.

"We need to take him to the sick place," Janad said in a panic.

"Yeah, you go ahead. We're busy here," RJ said waving her hand in the air dismissively.

Janad helped Topaz to the sick bay. He sat on the table, and she went to get the things she had seen Poley clean David's wound with. Topaz took off his shirt; she could see the pain etched into his face.

"I can't believe that your friends are so unconcerned about you. They are very cold."

Topaz laughed as she started to clean the wound. "Are you worried about me, Janad?" he asked.

"Why wouldn't I be? I've seen men die from less," she said.

Topaz laughed again. "Great bedside manner you've got there. Don't worry about me, Janad." As she started to get the stuff to dress the wound he added, "and don't dress my wound. Just watch." He pointed at the wound, and she watched in amazement as it started to close. In seconds his skin was completely healed. Janad thought she now knew what these beings were.

"You're all gods!" she gasped.

"No, Janad, not gods. Although you can call me that if you like." Topaz smiled broadly at her. "I took a potion. That potion has made my cells regenerate themselves whenever they are damaged. That doesn't make me a god. It just makes me the end product of an experiment, and that's really all Poley and RJ are, too. Levits and David are normal just like you. The proof of that is that David is so sick right now. Everything has a logical explanation, just like I can tell you right now without fear of contradiction that your King is not a deity, and that whatever is making light and bringing water to your homes and belching out clouds is more of machine than god."

Janad thought about it for a minute then shook her head. "No, you're wrong."

"Don't you understand, Janad? There are no such thing as gods," Topaz said.

"But the people, *my* people, believe in these gods, and therefore they have power. That power makes them gods," Janad concluded with finality.

"Well, I'll be damned," Topaz said appreciatively. "That's pretty sophisticated reasoning for someone who's supposed to be a primitive."

"You have powers, and therefore you must be gods," Janad said on a final note.

Topaz sighed. "I take back what I said."

Levits had taken Poley's place on the bridge, and Poley was trying to figure out how to turn off the force field around the gold when Topaz walked back in.

"You all right?" RJ asked, hardly looking up from where she was looking over Poley's shoulder.

"Fit as a fiddle," Topaz said. "I'm afraid your caviler attitude about my injuries upset Janad. But now that she sees what I already knew—that I am a god—she has gone back to the mess hall to eat. She's a very good eater, that girl."

"So, you're a god?" RJ asked with a smile.

"Actually she thinks we're all gods. I think we'll be hard pressed to prove otherwise to her," Topaz said. "I rather like the girl; she grows on you after awhile."

"He'd like anyone who thought he was a god," RJ said to her brother.

Poley smiled and nodded absently and added, "I have the force field off."

"Well, duh!" RJ said. She could feel the slight electric charge in the air when it had been on. The absence of that charge was obvious to her.

Poley put his ear to the safe and started to turn the tumbler.

"Funny," Topaz said. "All this high-tech shit, and it all comes down to a simple combination lock. The same kind we had on our school lockers when I was a boy."

In a matter of minutes Poley turned the handle and opened the door.

"Holy shit!" Topaz exclaimed.

"I guess the price of slaves has gotten really high," RJ said. "There's got to be..."

"One thousand, five hundred sixty-three pounds," Poley said.

Topaz shook his head in disbelief. "That's worth..."

"Seventy-five million, four hundred and eighty thousand credits," Poley said. "Too bad it's radioactive."

"Radioactive!" Topaz and RJ screamed in unison. RJ ran over, slammed the door closed and locked it.

"That would mean this fucking gold is from the planet Stashes. They found a vein of gold there right on top of a shitload of plutonium," RJ said thoughtfully.

"The safe is lead-lined. That's why no radiation leak showed on any systems check," Poley said.

"Freaking Reliance," RJ hissed. "Are there no depths to which they won't sink? They're trading soldiers for radioactive gold and cheap textiles."

"And think about this," Topaz said. "What do primitives do with gold?"

"They wear it," RJ answered, eyes widening as the realization struck her.

Topaz nodded.

"We've got to stop them," RJ said with conviction.

It took them several hours to fish all their things from the river in the dark. Their reed boat was in tattered ruins and beyond repair.

We could build another boat, Haldeed signed, then hung some more of their wet things on a bush to dry.

"No, I think it's a sign that we should walk inland," Taleed said.

A sign from the gods? Haldeed signed not without a healthy helping of sarcasm.

"Gods!" Taleed made a hissing noise as he picked up a rock with his toes and slung it into the water. "I do not believe my father is a god, Haldeed. I know for a certainty that I am not. Nor do I believe that whatever the priests hide in their caves is a god. If there were true gods, they would not show themselves, but would stay out of sight. They would make the world work, not order men to be maimed or wars to be fought. If they chose to meddle in men's lives, why would they not make things perfect? Why would they keep our planet barren, order us to have as many children as we can, and then order up wars? I say that if there are gods, then they care not for man one way or the other. I certainly don't believe that the priests speak their will. I'll tell you better than that—I do not believe that my father believes it—or even that the priests do."

Careful; do not anger the gods, Taleed, Haldeed warned.

"We have already angered my father, Haldeed. False gods have no power," Taleed declared.

We were nearly drowned in the river, Haldeed reminded him.

"No god made a waterfall appear on the river. It has always been there. How can our failure to pay attention be considered godly power manifesting itself? Furthermore, we didn't drown," Taleed said.

I almost did, and your power saved me, Haldeed said signing in an excited way.

"Don't be ridiculous, Haldeed." Taleed said. "I simply used my head. I sucked air into my lungs, and then I breathed it into yours."

You truly don't believe in the gods? Haldeed asked.

"I very truly don't," Taleed answered.

Their things hadn't quite dried when it started to rain. Taleed saw the look Haldeed gave him and frowned hard. "This is *not* punishment from the gods, Haldeed. It's just a little rain. Surely a god would be more creative then this. Getting wet is less like a punishment and more of an annoyance"

If you say so, Haldeed said and continued to pack their wet gear into their backpacks.

They walked down the river till they found a well-used path. This they knew would lead them to a village. But they wouldn't stop there; oh no. If the royal guards came down the river looking for them, they would of course look in the town closest to the river. So they would continue to travel inland. They knew the further they got away from the river the better off they would be. The rain was coming down hard, and the river would come over its banks soon. In fact, it wasn't rare to look up after a storm upstream and see a wall of water coming at you. That was the way it was here—weeks, sometimes even months, without rain—and then torrential downpours that could last just as long.

They walked a little faster as the sound of the river got louder. It was still dark, so they walked around the back side of the village and continued on up the road before walking into the thick underbrush and making camp. They were soaked. Their tent and their bedrolls were soaked. What little food they had left was wet. It was raining so hard and, it was too dark to look for more. Cold and wet and hungry, they crawled into their tent and tried to sleep.

It rained all through the daylight hours. Haldeed got out and foraged for food in the downpour, giving up any notion that the rain would slow up soon. No way of making a fire, and all he found was some *carotte* root. It came up easy, and he simply left it hanging in a small bush until the rain had washed it clean. It didn't take long.

Haldeed held the root for Taleed to eat. Taleed chewed the horrible-tasting root and made a decision. "OK, Haldeed. I've had it. Ours is neither a moderate nor a very forgiving world, and neither you nor I have ever been taught how to survive in it. I say we get up this very minute and walk up the road. At the very next village we come to we will find lodging, buy ourselves a good hot meal, take a good hot bath and sleep in a warm, dry bed." Before he had finished speaking Haldeed had dropped the root and started packing.

It was the middle of the night when they came to the small village of *Are'ne*. The inn, however, took them in at once. They had a backpack full of *bercer-roc* and that bought hospitality even when someone might not feel like giving it. The huge rock tub in their room was filled with hot running water fed by reed pipes from the temple. They bathed together, each one relishing in the warmth of the water and the feeling of being really clean for the first time in days. Two bowls of steaming legume soup were brought to them and they practically inhaled them. Then, feeling warmed inside and out and dry for the first time in two days, they crawled into bed and went to sleep.

Levits felt like he was the one who needed to be heavily sedated. He was circling one of the six moons of the planet, trying to find a safe place to land, when there really weren't any. Finally he found a suitable crater and started to descend towards it, trying to ignore RJ and Topaz's constant chatter.

"So, riddle me this. It's a huge planet, and they are living on a very small part of it—no way are they crowded. So, why have they picked the most inhospitable place on the planet to inhabit?" Topaz asked.

"The oceans, while teeming with life, are constantly in turmoil, spawning literally hundreds of hurricanes and causing erratic weather patterns across the planet's surface. Then there are the several thousand active volcanoes which dot the planet's surface. Topographically it may appear that they have picked the most inhospitable region, but, in truth, they have probably populated the only truly habitable spot available," RJ answered.

"Would you both shut up!" When there was silence, Levits took a deep breath. "I just don't know…"

"You're doing fine," RJ said. "It's easy."

"If it's so easy, then you do it," he snapped back. He drew a deep cleansing breath. They didn't understand what they were asking him to do. As he had explained to them, this ship hadn't been meant to actually *land*. It was meant to go from one space station to another and be tethered up. The troops would be offloaded onto the station then sent into smaller, faster ships to do battle either in the air or on a planet's surface. It was a pack animal, and, as such, it was never meant to do such delicate maneuvers as landing on a specific crater of a specific moon. He wouldn't have felt so bad landing on a planet. In a ship like this, the crew could easily survive a minor crash. That is, on an inhabited planet with things like food and air. Not so crashing on a freaking moon made of rock with no breathable atmosphere. Here, anything less than a perfect landing could mean disaster—even death. The only plus was that there was less gravity.

He slowed the ship still more and lowered it slowly down onto the surface of the moon without so much as a bad shake. Once he had successfully settled the ship on its landing gear he set the stabilizers, retracted the gear and anchored the ship. Only when he had checked all his readouts and knew for certain he had executed a safe landing and secure anchorage did he start to breathe again.

"See? I knew you could do it," RJ said smugly.

Levits turned on her, madder than hell. "You know what, RJ? Everything is not some big freaking joke. Do you have any idea how much I hate being responsible for all of you?" He unbuckled himself, jumped up and stormed off the bridge.

"Wow! Who shit in his cereal?" RJ asked of no one in particular.

"I think you did," Topaz told RJ in a scolding tone. "You might try being a little more sympathetic. You know that was damn hard to do, and you know he was worried about doing it."

RJ shrugged; she supposed she could be more sympathetic. After all, she knew he wasn't thrilled about being in space, and she knew how he felt about being in a position of authority. Still…"He's got to get over it sometime."

"Physician, heal thyself," Topaz mumbled.

RJ pretended not to know what he meant and ignored him. She checked to make sure that all communication links with the Reliance were completely closed and that the ship's cloaking device had been activated. Now they would just have to hope that the Reliance wouldn't do a thorough reconnaissance of the planet's moons when looking for their missing ship.

Working in their favor was a strange planetary phenomenon. Beta 4 periodically radiated anomalous but powerful magnetic pulses. These pulses affected the planet and space immediately surrounding the planet, causing transmissions and other signals to either bounce or fluctuate erratically. Communication and locating devices were functional, but not reliably so. Scans might indicate objects where there was nothing, and it was just as likely that things that *were* there might not show up. If the Reliance wanted to find the ship, they would have to send out a manned reconnaissance vessel to actually look for it. Not only was that improbable without some indication of an explosion, but it was a big moon, and after all, the ship *was* cloaked. It would be difficult if not impossible for the Reliance to find them in this particular location.

Everyone but David had been on the bridge, strapped in just in case there were any problems. David had been strapped to his bed. RJ unbuckled her own belt and stood up. She stretched as if she had just woken up from a nap. "I'm going to go un-strap David."

She left the bridge and started down the hall for David's room. When she walked in the door she did a double take. The straps were broken, the IV was dripping on the floor, and David was gone.

"Oh shit!" she trumpeted, and within seconds the others were at her side.

Topaz looked in the room and visibly shrank. "Oops," he said.

"Oops!" RJ slapped a hand to her forehead. "Freaking oops! He had advanced space sickness, you forgot to sedate him, and you're saying *oops*!"

"Sorry?" Topaz added with a shrug.

"Great!" Levits looked at RJ. "What now, Great Leader?"

RJ temporarily forgot about the task at hand. "Why are you so pissy with me lately? If you didn't want to go this badly, you should have stayed on Earth. I told you I didn't want you here…"

"And I told you why that wasn't an option, but you weren't listening. You never listen to anyone unless they're saying what you want to hear!" Levits screamed back. "We all had to come because—like it or not—you *need* us. You couldn't do it on your own. You'd screw it up, and we'd have the Reliance breathing down our necks again."

RJ shoved him, and he hit the wall.

"You know what you are? You're a freaking bully!" Levits pushed away from the wall and got right in her face. "Pushing everyone around, knowing they can't push back."

RJ looked like she was close to shoving him through a wall. The truth really did hurt, and, as a general rule, if you hurt RJ, she hurt you.

"Wow!" Topaz screamed holding up his hands. "If you two could just put this pissing contest on hold, one of our crew is wandering around the ship in a psychotic daze."

RJ took a deep breath and glared at Levits who glared right back. "All right," RJ said taking a deep breath. "Topaz, you and Poley and the girl…"

"I have a name," Janad protested.

RJ gritted her teeth. "You guys go that way. Levits and I will go this way."

Topaz gave her a strange look, which she ignored. She was not going to try to explain the logic behind this division. It should be obvious.

Just then a crashing and banging began in the direction of the mess hall, so the splitting up became irrelevant and they all ran to the mess hall instead. They followed a trail of David's torn clothing down the hallway. When they reached the room they found David standing buck naked in the middle of one of the tables with a stack of pans in his hands. When he saw them he started laughing, and then he started hurling pans at them. One of his arms hung funny. No doubt it had been pulled out of socket when he'd broken his restraints.

"Ow! That's gotta hurt," Levits said, making a face as he looked at the arm. He jumped out of the way of a flying pot just in the nick of time.

"Go away! All of you go away! You're trying to kill me!" he screamed. Drool ran down his face and dripped off his chin. "Doesn't matter. We're all going to die anyway, but I'm going to kill all of you first. Take this! And this!" He started throwing pans again. When he ran out of pans he squatted and shit in the middle of the table.

"God!" Levits said pulling a face. "So much for worrying about an impaction."

Then David reached down and grabbed the fresh turd.

"Oh no!" RJ yelled as she realized what he was about to do. She ran forward and jumped through the air grabbing him. They both landed on the floor, but unfortunately, that just seemed to help David to sling crap all over all of them and the room.

"Shit!" Levits screamed, unable to do anything but stand with his hands out looking down at himself.

"Precisely," Poley agreed.

Topaz ran up and gave the squirming man a shot with the pocket medic. RJ got off of David only when he was still. She put her foot on his shoulder, grabbed his filthy hand and pulled his arm back into socket. She looked down at her shirt and chain, which were covered in shit, and then turned to glare at Topaz.

"Sorry," Topaz said again. "Guess this gives a new meaning to 'mess hall'."

"I'm fucking covered in shit!" Levits stated the obvious at his usual high decibel range. "God! This just gets better and better." He stomped off in the direction of the showers. RJ picked David up and followed Levits.

"He's more trouble than he's worth," Levits said to RJ over his shoulder.

Right then, RJ was inclined to agree with him. She knew that David couldn't control what he was doing, but there was something about having human feces slung all over you that just made it impossible to look at the big picture. It was funny; blood didn't bother her, but shit was another matter completely.

The showers were communal. She cleaned David off then lay him down on a bench and covered him with some towels. She went back to the showers and stepped in with all her clothes on, trying to rinse as much off them as she could.

"If I didn't already hate the bastard I'd hate him now," Levits said standing beside her in the shower rubbing the soap against his nude body hard and fast, working up a huge amount of lather.

RJ was silent. She stripped her chain and clothes off and stepped into the shower stream. She held her hand out to Levits, and he handed her the soap grudgingly. He watched as she lathered up. He smiled in spite of himself. Looking at her, he almost forgot all about the whole shit-slinging incident. He noticed she was scrubbing herself every bit as hard as he had been, so obviously she was just as creeped out.

She handed the soap back to him and their hands touched. Their eyes met. He quickly took the soap and looked away. "I had a dream the other day—or night—or what ever it was."

"You did?" RJ asked conversationally.

There was something about being in a shower naked with someone after having turds thrown all over you that sort of washed all other inhibitions aside. "Yes," Levits continued, "I dreamt that you and I were making love."

RJ laughed. "Really? Was I any good?"

"Very good, right up until you pulled my penis off," he said.

"Well, that's a hell of a finale," RJ laughed.

"Remember the other day when I brought up that thing you and I said we were never going to talk about again?" Levits asked.

"You mean about us almost having sex," RJ said.

"That would be it," Levits answered.

Before he could finish what he wanted to say, RJ said, "I once did body detail. The bodies had been left to sit in the rain and then the sun for about a week. The flesh was swollen, putrid, and full of fluids. It slipped when you tried to grab a body. Some of the bodies would just come apart when you went to pick them up. I don't think I felt as dirty then as I do right now," RJ said.

"Nothing quite like human excrement, is there? I realize he has space sickness and all, but of all the things to do, *Gee...od!* this has got to be tops..." He realized then what she had done. Once again she had successfully changed the subject. He looked over at her and smiled. "You almost succeeded."

"Not quite, though, huh?" she said. She held her hand out and he handed her the soap again. "I'd rather not talk about it, Levits. That's usually what someone means when they say, 'let us make a pact to never speak of this again.'"

"Ah, but see, I'd rather we did, and since this wasn't something you did by yourself I think I have just as much right to talk about it as you have not to talk about it." he said. "Ever since it happened we have been at each other's throats, and since I had this dream I think I know why..."

"Because you're afraid I'll defrock you?" RJ asked with a crooked smile.

"Try not to make a joke for a few minutes. Please try to talk to me seriously and without getting angry," Levits said heavily.

"That's asking an awful lot," RJ said with a grin.

Levits shot her an angry look

"All right," RJ said reluctantly. "I guess we do need to talk, but do me this one little favor. Let's not have this conversation when we're in the shower naked washing dung off our bodies. Let me get clean, take care of David, and I'll meet you in your quarters."

Levits nodded silently, hoping that he didn't lose his nerve between now and then.

Janad and Poley had helped him clean the crap up out of the mess hall, and then they had headed for the showers. From the ease with which the girl stripped in front of them Topaz surmised that she, like his military friends Levits and RJ, was used to public bathing. While Poley had a fear of being immersed in water, he was used to showering to get clean. It was obvious from the way the girl was looking at Poley that she either didn't understand what he was or simply didn't care. Stewart had been living vicariously through the robot, and he had not only made him fully functional but had given him an inhumanly large *schlong*.

Topaz still didn't feel completely comfortable showering with other people, but he wanted the shit off, and he wanted it off now. The girl was beautiful, well muscled, and perfectly proportioned. Topaz didn't even try to act like he wasn't watching her. She looked up at him caught his eye and smiled.

"It doesn't bother you that I'm watching?" Topaz said.

"It would only bother me if you seemed displeased with what you saw," she said with a grin. "You have a pleasant body."

"Thanks." Topaz realized, not without embarrassment, that he had an erection. He hung a washcloth on it, and the girl laughed.

He deduced from her reaction that bathing was a time of playful interaction for her people.

"I can do that," Poley said proudly. He immediately got an erection and hung a bath towel on it.

"Showoff," Topaz grunted.

Levits didn't know how she had managed it, but she was in his room before he was. She was dressed, but he was so used to seeing her in the chain that she might as well have been naked without it. She was just standing there waiting for him. Her arms were crossed across her chest; there was a cool, expressionless look on her face. Obviously she wasn't going to make this easy.

Levits was instantly pissed off. "You haven't come here to talk," he accused. "You've come here to shut me up."

RJ glared at him and for a minute he was sure she was going to stomp out of the room. Then she uncrossed her arms and tried to look less severe, which, judging from the look on her face, must have caused her some sort of physical pain.

After a moment she gave up and just started yelling, "God damn it, Levits! How the hell would you like me to look? Would you like for me to look as uncomfortable as I feel right now? I don't want to talk about it. I thought I made that clear months ago."

"And so we haven't talked about it, and has that helped? No. In fact it has turned us into what we are today; two people who can't be in the same room without fighting. The tension between us has escalated to the point that everyone knows it's there. Even that alien girl knows that there is something between us. We act like people who hate each other, and I don't hate you, RJ. I never could."

"And I could never hate you, but how am I supposed to react when everything I say pisses you off?"

"Have you listened to the way you talk to me, RJ? Are you even aware of how you have been treating me? Like I'm your subordinate, like I'm completely inconsequential."

RJ thought about that for a minute. "I wouldn't talk to you that way if you'd quit contradicting me every time I open my mouth. You disagree with me before I've even had a chance to finish what I'm saying. If I say I'm hungry you jump up and yell that you can't hear my stomach growling," she defended.

"I wouldn't disagree with you if you weren't such an arrogant bitch!"

"I wouldn't be such an arrogant bitch if you weren't such an ignorant asshole...Wait a minute!" RJ took a deep breath. "We're doing it again. Arguing over who's more to blame isn't going to fix anything."

Levits nodded his head in agreement, took a deep breath and tried to continue in a calmer manner. "This all started when you pulled away from me."

RJ sighed. "You see, now that's a big problem, because the way I see it you pulled away from me first."

Levits started to disagree loudly and then remembered his dream. In the dream he admitted that he had pulled away from her, too. He quickly analyzed his dream. When he realized what the dream really meant he admitted, although only to himself, that he was in fact the aggressor in their confrontations.

"Only in my head, RJ. I had a doubt, a doubt I would have overcome if you hadn't physically pulled away from me," Levits said. Then added, "So it was your fault."

"My fault! How is it my fault?" RJ said. "For me pulling away in your mind is the same as physical removal; it feels the same to me, maybe even worse."

"Admit that you've been screwing with my head for years. I don't know what you really want, and quite frankly I don't know if I can handle you sexually, or emotionally for that matter. You know how I felt about Sandy, and you know she didn't feel the same way about me. I don't really know how I feel about you, all I know is I don't want to wake up one morning and realize I've fallen in love with you and that you're in love with someone else. Especially if that someone else is David Grant."

RJ laughed, and was immediately less tense. "Levits, I could never love David. I don't think that I ever really did. He was the first person besides Stewart that I was ever close to, and between you and me, my father wasn't the warmest guy in the world. I wanted to love David, and since I didn't really understand what love was then I thought that I did. I know better now." She took a deep breath. "I think it's obvious that the reason we are fighting all the time is because we aren't having sex. I admit it. I just haven't wanted to get that close, especially to someone I care about. I wanted to separate myself from everyone and everything, but you wouldn't stay behind, ya bastard, so since you're here bothering the hell out of me, we might as well at least be having sex."

"Once we leave the ship there's probably not going to be another chance for awhile," Levits said swallowing hard.

She made the first move, walking up to him and draping her arms around his neck. "If you're really worried about me shredding your manhood..."

"I'm not." He put his arms around her and pulled her to him. He brought his lips down on hers and she responded. "So can we close the door?"

"No, but I'll make sure you forget that it's open."

Topaz, Janad and Poley were in the rec-room. Poley and Topaz were trying to teach Janad how to play the complicated game of bottle caps.

"So you throw the bottle-cap into the cup and that's it?" Janad said.

"You have to make it from the spot the last person made it from," Poley reminded her.

"And if you miss you have to take a piece of your clothing off very slowly," Topaz said. Poley started to contradict him. "That's the space rules, Poley."

Janad nodded, and threw the cap in.

"Beginner's luck," Topaz assured her.

They all heard RJ's screams of ecstasy. Topaz looked at Poley and smiled. "Maybe they'll stop fighting now."

"I wouldn't bet on that," Poley said. He made his shot.

Levits walked into the rec-room looking disheveled and exhausted, and grinning from ear to ear. He didn't even seem to notice the fact that Topaz was sitting wearing nothing but a smile.

"So I see you lived through it," Topaz said.

Levits smiled stupidly his head lolling to one side. "So far."

"I'm so happy," Poley said.

"OK, whatever, little tin dude," Levits laughed. He seemed to stop and think for a minute. "I wanted to tell you guys something, now what was it?" Levits seemed to be in deep thought. "Oh, yeah! I slept with RJ." He laughed, went to the drink machine, took out two bottles, unscrewed the caps and tossed them to Poley who caught them.

"It didn't sound like you were sleeping," Topaz said with a broad smile.

Levits just laughed, took his drinks and left.

"That was very primal," Poley said thoughtfully.

"How so?" Topaz asked.

"The male of the species foraging for food to feed the female and the ritual equivalent of pounding on his chest in the presence of the other males to let them know to stay away from what he now considers to be his female," Poley said.

"Very good observation, Poley," Topaz complemented.

Janad just shrugged, bored with all of it. She tossed one of her bottle caps at the cup, and she missed for only the third time. She had taken off both her boots already, so she took off her top slowly as previously instructed.

Topaz smiled.

"While your courtship behavior is more juvenile," Poley observed.

"Here's a clue for you, Poley!" Topaz turned glaring at him. "You don't have to speak all your observations out loud." He jumped up, grabbed his pants off the floor and put them on quickly. "I have to go check on David." He left.

Poley shrugged and tossed his bottle cap. It went in the cup; it always did.

"Do you always hit it?" Janad asked.

"Yes," Poley said matter-of-factly.

"So why do you play?

"Because I like to win," he informed her.

He still made Janad uncomfortable, but she no longer feared him.

"What's wrong with you?" Janad asked.

"Nothing's wrong with me," Poley said in confusion. "I'm perfect."

"That's it!" Janad exclaimed.

Chapter Seven

Haldeed woke up first. In the distance he heard machines, big machines. Sounds he had only heard a few times in his life but recognized all too well. He ran to the window and looked out. In the distance he could see a huge flying machine carrying something even bigger below it. He watched in horror as it got closer and closer, and he realized what it meant.

Haldeed ran back to the bed and shook Taleed till he started to stir.

Taleed woke up smiling. He'd slept well enough and long enough that even being awakened with a shake couldn't dampen his spirits. He was warm and dry and well rested, he stretched and thought of the wonderful breakfast he would eat. "See, Haldeed? We have made it. We have escaped, and no horrible fate has befallen us. We haven't angered the gods, and no punishment will come to us," he said smugly

He heard a strange noise, and then Haldeed was frantically pulling him towards the window. Taleed followed reluctantly; he didn't want anything to rain on his parade. He looked out the window and sighed. "Damn! I should have kept my mouth shut."

They dressed and packed quickly and started for the back door. They could hear the village priest in the middle of the town telling the people that the gods had ordered that some of them go to shed blood on a distant world for the glory of the gods. Haldeed started to go towards the town square, but Taleed elbowed him in the other direction.

"We cannot give up now, Haldeed," Taleed whispered in Haldeed's ear. "Not when we have gotten this close. We certainly can't allow ourselves to fall into Reliance hands."

But Taleed, how far will we get when the very gods seem to be
pitted against us? Haldeed signed in despair. *How can we escape*
the Reliance and their machines? If we go to them and tell them who
you are, they will surely take us back to your father. The worst that
will happen to us is we will be scolded.

"No! No, I will not go back. Do you hear me, Haldeed? I
would rather be a slave to the Reliance than a slave of the
priests. If you are right and the gods are true, then no harm
can come to me because I am then a god. I am the chosen, and
I shall make sure that no harm comes to you. Now come on,
Haldeed, let us not give up without at least the hint of a fight."

"What the hell are we loading all this shit for?" Levits asked,
putting yet another pile of pans into the skiff.

"The girl told us they trade goods from their planet for
metal. We may need items of value to trade. Theirs is a metal-
poor planet, therefore anything metal is going to be of value."
She threw the second broken security droid into the skiff. "The
cloth, while of some trade value, is mostly there as a cover for
the gold, and we sure as hell aren't taking that gold to the
planet."

Levits nodded his head in agreement then smiled.

"What?" RJ asked. Then, feeling why he was smiling, she
smiled herself. She felt better than she had felt in a very long
time and much more relaxed.

"I was just thinking about how surprised David's going to
be when he wakes up and finds out everything has changed."
He looked at her his face getting suddenly red. "RJ, I just
wanted to say that I...Well that you really are..."

"What?" RJ asked with a crooked grin.

"Infuriating," he said with a laugh. He leaned over and
kissed her check. "Did you...could you..." Levits damned
his tongue. He didn't usually have any trouble talking; he sure
as hell hadn't ever had any trouble talking to a woman. Except that this wasn't just any woman. This was RJ. It was
unnerving to know that she knew exactly how he felt and that

he had not a clue how she felt. "Damn it, RJ, do you feel anything at all for me?"

"Of course I do," RJ turned her head and kissed his lips, "and yes I could." They were in each other's arms and on the floor of the ship in a matter of minutes.

Topaz coughed loudly. "All right. I hate to be the one to rain on young love, but it really is important that we get David to the surface as quickly as possible."

Levits rose up on his arms and looked down at RJ. "See? He's nothing but trouble." Levits got up and put down his hand to help RJ up, although it wasn't necessary. She took his hand, and allowed him to pull her against him as she reached her feet. He kissed her, and then they parted.

Topaz set down the load of pans he held. "Janad and Poley have another load, and then I think that's about got it. I've loaded all the medical supplies I could find. Who knows what we might be exposed to?"

"Lovely," Levits said taking a seat at the controls and giving them a quick once-over.

"All right. All that's left is to get our space suits on, make sure the helmets are safe, and it's time to bug out of here," RJ said. "I'll go get David. See if you can get a fix on where the Reliance set down their transport station on the surface."

"We were in luck," Levits said from his seat at the console. "We seem to be in a pulse-free window, and I've already got the coordinates locked in."

"Let's just hope this pulse-free window doesn't allow the Reliance to track us," Topaz said.

"We know their position in space; they don't know ours. It's damn hard to track something if you don't know it exists, much less where it's coming from," RJ said.

Topaz nodded. That made sense. "It won't take them long to set up the trans-mat unit, and then they will be transmatting the Beta 4 humanoids to the station. That's one more reason to get this show on the road."

RJ nodded in agreement and went to get David. Topaz and Levits started to put on their space suits. Levits got in his long before Topaz did, then he turned and, without a word started redoing the seals on Topaz's. Yesterday this would have precipitated a continuous stream of loud, noxious insults out of Levits' mouth, but today he just unsnapped and resnapped the seals. Topaz was glad to see Levits smile and even happier to see that the spring was back in RJ's step.

Janad and Poley brought the last load of pans. Poley helped Janad into her space suit.

"Aren't you going to put a suit on?" she asked.

"I don't need one," Poley said.

"But don't you *want* one?" Janad asked. "They're pretty. It will make you look like a god."

Topaz laughed. "Honey, with the *schlong* Stewart stuck on that boy, he already looks like a god. However put the suit on anyway, Poley; it may help you with the natives."

RJ arrived carrying David, and Levits helped her slip his sleeping form into a suit, but not without mumbling. "Bastard, sling shit all over me, I ought to leave your seals open." They slipped his helmet on him and secured it, then lashed him into a stretcher-type affair at the back of the flight deck, which was there to haul wounded back from the front.

They sat down and strapped in. Levits started the countdown, the bay doors opened, and as he got to 'one,' the skiff was shot from the mothership like a spore out of mold.

"Yee-haw!" Topaz screamed. "Now this is how it oughtta be. This is like *Star Wars* shit, man!"

Levits just smiled and shook his head. He actually felt more comfortable flying the skiff than he had the troop carrier. That had just reminded him too much of his own personal terrors.

"Don't rejoice yet, Topaz; you haven't experienced reentry. In a ship the size of this skiff and a planet with that kind of gravitational pull, it will feel like you are being shaken apart," Levits informed him.

"Bring it on, baby! Bring it on!" Topaz said excitedly.

"Just pray the Reliance doesn't get a bead on us, Old Man," Levits said. "I'm sure even their temporary satellite has fighter ships, and this skiff has one forward plasma cannon and one aft laser."

"They aren't likely to see us, much less get a bead on us," RJ reassured them. "They're on the other side of the planet, and, as I said, they don't know to look for us. I think you can relax and enjoy the ride."

Topaz laughed heartily. "You know, I've just got to say it. You two are so much easier to get along with when you're getting laid."

Janad started laughing loudly. "Oh! *That's* what they were doing."

They had run into a line of Reliance men just when they were sure they had gotten away, which made it that much harder to take when they were herded back towards the village square where the priest and the Reliance box were located.

"You now go to heaven to fight the gods' battles there. Do not be afraid to serve the gods. Do not be afraid to leave behind your old ones and your children; they will be well cared for."

They pulled the warriors from the group, easily recognizing them by their clothing and trappings. They started herding them towards the transport station.

The gods are punishing us because we ran away, Haldeed signed in fear.

"They are only taking the warriors. We wear the clothes of peasants, of workers; we will not be chosen. If our gods serve up our people to these aliens, then I say damn them. I will not serve such gods, and I most certainly will not become one." Taleed looked down to make sure his fake hands were still in place and looked real enough. He hoped the beards he and Haldeed had grown on their trip would hide their identities. However, it was obvious that Haldeed wanted badly to tell the captors who they were, give up and go back to the palace rather than risk being sent to heaven.

Better the demons you know, Haldeed signed at the end of a long string of frantic signing.

The priest walked right up to them and Taleed swallowed hard.

"You there," the priest said pointing.

"Us?" Taleed asked trying to keep fear from entering his voice.

"Yes, you…You are new in our village. You are young and healthy; are you not warriors?"

"No, holy one, we are but poor farm workers moving on to follow the crops."

"I do not believe you." The priest waded through the crowd towards them, and Taleed inwardly cringed.

All the priests throughout the land knew what the Chosen One looked like. Once a year they all came on a pilgrimage to the holy city and gazed upon his father and himself. If the priest got too close he would recognize him, and their adventure would end.

Suddenly there was a loud roaring sound and a bright light streaked across the sky. All stopped as everyone turned to look at the sight in awe and in wonder. The Reliance men looked up also and became immediately defensive, which told Taleed that whatever this was it had nothing to do with them. There was a loud noise and sparks flew from the box in front of them. The Reliance men scattered looking for cover and the villagers just ran. The priest who had questioned them dropped to the ground prostrating himself and started praying loudly. He was throwing his gold chains in the air as if offering them to the gods.

Haldeed pulled on the stunned prince's arm dragging him to safety behind one of the carved rock dwellings.

A white ship just like the one the Reliance people had arrived in set down gently on the ground in front of them. The Reliance's flying ship took off, firing rays of light down at the other ship. There was another loud noise and the Reliance ship exploded and fell out of the sky. Two gods with solid silver bodies stepped out of the newly arrived ship. The Reliance people still on the ground fired upon the new arrivals, but the gods were also armed with weapons of light and did smite any of the aliens who dared to show their faces. The people, realizing that their gods had come to save them from the claws of the Reliance, turned on the Reliance men and fought as they had never fought before. In minutes all the Reliance men were dead. The priest quickly moved and prostrated himself on the ground again. This time he fell before the gods and made an offering of his last gold chain.

RJ looked down at the prostrate man with tell-tale burns all over his head and his hair falling out. She looked at Poley who nodded.

"Janad!" RJ screamed back towards the ship.

Janad ran out to stand beside her as the others walked out of the ship.

"Yes," Janad said.

"Tell this man that all this gold is tainted and must be destroyed at once," RJ said.

In her native tongue Janad told the man what RJ said. He spat back a stream of utterances at her; she frowned.

"What did he say?" RJ asked.

"He said that these gold chains were gifts from our god and therefore could not be poisoned," Janad said.

"Tell him that the chains he is wearing is causing his hair to fall out and is making the boils that he has been afflicted with. Tell the idiot that he has radiation sickness," RJ ordered.

Janad told the priest what RJ had said, but he shook his head frantically and spat out another sentence.

"He says you are demons sent to tempt his faith in the gods, and that he therefore revokes his gift of the gold."

"Tell him I said...ah fuck it." RJ aimed her laser and shot him in the head. The old priest fell over dead. RJ removed her helmet.

The villagers looked at her in shock and horror.

"Damn it, RJ," Topaz cursed running up to her. "I might have learned much from him. Now all you have done is turn the villagers against us."

"By killing their spiritual leader I have proved the impotence of their gods, and they will not dare to anger me. Besides I doubt very seriously you would have gotten anything of value from that imbecile," RJ said. "Janad, tell the people that we mean them no harm, but that we will not tolerate such disrespect. We have come to save them, but only if they prove themselves worthy."

Janad screamed the statement to the general population.

Topaz stared at her, mouth open.

"Tell them that the Reliance is evil and is trying to kill their gods," RJ ordered Janad.

Janad made the announcement.

"What are we going to do with this radioactive waste?" Levits asked at RJ's shoulder.

"One thing at a time," RJ said. She handed him her helmet. He looked at his hands now filled with helmet, his own and hers, then turned and unceremoniously threw them into the open door of the space ship. RJ smiled at him before continuing. "First we have to make sure that these primitives don't turn on us the way they did the Reliance.... Janad, tell them that we will protect them from the Reliance and from the anger of their gods, but that they must do as we tell them."

Janad shouted the message, noticing that the people drew ever closer.

RJ noticed the stunned look on Topaz's face and asked, "What's wrong with you?"

"RJ, that isn't an alien tongue Janad is speaking," Topaz informed.

"Sounds alien to me," RJ said thinking he was probably flaking out again.

"It would to you. RJ, the language that girl is speaking is

French, an Earth language that hasn't been spoken in well over six hundred years."

Topaz was following RJ and Janad to the 'temple.' Levits and Poley had stayed to guard the skiff and keep an eye on David.

A group of village children were closely following them. RJ tried to ignore them, but they were bugging the piss out of her.

"It's a good thing I can't have kids," RJ said pulling a face as one of the smaller ones reached out and touched her. "I don't think I have the maternal instincts necessary to stop myself from killing them if they annoyed me." Since the one child had touched her without disintegrating, the others had moved still closer. RJ turned quickly threw her arms around wildly and growled at them. They screamed and scattered in all directions. RJ laughed triumphantly and kept walking.

"Have you heard anything that I've been saying to you?" Topaz asked.

"The natives speak French, blah blah blah. They must be decedents of Earth-born humans, blah, blah, blah, blah, blah," RJ said continuing to follow Janad.

"Aren't you interested in the least? How did they get here? From where does their belief in a handless god come? What about their god that makes clouds?" Topaz rattled out.

"I'm not interested in anything right now except getting any tainted gold out of this village and getting out of here before Reliance troops show up to find out what happened to their transporter. I don't care how they got here, and I don't know where they came up with their armless god, but I'd say *that's* where they got their belief in a god that makes clouds."

As she spoke, RJ nodded towards the middle of the village where there stood a huge rock. Carved into the rock was the 'temple,' and spewing from the top of the temple was a steady stream of steam.

"Well, I'll be damned!" Topaz said in awe.

Two guards stood at the door to the temple. When they saw RJ and her party they moved aside, indicating by their actions that they were welcome to enter.

Janad stopped at the door. RJ turned and looked back at her. "Come on."

"It is forbidden for any mortal save the priests to enter the temple, and…"

RJ grabbed her by the arm and pulled her inside. "It's bullshit, all right, Janad?" RJ said. "You're a bright girl; you've been in a spaceship. If a machine can power through space and move you across galaxies in a matter of days, how much simpler is a machine that makes lowamp electricity? You hear that noise?" Janad nodded. "That's the sound of a machine. You know what a machine is, so you know that whatever is in the heart of this *temple* is more of machine than god."

Men, obviously priests because of the rule, were running around wearing simple workman's coveralls, carrying tools and wearing tool belts. When they saw the three who entered, they dropped to the ground and prostrated themselves. Most of them clearly bore the signs of radiation sickness.

"Damn," RJ laughed. "I could get used to this."

"Didn't you get enough of it back on Earth?" Topaz asked sarcastically.

"I have never seen the priests in their holy garments or carrying their holy instruments before," Janad said in a low and reverent voice.

"Those are work clothes, and they are carrying simple tools." RJ sighed. "Don't you get it, girl? Your priests are nothing but mechanics."

"How do you suppose these people came to worship what is obviously a steam engine?" Topaz asked.

"Obviously because they have been kept ignorant of the fact that it is an engine. It's simple, Topaz. The people no doubt make sacrifices of food, clothing, and items of wealth to the priests. The 'priests' figured out early what a good gig this was, and have become wealthy making sure the people didn't find out that their 'temple' is nothing but a power plant," RJ said.

"Yes, but who gave them this technology? The tools they have are obviously old, some even show visible signs of damage. As you have pointed out often, they have little metal on this world. So who brought them the materials and the technology?" Topaz asked.

"Well, obviously it was some armless, deranged, black, French man," RJ said. "I really could care less." One of the priests was wearing one of the radioactive gold chains, and RJ reached down as she passed his bowing form and took it off in her gloved hand. "Again…all I want is to gather up the tainted gold and leave this village before the Reliance gets here in force."

"Ah! Here we go." They entered what must have been the very center of the Temple, and there sat a thermo-electric generator belching the steam that went out the vents in the roof. It was nearly covered with the gold chains, and it was surrounded by several gold bars and thousands of little black stones.

"I have never seen so many *bercer roc*," Janad said pointing at the stones.

"Janad, go back to the ship at once," RJ ordered.

Janad didn't have to ask why; she knew. They had said there was something wrong with the gold metal and that it was making the priests sick. She didn't have to be told twice. She practically ran from the building.

"If the Reliance just got here, where did all the gold come from?" Topaz asked.

"No doubt they made payment before returning for the warriors," RJ answered.

"So, the priests also believe that the generator is a god," Topaz said.

"Yep," RJ agreed. "No doubt they think that their work keeps the god happy, and keeps him making energy for their villages. No doubt the maintenance work they do has become complex ritual."

"So what now, *Kemosabe?*" Topaz asked. "Radiation isn't exactly healthy for us, either."

"We aren't going to be around it long enough for it to matter, and we aren't going to touch the shit," RJ said. "So, Topaz, can you speak French?"

"*Oui, je parle Francais,*" Topaz said.

"I'm going to take that as a yes," RJ said with a smile. "Call the priests in here, and tell them we have come to cure their affliction."

Poley worked at the controls on the Reliance transport station as the priests loaded first the gold and then the body of their high priest and the bodies of the dead Reliance men into the transporter as RJ had ordered. Levits had already very carefully gathered the weapons, not trusting them in the hands of the primitives, and carried them to the ship.

"Hurry, Poley," RJ ordered.

"I always hurry, RJ," Poley said. "I do things without delay; you know this."

"You know what that generator was, don't you, RJ?" Topaz asked excitedly.

"It looked like one of the thermo-generating plants they used to send out with early colony ships," RJ said without enthusiasm.

"It was one of the old thermo-generating stations they used to send out with early colony ships. They had all the equipment for drilling and setting up a power station. All of the equipment to civilize a planet. The only problem is that by the time they started working on earnestly colonizing the planets there were very few pure black people left," Topaz said thoughtfully.

"Uh huh," RJ said watching only the completion of the operation at hand.

"RJ, are you listening to me?" Topaz asked excitedly.

"As well as you are listening to me," she said with a smile.

"There, it's done," Poley said, closing the panel up and moving away from it while giving his sister what could have easily been interpreted as a pouting look.

The last priest set down his load and stepped out of the transport station.

"Tell them to stand clear," RJ said.

Janad did, and the people moved way back.

RJ took a timed charge from her pocket. She set it, then threw it in. She punched a button, and the whole lot disappeared.

RJ grinned impishly as she turned to face her friends. "That ought to slow down their operations for a while. Poley, dismantle the unit and bring the transmat components with us."

Poley nodded and started the task of disassembling that which he had just assembled.

Topaz started to administer treatments for radiation sickness to the priests with the pocket medic, telling each one to "Go now and sin no more." He obviously thought this got funnier the more often he did it.

However, for RJ, it had ceased to be funny at least twenty minutes ago.

"Topaz, find out which one of them is now in charge," RJ said.

Topaz nodded and asked the question of the next man in line. He made wide hand gestures as he spoke, then pointed to a big man towards the back of the line. RJ nodded grabbed Janad by the arm and headed for the man. He glared at RJ with cold eyes that let her know instantly that he considered her neither god nor friend.

"Tell him that the gold with which the Reliance has been trading is poisoned…"

"I understand that," the priest said in the Reliance tongue.

"Well, this certainly makes things easier. Listen to me. The Reliance is taking your people to Earth to be killed…"

"It is the gods' will," he said.

"That," she said pointing towards the Temple, "is a *machine* in there. It takes superheated steam from your planet's core and makes electricity. If you didn't repair the equipment, your god would die," RJ said.

The priest held his hands over his ears, and RJ sighed thinking about putting a plasma bolt in his head, too. She grabbed his hands and pulled them off his ears. He frowned when his struggling got him nothing but sore wrists.

"OK, here's the scoop, Shit-for-brains. You either listen to me or I pull your arms out of your body and beat you to death with the bloody stumps. I don't have time to tear through your stupid-assed religious dogma. I realize that you don't care about your people, but I *do* care about *mine*, and right now the Reliance is taking your people from your planet and sending them to mine to kill my people. I'm not going to let that happen. The Reliance will come back here. They will try to take your people away. You will not tell the people to go. You will tell them to fight the Reliance and drive them away. You will accept no gold from your gods or anyone else, because if you do a great plague will fall upon you, and you will all die even as you were dying when we arrived. If you help the Reliance I shall personally come back here, lay your temple to ruins, and crush your skull with your god." That said she picked him up and threw him several feet through the air so that he landed on his back in a pile of some sort of animal waste.

"Let it never be said that you can't be diplomatic when the need arises," Topaz said sarcastically.

"A kind word turneth away wrath," RJ said with a smile. Then she turned and headed back towards the ship. She emerged a few moments later with a stack of pans that she handed out—not to the priests, but to the people. The people took the pots and pans, holding them reverently. "Janad, tell them that they are to use these gifts in good health."

Janad told them, and they looked pleased.

"Tell them that they must always fight the Reliance. Tell them that the Reliance tried to poison their god."

Janad told them, and they looked upset and started chanting angrily.

"They must pick a reliable person to go to the next village and tell them what they saw here today and all that they heard. They must tell them that the priests must take the gold off their bodies and away from their god. They must take it far away and bury it in a hole marking it with a sign that warns others of the danger," RJ said. "It must be taboo forever."

Janad nodded and translated RJ's instructions. The people as a whole nodded their heads in agreement that became more enthusiastic as understanding dawned.

"That village must in return send a runner to the next village, and so on and so forth," RJ said, waving a hand dismissively. She hated to be bothered with trivial details. Life would be so much easier if people could learn to just follow a plan out to its logical conclusion on their own.

Janad relayed the message.

"OK, then. Let's get the hell out of here," RJ ordered.

Janad started to tell the people.

RJ grabbed Janad, putting a hand over her mouth and dragging her against her. "Don't tell them *that*, dummy." RJ laughed. Janad nodded and RJ released her.

Topaz was finishing the last of the injections, so RJ moved towards the ship and Janad was following.

"Maybe Janad would rather stay here, RJ," Topaz said.

"I wouldn't," Janad said.

"What we are doing is going to be dangerous," Topaz said.

"Yes, much more dangerous than staying here to fight the Reliance when they rush in here any minute now, all pissed off," RJ said sarcastically. "Now get your shit together and let's go."

We were saved by the new gods, Haldeed signed.

"They are no more gods than I am, Haldeed. There ship was no different than that of the Reliance. As for their appearance, you forget that my father has such a suit. They are just clothes—nothing more, nothing less. Something worn I suppose in space travel. There is no magic in them," Taleed whispered. "We must go with them when they leave."

What! Haldeed exclaimed with flamboyant hand gestures.

"You do not know the Reliance tongue as well as I do. I heard her say that the Reliance is coming back here, and we must not be here when they arrive. I do not believe they are gods; however, I believe from their actions that they know what is truly going on," Taleed said.

If we approach them they will kill us, Haldeed said excitedly.

"If we stay here, the Reliance may kill us or worse. What's the worse that could happen? If it looks like they mean to do us ill, I will tell them who I am, and then they dare not harm us," Taleed said. "Come, Haldeed. Quickly! They are getting ready to go."

Taleed started moving through the crowd, and Haldeed followed reluctantly.

The white headed woman went into the ship, and came back out shortly and whispered something angrily to the tall, thin, dark-haired man. He just shrugged and looked like he was just as angry with her. Then she stripped her suit off. The stiff-moving man took his suit off, and so did the girl who was the right color. These three walked away fast as the others climbed into the ship. In seconds the ship had lifted up and was gone.

Taleed switched directions and started after the white-headed woman and the two that had gone with her. They were walking so fast that the young prince and his companion had to practically run to keep from losing them. The strangers seemed to plow a trail through the tall brush as if it were nothing.

Sergeant Bradley and his crew of three men were in a level-three maintenance tube repairing a broken conductor cable. It was hot and the air damn near non-existent.

"Well, gee! Couldn't you just do this forever?" Harker said, stopping his torch just long enough to raise his visor and wipe the sweat from his face.

Sergeant Bradley smiled. "Yeah, they say the place to be in the military is in the combat forces, but they don't know what they're missing out on. We in maintenance know what real joy is."

"This guy Briggs...We've worked on some shit details before, but this guy has no respect for maintenance at all," Harker said.

"Let the station start falling apart, and he'd grow some in a hurry," Sergeant Bradley said as he moved to hold the cable steady. Hotter than hell, and he was forced to wear three thicknesses leather gloves.

"Why the hell can't we use laser tools?" Harker asked.

"Has something to do with some idiot not using the right kind of reflecting shield and cutting a hole right through the hull of a battle cruiser causing an instant depressurization which caused the death of twenty people," Sergeant Bradley explained. "Of course 5 or 600 maintenance personnel have died of heat exposure in these freaking maintenance tubes since, but, hey! we're expendable."

Bradley and the other two men hefted the cable into place as Harker continued his weld.

"You know what's wrong with the Reliance don't ya?" Harker started screaming over the spitting of the torch. "They let little jerk-offs like Briggs be in control."

"Between you and me, there are too many people who have never gotten their hands dirty making the decisions that make the rest of us work harder," Bradley agreed.

"Guys!" one of the other men interrupted, then added in a whisper, "The walls have eyes and ears, you know."

"Not down in the service tubes," Harker said. "The idiots up topside don't consider us bright enough to be a threat. When we were given our tests at nine they concluded that we weren't bright or ambitious enough for combat or officer ranks, so they condemned us to spend our lives fixing the shit that they break. They aren't afraid of any rebellion coming from us; they aren't afraid of us at all"

"He's right, though, Harker, better watch what you say. With someone like Briggs at the helm, damn near anything can be seen as treasonous. He just looks for reasons to execute people. Given free rein, I really think he'd take out everyone just to make a point," Bradley warned.

"Don't you ever get tired of it?" Harker said. "Tired of all the shit…"

"Better stop right there, Harker," Bradley said. He looked at Harker, then cut his eyes towards the other two men. Harker nodded his understanding and fell silent.

Just then the whole station lurched. Since three of them had hold of the cable at the time, it ripped out all the work they had just done. The ship rocked for several seconds, warning lights started flashing, and sirens started wailing.

"What the hell!" Harker screamed. "Are we under attack?"

"Here?" one of the other men screamed. "Why would anyone fire on us here?"

"Maybe the New Alliance found out what we're doing," Sergeant Bradley said.

"What the hell do we do now?" Harker yelled.

It was a good question. If they were under attack, their adversary was bound to start firing at the belly of the station, knowing that was where the main drives were. On the other hand, from their position, there was no way of knowing which direction might lead them to safety and which might lead them into tunnels full of fire or deadly gas.

The station seemed to stabilize.

"Whatever it is seems to have stopped," Harker said.

Bradley pulled his computer from his pocket and powered it up. "The damage appears to be localized in the transport area. A huge explosion and a hull breach right after a materialization. The emergency hull repair activated and seems to be holding, but the damage looks extensive."

"Could it have been caused by that damned magnetic pulse?" Harker asked.

One of their early transportations from the planet had gone very badly when a magnetic pulse from the surface had happened in the middle of transporting humanoids from the surface. Instead of viable humanoids, they had ended up with a sort of humanoid mush that had taken them the better part of a day to clean up.

"No, we have learned that the pulses are never closer than fifteen minutes. Since then we only send or receive right after a pulse. Besides, you saw what happens when a pulse interrupts the signal, and it doesn't cause any kind of explosion. I'd say someone sent a bomb on the transporter. You guys finish this job. I'd better get topside."

Just then, his communicator buzzed, and Captain Briggs' voice screamed, "Sergeant Bradley! Where the hell are you? We've had a problem in the transport bay."

"On my way, sir," Bradley said. He looked at Harker, pulled a face, and Harker smiled.

"Good luck," Harker said. Bradley nodded and left.

They got back to work finishing the project that had been interrupted. None of them harbored any notions of getting much sleep for the next few days. This time in the tunnels was probably going to seem like a vacation by the end of the week.

When they finished, Harker climbed out of the tube last. "You guys go on up. Tell Bradley I'll be there in a minute; I've got to take a crap."

He watched as they left and then quickly walked in the other direction. A hand reached out, grabbed him and pulled him into a service closet. The door closed and he found himself in total darkness. He felt hands undoing his belt and lips on his. He kissed her and then said, "I sure hope that's you."

"It is. What about Bradley?"

"I think he'd come over with us," Harker said. "I've known him most of my life. He hates the Reliance as much as we do, even if he is afraid to say so. Were you able to reach the New Alliance?"

"No. Damn it, their computer is hard to break into, and I have limited time. I have to be damn careful I'm not caught. I thought about just fixing the manifests to show what we are really shipping, but we've all been briefed over and over about the secrecy of our mission here. If they traced it back to me..."

"What happened to the transport bay? Bradley said it might be a bomb. Do you think it could be the New Alliance? That maybe you *did* get through somehow?" Harker asked.

"I wish I could say yes, but I just don't see how."

"I don't have much time," he said huskily.

"Then let's not waste any more time talking. I like you when you're all sweaty."

David had woken up groggy and disoriented. When he saw where he was a terror entered him—a fear like no fear he had ever known before. He had to get out of the ship and out of space. He had taken the belts off and stumbled from the ship. The 'aliens' in the silver suits were busy trying to get new victims to torture in space, and so he snuck past them and just started walking, happy to be walking on good-honest dirt. Glad to have something real and solid beneath his feet.

They had drugged him. He didn't know how or why, but he knew he'd been drugged. Nothing seemed to make any sense in his head, and he couldn't trust his mind to know the difference between what was real and what was illusion. He wasn't even completely sure of whether he was awake or asleep, alive or dead. He just knew he had to get away, far away from those Reliance thugs who were trying to make him believe they were his friends. He stumbled through the brush; his legs felt like they weighed a hundred pounds each. He fell at one point, and it was all he could do to pry himself off the ground. Behind him he could hear them calling his name, and he doubled his pace, but they were still closing in on him.

"What a giant pain in the ass!" Levits screamed at Topaz, mostly because he was the only one left to scream at. He lifted off and moved in the direction of the coordinates RJ had given him.

"She screams at me like it's my fault. That freaking pain in the ass!"

"Who?" Topaz asked with a smile, "David or RJ?"

"They're both pains in the ass, but right now I was talking about that giant sphincter wart, David Grant," Levits hissed. "I wish to God that we had left him on Earth."

"She wanted to leave him on Earth; he wouldn't stay any more than you would. If it's any consolation, I'm sure he's wishing he'd stayed home about now," Topaz said.

"It's not," Levits snarled. Suddenly a warning siren went off, and the ship started lurching from side to side. "Damn it all!" He looked down at the controls. Red lights were flashing.

Topaz quickly put on the seat belt he had earlier shunned. "I don't suppose that's the celebration light or the happy hour buzzer. And I'm willing to bet that *Damn it all* isn't just some funky little Reliance astronaut toast."

"Our fuel cells are low. We're losing power and altitude. Apparently the ship was never meant to actually *fire* the weapons. Suck-oid obsolete Reliance equipment! We were at full power when we left the ship, and now we're completely out of fuel. We're going to have to put down right here." Then they basically fell out of the sky.

Topaz looked at Levits, who was shaken but not hurt. "Well, that sucked," Topaz announced.

"More than you think. Barring a miracle, we're now stuck on this freaking planet."

RJ listened to the discouraging report Levits gave her and frowned. She took a deep breath and talked over his yelling. "Are you all right?"

"I'm…Yes, I'm fine." He sounded a bit taken aback by her question. "RJ, how are we going to get off this planet?"

"We'll hijack a Reliance vehicle if we have to. We'll find a way. It's a pain in the ass, but there's no reason to panic as long as you're all right." RJ paused. "We've been in tighter spots…I'm sorry I screamed at you. It's as much my fault as anyone's that David got away."

"Are you OK, RJ?" The tone of Levit's voice was both puzzled and concerned.

RJ laughed. "Yeah, I'm fine. Over and out."

"Out."

RJ looked at Janad. "You and Poley go on. You should catch sight of the deranged butt hole any minute. I'm going back up the trail to check on something."

"Be careful," Poley warned.

RJ smiled over her shoulder at him as she walked away. "Aren't I always?"

Janad smiled and started back on David's trail. Now she really felt like she was at home. Out here in the forest, stalking prey—it was what she had been doing since she was a child. She caught sight of their quarry and took off running. The stiff one followed her, matching her step for step, and she had the impression he could outrun her if he wished to. For someone whose every movement seemed labored he certainly was fast. None of the men of her village could keep up with her for more than a few feet. When David saw them he ran faster, but he was slow, and they would overtake him shortly.

"If we don't hurry, Haldeed, we will lose them," Taleed said excitedly as he started to trot along. "Already the trail grows stale."

Haldeed moved quicker to keep up with his friend, although his heart was definitely not in it. He didn't think it was wise to chase after gods. In fact he thought it was a bad idea all the way around. He'd tell Taleed so, too, if Taleed would just turn around so that he could see him.

Suddenly Taleed came to an abrupt stop, and Haldeed ran into him. When he looked up, he saw the white-headed god's blue eyes boring into him. He dropped to his knees and prostrated himself.

The white-headed woman looked at Taleed and spoke plainly. "Your friend thinks I'm a god; why don't you?"

For a moment Taleed thought about pretending that he couldn't understand her, but something told him that she'd know he was lying, and that if he lied to her she wouldn't be pleasant to them. "Because I know your language and I heard what you were saying. You're no god," Taleed said in the Reliance tongue, sticking his chest out forcefully.

Haldeed knew Taleed, and knew that he was probably as scared as he had ever been, but he was standing tall, looking strong and confident even if he felt neither.

"I could show you things to make you believe otherwise. Show you things that would prove to you that I am a god. At the very least, I could prove to you that you should treat me with respect and with fear." She took one finger and punched it into Taleed's chest, and he moved backwards under the force. When he looked at her again, he wasn't looking quite as confident, and she demanded, "Why do you follow us?"

Taleed swallowed hard. "We saw your power and how you fought against the Reliance to save my people."

The woman smiled. "Your people?"

"I meant our people. I know your language, but I'm not accustomed to speaking it. Me being a poor migrant farm worker," Taleed said, changing his earlier decision not to lie to her.

She laughed and shook her head, and then her eyes seemed to fall on his fake hands. Taleed quickly put them behind his back. "Does he not speak Reliance?" she asked nodding her head towards Haldeed.

"He understands your tongue, but only a very little, and he does not speak at all. He is a mute," Taleed explained.

"Quit bowing and scraping and get out of the dirt," she ordered Haldeed. "Your friend is right. I am no god."

Haldeed got slowly to his feet but still would not look into the face of the woman. She might not be a god, but she had power. He didn't want her to catch his gaze and hold it; he feared something awful would happen to him if he made eye contact with her.

"What is it that you want from me?" she asked Taleed.

"Only to help you. I know people, people in very high places," Taleed said. "People who might not listen to you, but will most definitely listen to me."

"The priests?" she asked.

"Among others," Taleed said.

"Isn't that a little odd for 'poor migrant farm workers'?" she asked with a sly smile.

Taleed thought quickly. "You will need someone to translate for you."

"I have two people who can do that already, and I'll be able to do it myself by tomorrow afternoon."

"Someone who knows this planet, then," Taleed insisted.

"I have one of those, and I'd bet a whole fistfull of little black rocks that she knows a hell of a lot more about your planet than you two do," she said.

"My friend and I could be of great assistance to you. I lied about being farm workers. It is true that we are wearing peasant's clothes, but only to avoid being captured by the Reliance. I promise you that we truly do know people in high places."

She smiled more broadly. "Ah, but what is it that you think that *I* can do for *you*?"

"My friend and I are, in reality, adventurers. We believe that you will show us an adventure, and that you can keep us from being captured and sent to another world to fight a war. That is all."

She laughed then and said. "That is utter crap. What greater adventure could you ask for than to go across space to another world and fight a war? Perhaps you had better come with us, though. At least till I figure out what the hell you really are." She turned then and ran. They followed.

They ran as fast as they could and still could not catch up to her. Haldeed realized she could get away from them any time she liked. She *was* a god; Haldeed didn't care what she or Taleed or anyone else said.

Janad ran and pounced, flying through the air to land on David. Unfortunately, she didn't fully understand the extent of the problem he was having with his center of balance, so instead of just falling, he stumbled first, and in trying to make sure he didn't get away from her Janad managed to pull them both into the rain-swollen river.

Poley wouldn't go into the water. He stood on the bank and watched as the girl struggled with David in the water, fighting both the current and the deranged frightened man who seemed intent only on drowning them both.

"Poley, help me!" Janad screamed as she struggled to break the surface.

"Think rationally now, David. You've been sick. Janad is only trying to help you," Poley said, following along on the bank as the current washed Janad and David further downstream.

"That wasn't exactly what I had in mind!" Janad screamed as David dunked her under the water and held her there.

"Now David, Janad is human in origin. As such she must have oxygen. If you do not let her up, she will drown," Poley said.

David laughed wildly. "That's sort of the plan, Tin Pants!"

RJ ran past Poley and dove into the water. She easily pulled David off Janad. Janad came up coughing and started to float down the river. RJ caught her in her free hand and threw her to Poley who caught her. RJ grabbed David around the shoulders, successfully holding his arms to his sides, and hauled him out of the water kicking and screaming.

"Let me go! You're all trying to kill me!"

RJ flung him away from her. "No one's trying to kill you, David. You're not our favorite person right now, but we aren't trying to kill you. You know me; you know that if I wanted you to be dead, you'd be dead," RJ said.

David stumbled forward and collapsed. Sitting on a rock, he put his face in his hands and started to cry. RJ walked over to him and patted him on the back. "You're all right, David. You just need to calm down. You've had the space sickness, and we had to sedate you. We're on a planet now, so you should start to feel better soon."

David nodded and seemed to have calmed down.

As soon as Janad caught her breath, she jumped out of Poley's arms and popped him in the forehead with the palm of her hand—which hurt her arm and seemingly did nothing to him.

"You! Why did you not help me?" she demanded angrily. "I was almost drowned."

"I couldn't," Poley explained with a shrug.

"He doesn't function at full capacity if he is submerged, so our father programmed him with hydrophobia," RJ said matter-of-factly.

Janad gave her a confused look, proving that she still didn't really understand what Poley was.

"He's afraid of the water," RJ explained simply.

Janad looked at Poley, pointed and laughed.

Poley gave the girl a confused look. "It isn't right to laugh at someone's fear. Is it right, RJ?"

"No, it's not, Poley," RJ said. She looked down, momentarily forgetting everything except the fact that her clothes and her chain were wet and how much she hated it when her clothes were wet. "I'm freaking soaking, dripping wet. My blaster's wet; I'll have to take it apart and dry it out. Why can't anything be simple? Why can't anything be easy?"

"Many things are simple. Many things are easy." Poley supplied.

"Poley, I wasn't talking to you," RJ said shortly. "I wasn't asking you a question."

"Then who were you talking to?" he asked.

RJ gritted her teeth. "No one, Poley. I wasn't talking to anyone."

"Oh," Poley said simply.

RJ ignored the judgmental quality in Poley's voice. "Put your little tin ego away and go medicate David."

"Am I to assume that you are talking to me now?" Poley asked.

RJ laughed. "Sarcasm, Poley?" She smiled at him and moved to slap his back. "That's very good! You just became a smartass. Now, could you just please medicate David?"

Poley moved towards David, and David jumped to his feet. Or at least he got to his feet as quickly as he could on this planet.

"No!" David screamed, backing away from Poley. "Quit doping me up. Quit drugging me. I know what you're trying to do. You're trying to brainwash me. But I'll never tell you where the rebel base is on Alsterace Island on planet Earth. Never!"

David tried to run, but Poley caught him easily. He took the pocket medic from his pocket and set it with one hand while holding David with the other. He placed the device against David's arm.

"No, please…" David felt a slight stinging sensation. His vision started to clear; he could almost feel the confusion draining from his mind. He didn't feel like he was going to vomit any more. "I…I feel fine!" David said in surprise.

"Yeah, now all you have to go through are the chills and you should be right as rain," RJ said.

"What the hell happened to me?" David asked, then added almost as an afterthought, "Where are we and how did we get here?"

"You had space sickness. We didn't notice your symptoms till it was too late for the medication to do you any good as long as we were in space, so we sedated you and brought you with us to the planet's surface."

"I still feel very heavy—like it's harder to move," David said, experimentally lifting his foot.

"That's because it is," RJ explained. "This planet is more massive than Earth and therefore has a stronger gravitational pull. For all practical purposes, you are a good twenty-five pounds heavier here than you would be on Earth."

"You threw shit on us," Janad said, glaring accusingly at David.

"I did what?" David shrieked.

"He tried to drown her, and yet she's more upset about the dung," Poley said in an interested tone.

"I did what?" David asked again.

"Never mind. Suffice it to say, you haven't been yourself lately." RJ started walking, and the others followed. "Oh, and it would probably be a good idea to steer clear of Levits for a few days," RJ added over her shoulder.

Taleed and Haldeed caught up to them then, huffing and puffing.

Janad met them with a big butcher knife she had obviously taken from the ship's galley in her hand, and they skidded to an abrupt halt.

Janad screamed something in their language.

"They're all right," RJ said. "Some local adventurers who want to help us with our quest. Come on, let's go find the others."

Chapter Eight

"So, the way I see it, we're basically screwed," Levits said.

"I'm freezing my ass off over here," David said, his teeth chattering in spite of the dry space suit and three solar blankets he had wrapped around him and his close vicinity to the fire.

"It should pass in a couple of days," Poley informed.

"That's very comforting, thank you," David said sarcastically.

"Shut up, shit boy," Levits hissed from where he sat across the firefrom him.

"All right. What happened with the shit?" David asked.

Levits started to tell him in what would, no doubt, have been very colorful language, but Topaz stopped him.

"Let's not go back there," Topaz said putting a gentle hand on Levits' chest.

"Ever," RJ added. She sat down behind Levits, and he laid his head against her chest. She wrapped her arms around him and kissed the top of his head.

"What the hell is going on?" David asked, wondering if he was still hallucinating or had indeed ever stopped.

"They have sex," Janad informed him.

"Really?" David asked, looking at RJ.

"Yes, really!" Levits hissed, apparently taking immediate offense at the note of disbelief in David's voice. "You got some problem with that, shit boy?"

David was stunned silent for a moment, but finally found his voice. "Ah, no...Not at all." It was a lie, and probably not a very convincing one.

He was shaking all over, and now suddenly his stomach hurt and he felt heartsick. Neither of these latter symptoms had anything to do with his disease. RJ hadn't been ready for a relationship. He admitted now, if only to himself, that he had harbored some hope that RJ still loved him. That when she was ready to have another relationship, it would be with him. He tried very hard to hide what he was feeling because it just wasn't appropriate. He didn't get along with Levits, but he didn't dislike him, and if he was sure of nothing else, he was sure that Levits loved RJ. David didn't really love RJ, not at least with the sort of passion he knew to be romantic love. The truth, was he thought he would never feel that way about anyone ever again, and RJ would have been the next best thing. At the very least he knew he could trust RJ. He wasn't sure he could ever really trust anyone else. So, now, the way he saw it, he was doomed to go through his life alone.

"David, are you all right?" Topaz asked, making David realize just how long he had been silently staring into the center of the fire.

"No, I'm not all right. I feel like crap, I'm freezing to death, and everyone keeps reminding me of the hideous things I did when I was delusional. I think I'm going to go in the ship and lie down." David started to get up.

"I'll help you," Poley offered.

David was about to snap at him that he hardly needed help lying down, when Poley reached down and helped him to his feet. He realized he actually *did* need the help, or at the very least he was glad to have it. Poley helped him into the ship and helped him to lie down on the cot, and then he covered him up with the three blankets.

"Thank you, Poley," David said, surprised at how tired he suddenly felt.

"You're welcome," Poley said and turned to leave.

"Poley?" David called after him.

Poley turned to face David. "Yes."

"Poley…Do you think RJ is happy with him?"

"Who?" Poley asked.

"Levits." David said, trying not to scream. Sometimes the obvious seemed to go right over the robot's head.

"She seems to be. Yes," Poley answered. He turned and left the ship.

While a human might have sensed that David needed to talk, Poley had answered David's question and since David said he wanted to sleep, Poley was leaving so that he could.

David stared up at the ceiling and started to feel trapped—like he was back in space. So he quickly looked out the open door. He took a breath and made himself calm down.

I can't begrudge them whatever happiness they can find. Even if they chose to find it together. It was foolish and selfish to think that RJ and I would wind up together. Levits cares about her at least as much as I do. He even loves her, and I don't. Not really. I'd like to, but I don't and I never will. So I have to be rational. But she's the only almost human woman in my life, and I just don't feel like being rational.

He had just decided to stay up all night brooding about it when he fell asleep.

Haldeed and Taleed stood several feet away from the others. It had gotten dark fast, but soon *Grande Lune*, the largest of the six moons, would be up. The second brightest of Beta 4's moons, and this early in its cycle, it would light things up so bright that it would almost—but not quite—blot out the light of the smaller moon in this cycle, *Azure Lune*. Between the two of them the night would be almost as bright as day.

"I think she knows who I am," Taleed said.

Who, the girl? Haldeed signed.

"No, the woman, the white-headed woman, the one they call RJ. I think she knows who I am. But how could she know, Haldeed? How did she figure me out when no one else—not even the Reliance men did?" Taleed asked.

She is a god, Haldeed signed frantically.

"Look at the facts, Haldeed. She's no god; she even said she wasn't…"

Haldeed cut Taleed off with a shove—something he hadn't done since they were boys.

No! You *look at the facts, Taleed,* Haldeed signed. *You are lying about what you are. She came from the sky. She was wearing the silver suit of the gods. She did utterly smite the enemy of the people and cleansed the temple of the poison gold. She runs too fast to be mortal. She doesn't look like us, and she doesn't look like them, either.*

"There is another people I have heard of. The ones who fight the Reliance. It is said that they are white-headed, blue-eyed and bronze-skinned. She must be one of those," Taleed said. He glared back at her. It hurt to know that she had already figured out his clever ruse. That his "hands" hadn't fooled her. It had been nice to be seen by others as normal. It bothered him to think that his disguise hadn't fooled her for even a minute. "They are all strange, all different. I admit I don't know that much about the Reliance people, but these seem even stranger than those."

All the more reason we should leave here and go back to the palace, where we belong, Haldeed signed.

"I'm staying with them till I find out why they have really come here," Taleed said stubbornly. "I don't understand everything that they say because they speak too fast and use slang words, but in a few days I shall know everything that they are saying. In a few days I will know what they are really doing here." He looked at his friend, pleading for his understanding. "I...I have this odd feeling, Haldeed, that my destiny is tied up with these strange people. If I leave now, I may never reach my true place in the universe. I may die without fulfilling my destiny. And if I leave now, I will never know one way or the other. I will always wonder whether this was the road I should have taken and didn't."

I do not understand you anymore, Taleed. You say you do not believe in the gods, but now you talk of destiny. Surely, if there are no gods, then a man makes his own destiny. Why risk your life on the off chance that your destiny may be linked to these people? If you truly do not believe that someday you will be a god, if you are never to be any more than a man, why worry about your destiny at all?

"You make good arguments, my brother, but I still will not go. Perhaps there *is* a larger power. If there is, then truly it has guided us to be here with these people now, for what were the odds that we should all be in that one place at that one time?" Taleed said in a passionate whisper.

Haldeed reluctantly nodded his head. Whatever Taleed wanted to do Haldeed would do, whether he thought Taleed's actions careless or not. Haldeed didn't need to find out what his destiny was. His destiny was to serve the young Prince. His destiny was written in stone, even as his tongue had been cut from his head.

Taheed glared down at the old priest. "Are you calling me a liar, Ziphed?"

"No, Your Majesty, but, well...Where is the Prince? He has missed his last three lessons, and...He has made a habit of running away, My Lord. His manservant Haldeed has also been noticeably absent from the palace grounds," Ziphed said with as much reverence as he could muster.

"Just because he's not here doesn't mean he's gone!" Taheed screamed. He played his words back in his head and shook it as if to clear his thoughts. "What I mean to say is just because he's not on the palace grounds doesn't mean he's left." He played these back as well and decided they didn't sound any better. "All right! All right! You pompous old snit! The Prince has run away again. In fact, he has been gone longer than ever before, and we have no idea where he is. Perhaps you made some mistake. Perhaps he was not the Chosen One at all. I've had twenty sons born this month. Test them see if one of them isn't The Chosen."

"For all the generations since the soul of The Ancestor first moved, the Priests in the Service of the God of the Clouds have picked the Chosen One, and never have we been wrong. He must be found and brought back here, or we will all lose face." Ziphed sounded more thoughtful than angry.

"Let me worry about my son. You worry about curing this disease," the King said looking at his mottled skin. "We look and feel worse with each passing day, and yet the commoners walk around with no sign of this plague on their flesh."

"The two are linked," the priest said. "The God of the Clouds punishes us all because we have let the Chosen One escape. Worse, we have made him so unhappy that he feels he can only be happy by leaving us. We must find the Prince. Only then will the gods intervene on our behalf."

"Then we shall find him," the King/God said. "I shall double my efforts." He pointed his stump towards the door, and the priest knew better than to stay.

"If I'm a god, then why is my flesh rotting?" he asked his mute manservant, who just shrugged. "Perhaps my son is right." He stared out the huge window at the night sky full of the glow from two moons, both full. The smaller one, whose name he could never remember, cast a pale blue light. He often thought of himself and the Chosen as these two moons in this cycle. The one brighter and overpowering the other, but the other different and therefore more impressive. As the large one faded, the blue one came into its own radiance—the smaller one waiting for the bigger one to cycle out so that it could shine alone.

"If my son is right, Yashi, bringing him back will not save me. It will not save any of us that have been so afflicted."

If Yashi could have spoken, he would have pointed out that *he* wasn't sick. He would have told the King that he thought their ailment was related to the gold metal the Reliance had traded for their people. After all, it wasn't until after they had fashioned chains of it and all the priests and the King had worn them that they had fallen sick. But he couldn't talk because having been chosen to serve god they had cut out his tongue. Also having been chosen, they had never taught him to write. He pointed frantically at the King's chain, making a gurgling noise.

"No, Yashi, how many times do I have to tell you? Gold metal is for priests and gods, not for servants. I would give you one anyway, as you are my dear companion, but the priests would be displeased," Taheed said.

Yashi sighed and slumped against the wall.

"So how radioactive is the gold?" Topaz asked RJ. She turned to look at Poley.

"Nine gray," Poley answered.

"So what does that mean?" Levits asked.

"It's dangerous but not immediately lethal. Exposure at a distance of several feet probably wouldn't even be detectable. More immediate exposure for a longer length of time is going to cause radiation sickness, and prolonged exposure will cause death," Poley said.

RJ let out a long breath shaking her head.

"What?" Topaz said seeing the look in her eyes.

"Don't you see, Topaz?" RJ said. She got up suddenly, practically dumping Levits on the ground. She started pacing back and forth with a look of concentration on her face. She was obviously calculating.

"What!" Levits demanded as he tried to get comfortable and regain his dignity, after having been dumped so unceremoniously on the ground. "God, I hate it when you do that. Start to say something and then stop. What, already?"

"The Reliance isn't just giving these people radioactive gold to get rid of something that would be otherwise useless to them. They did it on purpose to kill off the planet's leaders," RJ said. She stopped pacing and looked down at them. "They give them cotton and wool cloth, farming and cooking utensils, and gold. The priests make the distribution just as the Reliance knew they would. The cloth and utensils are distributed to the families of the people the Reliance takes away as a form of payment, and the priests keep the valuable stuff—i.e. the gold—for themselves. Of course they share some with the King, who is also a god. The people don't know about the gold. Or if they do, they no doubt believe it was gifted to the priests and their God/King by the bigger god. The one we all know is no more than a series of antiquated thermo-electric power plants."

"The King and the priests deck themselves out in this gold. They drape it all over the power plant and throne room where they live and work, slowly killing themselves with radiation," Topaz said with sudden realization.

"How does that serve the Reliance?" Levits asked in confusion.

RJ gave him an *I'm so tired of mortals* look and explained. "No leaders, no leadership. No leadership, no resistance. No resistance when the Reliance comes down, states that they have killed the people's impotent gods, and now they own the people. They send the war-ready population off to Earth to destroy the New Alliance and leave the rest of the population with the mess they have created. The only people left here to try to rebuild their civilization would be the old, the sick, the crippled, and the very young. They take generations of work on genetic uniqueness and perfection and destroy it in one generation. Then they continue to trade with the inhabitants for the items they want, screwing them worse than ever before, and making sure that they can never again raise an army that the Reliance might ever have to worry about."

"Could they do that?" Janad asked.

"Could they?" RJ huffed. "Hell, they already are."

"I never trusted them," Janad said of the Reliance. "Let's hope that the runner you sent out can make people believe him. Make them fight the Reliance. Many in my village also didn't trust the Reliance. No one wanted to go, but the priests...Well, they ordered it, and we are used to obeying the priests. We saw the Reliance weapons, how they pierced through even stone with nothing more than light." She looked over at where the two boys from her planet stood having their own conversation and she lowered her voice. "There was talk among my clan of revolt against the priests and against the gods. None of us thought it was right to leave the planet. None of us wanted to get into machines we didn't understand for reasons we didn't understand to fight a battle that wasn't ours. But, in the end, my people would not oppose the priests. They would not oppose the gods. They acted as if they had never had any doubts."

Topaz nodded. "It makes sense. When the priests tell the people that god orders them to do something, they are too afraid to revolt. They will turn off the voice in their heads that is telling them that something is wrong and follow blindly. Every evil thing that has ever happened on Earth can be traced back to religion. Faith, a belief in a higher power, can be a very helpful thing to people. It makes sense of things that are wrong in the universe and explains things that cannot otherwise be explained. But *religion*. Now that is a different matter all together. Religion is what happens when one group of people wants to take control of another group of people they consider inferior. You take a small child and you tell him *If you do this good thing I'll give you candy, but if you do this bad thing I will whip you.* Religion does that in the biggest possible way. *Do this deed and you will be rewarded with heaven and eternal life, do this deed and go to hell—or its equivalent—and burn forever.* Depending on the ultimate goal of the religious leaders, these commanded deeds could be anything. In this case it just happens to be *Go fight this war.*"

"That's very interesting, but not really very helpful," RJ said and continued pacing. Suddenly she turned in her stride and said to the native girl. "For the record, there is nothing stronger than light."

She stopped and looked in the direction of the two boys. She was silent and still, just watching them. As if sensing her eyes on them, they turned and started towards the fire.

"Well?" Levits asked, knowing what she had just been doing.

"The mute boy is afraid, probably believes we are gods. The other one...He puzzles me; he seems to have a great need in him. I think he thinks we can give him what he needs."

"Can she see in people's thoughts?" Janad asked, more than a little afraid. No doubt because she'd had thoughts she didn't want people knowing.

"Only their emotions," Poley informed her.

From the look on her face Janad obviously didn't feel very comforted.

"Did you have gold on this planet before?" Topaz asked Janad curiously.

"What the hell does that have to do with anything?" Levits asked.

"If they didn't, how did they know it had value?" RJ asked, giving him that *stupid-mortal* look again.

"Quit doing that to me! I think it makes me stupider," Levits said with a smile. RJ smiled back and shook her head.

"In the Holy of Holies, wherein lies the things which belonged to The Ancestor, there are an earring and a pendant of gold," Taleed said as he and Haldeed arrived at the fire. He had heard part of the conversation as he was walking over. "Once every cycle of *Luisant Lune,* the King dawns the Silver Suit of the Gods, puts on the Regalia, and rides through the streets in the Holy Vehicle. The priests follow behind him carrying Religious symbols of power…"

Haldeed threw his arms around and Taleed nodded.

"The people carry their sick into the street, and the priests give them potions and pray for them," Taleed said.

Haldeed made some more signs.

"They don't care about that, Haldeed," Taleed said dismissively.

"Try us," RJ said.

"Excuse me?" Taleed asked not understanding.

"What did he say?" RJ asked with a sigh.

"The Chosen One walks at the rear of the procession, and when his brothers and sisters see him they must bow down," Taleed said. "See? That information is of no use."

"You mean only the Chosen One of all the King's descendants has any importance? Only the Chosen One lives in the palace?" Topaz asked.

Taleed, Haldeed and Janad all laughed loudly.

"What's so funny?" Topaz asked.

"The King, our god, has over four thousand children," Taleed said. "The palace would have to be very large, indeed. Besides women aren't allowed in the Palace. Only menservants, the King, and The Chosen may enter the interior rooms of the palace. Even the priests are not allowed anywhere but the throne room and the outer halls."

"OK, I'll bite," Levits said. "How does a man sire over four thousand children if no women are allowed in the Palace?"

"He goes to the Temple and the priests bring him women in their cycles. A different woman every night. Some times more than one," Taleed said. "It is his duty to impregnate as many women as possible."

"Hell of a life this guy's got. He gets to have all the fun, and he doesn't have to put up with a woman," Levits said, giving RJ a meaningful look.

RJ glared back at him, not wanting him to be disappointed, and he smiled his very best, just kidding, smile.

"Is the Prince chosen because he is born with no hands?" Topaz asked.

RJ watched the boy carefully now; she even noticed the way he looked at her to see if she was looking at him. He knew that she knew. She wondered how he would play this out.

"No. He is chosen and then the priests cut off his hands when he is an infant," Taleed said bitterly.

"Christ on a crutch!" Topaz exclaimed.

"What does he mean?" Janad asked Poley in a whisper.

Poley shrugged and whispered back. "I don't know. I only know that he says that when he is shocked by something, or very agitated."

"It has to be a belief imbedded pretty deeply within them to maim an infant," Topaz said more to RJ than to Taleed.

"Or these priests are just some bloodthirsty bastards. Remember what you just said about religion. Create a god, cut off its hands and make it dependent on the priests for its livelihood. A handless man is helpless in a world like this," RJ said. She looked right into Taleed's eyes as she said it, and he glared back at her. "Such a man may want to go against the priests, he may even try to escape his servitude, but how far can he get without help? How can he take care of himself, and how can he hide? Who wouldn't know this handless man on sight?" She looked away from Taleed then, and back at Topaz. "Look at what we already know about them. They encourage their people to have as many children as possible and then have them wage war with each other to keep the numbers down. Thus ensuring survival of the fittest. They cut out the tongues of the palace servants so that they can't tell anyone what goes on there."

"How did you know that?" Taleed asked angrily. Perhaps at this point he just wanted her to expose him. RJ wasn't about to make it that easy.

"Someone must have told me. Or it just made a certain amount of sense."

"It is customary to cut out the tongues of the palace staff." Taleed obviously found her revelations annoying. "How do you know things which no one tells you? Do you read people's minds?"

Levits laughed and muttered under his breath. "That seems to be the question of the evening."

"It's just simple deductive reasoning," RJ said with a shrug of her shoulders. She walked over and threw some sticks on the fire. "You ought to understand that. From what I've observed while I've been here, you and your people are very good at it as well."

"Like I know that there is something wrong with your brother," he said, pointing at Poley, still mad and wanting to aggravate her if he could.

"He's perfect," Janad explained to Taleed.

RJ smiled at her answer. "Who told you that?"

"He did," Janad said. She got up and walked off into the brush.

"Getting a little full of yourself aren't you, Tin Pants?" RJ asked.

Poley shrugged. "I am perfect."

"If you say so. Remind me to come and borrow an ego circuit next time I'm feeling bad about myself," RJ said.

"I think you have quite enough ego, dear," Levits chided.

Taleed realized they had forgotten all about him, and this really aggravated him. He turned to Haldeed and said in his own tongue, "These people are fools. Perhaps we had better leave."

"Oh, no, you're our insurance policy," RJ said in his own tongue.

He frowned, really angry now. "I thought you didn't know our language," he said accusingly.

"I told you I'd know it by tomorrow evening. I just learned it a little faster, that's all," RJ said reaching in her pocket and pulling out a coin. She bent the coin around a link of chain to mark their victory today. "Going to have to get off this planet soon, or I'll run out of coins, and even I can't bend rocks," she said to no one in particular. She watched as the look on Taleed's face turned from one of surprise to one of total defiance. "Put all that out of your head. You wanted to join this party, and you know too much now for us to let you go. Get comfortable and enjoy yourself. You aren't going anywhere."

Janad walked up then, carrying some large, skinned and gutted reptile on the end of a sharpened stick. Apparently she had been hungry. She held it over the fire.

"Wow," RJ said taking a whiff. "That smells really good."

Topaz nodded his head in agreement. "Funny; I can remember a time when I would have been completely grossed out at the thought of eating a lizard."

"You can remember a time when rocks were soft, Old Man," Levits laughed.

"Why do you call him an old man when he is not?" Taleed asked, his curiosity piqued.

"Because I am," Topaz said with a smile. "I most probably predate your race."

"You think this race is that young?" RJ asked skeptically.

"Well, at least human influence on the race. Remember that I was alive when they first discovered interstellar flight, and humans couldn't have gotten here before that," Topaz said.

"You still think these creatures have human origins?" Levits asked curiously.

"Yes, they must," RJ said. "Besides the fact that they look like a human race that has disappeared, and speak an ancient Earth language, their cloud-making god is a human-made machine."

"Oh?" Levits prompted.

"It turned out to be an old thermo-electric generator. The kind they sent out with the old colony ships. It even still had the Reliance bar code on it," RJ explained.

"Are you saying," Taleed ran through everything he had just heard again to make sure he'd heard what he thought he had, "that my people are related to the Reliance people?"

"Yes," Topaz said. "Had to be. Ironic when you think about it. The white man is once again enslaving the black man, and once again it is your own chief who is selling you. But then they always have said that history repeats itself."

"What do you mean?" Taleed asked.

"And gravy!" Topaz said adamantly. "Gravy was always very important, especially with potatoes. No sense in even trying to eat potatoes without gravy—all dry and get caught in your throat and make you cough." Topaz started coughing until he was jerking around on the ground. Janad ran to try to help him as RJ rolled her eyes.

Suddenly Topaz quit coughing and sat up. He looked at Janad. "So, do you want to ride my pony?"

Janad had grown very fond of the old man and didn't understand the way the others seemed so unconcerned about him. Even if he did heal really fast. "What does he want?" Janad asked.

"Just say no," Levits said with a laugh.

Topaz stood up and started walking into the brush. "My hair is an absolute mess. Now if I was a hair brush, where would I be?" he mumbled. Janad started to go after him, but RJ grabbed her arm.

"Poley, go after Topaz. Keep an eye on him, and don't let him get too far," RJ ordered.

Poley nodded, got up and went after Topaz.

Janad looked at RJ and said with concern, "What's wrong with him? Does he have the same thing that David does?"

RJ let go of the girl's arm. "No, he's fine. He does this sometimes. It's nothing to worry about really, Janad. He's not sick. He's only insane."

Somehow Janad was not comforted.

Toulan bowed low as he entered the throne room.

"Well?" Taheed bellowed.

The Captain of the King's guard visibly cringed.

"My lord...We went down the *Agua'boue*, and we found spots where a camp had been made. We believe this is where the Prince made camp. "We...Lord we, found a broken reed boat which was destroyed at the bottom of *Agua'boue* falls."

"What are you trying to say?" the King bellowed. "Did you find any bodies?"

"No, My Lord, but..."

"Are you an unbeliever, Toulan? You know my son cannot die. He is a god. Now get out there and find him. He must have gone on from there on foot." The King got shakily to his feet and pointed at the door. "Now go. My time grows near, and he must be here to take my spirit."

The guard left, only too glad to do so. The King and the priests were afflicted with some disease. It had started simply with vomiting and diarrhea like many other diseases, but had quickly escalated to skin lesions and hair loss. Obviously they had enraged the God of the Clouds, and He had sat a plague upon them. They had lined their pockets and their necks with the people's blood. This was not the intention of The Ancestor, nor was it the intention of the god. It was the will of the priests, and the King/God had allowed himself to be lead by the nose by his brothers to keep the peace. Soon, the Reliance would swoop down and capture their prize, and the world as they knew it would be no more. As it had been written, so most it be.

Chapter Nine

Sergeant Bradley surveyed the ruins of the trans-mat bay from the supposed safety of his radiation suit. He was supervising the cleanup operation. He was in charge of maintenance on this space station; as such, someone had just made damn sure that he was going to be busy for several weeks.

What an incredible mess! Tainted gold, shredded bodies, and twisted metal everywhere. Not to mention the outside hull breach, which was way beyond their ability to repair. Thirty people, mostly soldiers and medical personnel had been killed, dozens of others wounded before the automatic safety system had been able to patch the hull. Unfortunately, someone had been caught up in it, his legs dangling from the patching substance. The corpse couldn't be removed without damaging the temporary seal, so there the body would stay until permanent repairs had been made. He, for one, didn't feel comfortable with the only thing between him and the vacuum of space being a substance that was basically sprayed out of cans, no matter how big those cans were. But he couldn't in good conscience send his crew into any place he wasn't willing to work himself. It was hard to know where to start when you had to tackle a mess like this. It was Bradley's job to make sure that as the debris was cleared away, they find out just what had been broken and fix it.

They had spent most of the day reinforcing the temporary patch because it wasn't trustworthy, and trying to divide the debris into two piles—human and not human. A crew was on its way from Stashes with the materials and the specialists to put a proper patch on the hull. The patch itself could take days. He still couldn't be sure how badly damaged the actual trans-mat system was because it still wasn't clear of debris.

To make matters worse the ship that was supposed to show up to pick up the latest batch of natives had never arrived, and all attempts to contact it both from the space station and from Moon Base had failed. They didn't know whether the ship had undergone some breakdown that was making it very late, had been lost in hyperspace, or had been abducted by the Argy. The damned magnetic pulses made it hard to be sure of anything, and, short of blowing up the planet, they had done everything that they could do to decrease its influence. The ship should have sent out a distress beacon if they had been attacked, and that would have been picked up by somebody somewhere, but Moon Base said that the ship had trouble with communications just prior to takeoff, and it might have undergone a complete systems breakdown. Shoddy maintenance! It would be the end of them all.

Someone tapped him on the shoulder and he turned. "Yes, Corporal?"

"The Captain wants to see you, Sergeant," he said.

Sergeant Bradley smiled broadly and punched the Corporal playfully on the shoulder. "Well, yes, of course he would. He couldn't possibly come down here with us grunts and check this crap out firsthand. Ten will get you twenty he will ask me a bunch of stupid-assed questions I don't have the answers to yet. Any word on the missing ship?"

"No, I'm sorry, Sergeant," Corporal Riley said.

"Well, at least that isn't one of my problems. Just trying to see what kind of mood the old man is in. Be a good fellow and keep an eye on this clusterfuck for me." He started to leave, then turned back around. "I don't have a clear picture yet of what actually happened, but between you and me this is what we deserve for giving those natives radioactive gold. I have pulled some shit details before, but between you and me, this is tops."

The Corporal nodded his head in silent agreement.

The Sergeant went into the temporary decontamination airlock they had set up. He unsuited, stepped into the showers then dried off and dressed quickly. What a pain in the ass this was! What a giant waste of his time. This was what com-links were for. There was no need for him to leave his post where he was needed and march up to the bridge so that he could tell some idiot Captain a bunch of crap he wouldn't understand anyway.

Briggs was a commissioned officer—an elite. He had never cranked the handle on a wrench. He didn't know one kind of power supply conduit from another. He knew space ships flew and space stations were stationary around a planet. He had no idea how they kept air in and space out. How they created gravity or even where his damn food came from. He appreciated the maintenance staff not at all. It never occurred to him that his safety and that of his entire crew was in the hands of the men and women who fixed all the things that they broke. The people who maintained the ma-chines that made sure they didn't go crashing into a sun and that made their air and gravity.

He walked to the bridge and entered. Captain Briggs swiv-eled in his chair to face him. "What took you so long?"

Ever have to go through decontamination, you old prick? Sergeant Bradley thought, but bit his tongue and answered. "I had to go through decontamination. I was working in the contami-nated area. In fact, the entire damaged area has been contami-nated by the radioactive gold we originally sent to the surface of the planet."

"Do I hear a hint of insubordination in your voice?" Cap-tain Briggs screamed.

Only if you're listening. "No, sir," he said quickly. Every day this job just got harder and harder. His last Captain had been a decent sort, a man who understood the importance of main-tenance and went out of his way to make his maintenance staff happy. So, of course, their ship had sustained minor damage during a skirmish over Stashes, and Captain Johnson had been killed when he fell during the attack and his head struck a sharp corner on the arm of his command chair. It was a freak accident really, not the way you would expect a combat veteran to die in a hundred million years.

Now he was stuck with this bastard Briggs who had lived his entire life behind a desk. He didn't have any clue how important the maintenance staff was, and he didn't care to learn. To him they were nothing more or less than glorified toilet cleaners, and he treated them like such, paying no heed at all to either their rank or their service record. Unless you lay around on your ass all day waiting for a chance to use your gun, he didn't consider you important at all.

"Do you know what happened to our transport bay yet?" Briggs asked impatiently.

"We found part of an incendiary device, could have been a timed charge. I can't be sure until we find all the pieces," Sergeant Bradley answered.

"You want to tell me where the primitives got explosives?" the Captain asked, seeming to calm down some.

Golly, Sir, I ain't supposed ta know nothin' like that. I'm jus' a darn toilet cleaner, don' ya 'member? I jus' fix things. "I have no idea, Sir. We'll have to run some tests first, see just exactly what sort of explosives we're talking about. I'm afraid it's going to take some time," Bradley answered.

"Time is what we don't have, soldier," the Captain snapped. "First we've got a missing ship, and now we have an attack on the station, and no doubt the ground troops have all been killed."

"We found pieces of some of them in the debris. They were sent back with the gold, along with a primitive with radiation sickness," Sergeant Bradley said.

"Whatever happened was quick. We only got one distress signal, and it wasn't clear," Briggs said turning his chair away from Sergeant Bradley so that Bradley had to look at his back. Bradley stuck out his tongue and almost got caught when Briggs swung back around quickly. "How many casualties did we take here on the station?"

"Ah…We can't be completely sure till we finish doing a head count, but I estimate about thirty of our people," Sergeant Bradley reported. He saw the security officer working at her station smile at him and then stick out her tongue, and knew that she had seen what he did and obviously approved. He kept the smile off his face only with an effort.

"Thirty! Why so many?" Briggs exclaimed.

Why the hell are you asking me? Don't you know a damn thing about the way this operation runs? Don't you remember it's me—the guy you think is completely unimportant? I fix things; that's it; that's all. However he apparently knew more than Briggs did. "We were expecting a bunch of natives. Guards had been ordered into the area and so had medical personnel. In fact I would say our medical staff was hit the hardest."

"Oh, that's great, just beautiful! Do you know how much time and money the Reliance spends training medics? They aren't going to be happy."

It always comes down to cost-effectiveness with these freaking Reliance goons, because they never have to peel someone's liver off a wall, or try to figure out whose arm that was. He was so engrossed in his own angry thoughts that he almost didn't hear what the idiot said next.

"I'm going to send an away team to the planet's surface. Till now, I have been reluctant to keep a military presence on the surface, but it may become necessary in the near future. We need to learn more about the planet, and we need to know exactly what happened with the transport station. One thing is obvious: for whatever reason, this village decided it didn't want to trade people for gold."

"Maybe they realized that it was the gold that was making them sick," Sergeant Bradley said, unable to keep the disapproving tone from his voice.

"Of course they didn't, Sergeant Bradley. They are stupid primitives, savages really. They worship thermo generators for Pete's sake! How smart could they be?" Captain Briggs screamed.

With any luck, smart enough to realize that you're the prick in charge and kill you instead of us.

"I suppose you're right, sir." Sergeant Bradley said. *Please tell me what dance you'd like me to do before I stupidly tell you what a pompous ass I think you are, and wind up spending the rest of my natural life in the brig.*

"Security officer Lieutenant Stratton will lead the away team. I want you to go with her," Captain Briggs ordered.

"With all due respect, sir, why me? I'm not a political; I'm not even combat. I'm the maintenance Sergeant. A huge hole has been ripped in our ship, and it's my job to see to the repairs..."

"I'm the Captain!" Briggs screamed glaring at him. "I'll tell you what your job is, and you will not question my orders. Do you understand?" Briggs levered himself out of his chair with an effort that made it look like he might have been velcroed to the seat, and stood to his full height of five-foot-four.

Gee, let me see...Yeah, I'm pretty sure you're a stupid fucking prick, so I'd say I've got it covered.

"Yes, sir..."

"You're a simple-minded person, Sergeant. I need someone who's simple to deal with these primitives. Someone who thinks like a commoner. No disrespect intended, Sergeant, but someone stupid enough to think like they think. Anyone who can handle the morons who serve under you in maintenance knows how to talk to primitives." It was pretty clear by the tone of his voice that disrespect *was* intended.

Well, go...o...lly, Captain, I'm overwhelmed at your faith in me. I feel honored that you think all us guys in maintenance are such a bunch of total ignoramuses. Let's disconnect the main gravitational transfusion junction and see what stupid fucks you think we are then.

"You will leave by shuttle at 0800 hours. Until then go about your duties...Oh, and assign someone else to oversee the work in the transport bay. A monkey with a pair of

pliers ought to be able to do your job here, so it shouldn't
be too hard to find a replacement," Briggs ordered. "You
are dismissed."

Sergeant Bradley saluted, quickly turned on his heels and
left. Outside the bridge door he started to mumble under his
breath all the things he would like to say to Briggs. There
was a bunch of static from one of the monitors overhead.
Usually this would have been of concern to him, because he
would have been in charge of making sure it got fixed, but as
of a minute ago anything to do with the maintenance of this
station had been changed to the list of *things that weren't his
problem.*

The monitors usually had a steady stream of station news
including who was to be where when, just in case someone
was confused about their assignment. On most ships or stations this sort of system was mostly a waste of technology,
but when you had a prick like Briggs running the show and
changing assignments and shifts at the last minute, it was a
necessary evil...

Bradley looked up; the screen had gone blank. And not
just that one but every screen he could see up and down the
hall. He felt somehow vindicated but then felt guilty because
he would be passing this and all the other huge problems off
to one of his subordinates. Just his luck—exciting things finally start happening up here, and he gets shipped planetside.

The screens all lit back up again, then went black again,
and then there was...What the hell was it? Some small alien
filled up the screen.

"People of the Reliance. Specifically personnel aboard
the satellite, Pam Station, which is in orbit around the planet
Beta 4. I am Mickey, President of New Freedom. Reports by
the Alliance are false; there is no hunger or sickness here, and
we are keeping a close eye on Reliance activities. For instance,
we are aware that currently the Council of Twelve has you
enslaving the peoples of Beta 4 and shipping them to Earth to
be used as shock troops to fight us. We ask each one of you to

look deep within your own conscience. Do you think it's right to use radioactive gold to buy these humanoids and to poison their leaders? To send them to fight us—the New Alliance—the same force that the Reliance couldn't overcome? To pit primitives against lasers and plasma blasters? What happiness has the Reliance brought you? We have sent one message to you already as proof of our intentions. Stop the inhuman acts against this world and against the peoples of my country, or we shall retaliate again—this time with severe prejudice."

The transmission halted, and the screens returned to their normal duty.

Bradley had to stop himself from laughing out loud when he heard Briggs screaming and slamming things around like an angry child.

The New Alliance must have one hell of a communications system, and one hell of a spy network. Not long after he heard Briggs start screaming, MP's started running down the halls, no doubt looking for the spy amongst them.

Bradley smiled. So there was a spy on board leaking information about their top-secret mission to the New Alliance? It wasn't him, and he didn't know who it was, so it also went on that growing list of things that just weren't his problem. He hoped they didn't get the spy and that this caused them to dissolve the operation altogether. But that little bit of hopeful conjecture was between him and his brain, and so far—try as they might, the Reliance hadn't managed to do away with free thought.

Except, of course, in the GSH's. No doubt if they didn't cost so much to reproduce and there wasn't this hidden fear that they would somehow break their conditioning and take over, the Reliance would completely phase humans out of the military—hell, maybe they'd do away with humans altogether.

By the time 0800 hours rolled around, there were already rumors flying about who had been arrested. He was on his way to his meeting with Lieutenant Stratton in the hangar when Corporal Riley ran up to him.

"Sergeant! They've just arrested Harker."

"What?" Bradley couldn't believe his ears. "What in hell's name for?"

"They think he's one of the spies, maybe even *the* spy," Riley informed him.

"That's insane. I've known Harker most of my life." Bradley looked at his watch. He didn't have time to go to the brig to check on Harker and meet Lieutenant Stratton in time. "Damn it all! Riley, run tell Lieutenant Stratton I'll meet her in a few minutes. I can't leave without checking on Harker."

"Why should I tell her you're running late?" He asked.

He only thought a second about making something up. "Tell her my best friend just got thrown into the brig. I just want to check on him it won't take me long."

Harker paced behind the bars like a caged animal. When he saw Bradley he ran up to the bars, grabbing them in his hands.

"Damn, Bradley, am I glad to see you," he said.

"What the hell did you do?" Bradley asked, wanting to sound supportive. It was hard because he was agitated. Whatever Harker had done had put Bradley in the position of doing something, that if found out might make him a suspect.

"You know we're constantly monitored?" Harker said.

Of course he knew, but sometimes he forgot. He thought about what he'd said to Riley earlier that afternoon and what he'd done when he'd been talking to Captain Briggs and cringed. When the Reliance was on this sort of witch-hunt you didn't have to do or say much to be hauled in.

"Yeah, so?" Bradley said. "You've never done or said anything that could possibly make them think you're a spy."

"They have a record of me talking to Barry when we were working down in the engine room. I was pitching a bitch, and I said something to the tune of how if I didn't get off shit detail I was going to hook up with the New Alliance and help them bring the Reliance down."

"Damn it, man!" Bradley exclaimed. "You can't say shit like that."

"I know that, man. I didn't *mean* it. I was just tired and hot and pissed off. Hell, I didn't even remember saying it till they showed me the recording. Can you help me?" Harker asked. There was fear in his eyes and in his voice. Bradley had never known his old friend to be afraid of anyone or anything, but he wasn't stupid, and he knew damn good and well that after the events of the afternoon they needed someone to blame. If Harker became that someone, they'd space him—no doubt.

"I...I don't have much clout, Harker. You know that. Besides which, I have to go with the away team down to the surface." He thought for a minute. "I'll talk to Lieutenant Stratton. She seems like she's all right. She might be able to help; after all, she is a security officer. Don't look so worried, man. You didn't do anything, and without proof they can't do anything to you. I have to go; I'm late as it is. You keep cool, and I'll see what I can do."

He reached through the bars and they clasped hands. Harker caught his eyes and held them. "Goodbye, Bradley."

Bradley laughed nervously as he withdrew his hand. "Cheer up, buddy, they can't convict you of something you didn't do."

"Bradley...you forget. This is the Reliance we're talking about."

Bradley unconsciously turned to look at the camera, and then he turned back to his friend and whispered, "Damn it, Harker! Watch your mouth. You're going to cause yourself even more trouble. I'll see you when I get back." He turned to leave.

"Thanks, Bradley," Harker said.

"No problem," Bradley said over his shoulder without turning. He took off at a run looking at his watch. If he ran all the way, he'd only be a few minutes late.

Bradley threw on his suit and ran onto the flight deck of the skiff. He looked at Lieutenant Stratton who was waiting patiently at the controls. She indicated the seat next to her, and he sat down, although he wondered why one of the Marines hadn't taken the co-pilot's position.

"I'm sorry I'm late, I had to…"

"It's all right, Bradley, don't sweat it." Stratton closed the hatches and started to power up the skiff. "Be a lot easier if we had a transporter planetside, but someone took care of that for us."

Bradley looked back at the others. There were only five of them going; that just didn't seem right. Five people alone with minimal armaments going to the surface of a planet full of obviously angry natives. A planet where there would be no other Reliance personnel, with natives who had not only gotten their hands on explosives but learned how to use them, and where communications were iffy at best.

Stratton must have read his mind.

"Captain Briggs seemed to think that if we showed up in force the natives might become restless," she explained.

"Restless! Try armed and dangerous and just flat pissed off," Bradley said in shock. "What the hell does he expect us to do down there, anyway?"

"Die," Stratton said in a whisper. "From what I understood, talking to the others, we've all said rather derogatory things of a personal nature about good ole Captain Briggs. Now, while he can't court-martial us unless we say it to his face, try to incite a mutiny, or bad-talk the Reliance, he can mark us *highly expendable* and send us on a near suicide mission."

"Great…and I thought Harker was in some trouble because he had been arrested," Bradley mumbled. "You'd think the bastard would have more to do with his time than sit around viewing surveillance tapes."

"Harker?" Stratton said in surprise.

"You know him?" Bradley asked.

"Heard of him, is all," she said quickly. "His name is familiar. I'm the security chief, and he certainly wasn't on any of my lists of possible suspects. Makes me wonder who Briggs is talking to concerning security."

"Could you put in a good word for him with the Captain? I know you said you're on his shit list, too, but…"

"My saying something might actually hurt his case," she said. "Sorry…Cheer up. I don't think even Briggs is going to do something as stupid as starting to space people over a suspicion, and our mission isn't nearly as dangerous as he thinks it is. All we're supposed to do is talk with the King, find out if he knows what might have happened, and then get his permission to investigate. Look and see if there is a suitable place for a grounded base on the surface.

"There are no telecommunications on the planet. All news is spread by runners, so it can take days for news to get to and from the most remote villages. There is a good chance that the King has no idea what has happened. In fact, there is a good chance that we will be walking into nothing but a very confused monarch who has no idea what we are even talking about when we explain to him that his people have attacked our transporter and our space station, etc," Stratton said. "The King and his priests speak our language, but they won't understand what we're talking about unless we keep things simple…"

"And that would be where I come in, because I, of course, am a moron," Bradley said shaking his head.

Stratton laughed. "Actually I think it takes a pretty intelligent person to know how to convey a message to someone who has no concept of the words and machines that we take for granted. How do you explain a transporter sabotage to someone who worships a thermo-electric plant?"

"How do you explain to a pompous ass like Briggs that if you poison these people's gods and they find out, they are going to be pissed?" Bradley asked with a shrug.

"RJ," Levits called out as he walked up behind her—you definitely didn't want to take the chance of sneaking up on her. You just might get yourself killed. He wrapped his arms around her. She placed her hands over his and leaned her head back onto his shoulder. "So…Are you going to try to get some sleep, or are you just going to stand out here and look at the moons?"

She laughed a little. "While I'd love to tell you that I was just looking at the moons, I was actually watching the sky. I really expected the Reliance to try a little harder than this."

"They would if they knew it was you," he said. "If they knew you were the cause of their problems they would have sent every shuttle on the station. They just think they have a primitive uprising, nothing to get too worked up about."

"Blowing up a big hunk of their station should have gotten their attention. Mickey should have made his transmission by now. That should have given them some clue," RJ said.

"Their minds don't work like yours. They're a little slow on the uptake sometimes. Do you have to be so disappointed that we're not under siege already?" He moved her hair and gently kissed the side of her neck. "Can't you think about something besides fighting for a few moments?"

"I was thinking that the blue color of the smaller moon is most probably caused by gases enveloping it," RJ said.

"Oh! How very romantic," Levits groaned. "I had something else in mind."

RJ laughed and turned in his arms to face him. "Yes, but if it's only going to take a few moments, it hardly seems worth the effort."

Levits shrugged. "What can I say? I'm only a mere mortal, and there is that added twenty-five pounds of gravitational pull. I just can't promise anything."

She moved away from him then took hold of his hand and started pulling him towards the solar blanket he had laid out under the shuttle. "Tell you what. You just lay there, and I'll do all the work."

Taleed looked across Haldeed to where the one they called Poley was leaned against the frame of the open ship door. He was pretty sure that Poley was asleep. He shook Haldeed until he woke up. Haldeed glared at him, obviously upset about being awakened.

"I think you were right, Haldeed, we should not stay with these strangers. We should sneak out while they are asleep and otherwise occupied." A few minutes earlier strange sounds had started to echo from under the ship, and Taleed didn't have to wonder what the alien woman and her mate were up to. They were obviously too busy to notice them slipping away.

"Poley never sleeps," Topaz said in a whisper making both boys jump. "And no matter how busy his sister is, she's not likely to miss you two clumsy boys trying to sneak away."

Poley had brought Topaz back to camp about thirty minutes before, and he had just walked in, lain down, and, Taleed thought, gone to sleep.

"Why can't we go if we want to go?" Taleed asked in an angry whisper.

"Because RJ said you can't." Topaz rolled from his side onto his back. "Do yourself a favor, boy, and don't cross RJ. She's a very good friend, but she's an even better enemy, and unless I'm mistaken—and I hardly ever am—you could use a friend. You already have enough enemies."

Taleed nodded silently, lay down and tried to get comfortable. It wasn't easy; all of their gear was still damp and the strangers hadn't had anything extra. He looked over once more at the man who guarded the door. This time he looked back at Taleed, and even in the darkness Taleed could see his smile.

He mocks me. I do not know what to feel. Haldeed, he already sleeps again. He is too tired to worry. He's more tired than I am because he has to do everything for the both of us because the priests have made me a cripple. He forced his eyes to close. *These people are so strange—so different. They know so much more than we do. Their technology is so superior to ours. I don't know whether to trust them or distrust them. I don't know whether I like them or despise them. I know that I don't like being told that I can't leave. That my decisions are not mine to make. If this is to be my new life, then it is no different from the life that I fled. I thought I didn't want to know what my life would be. I thought I wanted adventure and an unknown destiny, and now I cower like a child behind his parent and wish I knew what tomorrow was going to bring. I must stop sniveling, this is my chance, perhaps my only chance to break the palace bonds and make my own way in the world. I must not be afraid. My one true friend, Haldeed, is with me. I am not alone in this. I must be brave.*

But he didn't feel like being brave. He felt wet and cold, and the floor of the ship was hard. His thoughts strayed to the palace and his life there, and he began to wonder what he had hated so badly.

As they neared the planet's capital the dwellings came into view and Bradley did a double take. Obviously the city had once been a huge cave the size of a small sea. Some geographical catastrophe had sent the ceiling crushing in. The debris of the roof had been carried away, probably over many centuries, leaving what he assumed were huge, brownish-green-streaked stalagmites. The population had carved these stalagmites into dwellings, and they looked like...

"Looks like huge piles of shit, doesn't it?" Stratton said.

"Yeah," Bradley said with a laugh. Then suddenly the Palace came into view, and as they got closer and he was sure of what he saw, his mouth flopped open in amazement. "Shee...it!" He exclaimed.

It was an old colony ship, like the ones he'd seen in history books. Huge. Easily twice as big as similar ships today, and he knew why. The older ships had been almost completely filled with engine. From this angle it didn't even look damaged, but from the way it was sitting, with a huge stand of stalagmites behind it and a clearing several square miles long in front of it, he imagined that the entire side that wasn't visible as well as the belly of the ship had been destroyed. Few, if any, would have survived such a crash.

Stratton looked neither surprised nor shocked by what they were looking at, and he realized that she must have known what the "Palace" was.

"We are responsible for their religious beliefs, and now we are using them against them," Bradley said more to himself than anyone else.

"Yeah," Stratton said plainly. "A spaceship filled with high-tech equipment crashes onto a primitive planet just starting to use rock tools, and the next thing you know, there is a whole new god in town.... Apparently there was at least one survivor."

Bradley nodded silently as their craft landed in the clearing just in front of the "Palace," sending clouds of dust into the air.

"Suits completely off," Stratton ordered. "Apparently the natives worship the suits, and we don't want to appear as their gods, just as people doing business with them. When we step outside the ship stand still and wait. Apparently they will send an escort."

"Is...is it safe?" Bradley asked.

"The most dangerous thing on this planet is the radioactive gold we gave them," Stratton said with a hint of anger in her voice.

They removed their suits, opened the seals and walked out into the early morning sunlight. Bradley noticed that he felt heavy and remembered that the gravitational pull was heavier than Earth's. While he'd never actually been on Earth, he'd spent his life on space stations that were designed to simulate Earth's gravity.

He'd seldom been sent planetside, and it was a rare treat to step on dirt, smell "real" air, to see the sky above, trees and plants. He wondered why humans had ever left their home planet and journeyed to the stars. What had been their motivation? If you had everything you needed, why go anywhere else?

"Ran out of resources," Stratton said, seeming to read his mind for the second time that day. But it turned out she was just explaining the existence of the old Earth ship on this planet. "Too many people, not enough stuff, so they started sending out ships like this in search of new planets. Planets with resources that we needed. This ship must have gone off course. Beta 4 has nothing the Reliance wants. Nothing we need. Dirt and simple rock, that's about all that's here. No plutonium, no uranium, no suitable materials with which to make metal. It rains too much or not at all, and the soil is nitrite poor, so that the things these people call forests would be considered wasteland anywhere else. Then there are all the damned magnetic pulses that emanate from deep within the planet's surface, making communications and even some equipment run erratically. In short, it's not a suitable habitat for humans. It was more expedient for the Reliance to trade with the natives for items the planet actually did produce and that they found desirable than it was to try to colonize it."

"The natives seem to be doing fine," Bradley said, watching as the natives ran towards them.

"Only because they periodically hold wars to cut down their population. Otherwise there would be mass starvation," Stratton explained.

Bradley looked at her, his eyes growing large with realization.

"Why do you think the Reliance is taking them to fight their war?" Stratton asked. "Generations of selective breeding."

More natives seemed to appear by the minute, all talking and pointing. Bradley didn't touch his sidearm; they weren't acting in an aggressive manner, just a curious one. One of the men with them must have felt a lot more intimidated, though, because he raised his weapon and threw off the safety.

"Put that damn thing away, Jackson," Stratton said heavily. "The last thing we want to do is make them think that we mean them any harm. They are a race of warriors; treat them with the same respect you would have for an Elite. Their weapons may be primitive, but they are stronger than we are and well trained in the arts of war. There are thousands of them and only five of us. Better weapons won't save us against those kinds of odds. Use your head."

"This is plain bullshit!" Jackson grated out lowering his weapon.

"I'm inclined to agree," Bradley turned suddenly to face the three bodyguards the Captain had sent with them. He knew them by sight, but didn't know them personally. It was a big station, they were combat branch and he was maintenance; still, he felt safe enough to ask. "Any of you feel good about what we're doing to these people, or about all the finger-pointing that's going on back at the station right now?"

"I don't think any of us would be here right now if we agreed with everything the Reliance and that pompous ass Briggs is doing," Stratton said. "What's your point?"

"My point is that all I want is to be left alone to do my job and live what little life I have. I don't agree with what we are doing to these people, and I don't appreciate being given what that prick considers to be a very dangerous assignment just because I said something he didn't like. But here we are. Let's just do it, try to get it right, and get back to the station without pissing off the natives. I don't know about the rest of you, but after years in space and in the heart of war zones, I don't want to die on a third-class planet on the end of some primitive's spear."

"Agreed," Jackson said.

"I don't want to be part of giving radiation sickness to anyone," one of the men said.

"They'll do it with or without us, Decker," Stratton said sadly. "We screw this up and if the natives don't kill us it's a sure bet that the Captain will have us spaced when we get back to the ship. Then he'll just get someone else to do it."

"But at least it wouldn't be us," Decker said.

"Because we'd be dead, you stupid little dork," the third marine said. "Me being dead to save a bunch of bug-eating natives isn't an option. Let's just do whatever it is we're supposed to do and get back into space where we belong."

Bradley remembered him now from the mess hall. His name was Hank, and he was a smart-assed punk who was constantly mouthing off to someone. The kind of guy who was always aching for a fight, verbal or otherwise. Hank and Harker had come to blows once, and Harker wasn't the sort of guy who ran around spoiling for a fight; he just wasn't one to walk away from one that was shoved in his face. No doubt Hank had been put on this detail not because he had any principles, but because he had mouthed off to the wrong person.

"Let's just do it and get it over with," Jackson agreed.

The crowd in front of them parted and four priests covered in gold chains and the signs of radiation sickness in full bloom walked through the crowd to greet them.

"Damn," Jackson muttered from behind him.

"This is just wrong," Decker whispered.

Bradley looked at Stratton, and she frowned. "There has to be something we can do," she whispered.

Bradley nodded. "Give me a second." He ducked quickly back into the ship. He came back out a few moments later carrying the pocket medic.

Stratton nodded her head in agreement.

But Decker whispered, "You can't just slap a band-aid on it."

"We can slow it down," Bradley whispered. "Maybe the Reliance will change policy."

"Yeah, and maybe dogs will fly!" Hank laughed out.

"Fuck you, Hank," Jackson muttered under his breath.

"All of you calm down," Stratton ordered.

The priests bowed before them.

"Rise," Stratton said. "We have brought medicine for your illness."

"I knew the gods would save us," one of the priests said. Bradley assumed he was a big shot because he was wearing more of the gold and more actual clothing—long, purple cotton robes with full sleeves tied with a wide red sash.

"In return we wish to speak to your King," Stratton said.
All the priests looked at her in disbelief.

"Is there a problem?" Stratton asked.

"No female may enter the holy places. So you may not
enter either the Temple or the Palace. However if you wish to
have the honor of sleeping with our God…"

"No…That's all right," Stratton said quickly. She
turned to Bradley. "Briggs left out this little detail. Can
you handle it?"

"I'll try," Bradley said.

"All right then, I'll just stay here and have dinner waiting
for you boys when you get back."

Bradley smiled at the look on her face. She looked at him
and shrugged as if to say that this had just gone onto the list
of things that were no longer her problem, and started for the
ship taking Decker with her. Probably more to keep him from
saying or doing something to sabotage their mission than because she felt like she needed protection.

Bradley, Jackson and Hank followed the priests into the
Palace. Red warning lights flashed as they walked down
what had once been the main corridor of the ship, and warning sirens blared. The throne room turned out to be the
ship's bridge. The huge observation window, which had a
crack running through the full length of it, looked out over
the city. The King sat in what had once been the Captain's
chair. It was now strewn with small furs, lizard skins and
bright-colored fabrics. The room was decorated with
strangely shaped sticks, and dried plants hung in bundles
from the ceiling.

The King/God, who had no hands, wore a loin-cloth made
of reptile skin, a red shirt with a huge collar and equally huge
puffy sleeves. The King was draped in even more of the
tainted gold than the priests, so he was in far worse physical
condition. This became even more evident when a dry rack-
ing cough echoed from his lungs. He covered his mouth with
one of his stumps until the coughing spell ended.

Even a few years ago, such exposure would have meant certain death, but with the new medications extracted from that hole Stasis, it wasn't too late to save even this man who had lost most of his hair and whose skin was covered in oozing sores. Of course all the medication would do was slow down the inevitable if they didn't remove the source of the radiation—namely, the gold that all of these men were wearing in such abundance.

Bradley was glad when the sirens and warning lights were turned off. It was the sort of noise and light that put your teeth on edge when you had grown up in space, because such things meant imminent disaster. Here, they no doubt thought it was a way of greeting important guests.

The priest relayed the message Bradley had given him to the King, and the King looked with eager eyes at Bradley. Bradley walked forward and bowed before the King, then he stood up and held the pocket medic out before him. "My Captain sends medicine to help you with your illness." The King nodded and held out his arm, apparently not completely ignorant of the technology, and Bradley administered the drug to him.

"It will take time to work," Bradley said. He turned and handed the med kit to Jackson. "Inject the priests."

Jackson nodded and started injecting the priests who had lined up as instructed by the high priest. He hadn't finished injecting the fourth one when twenty more came running in the room and lined up behind him.

"Why have you returned evil for good?" Bradley asked the King slowly.

"I do not understand," the King said.

"We have traded with you in good faith. Now you have blown up one of our trans-mat units and have severely damaged our space station," Bradley informed him.

"I have not heard of this. Nor was this action ordered by me." He coughed again then continued speaking. "I do not believe we have weapons that could harm you...Perhaps your own people have done this terrible thing. Or perhaps the machine has malfunctioned, as machines are prone to do. Perhaps you should have your priests look into the matter. Perhaps they should consult with your god."

Bradley did not believe the man was lying. He really didn't have any idea what Bradley was talking about, which, since the incident had taken place roughly two hundred miles from here, and the planet had no form of telecommunications, was perfectly believable.

Bradley added that to the fact that The New Alliance had taken credit for the attack and came to the natural conclusion. Someone on the station really was a traitor to the Reliance. Someone—or more than one someone—was working with the New Alliance to try to stop the Reliance. Right now, Bradley wasn't sure how he felt about that.

"We would like your permission to investigate this matter," Bradley said.

"Yes, of course," the King agreed graciously. "We must keep good relations between our two peoples so that both may prosper. We have done nothing wrong and have nothing to hide. If you find that one or more of my people is guilty of any criminal act against you, then you may punish them in whatever way is your custom."

We are the ones committing the crime, and I'm very sorry. Bradley waited for Jackson to finish inoculating the last of the priests.

He bowed to the King, and the King dipped his head to him, and then they left the throne room and headed back for the ship. His insides felt like they were on fire. How could he live with what he had just done? These people trusted the Reliance, and the Reliance was using and killing them on a grand scale. How could he walk away and never mention that it was the gold that was killing them? How could he leave them to die?

There was only one real answer—there was nothing he could do to stop it. The Reliance did what it wanted to do; it had no conscience. It didn't see the individual. It was too big, and too many lives were at stake. Isn't that what they had drilled into him at school? The Reliance sometimes did things that seemed wrong because the individual was incapable of understanding the mysterious ways in which the Reliance worked. The Reliance always worked for what was best for the masses, and so if you thought they were doing something evil, you must be wrong.

The Reliance had supposedly gotten rid of religion, but all it had done was make itself into a god. A god they followed as blindly as these people worshiped thermo generators. They didn't understand where the power came from, or how it worked, so instead of trying to find out they just said it was unexplainable and worshiped it. To go against the Reliance was to go against god. So, just like these poor saps were wearing tainted gold to honor their gods, Bradley and the others were carrying out orders that they knew were wrong to honor theirs.

He almost doubled back more than once, but he had no right to make decisions for the others. Especially when Stratton was in charge, and he was acting in her stead.

"He says he had nothing to do with it and I believe him," Bradley said sitting beside Stratton as the others got in and the hatch closed. "He gave us the go ahead to investigate told us to punish the guilty party according to our customs."

"Those stupid fuckers," Hank laughed. "They're all eaten up with radiation sickness, and it never once dawns on them to take the damn gold off."

"Because they trust us," Decker said hotly. "They don't think we're trying to kill them. They aren't stupid; they're naïve."

"Well, we'll fix that," Bradley said heavily.

"Don't think I'm not going to tell command how you wasted medical supplies on those savages," Hank said. "After all I need all the points I can rake up so that prick Briggs doesn't keep putting me on shit patrol."

"You're a stupid dickhead," Decker spat at him.

"Let's just do this and get it over with," Stratton said taking a deep breath and letting it out slowly before she finished talking. "It's going to take a long time for me to get the taste of this mission out of my mouth."

The craft took off and they headed for the village where the transport had been sabotaged.

"Who do you suppose did it?" Stratton asked Bradley.

"I don't know," Bradley said. "Could have been one of our people, working with the New Alliance. Let's not forget that they took credit for it, and that they know what's going on here. They certainly have a reason to try to stop our little mission. I still didn't have an accurate body count when we left the station. One or more of our people who came down here might have stayed on the planet and rigged up the whole thing. You got nothing but arms and legs and body slime, it's hard to tell who's there and who's not. It's awful easy to throw your ID into a pile. Someone working with the natives could have very easily overpowered the patrol, especially if he had help from the New Alliance."

"And there's that missing ship," Jackson reminded them. "It might have been hijacked by the New Alliance and landed on the planet during a pulse. We'd be none the wiser. That ship could be here right now."

"He's right. Certainly those are all sound theories," Stratton said. The tone and dismissive quality of her voice led him to believe that she had a theory of her own and was basically dismissing theirs.

They were talking about the mechanics of the mission because most of them didn't really want to think about what they were really doing. Someone had defended these people, and now they were trying to find out who and get rid of them so that the Reliance could go right on raping them.

Stratton started trying to patch into command on the station to update the Captain on their progress. Instead of getting a channel out, Stratton wound up getting one in and the communicator started giving them the news of the day from the station. "Damned magnetic pulses," Stratton said, trying to readjust.

"No wait, I want to hear the news," Bradley said and the others mumbled their agreement. News broadcasts, however boring and repetitive, were high entertainment on the station. Right now Bradley mostly wanted to know what was going on with the investigations.

It was the same old crap, except for detailed information on the repairs and when they expected to be up and fully functional again. They were saying it would take less than a week.

"Two at the very least," Bradley said.

The radio announcement droned on, till it came to the end. "And finally today twenty-three people were arrested and charged with conspiracy in connection with the recent sabotage of the transport bay and station. At the head of the conspiracy was Corporal Harker, number ZX5568723, who, after one hour of questioning, confessed to the crime and has been spaced for his part in it...."

"No!" Bradley yelled. He was at a complete loss, momentarily unable to even pull one clear thought out of his mind. Then he felt the pain of loss and an anger that was almost tangible and was building by the second. He didn't even notice that the ship had lurched violently to one side.

Hank said something, but Bradley didn't really hear it, and then Stratton screamed something at Hank, which he also didn't comprehend. Then she was talking to him, but he was in a tunnel—a cone in which nothing and no one else existed. He could see Harker floating lifeless in space, could feel his pain, and suddenly he was hollering something without even being aware of doing so. He must have been unintelligible, because the next thing he heard was Stratton's voice asking gently.

"What, Sergeant?"

He knew then what he had said and he looked at her. "I said turn the ship around; we're going back," he ordered.

"Why?" Hank asked.

"Because we're going to tell those poor stupid fucks that the gold is killing them, that's why." It was Stratton who answered him. Bradley stared, at her dumbfounded for a minute, and then nodded his head in agreement.

"Man, you can't do that shit," Hank said. He looked at Stratton. "Who's in charge here, lieutenant? You or this toilet cleaner?"

"I'm in charge," Stratton said and turned the ship around.

"What the fuck are you doing?" Hank half-screamed, half-laughed. "Have you all lost your tiny little minds? This is mutiny. The punishment for mutiny is death."

"Apparently the punishment for saying anything they don't like is death, and we've all done that," Stratton said. Bradley was surprised to see that she seemed almost as mad as he was.

"You…I won't let you two soft spots do this. You're endangering all of our lives. You have no right to do this."

There was a familiar popping noise accompanied by a strange whiff of ozone, and then the sound of something large hitting the floor of the ship with enough force to make it lurch.

Bradley turned quickly to see Hank laying on the floor with a nice little burned mark right between his eyes. Bradley looked up at Decker who was standing with his laser rifle in hand. The green light on the butt of it was glowing showing that it had just been fired and was now powering back up.

"He…He was starting to pull his weapon," Decker said by way of an explanation.

"He's the least of our problems," Stratton said. She turned to look at Bradley. "A deadcrew man we can explain away easily, but if we actually go against the Reliance…Well, they'll kill us all. We go to the Capital and tell that primitive King that it's the gold that is killing them, if we warn them about what the Reliance is really doing here, there won't be any going back. Right now we can kick what's left of Hank out the hatch, let him splat on the ground for the local varmints to eat, and tell command he went AWOL. But if we go back to the Capital and talk to the natives, there won't be any going back to the Reliance. We'll be as good as dead."

"And if we go back we may be as good as dead anyway," Jackson said. "They picked up twenty-three people on that ship and accused them of conspiracy with the New Alliance. I don't think any of them are spies…"

"I know Harker wasn't," Bradley said. "He died because Briggs needed someone to blame, and dead men don't have any chance of proving you're wrong about them. This man was my friend, my best friend. I knew him. He was no traitor. He was a good man—a hard worker." He sniffed and dried the tears off his face quickly. "Briggs sent us down here in the hopes that we'd find out what he needs to know and get killed doing it. Between you and me, I think that if we do exactly what we're supposed to do here and go back up there and report to him, there's a good chance that he'll treat us just like he treated Harker."

"I'd rather die planetside than be spaced," Decker said. "And I sure as hell don't want to be party to what's going on here. I said that from the get-go."

The three men looked at Stratton. She suddenly seemed interested only in the view out her windshield.

"Well, it's up to you," Bradley prompted when he got tired of waiting for her answer.

She turned to face him and said. "I'm flying towards the Capital, aren't I?"

Chapter Ten

David had been asleep for days, so he guessed there was no mystery as to why he woke up before the others. He nodded to Poley as he walked past him at the door, and Poley nodded back.

Once outside the shuttle, David made his way towards a clump of bushes that looked like they needed watering. It wasn't cold, just that nice cool he associated with an early spring morning. He sighed with instant gratification as he relieved himself. A disgruntled and now wet lizard about the size of a small cat climbed out of the bush, and David jumped. It glared at David then moved slowly away.

"Sorry, dude," David said to the offended lizard and finished pissing. He had just fixed himself into his pants when he noticed that the sun was starting to come up. It wasn't all red and gold and orange like the sun of Earth. More purple and blue and grayish. It was only then that it finally dawned on him; he had flown across the vastness of space and was now standing on another world with a different sun, a different sky, different plants and different wild life. He walked a few feet away from where he had wet this strange new world and bent down and grabbed a handful of dirt. It felt exactly the same as Earth dirt. He was a little shocked to realize he didn't feel more excited than he did. In a way it was a little disappointing. He wanted to be full of awe and wonder, like a child who had found something new, like Topaz. Instead, he found that he was like Levits and RJ—basically oblivious to the wonder all around him.

Just another planet. No big deal.

They at least had an excuse; both of them had been on countless space runs and had been on countless planets. For them doing a mission on a strange planet was old hat, but it was a completely new experience for him, and yet try as he might, he didn't feel any joy, any awe, any sense of wonder.

It's different. So what?

He was clear across space, and yet he couldn't get the vision of Alsterace burning out of his mind, nor could he remove the stench of death from his nostrils. He supposed things could happen to you that were so horrible that they leached any ability for happiness from your soul. How could you ever be happy when you had endured so much pain? How could you trust anyone or anything when your own heart had lied to you? When the one person you had loved and trusted above all others had betrayed you and left you to bear the shame for her actions, it was hard to get worked up about something as mundane as a different sunrise. When you had taken a weapon and killed the only woman you had ever loved because she was a treacherous bitch, it was hard to enjoy anything at all.

He turned and started towards the firepit. He'd put some wood on the fire if there were still live coals. Fire was the same here, too. Fire, he decided, must be the same everywhere. He stirred the ashes and found some live coals deep down. He stacked some of the smaller pieces on the fire and decided to go look for some more deadfall. As he turned to walk into the brush, he saw RJ and Levits, curled up in each other's arms, asleep under the skiff. That was something he was sure he was never going to get used to. He stopped and watched them.

They looked content and peaceful. He hadn't seen either of them look like that even in sleep since before Alsterace was attacked. They had each lost the loves of their lives that night, and the damage to their psyches had been complete. Kirsty had deserved to die, and that didn't stop him from missing her, wanting her. Neither Whitey nor Sandra had deserved their fates; he could only imagine the hell that Levits and RJ had lived in over the last two years. Now they had found each other and this union was helping both of them to heal.

I have to be happy for her. She and I were never meant to be; if we had been it would have happened for us a long time ago. I don't love her. I never have. While she once loved me, there is no way she would ever love me again, not now. Not after what I did.

He walked quickly away into the brush. The place was filthy with lizards, but deadfall was a little harder to find. The largest trees in this so-called "forest" weren't even at tall as he was, and they were sparse. Mostly the land was covered in small bushes and cane-type plants.

Seemingly from out of nowhere, Janad appeared. She smiled when he jumped out of his skin after being startled by her.

"Looking for wood?" she asked.

"Yes," he answered.

"On the ground?" she asked giving him a curious look.

"Yes," he said.

She shrugged in a way that said she was never going to understand these humans. She went over to one of the bushes which still looked very much alive and had limbs of about three inches in diameter. She broke it off at ground level and started to break it into pieces. He remembered that she was stronger than him, but tried it anyway and found that it broke very easily. It was fibrous inside.

"The *buche'feu* plant breaks up easily but burns very long. Longer than most wood. Wood is hard to come by, but the forest is filthy with this stuff," she explained.

David nodded and broke off another limb. "You shouldn't sneak up on people like that," he said. For answer she just laughed at him. He shook his head and continued to work. After awhile they had a pile that she informed him would be more than enough for the day, and they headed back to camp.

As they walked up, RJ was walking into camp with a huge reptile on a stick.

"Janad, is this one edible?" she yelled.

Janad nodded her head excitely. "Yes! Very good."

"Great, more lizard," David muttered. He dropped his bundle of wood and found a rock to sit on.

Janad took the lizard from RJ and ran off. He guessed to clean and dress it.

RJ sat down beside him on the rock. "Feeling better?" she asked, looking up at the sun that was rising quickly into the sky.

"Yeah, but I still feel like I've put on fifty pounds. I suppose that's why they're so much stronger than we are," David said.

RJ nodded silently.

"So...when were you going to tell me about you and Levits?"

"What's to tell?" RJ asked. "I don't feel like I have to make an announcement to anyone about who I am or am not sleeping with. Do you truly believe I have been celibate these last two-plus years? I don't care who you're bedding, why should you care who I'm sleeping with?"

"Do you love him?" David asked.

"He loves me, and it has been my experience that when someone loves me I will love them eventually," RJ said. "I care very deeply for him; he saved my life. We share a common past."

"You don't always act like you like him a lot, and he certainly doesn't act like he loves you," David said matter-of-factly.

"Just because he doesn't kiss my ass—or I his—doesn't mean that we don't care for one another," RJ said simply.

"RJ, love isn't supposed to be work, it's supposed to just *happen*," David insisted.

"Love is always work, and nothing worth having ever just *happens*. I can't believe that after all you have been through you still don't get it." RJ got up and threw some more wood on the fire. "Nothing is ever as easy or as difficult as you make it out to be, David Grant. People have chemistry. If people have chemistry and they also care for one another, then it becomes love. You demand something that comes from nowhere and knocks you on your ass, but nothing is that easy. You demand that someone love you unconditionally; that they be always filled with passion and desire for you. Nothing is that difficult."

"Why is that difficult?" David asked.

"Because, in order to have that kind of love you would have to *give* that kind of love, and that's a hell of a lot of work." She sighed deeply, as if finding his lack of comprehension tiring in the extreme. "I just want to enjoy him. Why does our relationship have to grow into anything more than it is now if we are both happy with the way things are? I refuse to plan out where our relationship will go. To dictate to myself how I should or should not feel. Can't you see that by doing that you are just setting yourself up to be disappointed? This isn't some battle that needs careful analysis and planning. Even if it was, it would be my battle and not yours. Worry about your own empty, haunted life, and leave mine alone." RJ left then walking into the brush leaving David with his thoughts.

He carefully went over everything that RJ had just said twice and still had to admit that he didn't really know what she meant.

Topaz was gushing about the sunrise, the plants, the bugs, the lizards and some small fur-bearing creature he had caught a glimpse of running through the brush.

"Don't you have any birds?" Topaz asked the three natives.

"Birds." Taleed said the strange word and shook his head. "I don't know that word."

The other two shrugged.

"Animals covered in feathers that fly in the air like a...a space ship," Topaz explained.

"We have lizards that have feathers," Janad said and rubbed her stomach. "Very good to eat."

"You have flying animals on your world?" Taleed asked in excitement.

"Yes, many. And there used to be many more," Topaz said. "Overhunting, pollution and pesticides..."

"OK. I hate to interrupt Grandpa's story hour," Levits started, "but what's next? Are we just going to sit here camping until the Reliance finds us, or do you actually have a plan, RJ?"

"Sitting here till the Reliance finds us *was* my plan," RJ said, leaning forward from where she was sitting on a rock and tearing off a hunk of the not-quite-done lizard. She sat back down munching on the piece of meat. "I figure they have to come looking for us sooner or later. To do that, they are going to have to come down here. To get down here, they are going to have to bring a ship. They come after us, we kill them and take their ship."

"Good plan," Levits said approvingly.

"Unless they kill us," Taleed said, not understanding their cavalier attitude. They were not simple-minded like his people. They knew that the Reliance had weapons that were every bit as powerful as their own. They knew they weren't gods and therefore could be killed. "Surely you don't expect the seven of us to stand up to the might of the Reliance."

To his surprise the four aliens just laughed at him. The older one looked at him, and by way of explanation said, "Fighting windmills is what we do best."

"What is a windmill?" Taleed asked him.

"A huge monster with four rotating arms, beady eyes and sharp pointy teeth," Topaz said.

"You have those on your planet?" Taleed asked, his eyes wide.

"Oh, yes, thousands of them," Topaz assured him.

RJ rose to her feet and stretched. "Consider us giant-killers. We have fought the Reliance before many times, and we have only really lost once. The Reliance isn't likely to throw anything at us that we can't handle. Their downfall is their size; the Reliance is too big and too well organized to think on their feet. Besides, I said I wasn't a god. I *never* said I was *human*." She turned and walked off into the brush without another word, as if some destiny awaited her just beyond the line of their sight.

"What does she mean?" Taleed asked Topaz.

"Concerning what?" Levits asked almost under his breath. "All the double talk about the Reliance's impotence, or the fact that she isn't human?"

Taleed looked from Topaz to Levits and back again, indicating that he actually wanted both questions answered.

"Poley, RJ and I are all the result of different scientific experiments," Topaz answered, no doubt feeling that further explanation would be wasted on Taleed. "When you have only a few people to run things, they sit around and talk and get things done easily. The fewer people you have the more quickly decisions can be made. The Reliance, however, has a huge chain of command. RJ obviously believes that this means..."

"Why don't you just admit that you have no idea what the hell she was talking about?" Levits said with a laugh. He turned to look at Taleed. "Listen, kid...Do yourself a favor. Just believe what she says, and do what she tells you. She knows exactly what she's doing, and I've rarely known her to be wrong. Those who don't listen to her damage themselves and everyone else." He shot a look full of hate at David, then got up and walked in the same direction the woman had gone.

When he had gone Janad looked at David. "Why does he hate you so much?"

David took in a deep breath and let it roll out slowly before he answered. "Because I betrayed RJ and the New Alliance and caused the death of the woman he loved."

Janad didn't understand. Neither, for that matter, did Taleed.

"I thought *she* was the woman he loved," Taleed said in confusion.

"She is now," David said.

"I don't understand," Janad said shaking her head. "If what you say is true, why are you here with them now? Why did they not kill you?"

"Truly...I don't know." David stood up and walked away in the direction opposite from the way the others had gone.

"What did he do?" Taleed asked Topaz.

Topaz, of course, who lived to tell people what he knew told the whole story from the beginning of the New Alliance to their descent to this planet. The three child/adults listened intently, hardly even interrupting him with questions. It was only when the four of them had finished eating the entire lizard and Topaz had finished his story that he realized that it had been at least an hour, and the others hadn't returned.

"Poley, where are RJ, Levits and David?" he asked.

Poley pointed in the direction RJ and Levits had gone. "My sister and Levits are about half a mile away and have been engaging in sexual activities. They are quiet now, so I'm assuming they're done. "David," he pointed in the direction he had gone, "is about a quarter of a mile away, and is apparently chunking rocks into the river."

Taleed got up and walked over to Poley. He walked around him looking at his neck. "I still do not understand...How can a man have his head severed from his body and go on living?"

Poley made a face and rubbed at his neck.

"I told you...Stewart made Poley..."

"And RJ. I think I understand what RJ is, but...What is he? I don't understand."

"He's a machine," Topaz said. "An artificial intelligence, a robot."

"He can't be," Taleed said shaking his head. "He is a man. I see no difference between him and you or your friends."

"I didn't say Stewart didn't do a damn good job on the boy," Topaz said.

Taleed looked at Poley's hands. "You mean...you made him? Even his hands?"

Topaz had noticed that there was something wrong with the boy's hands. For one thing he didn't take his gloves off even when it was hot. For another the other boy had to feed him, which meant his hands must be extremely crippled.

"I didn't make him; Stewart did," Topaz answered.

"But if you repaired him when he was broken...You could build him?" Taleed asked excitedly.

"Well, of course," Topaz said egotistically, although in truth he wasn't sure that he could.

"Then you could make hands for me?" Taleed said raising his hands in the air.

"That's bionics, son, a whole different science," Topaz said. "One that is tricky at best and not really proven. You'd have to cut off your hands, and the hands you'd replace them with probably wouldn't do as much as the hands you have now."

"He doesn't have hands," RJ said, startling them all, both with her sudden presence and her statement.

Taleed turned and glared at her, and Janad, realizing what this meant, suddenly dropped to the ground and prostrated herself before Taleed. RJ walked the rest of the way into camp, reached down and grabbed Janad by the belt of her loin-cloth and hauled her to her feet.

"Get up girl; he's no god. Just some poor boy who's been maimed in the name of tradition," RJ said. "Isn't that true, Your Highness?"

Taleed glared angrily at her and spat out, "If you knew all along, why did you wait till now to expose me?"

"How would that have served me?" she asked.

"How does it serve you now?" Taleed asked hotly.

"Because you have something I want, and now I know I have something you want."

"What?"

RJ walked into the ship and appeared a few minutes later carrying one of the service droids. Its metal hands were dragging in the dirt. She threw it at the young prince's feet.

"I have hands. Topaz has the skill. Want to talk about a deal?"

Chapter Eleven

Stratton stared at the clock on the instrument panel of the flyer. Bradley and Jackson had been gone a long time. "I wonder what's taking them so long?" Stratton yelled back at Decker where he stood at the top of the ramp just outside the open hatch.

"I don't know, but this doesn't look good," Decker said.

From the windshield she could see what he meant. The "curious villagers" were carrying more and more weapons and beginning to appear less like a welcoming committee and more like an angry mob. Suddenly a huge scream came from them as a whole assembly.

"Get in the ship! Get back in the ship!" Stratton said, activating the switch that would close the hatch.

Decker jumped in, barely escaping the spear that rattled to the floor beside him where he landed on his butt.

"Shit!" Decker screamed as spears and rocks starting hitting the outside of the ship, making it almost impossible to hear. He got to his feet and ran to where Stratton sat at the console, trying to get through to Bradley and Jackson.

"Bradley, this is Stratton. We are under attack! Do you read? What the hell's going on? Damn it! If you can hear me, answer." There was nothing. "God-damned magnetic pulses!"

"It may not be the pulses," Decker said looking at the hail of rocks and spears thumping ineffectively on the windscreen and swallowing a lump in his throat. "He may not be in a position to answer us."

Stratton nodded. If Bradley had met with a similar welcoming party inside the Palace, he and Jackson were probably already dead. She made a quick decision and started powering up the ship.

"What the hell are you doing?" Decker screamed. "They may still be alive. We can't just leave them here."

"And they may already be dead. If we stay here, we'll be killed as well," Stratton told him. She got back on the comlink. "Bradley, we can't wait. We're lifting off. We'll come back for you."

"This thing was made to take re-entry and meteor showers. Rocks and spears aren't likely to hurt it!" Decker screamed. "We can wait."

"How long do you think it's going to take them to figure out that rocks and spears aren't going to damage us and go after tools? They have time and manpower on their side. If Bradley and Jackson are still alive, we will come back for them. For now we're going to run and hide," Stratton assured him.

"Fire the forward cannons…"

"If I use the armaments, we won't have enough power left to make escape velocity. The armaments on a skiff are for emergency use only!" Stratton said.

"And this isn't an emergency?" Decker screamed.

"Not yet," Stratton answered calmly.

"Call Briggs. Report what's happening and send for reinforcements," Decker pleaded.

"Oh, yes…That's exactly what we all want to do—escalate the problems down here. You know how the Reliance deals with primitive uprisings. They send bombers in to hammer the place level whether we—or Bradley and Jackson are here or not." She lifted off as the natives scattered.

"Then fire the cannons. If we aren't planning to go back to the Station anyway, what does it matter?" Decker asked.

"I'm not going to cut our options. I'm not willing to burn out bridges we may need." She lifted off. "If we shoot them, how are we going to prove that we want to help them? If we wind up being stuck on this planet, we had damn well better find a way to get along with the natives. The last thing we want to do is make them more hostile than they already are." She flew the skiff away from the palace and the capital city.

"In cause you didn't understand when we decided to defect, you were no longer in command," Decker said. "You left Jackson and Bradley down there to die."

"Right now, I'm in command of this skiff because I'm sitting in this chair and the only way you're going to get me out of this chair is to burn a hole in me like the one you burned in Hank. If they had it in their heads to kill Bradley and Jackson, they have already done so. If they are still alive, we will go back and get them. But we obviously aren't going to be able to sneak past anyone in this ship."

Decker nodded his head in reluctant agreement.

"Now buckle up. I'm setting this thing down," Stratton ordered.

Bradley looked at the ring of guards that had closed in around him and Jackson and then back at the King.

"What is all this?" Bradley asked. He heard but ignored Stratton's frantic call sounding from the transmitter in his ear.

"You said we would be cured," the King said. "We are not cured. Now you tell us you want the gold back. My people have traded with the Reliance in good faith for hundreds of years. Now you trade my people for gold and then order that we give the gold back to you."

"Listen to me…The Reliance has indeed dealt in bad faith with you. I don't agree with what the Reliance is doing and neither do these people with me. That is why—at risk of our very lives—we have come here to tell you that the gold the Reliance has given you is tainted. It is the gold that is making you sick. If you will only think about it, you will know that what I am telling you is true."

The King laughed, and the priests joined in. Then he stopped laughing and spoke angrily. "You think that since we do not have the technology of your people that we are stupid and simpleminded. We are not stupid. We know what you are doing. You are trying to trick us so that you have everything and we have nothing. We will no longer make trade with the Reliance."

"Good, you shouldn't," Bradley said. "Only listen to me. If you do not take the gold off your bodies and bury it in a deep hole far from your people, then you will die. You will all die."

The King laughed again. "I cannot die; I am a god. My soul will simply be moved into the body of the Chosen One."

The man Bradley assumed was the head priest shook with apparent excitement, then bent down and whispered excited words into the King's ear. The King's face at first looked amazed and then, if it was possible, more angry than before. He arose shakily from his throne and walked around Bradley and Jackson, looking them over.

"So," he said at length. "This is the game that you play. You bring some illness here to afflict me, and then you kidnap the Chosen One so that when I die, my soul will have no where to go. Your own evil shall be your undoing. Guards! Take their weapons and throw them into the dungeon." He stopped and glared into Bradley's face. "When your Captain returns my son, then I shall return you two."

"We do not have your son," Bradley assured him. "Our Captain will not bargain with you; it isn't our custom."

Jackson looked at him as the guards started to take their weapons, but Bradley shook his head. They couldn't fight their way out of here. Not right now. Even if they could, Stratton had just informed him that she was leaving with the ship, so there was nowhere to run. Jackson let go of his weapon reluctantly and the guards started to lead them away.

Bradley balked, turned back to the King and tried once more, "We don't have your son!" The guards began to drag them out. "It's the gold which is going to kill you. Think about it! When did you get sick? Damn it, we are trying to help you! You don't understand the ways of our people, or you would know that by doing this we put ourselves at great risk. Why not remove the gold from yourselves and see if you don't get better? See if I'm telling the truth or not. What could be the harm in that?"

"I will hear no more of your lies! Take them away!" the King screamed, waving his stumps dismissively.

The King sat on his throne with his head perched on one of his stumps thoughtfully.

"What are you thinking?" the high priest asked Taheed.

"What if...What if he's telling the truth, and it is the gold metal which is making us sick?" Taheed asked.

"How could metal make a man sick? Has the gold metal of your office that you have worn since taking over from your father ever made you ill?"

"No, but..."

"Did not the gods speak through us saying that it is wholly good and right that we should trade our warriors for gold and cloth? This illness is something brought by the Reliance so they may now take back what is rightfully ours. The illness will pass, the gods have said so..."

"Do you really think that they are responsible for Taleed's disappearance?" Taheed asked.

"I do not know. I cannot be certain. I will ask the gods when I return to the Temple tonight."

"While you are at it, ask where he is," Taheed commanded.

"I will ask, but you know that such questions often have answers which are not easily read, for the gods answer in mysterious ways...I will leave now, and return to the Temple. I shall talk to the gods and perhaps have answers for you shortly."

"Ziphed, my brother," Taheed called out to the priest's departing form.

The high priest turned to look at the King. "Yes, My Lord?"

"Why is it that I cannot talk to the gods? Would it not be more expedient that way? Wouldn't it be better if I asked the gods questions and they answered me directly?"

"You do not have the gift—few Kings have. It is a gift more suitably given to the brothers of the King, to the priests. It is our calling. When we hear the voices in our heads we know that the gods have chosen us to speak with them and to tell those who cannot hear them what is their will." Ziphed bowed and then left.

Taheed did not feel satisfied with Ziphed's answer. He got up and started to pace in front of the window. The fact that he felt well enough to do this proved—at least to him— that the alien's medicine was helping.

"How can I be sure of what the gods say if they do not say them to me?" Taheed asked. "One day he tells me that my disease is caused by the gods because they're angry that Taleed has run off. Now he tells me that the disease is caused by the actions of the Reliance, and that my son has not run off, but has been taken. The man in the dungeon says he no longer works for the Reliance. He gives us medicine that—while it does not cure, certainly has made us feel better. He says the gold makes us ill." He noticed then that Yashi was nodding and grunting excitedly. Yashi held out his arms for the King to see, and the King noticed for the first time that Yashi was not sick. "Yashi...You do not have the sickness!"

Yashi nodded more excitedly, and pointed to the chains on the King's neck and then to his own bare neck.

"Are you saying...Is that what you have been trying to say all along? Do *you* think it is the gold?" Taheed asked.

The mute nodded his head vigorously.

Taheed took the mass of gold chains from his neck and looked at them. He didn't feel any different, still..."If the priests say one thing one day and something else the next, then there is a chance that man is telling the truth. Who is to say that your council is not equal to that of the priests? If I am a god—and I must believe that I am—then my own judgment should be as good as any priest's—or better. Yashi, take these chains and all other Reliance gold from the throne room and bury it in the palace garden. Then go into the city to Jarish the Jeweler who weaves reeds into fine chains. Buy from him enough of the gold-colored reed chains to take the place of the real gold ones. In this way the priests will never know that

I did not heed their council. If I should get well while the priests remain ill, then the gold is poison and I will deal with the Reliance accordingly. "I begin to believe, Yashi, that I have been very poorly advised. If you and the man in the dungeons are correct, then I must think seriously what I should do—about many things. Perhaps I will tell the priests, and perhaps I will not. It depends mostly on what they tell me concerning what the gods have told them about my son."

Bradley paced back and forth behind the bars of the cell in what had no doubt been the old ship's brig. He and Jackson were not alone. Several of the cells were occupied including the one on their right. On a planet where metal was scarce, you would have thought this ship would have been torn down long ago and used to make tools. As Stratton had suggested some of the original occupants of this ship must have lived and obviously they had set themselves up as gods to the simple natives that lived here. The survivors and the natives made this place into some holy cathedral, thus keeping it from being cannibalized to make picks and shovels.

Stratton was suddenly talking to him again.

"Bradley, if you guys are alive, you'd better come back. We're not risking our asses to rescue cadavers, over."

The transmission was fuzzy; no doubt because of the thickness of the hull on this antique, but still audible. He just hoped his reply could get out.

He looked around to make sure none of the other prisoners were watching him and raised the wrist-com to his mouth, punching the button.

"Stratton, this is Bradley, we have been incarcerated in the old ship's brig. Repeat. We have been incarcerated. Do you read?"

"Barely," came back the reply.

He smiled at Jackson and held thumbs up. Jackson let out a relieved sigh and sat down for the first time since they had been put in the cell.

"Incarcerated is better than dead," Stratton continued. "Get back to me with the particulars—where the brig is located, how well guarded, etc., and we'll see what we can do about getting you out of there."

"I'll see what I can find out. Don't try anything crazy. No sense in all of us winding up in here or worse. Over."

"Not much chance of that; I'm no hero. I at least want to wait till dark. There are a lot of them, so the only way we're going to get you out of there is by using our heads, not with force or bravado. Over," Stratton said

"Keep transmissions to a minimum. Remember the natives aren't our only problem. If the Reliance finds out what we've been doing, they'll be on us like stink on a turd. Every time we use the transmitter we risk detection. Over," Bradley replied.

"With the pulses it's doubtful that surface to surface communications would be picked up by the station, but, just in case, change your channel to 00 opt 9. What the hell happened in there anyway? Over," Stratton asked.

"I will change my setting when we close transmission. Good thinking. They thought we were trying to trick them out of their gold. Suffice it to say that it just doesn't pay to try to be a nice guy. Over and out." He lowered his wrist and moved to sit beside Jackson.

"Well?" Jackson asked.

"We need to find out as much as we can and then radio Stratton. Realistically, I don't know what they can do. There are only two of them and about a gazillion of these bastards running around," Bradley said.

Jackson nodded.

"Yes, but none of them are the King's guards," the native guy in the next cell said in Reliance.

Bradley and Jackson both jumped, and then turned around to stare at the man. He was dressed as many of the other natives were, in a simple loincloth and sleeveless shirt made of rough brown fabric. His face shone with a friendly smile that was almost too big for his face.

"What do you mean?" Bradley asked him.

"The King's guards are highly trained fighters, and they know the palace well. But the King's guards all gone looking for the Chosen One, who has run away for these many times," he said in his broken Reliance.

Bradley found that he had to play back what the man had said in his mind to understand what he was actually saying.

"Run away?" Bradley asked.

"Oh, yes, he does it all the time," the native said and then fell silent.

"Why?" Bradley asked

The man looked at him silently and smiled.

"Why does he run away?" Bradley asked slowly, thinking that perhaps the man hadn't understood his question.

"You going to break out?" the man asked.

Bradley thought for only a second about lying to the fellow and then said, "Why do you ask?"

"I thought you would be smart men," he laughed. "I'm in here; I want out. You get me out with you; I tell you what I know and help us all get out."

"If we're breaking out, and you help us by telling us what we need to know, then we would help you get out as well," Bradley promised.

He smiled and nodded, then started talking. "Rumor has it that the Chosen One is very unhappy. That he doesn't want to be the King or a god. He has his own spirit and wants to keep it that way. For this reason he and his servant run away all the time. But this time he has been gone longer than ever before, much longer. So the King has sent away all of his personal guards to go out in search of the Chosen One and his companion. The men who fill the Temple now are not the King's guard. They are simple fighters from the town, chosen by the priests to fill in while the palace retinue is away. Since wars are not allowed in the holy city, these men have never even seen an actual battle. What's more, they get lost easily in the palace. This is why they are running around like crazy people. They are lost. If your friends on the outside were to dress like us, they could sneak in undetected, and we could all be out of here before they even missed us.

"Only one problem with that," Bradley said with a smile. "We are a different color than you are. Our friends are too, and one of them is a woman." Bradley noticed that the native's Reliance was getting better. Either that, or his ear was becoming accustomed to his speech, because he was much easier to understand.

"Yes, that could be a problem," the man said thoughtfully shaking his head. Then he snapped his fingers. "I've got it...They could dress like the gods."

"How could they do that?" Bradley asked. "What do your gods look like?"

"Like a man in a spacesuit," he said matter-of-factly. "You have spacesuits, don't you?"

Bradley remembered then what Stratton had said when they first got here about removing their suits. "Yes, but how...What are you here for anyway?"

The man laughed. "Sirs, you are looking at a defrocked priest. I read the holy books. I know what happened to the former inhabitants of this place. I know that this is a spaceship. I know that the voices that talk in my head and those of my brothers are a genetic legacy of insanity, and that they have nothing to do with hearing any god. I simply tell the voices to shut up. Sometimes they even listen. I tried to tell my brothers the truth, but they called me a blasphemer and threw me out of the Temple into the street, where I lived for many years as a common fish cleaner. But when my brother the King started to sell our people into slavery, I could remain silent no longer. I spoke openly against him and the priests. I told the people the truth about our so-called *gods*. They threw rocks at me for my trouble, and I was thrown into jail. So you see, I know the palace is just a spaceship, the cloud god is just a thermo generator, and our King is just a man whom the priests have maimed to serve their purpose. *And* I can help you get out of here."

Bradley was inclined to agree. Together the three of them started to form a plan.

Yashi was on his way back to the palace with a bag full of the gold-colored reed chains. The chains had become very popular since the priests and King had started wearing chains of the yellow metal. Yashi had been more than a little afraid that he would not find enough in Jarish's whole store to supply what the King needed, but the jeweler had enough—just.

Gradually Yashi became aware that he was being followed. He turned quickly and out of the corner of his eye he saw someone melt into the shadows. Yashi instantly knew who had sent the spy, and why he was being tailed. When he turned the next corner he stopped, laid the bag of fragile chains on the ground out of harm's way and waited. When the following priest rounded the corner, Yashi grabbed him and slung him against the building with force. The priest turned frightened eyes to Yashi. Yashi was a big, formidable-looking man made strong from years of doing the work of two.

Yashi looked at the priest with murder in his eyes. There was something about having your tongue cut out and branded a slave in infancy on the whim of a priest that just made you grow up hating them. Till now he had never dared to lay hands on one, but right now he was working for the King, doing his bidding. That meant that this priest was in fact spying on the God/King, and therefore Yashi, in his position as the King's hands, was well within his rights.

"Yashi, you are not to touch the priests! You let me go at once!" the priest screamed.

Yashi was unable to question the man because he had no tongue. Unable to question him, he couldn't be certain that the priest didn't mean the King harm. So he slammed him into the wall as hard as he could forty times and then buried his body in the same spot in the palace garden that he had buried the tainted gold. Then he took the chains to the King.

"Yashi...I was worried." The King looked him over. "Are you all right?"

Yashi nodded his head gravely.

"Good, I need to go to the bathroom."

Yet another reason for Yashi to hate the priests.

Stratton set the skiff down just outside the capital in a grove of short trees that didn't come close to hiding it, and she and Decker made their way through the city at night carrying their space suits. Ahead of them they heard some screaming and ducked out of cover just long enough to witness the violent murder of a priest. Stratton leaned against the wall, panting heavily, and looked at Decker, who looked like he was as close to throwing up as she was. They couldn't get involved; they were here to get Bradley and Jackson out of prison. That was their mission. Straying from their mission to try and help these people was what had caused all their problems in the first place.

When the big man carried his victim away, Stratton and Decker started to move again. The night was warm, which was why they had chosen to carry the space suits rather than wear them. They were somewhat climate-controlled, but without the addition of cooling packs—yet more weight—wearing them would still cause you to burn completely alive after just a few minutes of walking on a hot planet with a gravitational pull stronger than what you were used to. But carrying the damn things wasn't much better. They were bulky and hard to hang on to. When the antiquated spaceship was in sight, they stopped and donned their suits. Then, weapons in hand, they started for the ship.

As they got to the door, the two guards on duty dropped to the ground, prostrating themselves before them. Stratton smiled satisfied, and looked at the directions that Bradley had given her, and that she had programmed into her wrist-com. She was glad to have the map as they got into the belly of the ship. It was poorly laid out, and it would be far too easy to get lost.

All of the guards they passed had the same reaction to them as the ones they had passed at the entrance.

Decker looked at her and smiled. "This is too easy," he said. He had no sooner spoken the words than they went around a corner, and there stood a priest. He looked at them, pointed, and started babbling excitedly in his native tongue.

Stratton had no idea what he was saying, but from the reactions of the three guards with him it was obvious that he knew they were fakes, and that his words were enough to convince the guards, who immediately became aggressive.

The two guards closest to them ran forward, spears at the ready. She blasted one and the priest just for good measure as Decker took out the other two. Then she followed the computer-drawn map at a run to the brig, Decker right behind her. Five guards who had apparently heard the commotion down the hall seemed to be confused about how to react to them. They couldn't seem to decide whether they should be worshiping them or killing them. She smacked one hard in the face with the butt of her rifle when he got too close, and as he went reeling into the bars of a cell, she made her way to the control panel. She didn't bother to try and figure out which button controlled which cell. Bradley and Jackson might be in any of them, so she just opened them all, hoping to save time and further confuse the guards with a large-scale prison break.

Absolute pandemonium beyond her wildest dreams followed the release of the prisoners. The guards were running around trying to stop the prisoners, and the prisoners seemingly preferred open conflict with the guards to actually fleeing. In all the mayhem, it took several minutes for them to locate Bradley and Jackson, or, more accurately, for Bradley and Jackson to find them. There was a native man with Bradley, and from the way he clung to Bradley's shirt, it was obvious that he had no intention of being left behind.

Just as they all came together a guard came at them screaming with his spear raised. Decker fired his weapon and hit his target, but unfortunately not before the warrior had released his spear. The primitive weapon struck Decker square in the chest, and Decker went down—making it pretty obvious to all the guards that there were *people* in the suits, not gods. If the guards hadn't been so busy exchanging blows with the other prisoners, they would have no doubt come after them more effectively.

Realizing that they were running short on time, Bradley grabbed Decker's weapon as Jackson grabbed Decker and threw him over his shoulder. They made a run for the exit. The native had let go of Bradley and was now leading the way out. Stratton lost count of how many of them she killed as she moved up alongside the native and took point. She was glad to know that Bradley was watching their backs. He wasn't military, but he was more capable than most of the soldiers she knew.

Once out of the palace area, the native tugged on her arm and led them to a service hatch that opened into a cargo bay. He opened the door to reveal an ancient land rover. They all ran for cover in the storage compartment, and the native explained as he was getting in the vehicle and sitting down.

"It rolls, it runs, we can use it to get away."

Bradley jumped in the driver's seat and looked at the dashboard. It wasn't a difficult machine to figure out, and it looked as if it had been well maintained. He turned the key that stuck out of what he thought must be the ignition, and it started right up. Jackson laid Decker in the back and then unplugged the land rover. Stratton, who had been firing at the natives from the doorway, holding them off, jumped in as Bradley drove up next to her.

The vehicle wasn't very fast, but it was more than fast enough to outrun the spears and the natives on foot. Still, Bradley didn't dare to breathe again until they were out of the city. Stratton sat beside him giving him directions to where they had left the skiff. When he saw it, he got a strange sence of homecoming. He pulled the land rover over next to it and parked.

The native immediately jumped out of the vehicle and started to walk away fast. "Thank you! Thank you very much."

Bradley ran after him, catching hold of his arm. "Where do you think you're going?"

"To the next village. Thank you, thank you very much." He started to walk away again, and was brought up short because Bradley still had a hold on his arm.

"We still need your help. We know very little about your planet, and we do not speak your language. Because we tried to help your very ungrateful King, we may be stuck here for the rest of our natural lives. We're going to need a guide," Bradley explained.

The native sighed, looking resigned. "All right." He sighed again. "I'll help you." He started mumbling something in his native tongue. Bradley could only guess at what he was actually saying.

Jackson and Stratton had retrieved the pocket medic and were both bent over Decker in the vehicle.

"How is he?" Bradley asked walking over.

"Not good," Stratton said in a whisper. "The spear is close to his heart. It's more than a pocket medic can handle. He needs a doctor."

"Do you have doctors?" Bradley asked the native, who was still mumbling.

"The priests all know medicine," he said, walking over and looking at Decker and then walking quickly away.

Bradley grabbed his arm again. "And you're a priest."

"Was..."

"You still know how to doctor wounds," Bradley said, dragging him back over to Decker.

"That's bad," Jessit said. "Maybe Jessit would try to fix your friend, and maybe he would die anyway. And maybe when he dies you will blame Jessit, and then kill him or worse."

"What could be worse than killing you?" Jackson half growled at him.

"I can think of lots of things," Jessit said.

"I'll tell you what, Shit head, if you *don't* try to save my friend, and he dies, I'll figure out what one of those things is and do it," Jackson said heavily.

Bradley glared at Jackson, silently letting him know that he wanted him to shut up. "If you try to help him, I promise no harm will come to you whether he lives or dies."

Jessit nodded. "We will need light and medical supplies." He turned to Jackson. "My name is Jessit, J-e-s-s-i-t. Not Sheet-he'd, or whatever you said."

They had carried Decker into the skiff, and the native had familiarized himself with their medical equipment, checked out the wound, and then gone on a search for plants he said were medicinal. Bradley sent Jackson with him because he didn't trust Jessit to return on his own.

When Jessit returned, he carefully laid out several different leaves and twig-looking things, and a dead lizard as thick as a pencil and long as his palm. He did the same with the medical tools.

Then he stuck his hands on the spear, grunted loudly and shoved it through.

"What the hell!" Jackson started to rush forward, and Bradley grabbed him.

"The heads are lashed and grooved in such a manner that if you pull on them they come off in the body cavity, or pull his insides out with them. Neither is very good," Jessit explained. He rolled the injured man on his side, grabbed the head of the spear with forceps and pulled it out. Then he untied the spearhead and removed it from the shaft. Only then did he pull the shaft out. He slapped one of the leaves on the wound in Decker's back and applied direct pressure. It quit bleeding almost at once. He then rolled Decker back onto his back. After moving the clothing out of the way, he took a scalpel from the tools and made the incision bigger. Then he stuck his hand in the opening and started feeling around. "The heart is fine, but it is as I feared, his lung has been nicked and is collapsed." He withdrew his hand, picked up one of three hollow reeds he had laid out on the table and carefully inserted it into the hole he had found in Decker's lung. Then he stuck the lizard into the reed tube and blew.

"What the fuck are you doing!" Jackson screamed.

"The lizard will repair the damage in the lung," Jessit explained.

"A dead lizard! Come on, Sergeant, he's killing him for sure."

"The lizard is not dead. He is sleeping. At night when the temperature drops the *roseau* lizard falls into a deep sleep like a coma. Your friend's body temperature will awaken him. In trying to escape from the prison he finds himself in, he will run around finding holes. They will not be big enough for him to exit, and he will become frightened. When he becomes frightened his skin emits a medicine that seals lung tissue, and he will leave this medicine behind him, sealing the punctures. Eventually he will find the natural air entrance to the lung and come out in either your friend's nose or his mouth. You must tell your friend to bring him up and not to swallow him or in any way damage a creature which has done him nothing but good, for if he injures it bad luck will fall on him like a poorly made tent."

"That's crazy. Lieutenant...You can't actually think that...that...*lizard* is going to save Decker."

Stratton shrugged. "Our own medicines have come from sources just as strange. We have used maggots to help cure ganggrene and leeches to help remove clotting around reattachments. We know nothing of this planet. None of us know any more than basic first aid. This man obviously believes in this treatment. As primitive as his medical techniques may seem to be, he still knows more than we do. He's Decker's only shot."

Jessit, who had stopped working on Decker, looked at Bradley. Bradley nodded and Jessit went back to work. He removed the reed from the chest cavity, wrung one of the plants out over the incision and the wound started to foam. When it stopped foaming he wiped it clean and then stuck another of the leaves over the entrance wound and again all bleeding stopped. Jessit rose to his full height and wiped the sweat off his brow.

"Now we wait," he said.

Stratton gave Decker a shot of antibiotics with the pocket medic, thinking that it couldn't hurt.

"We need to move," Bradley said.

"Where to?" Stratton asked.

"Anywhere away from here. Before either the Reliance or the natives can find us," Bradley answered

Stratton nodded. That made sense. "We could go to the village where the trans-mat was sabotaged. If it was the New Alliance…Well, then maybe we could hook up with them. If not, and the Reliance finds us, it will at least look like we're trying to do our job."

"And if it wasn't the New Alliance, which is just as likely, then we will be walking into a village full of angry natives who will no doubt see us as the same sort of scum they have driven from their land and attack us, too," Bradley said.

"We could get close to the village, do a reconnaissance, and find out just exactly what did happen," Jackson suggested.

"That sounds good," Bradley said looking at Stratton. She nodded. "Have we severed all communication links with the station?"

"Yes, and the pulses should make it difficult if not impossible to trace the skiff's ozone trail. However with all communications shut down, they will assume we've been killed, and it will only be a matter of time before they send a full military away team including one or more GSH's to see what's happened to us. No doubt they won't be in a skiff, but a fully operational battle cruiser," Stratton assured him.

Bradley looked troubled for a minute, then he smiled as he suddenly had a brilliant idea. "We're doing this all wrong. Restore the link with the ship."

"Why...Are you nuts."

"No, actually. I just started thinking clearly," Bradley said excitedly. "Don't you see? If there is no form of communication from the planet to the station, then they can't know anything that we have done. We can tell Briggs whatever we think he wants to hear."

"How do we explain that we have been out of touch ever since our arrival?" Stratton asked.

"Tell him there was trouble with the ship on entry," Bradley said. "That I was just now able to repair the damage done to the communications system. Hell, blame it on the pulses. God knows we've been blaming everything that's gone wrong on them ever since we got here."

"What if he doesn't buy our bullshit and sends some one to check it out?" Jackson asked.

Suddenly Bradley started laughing.

"What's so funny?" Jackson asked.

"Well, just think about it. If they come to look for us they'll go to the Capital first, and just think what they'll be walking into," Bradley said.

Stratton laughed, too, then. "They'll be too busy dealing with the natives to worry about where we are, or what we're doing."

Chapter Twelve

"Of course you can," RJ said, obviously agitated, although Topaz couldn't be sure whether she was mad at him, or if she was mad because she couldn't find something she was looking for on the ship. "It should be easy. Simply take the hands off the robot and put them on the boy."

The others were outside sitting around the campfire roasting yet another lizard. RJ and Topaz had gone into the ship to look for tools with which he might work the magic she was demanding he do.

"Gee! It does sound easy. Whatever was I worried about?" Topaz said rolling his eyes and throwing his hands around in huge arcs. "We simply take the robotic hands that run with hydraulics, fiber optics and a power pack, and hook them up on a human who has blood and veins and a heart for power. Why anyone can see that they are completely compatible, and…"

"I wasn't thinking cybernetics, Smart Ass. I was thinking you could make them into a robotic prosthesis. Hook them up so that they open and close by movement command. You know, like the hands open and close when he moves his elbow. Fix them to some sort of harness that could go under his clothing," RJ said.

"Oh…Well, that does make sense," Topaz mumbled then screamed, "but it won't be easy! Not on a primitive planet with very few tools…"

"Blah, blah blah," RJ said with a crooked grin. "Stop talking, old man, and just do it. Poley and Haldeed will help you." RJ sat down at the instrument panel of the skiff and started working at the ship's computer, apparently giving up her search for whatever she'd been previously looking for.

"And just what the hell will you be doing while I'm building hands?" Topaz asked.

"I noticed something while I was looking around in here earlier today. I was trying to get a bead on any Reliance ship that might come into our air space. I was checking different channels, trying to intercept communications between the surface and the station…"

"Were there any?" Topaz asked.

"I'm sure there were; I just never keyed into the right sequence. And of course there is always that damned magnetic pulse. However I picked up something else…Listen to this," RJ ordered. She pulled up the audio, and a loud high-pitched whine filled the air for a few seconds and stopped.

Topaz covered his ears. "What the hell is that?"

"I think it's a distress beacon. It sends out a signal every three hours unless interrupted by a magnetic pulse. But it's not Reliance. It's like nothing I've ever heard. Come here," she ordered. Topaz moved to stand behind her looking over her shoulder at the screen as a topographical map created by bouncing sound waves off surfaces came up on the monitor. RJ pointed to a spot on the map. "I've traced the sound to this small mountain range here. Now, the skiff's power cells have powered up enough to move us to about here." She made a circle with her finger on the screen and it stayed on the map. "That should move you far enough away from here to keep the Reliance from landing on top of you, and it would put us about fifteen miles from the site—a good one-day hike even with the added weight that gravity puts on us."

"All right, but why? I've never known you to give into curiosity," Topaz said.

"It's some sort of *ship*, Topaz," RJ said in a disbelieving tone.

"So?" Topaz shrugged.

"Are you taking dullness lessons from David?" RJ snapped. "If there's a ship, it might have a viable power supply. It obviously has some sort of power or it couldn't send out a distress beacon. We need a power supply. Go to ship. Get power supply. Bring back. Ugh."

"What about your plan to wait for a Reliance ship to find us and then kill them and take their ship? That sounded like a pretty sound plan to me," Topaz said.

"It was and is, except that a ship should have come by now. Which means one of two things. Either Mickey's message to the ship has led them to the obvious conclusion that there are New Alliance rebels on the planet's surface and they are proceeding with caution. In which case we might have a well armed Elite assault team complete with a squadron of GSH come through the brush at us at any time. Or, we completely destroyed their station in our attack, and there are no ships to come down here."

"Or worse yet—some wildcard has thrown the whole deck off, in which case there is no preparing for what might happen?" Topaz suggested.

"Exactly," RJ said, nodding.

Captain Briggs paced the command deck with both his hands buried in his thinning hair. Everything was going to hell in a hand basket. First there was the missing ship. Then the attack on the transport bay. Then the message from the "President" of the New Alliance claiming responsibility for the attack. He sent an away team comprised of people he despised and considered expendable to the surface to find out what had gone wrong, and while he hardly cared what had happened to them, he really did need the information. He needed to know just exactly what had gone wrong on the planet and why. He had rounded up every single person on the ship who he had suspected of espionage and executed six of them. But apparently he hadn't corralled all the rebels on board, because as he was executing the last of the six someone had released all the others and riots had started all over the ship. He had spent four hours hiding in his quarters until the Elite guard had put an end to the riots and rounded up all those responsible.

The man who had replaced Bradley in overseeing the very real problem of the hole that had been blown in the side of the station had been one of the first arrested in the riots. With no real supervisor and with the rest of the maintenance staff making up roughly half of those also responsible and subsequently imprisoned for the riots, work to repair the damage done in the explosion had been slowed to a crawl. As if that weren't bad enough, the maintenance staff had sabotaged still other areas of the station so that absolutely nothing was running as it should be. Toilets were backing up and water was running down the halls. The garbage disposal had stopped working and garbage was building up in the halls as well. Vending machines weren't vending. In short, everything was a mess.

Now the crew from Stashes that had been brought in to fix the breach in the hull was orbiting the station, refusing to dock or to consider even unloading necessary materials until Briggs could prove to them that the station was completely under his control, and that there was no chance of yet another riot. Which of course he couldn't actually do because that little freak from the New Alliance was taking over his screens every hour on the hour, giving his personnel a message to revolt. Crew morale since he had ordered the execution of the "spies" was at an all-time low, and it was obvious that many of his crew would rather take their chances fighting the system than just letting it kill them.

He stopped pacing and went back to his command chair. He removed his hands from his hair and tried to straighten it. He took a deep breath, let it out and sat down. Ready, he nodded to his communications officer, implying that he was ready to try to talk to the idiot from Stashes again. The communications officer just stood there scratching his balls, apparently oblivious to the unspoken command.

Briggs could feel himself starting to lose control, so he took another deep, cleansing breath. "Hail the *Kryptonite...*"

"Sir, I've got a message from Lieutenant Stratton!" he yelled out excitedly.

"Well, don't just stand there like a moron. Patch her through..." This could be just what he needed to convince those moron Stashes maintenance men that he was back in control.

"Stratton calling Pam Station. Come in Pam Station," the Lieutenant's voice was breaking up pretty badly, but was still recognizable.

"Transmission is bad, but we read."

"Thank God!" Stratton said. "Entry did something to our ship's communications system. Bradley has been working on it most of the day. Between the damage and the pulses we've been unable to make contact." The transmission was starting to get clearer.

"Have you been able to find anything out?" Briggs asked.

"The King claimed to know nothing about what had happened. Not too hard to believe since the incident took place several hundred miles from the Capital. He gave us his permission to investigate the matter thoroughly. We are currently stationed just outside the village where the sabotage occurred. We are planning to go in under cover of night and do a reconnaissance mission. If the natives are fully responsible I think it would be foolhardy to trip in there and expect them to just give us the information we need. All that would do is get us killed. Since so far our data shows no signs of a second ship, I have to assume that it was the natives with the help of one or more of our people who came down to do the mission that sabotaged the transporter. No matter how they brag about it, there is no sign that it was the New Alliance. From what we have observed these natives are very fast learners. I imagine we are looking at a simple case of some disgruntled personnel somehow convincing the primitives to help them to sabotage the transporter."

"Great," Briggs said breathing a sigh of relief. "Get back to me as soon as you know for sure. Leave half your people at the ship and call immediately if you think you may need reinforcements. We'll hit that village with everything we've got."

"We're right on it, Captain. Over," Stratton said.

"Keep up the good work, Stratton. There's a promotion in this for you. Over and out."

Briggs leaned his head back so that his neck was resting on the back of his chair and laughed. "All right. *Now* hail that glorified toilet-cleaner on the *Kryptonite* for me."

They were donning night camouflage. "Is there really no trace of a second ship? No lingering ozone trail?" Bradley asked, zipping up the front of the coveralls.

"Who knows? On this planet none of our locating or communications equipment operates at 100 percent," Stratton said. "Frankly, I doubt it. I imagine what I told Briggs is more or less the truth."

"It's hard to believe that someone from the station would attack it," Bradley said thoughtfully.

"I agree," Jackson said from where he sat watching Decker. "An attack like that could have taken out the whole station if any of the safety systems had failed. Such a person would have to have no one they cared about on the station. They'd have to be a fanatic."

"I think there must be a second ship here. That spies told the New Alliance what was going on, and that they are here in their own ship," Bradley speculated.

"Well, on this planet, even with all this fancy equipment, there is only one way that we're going to know whether there is another ship here or not," Stratton said.

"How's that?" Jackson asked.

"See it," Stratton answered.

All geared up, Stratton, Bradley and Jessit left for the village. Jackson would stay behind to guard the ship and watch Decker.

The brush was thick here, and the mud was deep. Recent rains had left a small stream running through the middle of what might have at one time been a trail.

Their plan was a simple one. Jessit had told them that most of the people would be asleep. He would go to the Temple claiming to be a traveling priest and find out all that he could about the attack. Bradley and Stratton would search the village, paying particular attention to the area where the trans-mat station had been located, and look for evidence of another ship. If they found evidence of a landing they would know what kind of ship by the landing pattern it left in the dirt.

At the edge of the city Jessit turned towards the Temple while Bradley and Stratton headed for the coordinates where the trans-mat station had been. They used buildings and small clumps of bushes and trees as cover as they moved silently through the village. It wasn't quite dark enough for them to feel like they were actually able to use the "cover of darkness." In a few minutes they had found the location of the transmat station and the burnt, almost unrecognizable wreckage of the skiff that had transported it there. Not too long after that they found the landing place of another ship.

"It's one of ours, a skiff, just like the one we're using," Stratton said. The scanner in her hand displayed an infrared picture of the area and clearly identified the marks of a second ship. "There was another ship."

"How can you be so sure?" Bradley asked. "It could have just been from where that ship landed," he said pointing at the wreckage.

"That ship was taken out by a plasma cannon. One like the one that is mounted on our skiffs. It sure as hell didn't shoot itself," she said. "Someone must have hijacked the *Avonlea* and used a skiff to come to the surface, but what did they do with the ship? Where did they hide it? Even with the pulses, we would have found a ship in orbit around the planet by now." She was talking more to herself than Bradley. As she spoke, she started scanning the surface around the landing site.

"Maybe they let the skiff off and then moved the ship out of range of our detectors," Bradley said.

"Maybe." Stratton suddenly took a deep breath.

"What?" Bradley asked.

"Well, look at the boot prints. The natives wear a soft, padded-leather shoe. So everything with a heel has to be either Reliance personnel or whoever was in that other ship. Now this…" she made a boot print next to one the scanner clearly showed in the sand, "is an Elite boot print, and so is that one. Yet there were no Elites sent on this assignment. It's not my *own* print because it's considerably larger than mine. Which means that one of the people who came out of that ship was wearing Elite boots."

"So?" Bradley shrugged, not understanding the significance of her statement.

"So…I've only ever heard of one rebel elite," Stratton said.

"Don't be ridiculous! Anyone can get boots, and if you're a rebel you hardly care whether or not you're breaking the dress code." Bradley laughed. "Come on, let's go back to the rendezvous and wait for Jessit. With any luck, he'll be able to tell us exactly what happened."

They waited in the wet brush at the edge of town for so long that they were beginning to think Jessit had abandoned them. They sat mostly in silence, both of them having things on their mind.

"I wonder…*did* one of our messages get through?" Stratton mumbled, temporarily forgetting that she wasn't alone.

"Who…what are you talking about, Stratton?" Bradley asked. He'd been thinking about Harker and was glad to have a diversion, any diversion.

"Nothing," Stratton said nervously. "Talking to myself is all."

Bradley quickly tried to remember exactly what she had said. "No! What the hell were you talking about? Who were you trying to contact?" He jumped to his feet and turned to face her. She was silent, looking at the ground, and he knew. "You!" he said through clenched teeth. "You!" He reached down, grabbed her by her collar and started shaking her. "It was you? You were the freaking spy, and you let Harker die for it. You let them space Harker, knowing that it was you all along that leaked the information to the Rebels."

Stratton let her tears fall as she pushed away from him. "I didn't know they were going to space him! Besides, I didn't think any of our transmissions went through." She laughed then, though obviously not because she was amused. She wiped her face on the back of her sleeve. "We were trying to get you over to our side. You idiot! You were so sure Harker wasn't involved. Harker *started* the rebellion on the station, Bradley! He recruited me, not the other way around. He was baiting you, baiting everyone, trying to see where their loyalties lay. Between him and me, we have half the maintenance staff and one third of the combat units on the station ready to revolt. But it wasn't enough to ensure success. To do that, we would have had to infiltrate the entire station, and that was going to take time we didn't have, so we started trying to reach the New Alliance. But we didn't think we were having any luck—and then the transport bay was sabotaged. Everything happened so quick after that. Harker was arrested, Briggs sent us planetside." She cried harder then. "I didn't even know they'd arrested Harker until you told me. I didn't even get to say goodbye." She sat back down on the ground and buried her face in her hands. Bradley sat down beside her and put his arm across her shoulders.

"I'm sorry...I should have known. Just this morning...Oh, God! Was that only this morning? Harker was saying very insubordinate, damn near treasonous things. So was I, for that matter. I just can't believe...Harker—a rebel leader! I mean it, just doesn't compute! He just never seemed to have that much ambition. Why wouldn't he just tell me what he was doing? I would have helped. At least, now I'd like to think I would have. Maybe not, though. I've always been happy to just do my job and stay out of harm's way. Maybe Harker knew me better than I know myself. But I do know this—I wouldn't have ratted him out."

"Maybe not on purpose, but once you know something...The Reliance has ways of making people talk. You can swear you'd never talk no matter how badly you were tortured, but the truth is you never know what you'll do when you've got a blade to your privates." Stratton sniffed and wiped her face on her hands and then wiped her hands on her pants.

Bradley nodded and took a deep breath. In less than a day his whole life—his whole way of looking at things—had changed. Absently he picked up some dirt in his hand and marveled at the fact that, as much as it had apparently rained, the ground was not mud. There was mud in the low spots, but any place with even moderate drainage was already starting to dry out. It was a testament to how poor the soil was and how long it had been since the last time it had rained.

"I've hardly ever been planetside," Bradley said conversationally. "I was born and raised on Frank Station, you know."

"No, I didn't," she said, knowing how unusual it was for a maintenance unit to have been raised on a space station.

"Yes, my parents were both air corps. I was supposed to grow up to be air corps, but the test showed I lacked the intelligence and fortitude to be anything but maintenance class. So at nine, they sent me away from my parents to maintenance school. Since I had lived so long in a space station, it was decided that I would be trained to maintain stations and starships so my early education wouldn't be wasted. I remember my mother cried as I boarded, but my father couldn't even look at me. He was that ashamed of me because I was going to be in maintenance. I never told anyone this before, but for years I cried myself to sleep every night because I wanted to fly so much.

"One day, years later, we were being trained in the hangar and I overheard one of the pilots bitching about his fighter— how it was losing speed whenever he punched it. For the first time since my father had looked away from me with shame in his eyes I felt good about myself, because, you see, I was a green-assed seventeen-year-old kid, and I knew what was wrong with his fighter—and he didn't. He could fly it, but I could fix it. I realized that—no offense—a trained rat could fly a fighter, but it took some real smarts to know how to fix them.

"I realized that day that those tests they had given us didn't show that I was too stupid to be a pilot, they showed I was too smart to be wasted on jockeying a ship, even too smart to be in combat. See, everyone looks down on us because we're 'just' maintenance, but the truth is that without us ships don't fly, toilets don't flush, and people are swimming in their own filth. The thing they don't want you to know—the real secret that the Reliance is hiding from everyone—is that the higher up you go, the stupider people get. Briggs is Captain because he's too stupid to be trusted to do anything that really matters."

Stratton nodded silently.

Bradley changed the subject. "So, do you think Jessit cut and ran on us?"

"I don't know, but maybe we should go look for him," Stratton said.

"Beats sitting here getting our butts wetter." Bradley stood up and then reached down and helped Stratton to her feet. He just stood there for a second. "So, were you and Harker.."

"Yes," she said with a choking sound in her voice.

"Then I'm really sorry," he said.

"I'll do better if I just don't think about it. Let's go look for that native."

"Who, me?" Jessit said.

They jumped about a foot in the air then turned to glare at him. He just shrugged.

"Where the hell have you been?" Bradley demanded.

"You didn't think I was likely to get a straight answer from a bunch of priests, did you? One had to tell the story of the explosion while pontificating on the deep religious meanings of the events, and then all the others had to disagree with him about it. I'm lucky I got out of there when I did." He started walking in the direction of the skiff, and Bradley and Stratton followed.

"So what happened?" Bradley demanded.

"Would you like the plain, the metaphysical, or the deeply religious version?" Jessit asked turning to look at them and smiling. He seemed to walk backwards in the dark with as much ease as he walked forward in the light.

"Just the simple truth, please," Stratton said smiling back.

Jessit imparted all that he had learned. They were almost to the skiff before he finished.

"...She apparently knew the gold metal was making them sick, and she sent it and the dead bodies and some device away with the box. Then she and her friends left."

"What did she look like?" Stratton asked suspiciously.

"The air must be too thin here. You aren't thinking clearly. It's not her. It *couldn't* be her," Bradley said with a laugh.

"They said she was like no person they had ever seen before. Her hair was as white as starlight..."

"It's her. It's got to be her," Stratton said, a trembling in her voice

"Is she a god then?" Jessit asked, no doubt confused by the sudden fear that had entered her voice.

"It's not her," Bradley assured Stratton. "Why would she be here? Here, in the middle of space, on a third-class planet."

"Where else would she be? If our message got through to the New Alliance, if she learned what the Reliance was doing—and we know that the New Alliance knows because they sent a message to the station.—where else would she be? It would be just what she would do."

Jessit stopped and they almost ran into him. He reached into his loincloth, and they both just stared at him in amazement. He pulled a folded piece of parchment from his pants and opened it slowly. "Maybe this will help. I pinched it from one of the priests."

He held it out to them, but neither was in any hurry to take it, considering where it had been. Finally Bradley took it and held it at the corner between his forefinger and his thumb, with his light on it so that they could better see it. It was a beautifully sketched, well-crafted drawing. Bradley and Stratton looked at the drawing and then at each other.

"It's her," Bradley said. "Right down to the chain with the bent coins. My God, it is the platinum bitch of Alsterace. It's RJ."

"Who is this RJ?" Jessit asked. "And, why do you sound so afraid?"

"Because she *is* a god," Bradley answered.

"Tell me you're freaking kidding," Jackson said, looking at the picture he held in his hands.

"The part about it being in his pants, or that it's RJ?" Stratton asked with a smile, having regained at least part of her sense of humor.

Jackson sat down in one of the seats with a thud and just looked at the picture. "Freaking RJ! Here on this planet. With us."

"I am confused," Jessit said from where he sat cross-legged on the floor of the ship. "You say that you are against the Reliance, and it is obvious that she, too, is against the Reliance."

"True," Bradley said.

"If you are on the same side, then why do you fear her?" Jessit asked.

"Because…" Bradley didn't really have an answer; it was a damned good question. "She might not believe that we are also fighting the Reliance, and she might kill us…"

"That's bullshit," Stratton said. "She's one of *them*. She would know we were telling the truth. *That's* why we're afraid of her, Jessit. Because she's something that shouldn't exist, the product of some mad scientist's experiment. A being that can sense our very emotions, can run faster, and jump higher than we can. She is also stronger than we are. This gravity that has worn us down wouldn't even faze her. The spear that has almost killed Decker wouldn't have even nicked her skin. She needs very little sleep, and very little food. She is like a machine, except that she feels all the same emotions that we feel. She believes utterly in her cause and will execute any plan to stop the Reliance ruthlessly. She cannot be stopped."

"She sounds like the sort of being you would want on your side," Jessit said, still not understanding their fear.

Bradley laughed nervously. "Well, you sure as hell wouldn't want her against you. It's just…" Bradley shrugged, he didn't know how to explain it.

Jessit jumped up as sudden understanding filled him. He looked at Bradley and clapped his hands together in excitement. "It is like my people. They believe in our gods and praise them, but they don't really want to *see* them, they are afraid of them."

"Exactly," Bradley said. "That's *exactly* what it's like. But, scared or not, I think we all know that it's in our best interest to find RJ and pool our efforts."

"Damn, I was afraid you were going to say that," Jackson said, burying his face in his hands. "RJ, man, freaking RJ! How do you know she won't just kill us outright?"

"We make damn sure she knows we aren't a threat to her," Bradley said.

"Hell, she already knows that. She could kill us all and never even work up a sweat," Jackson moaned.

"You know what he means," Stratton said. "Between us we know everything about the station, and Jessit knows everything about this planet. We could be valuable to her. RJ isn't stupid, and if we hook up with her, we'll have a hell of a lot better chance of making it when Briggs finds out what we've been up to here."

"It won't be easy to find her," Bradley said.

"Easier than you think," Stratton said. "They fired their cannon at least twice, and that means they're low on fuel. They couldn't have gotten very far, and we know which direction they went in when they left here. We simply fly in that direction and look around till we find them."

Behind them, on the stretcher, Decker started to cough. They all turned quickly. His eyes opened, and Jackson went to his side.

"Well I'll be!" Jackson turned around, holding the lizard by the tail as it twitched. Jessit quickly walked over and took the lizard from Jackson. He looked at Jackson, and Jackson didn't have to ask what he wanted. "All right, all right, I'm sorry, man." He laughed as Jessit smiled smugly and walked out of the ship, talking to the lizard. Jackson shook Decker gently. "Hey, bud! Can you hear me?"

"Yeah," he crocked out. "Man, what happened to me?"

"A native hit you in the chest with a spear, and a witch doctor saved your life," Bradley said.

"Great..." Decker forced a smile, and then made a face. "I've got the damnedest taste in my mouth."

Levits stood beside RJ in the first light of dawn and looked up at the mountain ahead of them.

"You didn't tell us it was a fifteen-mile hike straight *up*," Levits said, shaking his head. His back still hurt from the rather rough, powerless landing he had made just a few hours ago because RJ insisted on pushing the power cells as far as she pushed everything else.

"It's not straight up. More on an angle like this," RJ said holding her hand at about forty degrees.

"Gee! And I thought Poley was supposed to be learning from you, not the other way round," Levits hissed. He glared at David who was laughing. "What are you doing, Shit Boy? Trying to make points by laughing at her lame-ass attempt at humor?"

David shrugged. "It was funny."

"You can both stay here if you'd rather," RJ said. "Bringing the power supply down the mountain, if it's compatible, shouldn't be that hard. I could probably do it myself."

"Oh, no you don't," Topaz said walking out of the ship with the droid and some tools. "I have enough on my plate without having to babysit David and Levits as they pout and fight and just basically make everyone around them as miserable as they make each other. No! You take them with you. You can leave Janad if you like. She's pleasant company, and easy on the eyes, but you take the testosterone twins with you."

"We're all going, Old Man, so don't get your shorts in a wad," Levits spat back.

David looked through the binoculars at the spot where RJ assured him the ship was. "I don't see any ship."

"I believe it crashed so long ago that it is now buried in the mountain," RJ explained.

"I believe we are climbing up the side of a barren freaking mountain for no good reason," Levits mumbled.

RJ took his hand and kissed his cheek. "It will help you adjust to the planet's gravitational pull quicker."

"Oh, joy!" Levits said, but he managed a smile. "All right, let's get climbing. I'd like to have a good chunk of it done before it gets hot this afternoon."

RJ and Janad loaded packs on their backs, and they started up the mountain.

Levits looked fleetingly at David. "So, do you suppose they're bringing us along just because we're pretty?"

David laughed, and then he looked at Levits in shock. "Do you realize that you just said something to me that wasn't hateful?"

"Yeah, well, don't expect it to happen again anytime soon." Levits rushed to catch up with RJ, leaving David to bring up the rear. Which wasn't a bad place to be considering that being in the rear gave him the perfect vantage point from which to watch Janad's ass—which was looking more attractive with every passing day.

Taleed and Haldeed watched with great interest as Topaz and Poley worked on constructing the mechanical hands. "I am going to have hands. Haldeed. I'm going to be able to pick things up on my own. Do all the things that normal men do," Taleed said.

Haldeed nodded.

"I only wish there was some way to give you back your tongue."

Haldeed made hand signals.

"Oh, my brother, you are indeed the most gracious of men."

"What did he say?" Topaz asked curiously.

"That he doesn't need his tongue…"

"Obviously he and I haven't dated the same women," Topaz said. Poley looked at him curiously. "Don't ask, Tin Pants, just pass me the laser cutter."

"He says that speech is not as important to him as hands are to me," Taleed finished, completely ignoring Topaz's interruption.

Topaz started cutting the hands and metal arms from the body of the droid. Without looking up from his work he asked, "So you have lizards and small marsupials. Nothing bigger than a small goat. In fact there is nothing more complicated than some small mammals, and then we have man. Now your people have human origins; we know that. We also know how your human ancestors got here, or at least I'm fairly sure. However, there was something else in your DNA—or at least in the sample I took from Janad. Something very different, and yet familiar. Obviously there was another humanoid species on this planet already when the humans arrived. But where, oh where, is the missing link? Huh? Can you tell me that?"

"I don't even know what you're talking about," Taleed said with a sad shrug.

"I, too, have noticed the lack of suitable animals from which humanoids could evolve. Another race must have crashed on this planet hundred of years before humans did," Poley said.

"Why hundreds of years before?" Topaz asked.

"Because otherwise they would not have given in to the whims of the humans. The other race would have had to be here long enough to have forgotten about the technology that brought them here. They must have become primitive first, otherwise they wouldn't have allowed the deranged, brown, handless Frenchman to take over," Poley said.

"I was just going to say that," Topaz said angrily.

"I don't think that you were. Any more than you have deduced that the ship my sister now goes to check out is probably the same ship that brought the first people to this planet," Poley said.

"Ah, now! Ya did that on purpose," Topaz said, slinging the tool he'd been working with into the dirt. "If you had given me half a minute more I would have come to that conclusion myself."

They had stopped to rest on a rock outcrop that made a good seat.

"Ah! I can feel...myself adapting...to the gravi...tational pull...with each step," Levits said, trying to catch his breath. He glared at RJ who sat beside him. "Could you at least *pretend* to be winded?"

"I thought I only had to do that during sex," RJ said with a smile.

David laughed, and Levits glared at him. David just shrugged.

"How much further?" David asked. He felt like his blisters had blisters.

"We aren't halfway yet," RJ said.

"I hope whatever we find is worth this freaking climb," Levits complained.

"I hope whatever it is, it's worth listening to you bitch for a whole day," RJ said standing up. She put down her hand, and he allowed her to help him up.

"If he didn't bitch she'd be asking what was wrong with him," David whispered to Janad as they both stood up. Janad laughed and nodded.

"I think it is the way they communicate their love for one another," Janad whispered back.

"That and screwing all the time," David laughed out. Levits turned around and glared at David as if knowing that he was the brunt of some joke. Then he turned right back around and started arguing with RJ again as they started to climb.

"Topaz told us everything that happened," Janad said. "About the war. What you did. It wasn't your fault. I mean...It was, but it wasn't. You did something stupid. We have all done something stupid in battle that has caused someone else's death. You cannot expect them to forgive you, but you have to forgive yourself."

How could he explain to her that not everyone had fought in a battle, much less been responsible for the death of another? Hers was a culture that lived at war.

"I have tried to forgive myself, and for most things I can. But for the pride...No. I let my own pride get in the way of the truth. I let it make me believe that I was more than I really was. I thought that I knew better than RJ. Worse than that, I wanted to prove her wrong. I can blame Kirsty for tricking me, and Jessica Kirk and the Reliance for the actual death of my troops and the destruction of Alsterace. But they couldn't have done that except for my own faults. Except for the flaws in my own personality that allowed me to be blind to reality. You're right about the things that I did that were stupid, but the things that I did because of my pride, my ego, my need to be in control...I can't forgive myself that because if I do...If I forgive myself for the things I did because I wanted to be better than RJ, then there is a chance that I might repeat that behavior. I just can't take that chance. I don't ever want to be that person again."

"Who do you want to be then, David Grant?" Janad asked carefully.

It was a very good question. He sure as hell didn't like who he was now. "I...I want to be the man I was before. Not the man I was when I first meet RJ. Then I was just a green kid who didn't understand anything. No, I think I want to be the man I was before RJ and Topaz turned me into the mouthpiece for the Rebellion and I began to get full of my own power. I want to return to the me I was when I truly only cared about making my world a better place and freeing my people." David smiled. "I was happy then, and they were all happy with me."

"Then be him," Janad said. "*Be* that man."

"How? Too much has happened..."

"Just remember what it was that you liked about him and imitate it. Before you know it, you'll be your old self again, but you'll know all that you know now."

RJ had overestimated the resilience of her human counterparts, and when Levits' bitching reached a crescendo, and even Janad started to stumble in her stride, she knew they had to stop and make camp. They had just come to one of the many shelves they had encountered during their climb, and RJ decided this was as good a place as any to put down.

"That's it!" Levits flopped to the ground like a rag doll. "I'm not going to take another step. Leave me here for the lizards to eat; I just don't give a damn anymore. I am sick to death of..."

"All right. This is as good a place as any," RJ said, deciding to let Levits think he had won the argument they weren't actually having. She took off her pack, and saw Janad gratefully drop hers to the ground.

"Freaking mountain climbing! I'd rather stay on this damn planet forever than climb one more inch. In fact, I would have just as soon we all stayed on Earth in the first place," Levits said, continuing his angry prattle. "But, oh, nooo! Let's all fly across the vastness of space to try and make the Argies our allies. Oh! But no! Wait a minute! Let's stop and make a side trip to a third-class planet where we can eat all the lizard we want and go freaking *mountain climbing!*"

RJ moved and flopped on the ground beside him, laughing.

"Now what's so damned funny?" Levits asked hotly.

"I said we'd stay here. You already won," she said, turning to look at him.

Levits smiled back then. "I know, but you can't just cut a man off in the middle of his bitch like that. It could do irreversible damage."

"I don't know why you're bitching in the first place," David said flopping to the ground. "This climb is every bit as bad for me as it is for you. It's not like we're having to use ropes and picks. You make it sound like we're clinging to the side of a rock face hanging on by a thread."

"Bite me, David," Levits said. "Look me in the eye and tell me you could have taken one step more."

"I didn't say that I could. I'm just saying that I wasn't bitching about it and everything else," David said. "The way I understand it, the gravitational pull of this planet adds about twenty-five pounds to you and me. I hate to be the one to point it out, but Janad is carrying more than that in her pack, so except for RJ we're all basically in the same boat. While I admittedly did my fair share of bitching, I didn't hear Janad complain even once."

"Perhaps I should give you a gold star," RJ said to Janad.

"What does that even mean?" Levits asked pulling a face.

RJ looked thoughtful for a moment. "I don't know exactly. It's something I've heard Topaz say. In the context in which he uses it, it means you've done very well."

"Thank you," Janad said.

"How about a little praise for me?" Levits asked lightly.

"She could give you a gold star for bitching." David laughed out.

"And give you one for being a shit-slinging moron," Levits snapped back.

RJ took Levits' chin in her hand and forced him to look at her. "I could think of something I could give you a gold star for," she said huskily then she kissed him. Within seconds they were rolling around in the dust, Levits apparently forgetting how tired he was.

"Chain, RJ, chain," Levits said, and unbelievably the thing went flying through the air like a discarded piece of clothing.

David got up and dusted his hands off. He looked at Janad, "Ah, maybe we should go get some firewood now."

"Huh?" Janad asked, her eyes riveted on the couple ripping at each other's clothing. David walked by her and, with a laugh, grabbed her by the shoulder, hauled her to her feet, and started pulling her along after him.

"Come on, you perv," he said. He didn't feel like walking another foot, but he didn't feel like sitting there and watching Levits and RJ screw either. It was enough to know they were doing it without actually having to watch.

Janad was dragging on his arm, turned as she was to watch RJ and Levits till the end.

"Would you come on, Janad?" David said. "I can't believe him! He bitches all day about being so tired he's going to die, and now he's...Well, you know what he's doing."

Janad sighed and started to walk to match his stride. "Why does it bother you so much to see them together?"

"Because...It isn't our custom to watch other people having sex," David said.

Janad laughed. "It isn't our custom, either. That doesn't mean it isn't entertaining."

David laughed then. "Yeah, I would imagine that RJ and Levits can put on quite a show." David stopped laughing then, remembering another time and place, and another friend who wanted to watch RJ do it. "People shouldn't intrude into affairs between two people. It should be private."

"Then they should go someplace private to do it," Janad said with a shrug, bending down to pick the top out of a plant that she started sucking on.

"True enough," David said with a laugh. "Still, RJ has an Argy's libido, and when she gets turned on...Well, I think she just sort of forgets where she is or what she's doing."

"What about your...libido?" Janad stumbled a little over the word, it apparently being new to her Reliance vocabulary. She picked one of the plants and handed it to him.

"It's healthy enough," David said. He sucked on the end of the plant as Janad had done, and a sweet liquid covered his tongue. He smiled approvingly and continued. "I've sort of had to put it in drydock if you know what I mean." From the look on her face she didn't.

"You know...When I first met you, and I punched you in the nose...I thought all Reliance people were repulsive looking. With your pale, fish-belly skin you looked disgusting to me. But now...Well now I find that I have an appreciation for you. I find you to be...very beautiful," Janad said nervously.

He wouldn't have put it exactly that way, but he'd had the same feeling. When he'd first seen her, all dark and wild-looking, he had thought her completely alien and her appearance horrid and even frightening. Now, looking past his initial fears, he saw a dark, beautiful creature whose intellect was far from inferior to his own, and who had a far superior grasp on who she was in relation to the universe than he ever had or probably ever would have.

"I think you're beautiful, too," David said.

Janad moved to stand with her chest pressed against his, blocking his way. She looked up at him expectantly, and he kissed her. She kissed him back, and they kissed for a long time. When their lips separated they looked at each other for a long moment then David grabbed her hand and started pulling her towards a wooded area. She followed him, laughing.

RJ stirred the coals under the spitted lizard. She looked up at David and smiled as he walked back into camp with Janad close behind him.

He sat down across the fire from her. Whatever energy he'd had after their climb he had just spent. Janad knelt down behind him and wrapped her arms around his neck.

RJ smiled broadly. "I thought you were going to get firewood?" RJ said.

"We had sex instead," Janad said bluntly.

"Yes, I had figured that out," RJ said, grinning at David.

"What?" David said feeling suddenly very vulnerable and exposed.

"Nothing," RJ said with a shrug.

Levits walked back into camp, zipping up his fly. He looked at Janad and David with a smug, all-knowing smile that made David want to slap him more than he normally did.

David untangled himself from Janad, jumped up walked over and grabbed RJ by the arm. "Come on. I need to talk to you."

RJ shrugged, got up and followed him a little way away from the camp. "What's wrong? I figured after you got your winky taken care of…"

"My what?"

"Your winky. That's what Whitey used to call his…I would have thought you would be in a better mood than this," RJ said. "Was the girl not any good?"

"Too good," David said. He lowered his voice. "Remember how when I was with Kirsty you told me that I had to have known it was different. That I should have known she wasn't human."

"Yeah, but we already know that this girl is some sort of hybrid…"

"Yes, but I've been with Kirsty, now, and I know why she was different. And…that girl…it's the same…her…well, you know…If I didn't know better, RJ, I'd swear that girl was an Argy hybrid."

RJ looked thoughtful and started pacing. "Now that makes a certain amount of sense. We know that the Argies and humans evolved at about the same pace, the Argy being only slightly ahead of the humans. A couple of hundred years at best, but that would be enough."

David snapped his fingers. "Damn! In the infirmary Topaz said that there was something familiar about Janad's DNA. That must be why…"

"Because, except for the obvious trappings of my genetic engineering, my DNA and Janad's are the same," RJ said thoughtfully. Then she added, "And we know that this planet wouldn't get around to making humanoid life on its own for another billion years, if ever…"

"How do we know that?" David asked.

"Because this is a *class-three* planet," RJ said, the words *dumb ass* implied by the tone in her voice. "The flora and fauna are very primitive, and there is nothing here that could have evolved into anything remotely humanoid. If the ship we find…"

"If there is a ship," David said skeptically. He had been looking through the binoculars all day, and while he could clearly see their ship in the valley below, he could make out not even a lump that looked ship-like on the mountain above them.

"Oh, there's a ship all right. Whether we can get to it is another story," RJ said. "But if it is an Argy ship, that would explain everything—including Janad's Argy-like vagina…"

"Damn it, RJ! Do you have to be so uncouth?" David said making a face.

RJ laughed. "If I live to be a thousand—and in all likelihood I will—I will never understand men. You can stick your winky in it, but you can't talk about it, at least not to a woman who has all the parts you apparently find so embarrassing." RJ smiled then. "So…Did you enjoy her?"

"Don't be stupid," David said with a stupid grin. "I said she was like an Argy woman. Of course I enjoyed her." He looked thoughtful then. "RJ…" He decided to let it go.

"What?"

"Nothing," David said quickly.

"Nothing me no nothings. What!" RJ demanded.

"You…What about the big picture, RJ? I mean what the hell are we doing here? Are we still trying to get to Argy? It's not like you to flip from one plan to another. It's not like you to be so…"

"Relaxed?" RJ supplied for him. "Screwing in the middle of camp and all. Going off on what is basically an archeological expedition and will probably yield nothing of value, when we are on a strange world far from Earth and far from our intended destination? Giving an alien prince robotic hands when I don't really know how I'm going to use him yet? You figure that it's not like me to do anything without a damn good reason, so you figure that as usual I have figured out everything and I'm just keeping everyone else in the dark."

"Well, yeah," David said.

"Want to hear something really scary?" RJ whispered.

"Not necessarily," David answered honestly.

"Well, too bad, because here's the truth. The truth is that my mind doesn't work as well as it used to, and calculations I used to make easily have become difficult. At this point in time I don't really have a game plan," she said plainly. "We haven't been able to make contact with Marge or Mickey since the first day we got to the surface of this planet. I haven't been able to tap into the Reliance's communication systems back on the station or pick up any of their transmissions to this planet if there have even been any. So I have no idea what the Reliance is up to. This planet has no communications more sophisticated than village runners. I can *guess* at what the Reliance is doing. I can *guess* at what the locals are doing, but I can't really know. So taking all those things into consideration, I'm not looking at the big picture right now. I'm playing things out as they are thrown at me and hoping for the best."

RJ without a plan. It was quite possibly the most frightening thing David had ever heard in his life.

Chapter Thirteen

Taheed felt better today than he had yesterday. He knew it had little to do with the intervention of the gods. It was all due to the medicine the Reliance men who had escaped from his dungeons had given him and removing the tainted gold from his body.

He looked at Ziphed, who looked worse today than he had the day before, even with the Reliance medicine, and waited to hear what the "gods" had told him concerning his son, the gold, and the Reliance. Ziphed stood silently as if waiting for something.

"Well?" the King asked. "Did you talk to the gods as I asked you to?"

"Yes, Sire."

"And what did they tell you?" Taheed was growing impatient.

"Concerning the matter of your son, the Chosen One, they have said that it was indeed the Reliance which kidnapped him and who brought this plague on your house. Then they sent those men to try to steal the gold back. The fact that they escaped from your dungeon last night proves their guilt."

"And where is my son?" Taheed asked. "Where is the Chosen One?"

"The gods say he is being held between two moons. We have been pondering the meaning of this all morning and hope to soon have a revelation concerning what it could mean," Ziphed said.

Taheed inwardly stewed. How many years had he heeded this man's council? He felt like an idiot to realize that he had been fooled—that his whole life had been a farce. "Is the gold tainted?" he asked.

"Of course not," Ziphed assured him. "Metal can carry no curse, no disease. That is why it is holy above all other things."

Liar! You and I are the proving grounds, brother. I grow stronger each day as you grow weaker. Taheed bit his tongue. The priests were powerful. If he told them what he knew was the truth, they would only argue with him. They might even rise up against him. However, if he withheld his knowledge from them, their own lies would kill them. A fitting end for treacherous men.

"Then my decision is this." He took in a deep breath as much to calm his angry soul as to contemplate his words. "We will cease to trade with the Reliance until they lift this curse from our bodies, apologize for their treachery, and return the Prince to the palace."

Ziphed was obviously unhappy with the King's decision. "But, Sire…We rely on the Reliance for so many things. From the implements we use to till the ground to the pots we use to cook our meals. The bulbs that light our homes and our streets. We…"

"Ziphed…We can not trade and hold simple commerce with a people who steals away the Chosen, puts a curse on our heads, and tries to steal back that for which they have already been paid." Taheed felt quite happy with himself. He had let the priest hang himself with his own lies. Perhaps the charlatan should have argued with the gods over their findings. "Since they have the Chosen One, it is in their power to return him. Since they have caused this disease, they can cure it, and certainly it is in their power to apologize for their attempted act of thievery. When these things have come to pass, we will once again trade with them. Having proven that we are not the fools they have taken us for, they will perhaps treat us with greater respect. We have to force their hand, my brother. Don't you see? This is the only way to force them to give us the cure to this disease and return Taleed. My will has been spoken. You may go."

Ziphed nodded and left the throne room mumbling.

Taheed picked up the reed chains at his throat with one of his stumps and looked at them. "Ah, my brother, we shall see who has the last laugh. For my burden is lighter than yours, and I know what you will not see. The gold is indeed tainted, and the men whom we imprisoned are our friends, not our enemies. My son has not been captured by the Reliance, but has gone off on yet another of his adventures. Yet still you would fool us all saying that you have spoken to the gods. You fool yourselves most of all because the gods have failed to tell you the one thing that could save your life."

Yashi grunted and he looked at him. He pointed in the direction that the priest had gone and then at the chains around the King's neck.

"No...I'm not going to tell them. Why should I?" Taheed asked. "If they truly have the gods' ears, then everything he says is true and it is only a coincidence that I am healing. If, on the other hand, the priests are only pretending to talk to the gods, then everything they have ever told us has been a lie, and I was blind. Willfully so, because until now everything has gone my way. It was only when my luck went bad that I began to see the truth. As long as the priests' ways worked for me I was happy with them. Now I see that my son Taleed has spoken the truth. That our whole way of life, all our beliefs, are nothing but a system set up to serve selfish priests. And spoiled kings who wanted to believe that they were gods have allowed it to go on for centuries." He drew a deep breath. "If all of this is true, then perhaps the Reliance has, through their treachery, done us a great service."

Topaz looked at the prosthesis. It wasn't complete yet, but he thought he had most of the kinks worked out of the basic design.

RJ had called in yesterday just before dark to say that they had stopped for the night and would continue their ascent today. He wished she was here so that he could gloat over his handiwork. The two youngsters were in awe of everything, and Poley was no fun at all.

The apparatus wasn't the most handsome thing he had ever created. He had cut down the gangly arms of the droid to the length of the young prince's arms. Velcro straps would hold the arms in place along the prince's own arms, putting the hands in just the right position to be useful. Sensors at the elbows would indicate when the prince had moved the elbow. The hand would close when the elbow was flexed and open in degrees as it was relaxed. The power pack was small, and would ride on his back right between his shoulder blades. Hydraulics would allow the boy to stretch to reach for something without shifting the entire apparatus or tearing it free. Fortunately, the droid had been constructed of a lightweight—but very durable—titanium alloy. The whole apparatus didn't weigh more than five pounds, yet it would be strong enough for the prince to crush a rock, and it would survive most impacts.

Poley was wearing it.

"Try to close the right hand again," Topaz said after making an adjustment.

Poley moved his elbow, and the hand slammed shut, crushing the rock he was supposed to be picking up.

"Damn," Topaz sighed. "Hold your arm like this." Topaz held his arm up so that it was even with his shoulder with his forearm hanging down. Poley complied and Topaz started making adjustments again.

"If you would just slide that one hydraulic…"

"Poley! Who is doing this, me or you?" Topaz asked hotly.

"I thought we were doing it together," Poley said.

"Well, we aren't. I'm doing it, and you're helping. If I need your advice I'll ask for it," Topaz snapped. He looked at the elbow link again. "I think I'll just slide this one hydraulic back a little bit to pull off the tension."

Poley made a noise that sounded a whole lot like a disgusted sigh.

"What did you just say, Tin Pants?" Topaz asked.

"I didn't say anything," Poley answered.

Topaz laughed and rubbed Poley's head. "Ah, my little wooden head, you'll be real boy someday."

"I am too intelligent to be humored," Poley objected.

Topaz just laughed louder and then focused on his work.

"How's it going?" Taleed asked from behind him.

"Great, I'm almost finished," Topaz answered. "Of course it could take weeks to get all the kinks worked out so that it works right for you."

"I am very excited," Taleed said. "You don't know what it's like to have to rely on another person for everything. I love Haldeed, he is my friend, better than any brother. It distresses me to have to ask for his help for everything. It upsets me that he can't have a life because he has to be my hands."

Topaz nodded silently and continued to work.

"This is like a dream come true for me. To think that I will be able to pick up sticks, throw a ball. It's amazing!"

"Yeah, well, don't expect too much right away. It will take awhile for you to figure out how they work. I wouldn't try anything too difficult at first. The one thing I can't simulate is a sense of touch, so jacking off probably wouldn't be a good idea," Topaz explained.

"What's that?" Taleed asked.

Topaz laughed. "Don't worry about it, kid, it was just a joke. Why don't you get your buddy up and you and he can go gather up some wood and get the fire going. Maybe catch us a lizard or two for breakfast."

"We are close to a river. We will bring you something better than lizards," Taleed said excitedly. He ran off to get Haldeed. He went into the ship and shook him until he woke up. Haldeed yawned and looked up at him sleepily.

"The old one has ordered us to get some wood for the fire and to get breakfast. I was thinking we could fish some *colimaçon* from the river," Taleed said excitedly.

Couldn't it wait? I'm tired? Haldeed signed.

"How can I ask him to wait when he makes me *hands*, Haldeed? I shall have hands, and you my friend shall have your freedom," Taleed said.

Haldeed nodded, resigned, and got up. He pulled his shirt on, tightened his loin-cloth, grabbed his boots from the floor and followed Taleed outside. He sat on the ramp of the spaceship, pulled his boots on and started lacing them. He looked to where the two aliens were busily working on Taleed's hands. Then he looked back at Taleed's face, which was filled with a joy that he had never seen there before. He automatically started to adjust Taleed's clothes.

"Hurry, Haldeed! I want to show my appreciation," Taleed said.

Haldeed stood up and started following Taleed to the river. "We can make some traps and put them out while we are looking for wood, and when we come back they will be full."

Haldeed sat on the bank and carefully wove the reeds into a trap. "Can't you go any faster?" Taleed asked.

It takes time, Taleed, Haldeed signed back.

"Haldeed…is something wrong?" Taleed asked.

Haldeed shrugged and started to say nothing, but then he put down the work he was doing and started signing faster than he had ever signed before.

"Whoa! Slow down, Haldeed. I cannot understand you."

Haldeed slowed down. *I am very happy for you, Taleed. I know this is all that you have ever wanted, but as you say they cannot give me my tongue back. You talk of my freedom as if it is a good thing, and I know that you believe that it is, but what will happen to me? I can talk to no one but you. Only you understand me. All I know how to do is to take care of you. I don't even know the warfare skills that even the smallest child knows. I have no other skills. No other friends. You are my life; I have nothing else.*

Taleed laughed then and placed his stump against Haldeed's shoulder. "My dear friend, do you truly think I would abandon you? I would not; I could not. We will teach you to read; there is no one to stop us now, and then you will be able to talk to anyone. Or perhaps these people can find some way to give you speech. Surely if they can build something as complicated as hands, a simple thing like restoring speech should be easy for them. But no matter what happens, you and I shall never be separated. We will always be together. If I had ten arms and as many legs I would still need you, Haldeed. You are not just my hands; you are my friend."

Haldeed smiled then, all worry seeming to vanish from his face. He worked quickly at making the traps and dropped them into the water, securing the strings to tree limbs. Then they went off in search of wood. Haldeed broke down a *feu bu'che* plant. Taleed held out his arms and Haldeed loaded him up then grabbed an armload for himself.

"Soon I will be stacking wood on you, Haldeed," Taleed said. They started back for camp.

Haldeed grunted loudly and dropped the wood he was carrying. He pointed into the sky and Taleed saw it, too. A ship just like theirs was coming in fast.

"We must warn them, Haldeed!" Taleed dropped his load of firewood as well, and together they ran towards the camp. The ship landed long before they could reach the others. Taleed and Haldeed jumped into some bushes for cover, hoping that Poley and Topaz had heard Taleed's screams of warning. Neither Topaz nor Poley were in sight. Haldeed took hold of Taleed's collar and pointed towards a lump of brush closer to the craft. One that would offer more coverage while giving them a better vantage point. Taleed nodded and followed where Haldeed pulled him.

"Can you see Topaz or Poley?" Taleed asked Haldeed in a whisper. Haldeed shook his head quickly and pointed at their ship's door, which was now closed. Taleed nodded; it made sense. The old man and the robot had taken refuge in the ship.

The hatch on the second ship opened and three Reliance people walked out with their arms raised. The biggest one, a male, immediately started screaming. "We are unarmed! We have defected from the Reliance and seek asylum." Now one of Taleed's people was walking out of the ship after them, looking scared and ready to bolt. "We are alone except for a wounded man in the ship." The man lay down with his face in the dirt, and the others followed his lead.

The ramp from their own ship lowered slowly and Topaz and Poley walked out, both holding weapons.

"Poley, check the ship," Topaz ordered. Poley nodded and ran towards the newly arrived ship.

"Come on, Haldeed, we may be able to help," Taleed said. Haldeed nodded and together they ran out of the brush to stand beside Topaz, one on each side, trying to look as formidable as possible.

"Ah, boys! You're here right on time. Search these thugs for weapons," Topaz ordered. "I'm warning you, make one wrong move and I blast you to smithereens. So if you're feeling froggy, go ahead and jump. Make my day."

Haldeed and Taleed went to search the four prone people as Poley walked out of the ship carrying three rifles over his arm.

"Are you sure my sister left you in charge, Topaz?" Poley asked.

"Well, of course she did," Topaz said haughtily. "Do you really think she would leave *you* in charge?"

"Yes, I really do," Poley said.

"Well...she didn't, so there."

"My prince," the man of his people said as he prodded him with his stumps.

"Prince!" the big man exclaimed from where he lay on the ground.

"They have no weapons," Taleed reported.

"All right. I guess you can get up," Topaz said grudgingly. "But don't try nothin' or I'll bore a hole right through ya."

They got up slowly.

The big one looked right at Taleed. "So, *you* kidnapped the Prince," he said.

"We didn't kidnap him," Topaz said in an agitated voice. "We *found* him."

"Actually he found us," Poley corrected.

"I was not kidnapped," Taleed said angrily. "Is that what they are saying? That I was kidnapped? I ran away, and they all know it. I run away all the time. Isn't that true, Haldeed?"

Haldeed sighed deeply and nodded his head.

"Is it true that you defected from the Reliance?" Topaz asked skeptically.

"Didn't you?" he asked.

"I asked first," Topaz said with a sly smile.

"Yes...None of us were very pleased with the whole tainted-gold thing, and then our Captain started rounding up our crewmates on the station and having them spaced for treason. There comes a point when you get tired of being a pawn in their game. I guess for us that time was when we were sent on a dangerous mission because the Captain was mad at us because we all said mean things about him. When he started spacing our friends for doing less than we had done...well, we kind of entered the *damned if you do, damned if you don't* category. So here we are."

"How did you find us?" Topaz asked suspiciously.

"We went to the site where the transporter was sabotaged," the woman started. "When we realized you had fired your plasma cannon at least twice, we knew you couldn't have gotten far."

Topaz nodded; it made sense. Their story sounded plausible. You might not rock the boat to pull someone else in as long as you were safe inside, but if you knew there was a good chance you were going down anyway...

"I know this man," the Prince said pointing to the man who was one of his people. "He was a priest. The priests had him imprisoned for blasphemy."

"Yes, we met him in your father's prison," the big Reliance man said. "Why do you bother with this interrogation, though? We know that RJ is with you. Simply have her scan us to see if what we say is true."

"How do you know that?" Topaz asked curiously.

The man reached in his pocket, and both Poley and Topaz raised their weapons to point at him.

The man stopped temporarily. "I'm just going to take a picture from my pocket." He pulled it out slowly and draped it over the end of Topaz's weapon. Topaz reached out and took it. He looked at the picture and then handed it to Poley.

Poley looked at the picture and smiled. He held it up for Haldeed and Taleed to see. "It's a picture of my sister."

"Yes, Tin Pants, it's a picture of your sister," Topaz said with a sigh. "Where did you get it?" Topaz demanded.

"It was drawn by a priest in the village where you attacked the transporter. So where is she?" he asked. From the sound in his voice, he didn't really want to see her.

"It just so happens she's not here at the present," Topaz said. He raised his wrist-com to his mouth. "RJ, this is Topaz, come back."

They had just reached a cave. RJ was getting ready to check it out to see if it opened into the ship when she suddenly changed directions, ran over to David and grabbed the binoculars from around his neck. She climbed up on a pile of rocks and looked down into the valley below.

"What the hell is it, RJ?" Levits asked.

RJ didn't answer. "Well, I'll be damned," was all she said.

"What? What the freaking hell is going on?" Levits yelled up at her.

"Oh, it would just fucking figure! The minute I leave camp…" RJ cursed. "What…well, I'll be damned," she said again.

"God damn it, RJ! Tell us what is freaking going on," Levits demanded, losing what little patience he had.

"Shut up, Levits!" RJ screamed back. "I don't know yet."

Her com-link squawked and she answered it. "I'm here; did I just see what I thought I saw? Come back."

"Four former Reliance personnel and a native priest—all defectors. What do you want me to do with them?" Topaz asked.

"Are they for real?" RJ asked.

"Now only you would know that for sure. They seem to be. One of them is wounded—they said in a prison break."

"Is their ship fully operational? As in get us the hell off this planet when the time comes?"

There was a pause, and then Topaz answered. "Yes, fully functional. So I'm asking you again, what do you want me to do?"

"See if there is anything you can do for their wounded man. Have Poley keep watch on them; don't let them have any weapons. As long as we're this close, I'm going to check this thing out. We'll be back as soon as we can. If they even bitch about dinner, shoot them. Don't take any chances. Over."

"Got you, RJ. Be careful. Over."

"RJ...Damn it, what's going on?"

RJ hung the binoculars around her neck and started down the rock. When she got down to the others, she stood in front of Levits and asked, "How am I supposed to find out what's happening and answer you at the same time?"

Levits took a deep breath. He supposed there was some logic in that, but still..."I'm sorry. So...What the hell is happening?"

"Some defecting Reliance personnel have just landed a fully operational skiff in our campsite." She looked at David with meaning. "Now do you see what I was talking about? How can I be expected to make decent plans when things like this keep happening?"

David smiled.

"Well, what the hell are we waiting for?" Levits said. "We no longer need what might or might not be here, so let's get back down this mountain and get off this rock."

RJ, however, was completely ignoring him. Instead of heading down the mountain, she was stepping into the mouth of the cave, flicking on the illuminator on her com-link and looking around. "We're this close; we might as well see what is here. Who knows? We might find something useful."

"You just can't admit that you made us climb up this damned mountain for no good reason," Levits mumbled as they followed her into the cave.

"Well, there is that, too." RJ shone the light on what was obviously the open hatch of a ship. "Aren't you even a little curious about an ancient artifact that keeps sending out a beacon hundreds of years after everyone on it would have been dead?"

"Bitch loves to be right," Levits said, looking back at David and Janad. He had just spent the last hour of their climb bitching that there was no ship, just some anomaly caused by bouncing sound waves caused by the accursed magnetic pulse. The same thing that was making it impossible for them to get a long-range message in or out.

They walked into the ship. It was cold, and everything was covered in dust. It appeared to be as dead as a tomb.

"How did it get buried in the side of a mountain?" David asked curiously.

"From the way it looks, I'd say it hit the mountain with enough force to send the top of the mountain crashing down to cover the ship. This mountain is made up of mostly soft igneous rock, so it wouldn't have been that hard to loosen enough rock to cover the ship. There were definitely survivors, though."

"How do you know that?" David asked.

"Well, besides what we have already talked about—the fact that there is little likelihood of this planet having produced humanoids—there's the open hatch and the cave."

"Huh?" David said, not understanding the path of her logic.

"Someone had to open the door and dig out," Janad said to him.

Levits laughed. "Even the primitive is smarter that you are, David."

"They aren't primitives. Don't you get it, Levits? They are the product of two advanced, fully developed races. Their brains are at least as complex as yours," RJ said. "Naïve to our technology and culture, yes. Primitive? Absolutely not.

Have you not noticed how quickly they assimilate our language? How quickly they learn even complex ideas? They are
what the planet and some deranged, handless black Frenchman have made them. They have found a way to survive on a
planet on which most people would die. They have had their
religion hammered into their head from infancy, and yet both
Janad and Taleed have decided to go against everything they
have ever been told to try and find the truth when what they
were being told contradicted the facts. The average Reliance
citizen isn't as intelligent as these people are. Remember that,
while the Reliance has been running breeding programs for
generations, so have these people. The difference is that these
people have worked on the old, tried-and-true method of survival of the fittest, and that also means smartest. That's why
they solve problems so quickly. If you take too long thinking
in a battle, you wind up dead."

She stopped suddenly and shone the light on a panel. "Aha!"
she said.

Levits looked at it, as did the others. "So...some alien language. I wasn't expecting Reliance. The ship is obviously not
of Reliance design."

"That's not just any alien language," RJ said. "Do you
know what it says?"

"Well of course I don't, smartass," Levits answered.

"Well I do. It says, *Warning: do not open interior hatch when
airlock is open*," RJ read. "It's Argy."

"I didn't know you knew Argy," Levits said.

"I learned Argy for the same reason that Janad and her
people have been taught to speak Reliance. In case I needed it
behind enemy lines," RJ explained. "Most of your special-
forces Elite speak Argy."

"Then this *is* an Argy ship," David said.

"Yes, it is," RJ confirmed.

"What does that mean?" Levits asked.

"That all these people are hybrids. Argy and human. If it
wasn't for the obvious gene tampering that my father did and

our difference in coloring, Janad and I would probably be very much the same."

Janad looked around the ship. "If the First Ones came in this ship, that would explain why they were looking for salvation to come from the sky," she said.

RJ looked at Levits, who looked dumbfounded. "See? Not a primitive." They had entered the flight deck. RJ dusted off the control panel, flipped a couple of switches, and a hum started. The ship started to pulsate, and then the lights all came on and the sounds of computers and fans running filled the air.

"Why would they completely abandon the ship?" Levits asked looking around. "It doesn't seem to even really be damaged. Hell, before all the plants grew over the site, it was just covered with dirt and a few rocks. It probably could have flown right out. It doesn't make any sense. This ship is huge and seems to be fully operational. If nothing else, on a planet where metal is rare, why didn't they chop it into spear heads?"

"That's a very good question." RJ looked at the panels as if trying to find an answer there. "The ship would have been a symbol of home and of safety. It's not logical that they would just walk off and leave it. Like you said, if nothing else, why not strip it for parts? A chair is a chair whether it's on the deck of a ship or in a tent."

"A ship that crashes doesn't seem very safe to me," Janad observed.

"She's got a point there," Levits said. "Still...There is still a viable power supply here. I would have thought they would have at the very least taped that. Lights, generators...it just doesn't make any sense," he said again. "It's like leaving a vehicle halfway through a trip so you can walk the rest of the way."

RJ started to read the data that filled a screen. "Hey, I've activated the ships' log...Well, would you look at this shit?"

"I am, just looks like trash to me. What's it actually say?" Levits asked.

"This was an Argy prison ship. Apparently this ship was hauling prisoners to be interred on this planet. They were coming here to serve life sentences. This was to be a prison colony."

"A way to give them a death sentence without looking bad to the general public," Levits said, no doubt thinking of the world outside the ship.

"Crap!" RJ exclaimed, moving to stop the text rolling in front of her so that she could make sure she had read it right, even though there was really no point in it.

"What?" Levits asked.

"These people had all committed the same crime," RJ said.

"What crime was that?" David inquired.

"They were all rogue telepaths," RJ said. She sat down hard in the chair in front of the screen, oblivious to the cloud of dust she sent into the air. They could all but see her mind calculating.

"*That* was their crime—that they were telepaths?" Levits asked.

"Among humans empaths are rare and telepaths are almost nonexistent. Among Argy's, empathy is the norm and telepathy is not uncommon. But no one—human or Argy—wants anyone around who knows their every thought. Knowing someone's every emotion can be unnerving enough, but on a world full of empaths it's a given. On Argy, telepaths were supposed to register and wear a special apparatus that keeps them from reading the minds of others. Mostly they work in the military sector. The people imprisoned on this ship were all caught using their telepathic abilities without authorization, so…" She lowered her voice then almost talking to herself. "A shipload of telepaths lands on a third-class planet. For some reason they completely abandon the ship and everything in it, forcing them to live a primitive life on the planet's surface. They breed and start a civilization. In just a few generations they forget all about technology. They only know of stories handed down from one generation to the next about how they came out of the sky. So demented, handless black French guy comes along, and what do they do? *They all read his mind!* They realize that he knows things they don't know, and they decide he is the god he believes himself to be. Feeling himself superior to the primitives he has encountered, he breeds with as many as possible and puts in motion a breeding program that still exists today. So what happened to the telepathic/empathic gene? Did it get bred out or mutate? Janad appears to have, at best, minimal empathic abilities. The Prince certainly has no such gift, but what of the priests? What if they are priests because they are telepathic? What if they think they're talking to gods because they can read the thoughts of the King/God? There is only one thing that makes no sense at all...Why did they abandon the ship?"

When no one answered, RJ turned quickly around and found herself alone.

David hadn't realized that he was leaving the ship's bridge until he was lost in some long, dark seemingly endless hallway. "Hey! Guys, where are you?"

No answer.

"Janad, RJ, can you hear me? Hey! I'm lost in the ship!"

There was no sound except the echo of his own voice. He looked around quickly. Suddenly the light coming from his wrist-com seemed to be dimmer than it had been. He started back the way he thought he'd come, mumbling, "That asshole Levits is never going to let me live this one down."

Out of the corner of his eye, he saw something move. He walked faster, not caring to find out what it was. Then he caught a glimpse of something again and started running. "RJ! Can you hear me, RJ?" He hit his wrist-com, feeling like an idiot. "RJ, can you hear me? I'm lost in the ship!" There was nothing but static in reply. And then he clearly saw what was in the hall with him. It was a rat, a huge filthy rat. "It's just a rat, just a rat," he said. He hated rats. When he had been in the prison camp, rats were everywhere. They would steal the food right out of your hand if you weren't careful. At night if you finally fell asleep, they would come in and start chewing on you, literally trying to eat you while you slept. Then there was the vision he couldn't wash from his mind. Alsterace was still smoldering when he returned from what he had thought had been his ultimate horror. Dead, bloated and decaying bodies filled the air with a stench he was sure would never completely leave his nostrils, and rats, rats everywhere. Rats feasting on the dead. They were on top of and even inside the bodies, so many of them that the bodies appeared to be moving.

He had started running without even being aware of it. He forced himself to slow down. He was panicking. If he wasn't careful, he was just going to get more and more lost. He saw two more rats. "It's just a freaking rat," he reminded himself, then started screaming into his wrist com. "RJ! Damn it, RJ! Can you hear me?!"

There was still nothing but static. "Damned magnetic pulse," he mumbled.

He heard something moving at the end of the hallway, and he moved towards it. Maybe it was RJ and the others. Suddenly, the hall in front of him erupted in an ocean of rats coming right at him. He turned around and ran the other way until he reached a wall and came up short. He turned, grabbed his weapon and started firing.

Janad looked around her. She wasn't sure how she had come to be in this room, or even how or when she had been separated from the others. She shone her light around, trying to find a door, but there was none. How had she gotten in here if there wasn't a door? It didn't make sense. There had to be a hidden door. She started banging on the walls, trying to find a hidden panel or a button. She wished she had a wrist communicator like the others. Without it, her only option was to scream, and if she did that people would think she was scared, and she wasn't afraid. Not of being in a room with no doors and no windows. A room that seemed to be growing smaller by the minute.

She realized that it wasn't her imagination. The walls *were* closing in on her, and the air was getting thin and stagnant.

"David! RJ! Levits! Can you hear me?" she screamed. There was no answer, no sound, no smell—nothing at all to tell her where a door might be. And the walls seemed to move faster, making the room smaller and smaller. She banged harder and more frantically on the walls and screamed louder. "Help! Help me! Help!"

Levits heard something and walked towards the sound. Now he had no idea where he was in the ship, or where the others were. He got on his com-link. "RJ, I have managed to get lost in your little archeology project. Apparently the builders of this ship thought it was a good idea that there be no rhyme or reason to the layout."

There was no response.

"RJ...This isn't funny. Tell me where you are. Better yet, come and get me."

There was still no answer.

"Oh, that freaking David will have a field day with this," he mumbled. He thought he heard voices, so he went in that direction. "This isn't funny, RJ! All right, I admit it. I'm an idiot and I got lost. Now come and get me."

Then Levits smelled smoke. He turned around and saw that the hall he was in was engulfed in flame. He got on the com-link again. "Guys! When we turned this thing back on it must have caused a short! The ship's on fire! We have to get the hell out of here, except I don't know where you are. Hell, I don't even know where I am."

There was still no answer.

"Damned magnetic pulse." He forgot about the com-link and just started screaming. "We have to get the hell out of here. The ship is on fire!"

He ran around, frantically looking for some sort of fire extinguisher. Finding nothing and no one, he ran away from the flames, looking for RJ and the others and a way off this burning death trap. He couldn't find anyone, and the fire was getting worse. RJ could hear *anything*. Why couldn't she hear him? "RJ!" he screamed at the top of his lungs. "RJ!"

There was still no answer. She must be hurt—or worse. He doubled his pace, ignoring the smoke that scorched his lungs.

RJ tried her com-link for the fifteenth time. "Damned magnetic pulses." Then she found the monitors on the ship's console and started playing with the switches. Finally they came on. She started scanning the ship room-by-room and hall-by-hall. She found Janad first. She was being crushed in a room that was rapidly getting smaller. While RJ was busy trying to figure out where in the ship Janad was so that she could go to her aid, she found David being attacked by rats. Before she could find out where he was, she found Levits being consumed in a room full of fire and smoke. Even if she could locate their exact positions, there was no way she could save them all. As she tried with every skill she had to find the exact location of even one of them, she watched in horror as, one by one, they died. As she saw Levits engulfed in flames, she fell into a seat and started to cry. When she looked up the screens in front of her were blank, but then they flickered back to life and David and Levits and Janad were dying all over again.

RJ realized then what was going on, and why the occupants had abandoned this ship, never to return.

He was crouched in a corner, screaming, and the rats were rending his flesh. Suddenly, the pain ceased and he found himself crouched on the floor of the bridge. His gun was still in its holster. Levits was screaming and RJ was shaking him. Janad was rolled up in a ball, crying.

RJ left Levits and shook Janad.

David realized that RJ must have woken him up, too

"It's all right," RJ said. "It wasn't real. None of it was real."

"What the hell happened?" Levits demanded.

"It was a weapon," RJ answered, still badly shaken from her own experience. "A weapon that attacks the mind. The perfect weapon to use against telepaths."

"But I wasn't here," Janad said. She stood up and stretched her arms out. "I was in a room alone and the walls were closing in." She shook with remembered terror.

"No one left this room. We must have triggered the ship's defense system when we walked in. The weapon put us into a kind of sleep, a dream state. Apparently the prisoners tried to take over the ship before it could land. They caused the crash, and the ship's internal defense weapon was triggered automatically. It wasn't a distress beacon this ship was emitting, it was a warning to other ships that there were escaped prisoners on the planet's surface."

"Well, at least we know why they abandoned the ship," Levits said running his hands through his hair. "It was so real. I swear I can still smell the smoke in my hair and on my clothes. I don't understand how anyone could have resisted. How they could have gotten away."

"I imagine they were all well aware that such a weapon existed. As soon as I knew that what I was seeing wasn't real, I was able to fight the visions in my head and wake up. It wasn't easy, but it wouldn't have been impossible. The worst part would have been keeping people awake. I imagine they worked in shifts to get free of the ship. It explains why they left the ship and everything in it behind. They just wanted to put as much distance between them and the weapons as quickly as they possible could."

"What did you do to it?" Levits asked.

"I found the weapon, located the switch, and turned it off."

Even knowing the weapon was off, none of them were eager to stay on the ship. They were not at all happy to learn that the thing that RJ found she absolutely could not live without, among all the wonderful things on the ship to choose from, was the accursed weapon itself.

She was digging around under the console, occasionally pulling out little parts attached to fiber-optic cable.

"Just leave it," Levits begged. "We don't need it."

"Yes, we do need it. We do," RJ said. "Don't you see? Even I was rendered completely useless for several minutes. We may be able to use this weapon. If we get in a position where it would work perfectly, I don't want to be kicking myself that I left it here. Furthermore, I'm pretty sure that you don't want to be the one that I'm kicking instead because you talked me out of getting it."

Levits mumbled and walked away.

"I don't think people should use weapons that attack the mind," Janad said disapprovingly. "It's sneaky and underhanded. There is no glory in it. No courage, no bravery."

"Gee!" RJ said, never stopping what she was doing. "I never thought of it that way. I just figured that the object of war was to kill the other guys before they killed you. I apparently missed the fair-play class when I was in basic training."

RJ yanked the last of the components out and then started looking around at the top of the wall. She jumped up and grabbed something that looked like a normal surveillance camera. Then she started off down the hallway. They all followed her. Every few feet she jumped up and grabbed another of the camera-looking devices. Since they were all following her, all secretly afraid to be alone for even one minute after the ordeal they had just gone through, RJ handed the devices to them to carry.

"RJ...What do you want with surveillance cameras?" Levits asked as she loaded the third one on him.

"The weapon works in two parts. First by using sonic waves to interrupt the brain's normal function and causing sleep, then by stimulating the fear centers in the brain, causing your own brain to attack you. The components I pulled out of the console are the weapon itself. However, these surveillance cameras hold the apparatus which makes the actual sound," RJ said jumping up and pulling down yet another.

"How many of them are you going to need?" David asked.

"A few. Why?" RJ asked, jumping up and grabbing yet another one.

"Because we have to carry them down the freaking mountain!" Levits practically screamed. "We have to cart this weapon—which none of us feels very safe around, and you don't yet know what you are going to do with—down the side of a freaking mountain."

"What is with this word *freaking*?" Janad asked. "You say it all the time for everything. What does it mean?"

"It's the same as the word *fucking*," Levits said.

"If you mean fucking, why not just say fucking?" Janad asked.

"Because when you do, certain people higher up in the ranks get all tightassed and you can get demerits, even brig time," Levits explained. "Get your pay docked or spend a couple of nights in the brig for letting the wrong word slip in front of the wrong prick and you learn real quick to say something else. It means exactly the same thing, but for some reason they let it slide."

"Huh?" Janad said scratching her head.

"It's military stuff, Janad," David explained. "It never makes any damned sense. *Freaking* encompasses a whole range of emotions from frustration and anger, as in *The stupid freaking mountain*, to excitement as in *You've got such a freaking big wang*."

"Poley has a freaking big wang," Janad said.

"Yeah, well, that's technology for ya," Levits said with a sigh.

RJ turned to look. "Do you people ever freaking listen to yourselves? Let's just get what we freaking need and get back down the freaking mountain." Looking at them, she realized they were all carrying about all they realistically could. So she stopped getting cameras and started walking down the hallway, opening doors and looking in.

"What the hell are you doing now! Let's pack this damn crap up and get the hell out of here," Levits ordered.

"If they had this weapon on board, it's a sure bet they had some kind of device the crew could wear to cancel out the effects. Ah-ha!" She walked in the door she had just opened, and right up to one of the three mummified humanoid remains that were in the cabin.

"Well…This is freaking creepy," Levits said making a face.

"They're all wearing the same uniform," David observed.

"No doubt they were part of the crew." RJ checked them out closely one by one.

"What the hell are you looking for now?" Levits demanded. "Are we going to need mummified Argy's later? Maybe you're going to make a freaking potion."

RJ ignored him, choosing instead to talk more to herself than anyone else. "Damn! The prisoners must have stripped the crew of the apparatus…That would have made it a damn sight easier for them to get out. Smart…of course, if they had been very smart they would have looked for the weapon and turned it off like I did. Of course, criminals of any species are almost inherently stupid. Well, no sense hanging around here." She started walking back towards the bridge, and the others followed. "They obviously used the apparatus to escape from the ship, so they are doubtless on the surface of the planet somewhere."

"If they had the sonic disruptors, why didn't they use them to dismantle the ship? At least take *some*thing?" Levits asked.

"I imagine the units had a limited power supply. After all, in most cases they would only have to last long enough to put down an uprising, and with that machine in place, that shouldn't take more than a few minutes. They probably only had enough power to get out. They escaped with only what they could easily carry and could just grab," RJ explained. "With something like that thing playing in your brain, you wouldn't be thinking clearly, and most of them wouldn't have had the disruptors."

"If it's just sound, wouldn't ear plugs work?" David asked.

Levits laughed loudly and gave David a *you really are an idiot* look.

"Sound waves can penetrate practically anything," RJ answered. "You need something to interrupt the sound waves and change them into something harmless. We should be able to make something that will work fairly easily."

"Just to satisfy my morbid curiosity," Levits started, "what killed those people back there?"

"Well, they were tied into their chairs, there was no sign of blunt trauma to the head, no obvious laser marks on the clothing or skeleton, there was too much mummified flesh left on their bones to suggest that they had starved to death, so I would say off-hand that the weapon killed them," RJ said. They had reached the flight deck.

"Well, isn't that a lovely thought? Everyone gets to die from their own worst fear," David said.

"Oh, it's worse than that. The Argy are empathic, remember" RJ said conversationally. "They got to experience everyone else's fear as well." RJ pulled two backpacks from her own; she'd come prepared to carry a power supply back if they had found one. She used the radiation-proof bags she had brought to wrap the components of the weapon, and Janad helped her pack them into the backpacks.

"It can't work now, right?" David said as she slipped one of the packs on his back.

"Of course it can't work, you dildo," Levits said exasperated. "All the optics have been broken, and it's been disconnected from its power source."

"I was just making sure," David spat back hotly.

"You are such a dumb ass," Levits sneered.

David turned on Levits. "Get off my back, or I'm going to kick your scrawny ass."

"Why don't you go ahead and try it? I'll…"

"Get your ass kicked," RJ said. "David is bigger, stronger, and more experienced in hand-to-hand combat, so he'll kick your ass."

"I'd like to see him…"

"But I wouldn't. Nobody's going to be kicking anybody's ass." She held the second pack out to Levits, and he grudgingly put it on, mumbling the whole time.

RJ moved to turn the ship's power off.

"Hey! Why'd you do that?" Levits asked as he raced to turn the light on his com-link on.

"No sense in leaving it on to run the power out. Who knows; we might need this ship yet," RJ said. She looked back around her, suddenly feeling a reluctance to go. She had an illogical feeling that, for an instant, she had connected with the other side of her heritage. The only way she had ever interacted with them before had been by killing them on planets in galaxies far away from here. She took a deep breath and walked out of the ship. If they hurried, they should be able to make it down the mountain before it got dark enough to impair her companions' vision.

They had been walking a little over an hour when she realized that Levits was very purposefully not talking to her. She let David take the lead for a while and held back with Levits.

"So, what did I do now?" RJ asked with a grin.

He glared back at her. "You know what you did. You took his side."

"I didn't take his side," RJ said in disbelief. "All I did was tell the truth. He can kick your ass. You and I both know that you would have talked your way out of it anyway, because you have an aversion to pain. So in the end, the outcome is the same, and it was a lot quicker this way. You're smarter than he is; he's stronger. In all reality, which would you rather be?"

"You could at least pretend that you think I'm stronger," Levits said with a smile.

RJ smiled back and took his hand in hers. "I didn't ask you to pretend to be dumber just to make David feel better."

"RJ...What are you going to do with this damned weapon?" Levits asked, more than ready to change the subject.

"I really don't know yet. It could be modified to do any number of horrible things."

"Worse than what it does now?" Levits scowled. "I don't like the sound of that."

"Rather depends on who we use it on, doesn't it? Some people deserve a tortuous death..."

"I'm not sure *anyone* deserves *that*," Levits said, a cold chill running up his spine as he remembered the terror. "RJ, I'm curious. What was your fear? I mean...I didn't think you were afraid of anything."

"I'm an empath, too, Levits. I felt your fear—all of your fears," RJ said simply. That was all he needed to know. She didn't want to talk about her only real fear. They could all avoid their fears, but her fear was inevitable.

Chapter Fourteen

Haldeed didn't know what the defrocked priest and the old one were talking about; he only knew that it was slowing down progress on the prince's hands. This was frustrating Taleed, so that he was bitching at Haldeed. He and Taleed had been catching *colmaçon* all day, and they had enough for a feast. He had shelled and cleaned them and was now pushing them onto a spit to be put over the fire.

"Hurry, Haldeed," Taleed said impatiently. "I want to see what the old one is talking about that is so important that he has all but stopped working on my hands."

Haldeed just looked exasperated and worked a little faster at poking the snails onto the skewer. He didn't stop to explain to him that since Taleed was contributing nothing but aggravation, he could leave at any time. Haldeed grunted when he had finished the task, and together they walked over to the fire where Topaz was talking to the priest.

"So all the priests are basically schizophrenic," Topaz was saying excitedly.

"I don't know what that is," Jessit answered.

"They all suffer from this disorder where they hear voices in their heads," Topaz said.

"Yes," Jessit said shaking his head. "I have it, too, but I know it isn't gods that are talking to me…" He looked then at the young prince and fell silent.

"Speak freely. I have long believed that the priests spoke falsely, and everything I have seen on my adventure since I left the palace has only strengthened my belief. If you have any insight, please share it with us," Taleed said.

"Only that…."

Haldeed put the snails over the fire.

"My goodness! What a fine feast we will have," Jessit said smacking his lips.

"Jessit, please," Topaz begged with a sigh. "Try to stay on task. What were you going to say?"

Haldeed smiled. He thought it was funny that the old alien should be telling anyone to "stay on task," when Taleed's hands lay in the dirt at his feet untouched and unfinished.

"Well, it became obvious to me early on that the voices in my head couldn't be the gods. Why would the gods want me to have sex with my neighbor's farm animals? Or slit the throat of a merchant who overcharged the man in line ahead of me? I spoke to the head priest Ziphed about it. He said the gods spoke in mysterious ways, and that I must learn to interpret what they were saying to me. I knew then that everything that he said was only lies. Lies that he told when he interpreted things like *Have sex with the neighbor' farm animals*, and turned them into *The gods want us to fight with each other*. I mean how can you credibly translate having sex with your neighbor's animals into anything godly? Perhaps you could make an argument that it means the animals should be bred, or perhaps that the community as a whole should condemn or perhaps engage in acts of bestiality. But it hardly seems to me that the gods would waste their time talking about such trivial matters."

Haldeed couldn't make much sense of what the priest was saying, and from the looks on the faces of the three alien strangers, neither did they. They seemed more like the Reliance people he had seen all his life. The ones that had come to the Capital to trade hides and carvings, beads, art and sometimes meat for cotton cloth and metal implements. Cold and detached, like priests. Not like RJ and her people, who were more like the palace guard. Very serious at their posts, but cutting up, laughing, and offering mute palace servants a sip of wine they weren't supposed to have when they were off duty.

Haldeed understood what they had said about why they were here, but he wasn't sure that he trusted them. Their expressions were devoid of emotion. Their movements were stiff, their body speech unreadable. He wondered if this was part of some training they had undergone, or whether their world just repressed them so much that their souls had retreated from their faces.

The priest was still talking. "...I wasn't happy to just believe what they told me to believe. I wasn't happy to tell the people that they should believe what I didn't. In a glass case deep within the Temple is the Holy of Holies, a huge vault in which are machine-printed journals said to have been written by The Ancestor himself. No one save the High Priest is ever supposed to read them. So of course I read them right away. It wasn't very hard to gain access. I gave the guards a couple of bottles of wine once a week, and in return they opened the vaults and let me read the books."

"What was in the books?" Taleed asked forgetting at least for the moment about his hands.

Jessit laughed, then fixed the boy with a stare. "Ah, my Prince, it would be easier to tell you what was *not* in the books. They were the ledger of the man who would be king, the man who believed he was a god and easily convinced the people who already lived on our world that this was so. He wrote..." Jessit's eyes appeared to lose focus. Or perhaps to focus on something only he could see. His voice dropped into the singsong cadence of rote recitation, and he began.

My name is Paul Arquette. I have dictated this to the computer and had it printed out because it is important that my story be told. Also who knows what will become of the technology that accompanied me to this world? Who can trust that equipment when the very government that we have put our trust in has purposefully sabotaged it?

The Reliance...May their name forever be cursed!...sent us on a mission to colonize this planet. Now looking out at this vast wasteland, I know that we were never meant to survive. Of the eight hundred and seventy-two men and women who accompanied me on this pilgrimage, only I have survived, and I don't know how much longer I shall live. Both of my hands were severed in the crash, and in an attempt to keep from bleeding to death I cauterized them against the red-hot hull of the ship. It's funny how quickly mind and body will react. I wasn't even aware of doing it till it was done.

My shipmates litter the interior of the ship and the ground outside, and I am crippled and too weak to do anything but watch them rot. I feel ill. Perhaps I will go to sleep and never wake up. I think that is what I would like.

Day two—I woke up this morning feeling better but hungry. I found no viable food in any part of the ship. The mess halls and kitchen were on the starboard side of the ship, which was almost completely destroyed on impact. I wonder how it is that I am alive when everyone else has died, and when the very ship that has brought us here has been so damaged. The surgical unit was intact, and I found some ointment. I spent several minutes wondering how I would get it from the dispenser, and then I pushed the button with my knee. The ointment immediately started to heal my flesh, and the pain went away. I begin to think I may yet survive if I can only find something to eat.

I wish the dead people would stop looking at me. Every time I see one of them, they seem to be looking at me, accusing me of some crime, because I have lived and they have died. But it is only the Reliance who has betrayed us. First they took away my right to breed, and then they sent me here—sent all of us here—to die. It seems that they cannot be rid of our color soon enough. We have already served our purpose in their breeding program, and now we are just flies in their genetic ointment. Still, I never thought they would go this far to get rid of us.

Day Three— My hunger overwhelms me, and every day I realize more and more that a man cannot exist on a strange planet with no hands and no provisions. Today it rained, and I was able to stand at the edge of the ship and catch the water as it ran off. I kicked a big pot from the galley over and put it under the drip, so now I have drinking water. I found some edible food cubes deep within the rubble of the ship, and there are a few more that weren't destroyed in either the crash or the fire. Even the simple act of eating is almost impossible. I have to get down on my knees, lean *over—careful not to put any weight on my stumps, which are still healing—and lift a food pack with my teeth. Then there is the task of opening the foil pouch. After several attempts I simply stuck it in my mouth whole, chewed it up, and spit the foil pieces out.*

There is still foil in my teeth.

I kicked with my feet till I found the food cubes. I kicked till my feet hurt. I would like to take off my boots, but I cannot. Maybe if my arms were completely healed…But they aren't, and if I don't get some real food soon, they probably won't heal at all. I will die here. Without help I will die, and there is no one here to help me.

Day four—*They keep looking at me. Some of them are starting to bloat and to smell, but others deep within the ship—especially down where the ship has been buried in the earth—are so cold that they still seem alive. But I know that they aren't. I know that they are just bodies. Some of them have the faces of my friends, but they aren't there anymore, and they won't know. No one will ever know. I worked socks onto my arms, and it cushions them enough that I can use them as long as I don't push too hard. It doesn't take much pressure to push a button on a laser knife. I cut slabs of meat from the thigh of a young Corporal today; he didn't seem to mind. I found that there was a working microwave in one of the break rooms, and I cooked the meat. I looked at it for a long moment then I lifted the plate to my face and ate.*

It didn't taste like chicken.

Day five—*My stumps seem to have healed overnight, and the growling in my stomach has stopped. There is a voice in my head— several voices, actually. They are telling me that it is good to eat the dead. Maybe it is the spirits of my dead friends who want me to live. I found Jim today down on the lower deck. I thought that deck would have been utterly destroyed, but it was surprisingly devoid of any real damage. Apparently it was only the starboard side of the ship—the side that impacted the ground first—that has been damaged beyond repair. When we hit this strange valley, crushing the rock formations—which can only be described as looking like huge African termite mounds—before us, the ship was totally out of control, and it took the brunt of the impact. The rock formations* are now piled like a child's broken toys in front of and in some cases on top of the ship. Surprisingly, the observation window on the bridge, though badly cracked, is not broken. The voices tell me that others will come. The Reliance won't be happy to get rid of just a few of the blacks on the planet. They will only be happy when they have destroyed us all. They want to breed a race of one color, to bring about a feeling of unity and do away with racism by an act of genetic genocide. But there are too many of us, and it will take too long to breed us out. So they take away our breeding privileges. But some of us noticed that more people of color lost their breeding privileges than whites and we started trouble. So they round up all the troublemakers and tell us we can breed all we want if we will colonize this planet. They send us in a rickety ship that is sabotaged, hoping to exterminate us all and get away with murder. But I am still alive. Do you hear me, you stupid Reliance shitheads? I AM STILL ALIVE!

Day 27—I am a god. There is no other explanation for what has happened to me. Why else has everyone else died while I have lived? Why can I now hear the voices of the dead who live inside of me? I got five of the service droids running and programed them to take vocal commands from me. It wasn't easy; I had to use my teeth and stumps to hold the tools to fix the first one. We cleaned the decaying bodies away, and, using one of the land rovers that wasn't damaged in the crash, we carried them to a canyon several miles away and dumped them. We were able to get the freezer on line, and we have butchered all those bodies that had kept so well in the buried part of the ship. We have installed one of the dozens of thermo generators the Reliance sent for the proposed colony. I half expected them to be fake, but they seem real enough. If I ration, I should have enough meat to last me for years, and the freezer should last as long as there is steam in the core of this planet.

I am using the droids to find and test edible plants. After all, I may be a god, but I am still a human god, and humans are omnivores. So far, the droids have found twenty varieties that are safe for human consumption and packed full of vitamins. Unfortunately only one of these appeals to my French palate.

I grow to like this planet more with each passing day. The Reliance sent us here with a sabotaged ship in the hopes that even if some of us did survive the crash we could not live on this desolate planet, but this planet is not as desolate as they think. They will send more people here, and if even one woman survives that crash we will make a race here. We will breed, and breed, and become as numerous as the sands of the sea and then we shall track you across space and across time and we will make you pay! I will make you pay!

John Henry stood in the shadows, his prostheses in the hands of another man. His skin was painted brown, and he wore his silver space suit; he felt like a grade-A moron.

"I feel like a grade-A moron," he said.

"Just don't get it wrong, John. You know RJ would never ask us to do anything without damn good reason," his partner said. "We can't afford to screw it up now."

John Henry nodded. He looked at the message scrawled across his left stump. "My children! The time has come to fight! You must cleanse this planet with the blood of the Reliance. Rise up and smite your oppressors."

"You don't sound very god-like," his partner said, pulling a face.

"Just what the hell does a god sound like, Jack?" John asked in an angry whisper.

"Not like that!" Jack laughed. "Sound more forceful, more booming. Try it like...My children..."

"Hey!" a guard yelled rounding the corner of the building. "What the hell are you two up to?"

"Nothing," Jack said, shrugging.

The guard must have seen Jack's weapon then, because he raised his own to a firing position. "Better drop that gun, alien."

"What gun?" Jack asked with a shrug.

The guard moved closer. He looked John and Jack up and down. "What the hell are you two dressed up for?" His finger was way too close to the trigger.

John looked at Jack, and Jack looked at John. Then John slung his arm out and forced the barrel of the guard's rifle up, making the bullet fire wild. "Go!" Jack ordered, shoving John foreword.

"Shee...it!" John said running into the middle of the compound where the Beta 4 humanoids were just being led back to their barracks from a day of training. Seeing them John flung his stumps wide. "My children..." A bullet kicked up dirt a few feet in front of him, and he realized he had barely missed being shot. "Don't just stand there; kill these bastards!" John screamed, running into the sea of Beta 4 humanoids who grabbed the Reliance soldier as he ran after John. They beat the guard to the ground and took his weapon. John stopped moving again. He looked at the people all bowing before him. "Don't start that bowing crap! Kick these guys' asses, and let's get the hell out of here."

They seemed to smile as a whole, then they let out a loud battle cry and started taking the camp apart.

John found a fairly safe place and squeezed in to watch the battle in relative safety. The Beta 4 humanoids were kicking some Reliance ass. Apparently they had just been waiting for any sign to attack them.

John Henry settled in and got comfortable. "Ah...It's good to be god."

Chapter Fifteen

"Then one day, I don't remember which one it was," Jessit continued, "but it was years after the crash. These white-haired people with bronze skin and blue eyes found him. They thought he was a god. And, of course, so did he. He basically did to them what the Reliance had done to his people: he made all of their males stop breeding their females in their cycles, and he bred with all the females when they were fertile, making children that were all as brown as we are. He formed the Religion, and put a breeding program in place that would ensure that his race would survive but wouldn't become so inbred that they started to have genetic mutations. It's very complex, and one has to wonder if the high priests have always understood the program themselves."

"So, in fact, he was like a god because he did create you," Topaz said thoughtfully.

"Yes," Jessit said. "He and the priests."

"So here's something I don't understand," Stratton said. "From what you have said, and what little I have observed in your culture, women are more or less completely equal. Children are raised by both parents, men and woman hold the same jobs, wear basically the same clothing, and train and fight together. Yet woman aren't allowed to be priests. They aren't even allowed in the palace or the temples, why is that?"

Jessit laughed. "Ah! That's easy. Women distract men, and men distract women. A choice was made. Men would serve, and women wouldn't. Therefore we can't have them around to distract the King and the priests."

"It's probably simpler than that," Topaz said. "The Ancestor thought he was god and therefore perfect. That's why he put the breeding programs in place—to make everyone look like him. He was black, so he wanted them to be black. He was male, so therefore those who were male were *more* perfect, so he set them up as the priests."

"Yeah, well, here's what I don't get," Bradley started. He, too, had been listening to the native's story. "If Paul Arquette hated the Reliance so intensely, why did this people ever deem to trade with them? To even try to have friendly relations with them?"

Jessit smiled. "Ah…because the King/God's spirit is said to move to the body of the Chosen one. The King/Gods have all taken counsel from the priests. At some point the Reliance sent ambassadors to trade with our people. The high priest's voices told him it was a good thing. The other priests agreed, and when they told the King what the gods had told them, the King gracefully agreed. Of course the King/God never reads from the book of The Ancestor, so he wouldn't have known about the real history. And you and I both know he really did not possess the sprit of Paul Arquette. So he had no real problem with the Reliance, and we needed replacement parts for the generators, light bulbs, metal implements and things the Reliance had in abundance and that we could not make."

"So…the priests are all schizophrenic?" Topaz said again.

"No," RJ said. They had walked up unseen on the group huddled around the fire, and they all jumped. "Sorry," she said with a wicked grin, then continued with her train of thought. "The priests are all telepaths, although I'm sure, that being untrained as to how to handle the power, they do go quite mad. Basically these people are the descendants of a deranged, handless black French human and criminal Argy telepaths who had been sent to this planet as part of their sentence. By the time the deranged, handless black Frenchman got here, the telepathic gene had been mostly bred out. Then, by the time he bred in his own genes for several generations, the common Argy empathic trait all but disappeared. However, the priests have a separate breeding program. One that ensured that the telepathic gene remained active. Although, without knowing what it is, they believe that they are talking to the gods."

"Damn it, RJ," Topaz said. "I wanted to figure it out."

"Sorry, Old Man, but maybe now you'll be able to get back to work," she said, looking at the hands and their apparatus at his feet.

Topaz grumbled, got up and moved to pick up the prostheses from where he had laid them in the dirt. He turned to Taleed and shrugged. "Sorry," he apologized.

"I have gone a lifetime without hands; a few more hours aren't going to make a difference," Taleed said graciously.

RJ went over to the fire, lifted the skewer from the tripods, and pulled one of the fully cooked and steaming hot snails from it. She let it cool only a few seconds and then took a bite out of it. "Wow! These are really good! What are they?"

Taleed started to answer, and Levits moved quickly to put a hand over his mouth. "No. Don't tell us. I may actually enjoy it if I don't know." Levits let the boy go. He hefted the backpack from his back and sat down on the rock next to Taleed.

"Did you bring me anything?" Topaz asked, looking at the obviously full packs on each of their backs.

"Some very heavy, horrid weapon RJ simply had to have. Nothing of any real value," Levits said, glaring at RJ. RJ just smiled and returned the skewer to the tripods.

RJ looked at the strangers, sizing them up with a glance. One thing was obvious; they were afraid of her. She could feel their combined fear like a wave. They didn't know what she might do to them, but they were pretty sure they weren't going to like it, and just as sure that there was nothing they could do to stop her.

Of course they had a point.

"So...Who's in charge?" RJ asked of them as a group. They all looked at the biggest man in the group, as the native—who had no doubt come with them—struck a neutral pose as if to say he was with no one and knew nothing.

The big man turned and stared back at the woman. She looked up at RJ unblinkingly although her emotions gave her away. "Technically, that would be me. Lieutenant Stratton, First Division, Space Force." She stood up and held her hand out towards RJ.

RJ stuffed the rest of the meat in her mouth, grabbed the woman's hand with her greasy one and applied just enough pressure for it to be uncomfortable. The woman's face didn't falter, even as the fat from the meat dripped out the bottom of their joined hands, and RJ let her hand go. She wiped the goo from her hand onto her pants leg and smiled. Then she turned quickly on the big man.

"But you're basically in charge now," RJ said noticing the way he jumped.

"I don't think any of us are in charge now," he said, quickly composing himself.

RJ laughed heartily as she helped Janad take the heavy pack off. "He's a smart man. Give him a gold star," RJ said, smiling at Topaz. Topaz just shrugged as if to tell her that her little display of power was more irritating than it was amusing. She shrugged back, acknowledging his indifference and letting him know she didn't care what he thought.

"Do you have a name?" she asked their leader.

"Bradley. This is Jackson. Our wounded man is Decker, and the native is Jessit," he said.

RJ could feel his fear of her start to fade. He really was a smart man, and he knew that if she meant to kill them she would have done it already, and saved herself the trouble of getting to know them. "Levits, David and Janad," RJ said pointing at each respectively. "Apparently we are all on the same side, so as long as you do what I tell you, when I tell you, we'll be all right."

She spoke to Topaz over her shoulder, "Give them their weapons back."

"Oh, I don't think that's such a good idea," Topaz said quickly.

Levits dumped his heavy pack then grunted and walked into the brush.

"Who died and left you in charge?" RJ said angrily. Now was not the time to question her authority. Not in front of the new "recruits." She looked around, then looked at Topaz suspiciously. "Where is my brother?"

Topaz seemed to focus more intently on his work as if he hadn't heard her.

"Topaz, I asked you a question. Where is my brother?" RJ demanded.

"Ah...You don't have a brother. You have a sister, but..."

"Don't start your shit with me, Old Man," RJ hissed back. "Where is Poley?"

"He's watching them...You told me to have him watch them," Topaz defended.

"Watching them do what from where?" RJ asked hotly.

"Watching the camp, watching the prisoners..."

"Prisoners?" RJ asked, her patience wearing thin.

"Well, you're the one who always says you can't be too careful, and I was in charge..."

"Who said you were in charge? Why would I leave you in charge? You're crazy; you know that. In charge of what?" RJ said hotly. "In case of any Reliance defectors should happen to land a ship in our camp? Give me a freaking break!"

"I'm pretty sure you left me in charge, RJ. And, yes, in case something just like this should happen...I mean, someone has to be in charge," Topaz defended.

"Well, no offense, but it wouldn't have been you," RJ said with a sigh. She mentally counted to ten. "Now, what the hell have you done with my brother?" RJ demanded, taking a menacing step closer to him.

"I had him walk up on the little hill over there and keep watch. I figured he could see the whole camp, and if any of the prisoners..."

"Oh, just shut up, Topaz," RJ looked up at the hill, focused, and saw Poley. She waved at him and said, "Poley, get back down here."

She heard him answer, and then saw him start to run down the hill.

A few moments later Poley seemed to appear out of thin air. The four newcomers seemed a little shocked at the speed with which he had returned, and from the look on Bradley and Stratton's faces they had already come to the wrong conclusion. "He's not, you know," RJ told them.

"Not what?" Stratton asked.

"A GSH…He's not," she said simply. "However, he *is* my brother."

"Did you leave Topaz in charge?" Poley asked immediately, not allowing Stratton to respond to what RJ had said.

RJ sighed deeply. "Of course not, Tin Pants."

"Then it was just more of his crazy ramblings," Poley said matter-of-factly.

Topaz's head jerked up. "Crazy ramblings! Crazy ramblings! How would you like this little metal arm shoved right up your little metal ass?"

"I wouldn't like it," Taleed said. "I would like to use the hands."

Just then Levits walked back into camp. He had his underwear on, but he had the top of his pants wadded up in one fist and they were hanging around his knees. His other hand was cupped very close to his groin.

"What's wrong?" RJ asked with a sigh.

For answer, Levits started to laugh hysterically. "Wrong? What's freaking wrong? Oh, nothing's wrong. My life's perfect—couldn't get any freaking better. I'm stuck on this floating turd of a planet with you bunch of lunatics, and now…." He moved his hand away to reveal a small lizard about an inch long and almost as wide stuck on his leg. "What the freak is this thing, and is it going to move?"

"A vampire lizard," Jessit said moving forward. "It won't move until it's finished eating. It makes a hole in you and sucks your blood out through its tube-like mouth..."

"I don't want to know it's freaking lifecycle! I just want it off of me!" Levits hollered.

"Can you get it off?" RJ asked the priest.

He nodded. "Yes, but it hurts."

"It hurts now," Levits said. "Just get the bastard off of me. I'm *using* my blood, I *need* it."

Jessit nodded, walked over to Levits and smacked the lizard hard with the palm of his hand. Levits let out a scream, and the lizard fell to the ground, hissing up at them. Jessit picked the little beast up by its tail and tossed him into the fire where he made a satisfying little popping sound.

"Now we have to suck the poison out," Jessit said moving to do so.

"Poison!" Levits screeched. Then he grabbed the native's head. "Wait! Wait a minute. How bad is the poison?" He glared at David, who was trying hard not to laugh, but not really succeeding.

"It won't kill you, but it could make you very sick."

"Probably infection caused from the bite itself. Sucking on it probably removes the impurities," RJ said. "Better let him do it."

Levits looked at her appealingly, then looked to the spot where the bite was.

RJ looked at Bradley and Stratton. "So much for making a formidable first impression," she said. Rolling her eyes, she grabbed Levits' arm and started pulling him towards the area behind the ship. "You are such a big baby."

"You know what, RJ? Just once I wish something like this would happen to you," Levits said, and then they were out of sight.

David looked at Bradley and smiled. "I'm not an empath, but I know what you're thinking," he said.

"What would that be?" Bradley asked.

David smiled more broadly and answered, "How the hell did this band of lunatics beat the Reliance?"

Bradley smiled then and relaxed for the first time all day. "Wow! You read my mind."

Even shut up on the bridge he could hear the screams of the prisoners in the brig, although he wasn't quite sure whether the noise was real or imagined. He was spacing them as quickly as possible to make sure they didn't escape again. He had no qualms about executing the prisoners; he just wanted the job to be over so that the station could get back to business.

What a mess! Whatever happened to dying with dignity? he wondered.

"Could you please…" Briggs took a deep breath before looking back up at the screen and continuing. "I have told you that everything here and on the station is well under control. Please just dock and do the repair work as you have been ordered."

"You're correct. My orders are to fix the station. But I am not required to put myself, my ship or my crew in jeopardy to do that. To the contrary, unless you are in immediate danger, my first priority is to ensure the safety of my ship and my crew. The patch on the station is holding, therefore you are in no immediate danger. Your job is to make sure Pam Station is secure enough for my people and me to dock safely and make the repairs. You do your job, and I will gladly do mine…"

"How dare you tell me what my job is, you glorified mop jockey! Listen to me! Dock that ship and get to work before I write you up!"

The fat man in the work coveralls looked at him and smiled broadly. "What's that, Briggs? I can't hear you; we're breaking up. Must be that damned magnetic pulse."

It sounded more like he was scraping something across the transmitter.

"Gee! I can't hear anything you're saying."

"Damn it, man…I'll see you court-martialed! This is not some joke. My mission is in jeopardy."

The image faded out, and there was no audible response.

"They have cut transmission, Captain," the communications moron reported.

Briggs took in a deep breath and wondered why he had been surrounded by idiots. There was no problem on the station now; they had totally crushed the uprising. No doubt the maintenance people who were giving him all the trouble had managed to make contact with the Kryptonite, and they were refusing to dock as a sign of solidarity.

Well, that just wasn't going to work, not in the Reliance. Not with Captain Briggs!

"Get me a line with Admiral Berk. I'll get that fat jerk off his ass one way or the other," Briggs ordered. "We'll see if the moron is still laughing when Admiral Berk gets done with him."

"Yes, sir," the communications officer said. It seemed to take the idiot an hour to get Briggs a clear line with the Admiral.

"What is it now, Briggs?" the Admiral's voice sounded tired and angry. His features probably would have been impossible to read even if he had bothered to look into the monitor.

Briggs took a deep breath. It was hard not to tell the guy where to stick his attitude. When he had accepted the position on Pam Station with the duty of moving the Beta 4 humanoids to Earth for military training, he had been promised it was a cushy position that would propel him up the ranks. Now everything was falling apart through no fault of his own, and he was dealing with all these nightmares while the Admiral was curled up in some cozy office planetside. Briggs realized now that if the mission was successful the Admiral would get all the credit, and he'd get his crumb for being a "good boy." If the mission bombed the way it seemed destined to do without some help from Berk, he, Briggs, would be hung out to dry.

"Sir," Briggs saluted and swallowed hard. "We caught and executed the rebel spies who were directly responsible for the attack on the station and for giving top secret information to the New Alliance, and there was a minor disturbance among a few additional personnel. We have contained the rabble-rousers and things are now back to normal. My problem now is that the repair crew from Stashes is refusing to dock and do their job…"

"Briggs, handle these problems yourself!" Berk said hotly, looking up for the first time. "We have bigger problems than a few disgruntled maintenance workers. Your little Beta 4 natives have just gone crazy in their camps and are tearing the bases apart and killing all the Reliance personnel they can get their hands on. It's all Earth Forces can do to contain the bastards. It's obvious the rebels were able to infiltrate at some point and win the brown bastards over. Until a full inquiry can be made, your operation is closed down. So you see? Making Pam Station operational is no longer a high priority. Someone somewhere dropped the ball, and you better hope it wasn't you, Briggs."

"Sir, I assure you…I followed your orders to the letter! I gathered up anyone I even suspected of spying as soon as I knew there was any sort of problem. I feel as if I have acted admirably under these conditions. Nothing that has gone wrong is my fault. It certainly wasn't my idea to train Beta 4 humanoids to fight the rebels. It certainly wasn't my idea to trade them for radioactive gold. I was just following orders, and I really think…"

"Quit whining, Briggs. If I were you, I'd quit wasting time figuring out all the reasons none of this was my fault, and find some way to salvage what's left of the operation. Do something right, and it might even make you look better in front of the board of inquiry." The screen went blank, and the transmission ended.

"Well, that's it, then." Briggs sighed. He stood up and started pacing, burying his fingers deep in his ever-thinner hair. The worst had happened. The entire plan had fallen apart, and he was going to be blamed. Blamed for all of it. From the missing transport ship and the hole in the station to the Beta 4 natives' attack on Reliance personnel on Earth and the destruction of Reliance property. He was going to be blamed for it all, and at least his career, if not his life, was over. He walked back to his chair, sat down and took a deep breath.

"Yumby, stand on," he ordered. The Sergeant turned to look at him curiously. "Desperate times call for desperate measures. Power our weapons up and target the Kryptonite...Lieutenant Drex, get the Kryptonite on line."

The fat maintenance guy's face filled the screen again. "What the hell do you think you're doing, Briggs?" he screamed. "Our sensors indicate that you have aimed your forward gun at us."

"Yes, that's right, fat boy. And unless you dock and get your fat ass to work, I am going to blast your defenseless ship right out of the sky," Briggs said. "In ten, nine, eight..."

"All right, you freaking lunatic! But don't think I'm not going to report this."

"You have exactly twenty minutes to dock and commence work on the station. Transmission out."

"Lieutenant Drex, get me Lieutenant Stratton on the surface. I want to know what, if any, progress they have made," Briggs ordered.

"Yes, sir," Drex said.

It took quite a while to raise Stratton, and she sounded hurried and was obviously out of breath as she answered him.

Briggs didn't beat around the bush. "Stratton, it is customary to call in occasionally and inform your Captain of what—if indeed *any* progress you have made."

"Sorry, sir, the magnetic pulses..."

"Magnetic pulses! Magnetic pulses! I am sick to death of every incompetent buffoon on this mission using that as their excuse to screw up. You will get up here immediately and report every detail of information that you have learned about that planet."

"Sir...We aren't finished gathering information yet," Stratton said.

"Oh, yes. Yes you are," Briggs said. "The entire mission has been scrubbed, and all that remains is for me to try to salvage our previous trading agreement with those filthy primitive bastards and try to save my own ass. I need to be briefed in full about what you've learned about their culture, attitude, and battle readiness immediately."

Nothing but silence answered him for the longest time, and his anger flared again.

"Lieutenant, all that is left is for you to say *Yes, sir* and report back to the ship immediately."

"Yes, sir," she said.

The transmission closed.

Briggs screamed in frustration and slammed his fist into his console, causing warning lights to flash and sirens to wail.

"Get these fucking things turned off!" he ordered the crew.

"Sir," Yumby seemed reluctant.

"Spit it out, man!" Briggs screamed as the emergency alarms shut down.

"Well, sir…the station-wide emergency system which you just activated?"

"Yes?"

"Well, sir, when it comes on…the…um…the cells automatically…uh…open…in the brig," Yumby explained not without cringing.

"What!" Briggs screamed. "Why the hell would they do that?"

"It's a safety precaution sir," Yumby explained. "People in the brig aren't usually receiving anything more than discipline, and…"

"Are you telling me that all those lunatics are losse on the station again?"

"Not the whole station," he said with an air of pride. "I was able to close the cell block off before they had time to escape."

Briggs seemed to be relieved. "Good then; they're still locked up."

"Yes, sir, but...Well, they are mostly the maintenance people."

"So?" Briggs snapped.

"So, there are several maintenance hatches in the cell block, and they know their way around the service ducts," Yumby explained.

"Why would they put something so freaking important basically on the arm of my damned chair? How freaking stupid is that...Gas them!"

"But, sir...the ducts serve the entire station, and..."

"Yumby, you find a way to contain those prisoners, or I'll see to it that when I go down I take you with me. Do you understand!" Briggs screamed.

"Yes, Sir," he said. Then just stood there.

"Do it now!"

Yumby ran to his console and started keying frantically.

Briggs jumped up and started pacing, again pulling at what was left of his hair. "It's all coming undone. I have to think. What do I do now? What is my next move?" He was talking out loud, and when he looked up and realized that everyone on the bridge was staring at him as if he had gone round the bend, he yelled at them all. "Don't you have anything better to do than stand around on the bridge all day?" No one said anything; no one moved. "Well?"

"Sir," Drex started. "We work on the bridge."

"Oh...I know that! Don't you think I know that!" he said, momentarily stopping to glare at them all.

What next, Briggs? Everything is coming apart, and now all the lunatics who want nothing more in this world than to kill you are loose and running amok on the station again. If some broom-pusher doesn't kill you, it's a sure bet the Tribunal will fry you. You have to do something amazing and brave.

Suddenly he knew exactly what to do.

"I...I can't wait for Stratton to get back. I will have to go to the planet's surface myself without the information and try to save our relationship with the natives. Lieutenant Yumby, you're in command until I get back." He turned on his heel then and headed for the door. "Yumby, get me a crack team of Elites and three GSH's, and have them meet me in the hangar. We will be taking a fully loaded and fueled battle cruiser. If the natives won't talk reason, we'll at the very least teach them some respect."

"Yes, sir," Yumby said.

"Well...Get to it! While you're at it, call maintenance. When I get back I want that damned emergency control button to be...Somewhere else."

"Where, sir?" Yumby asked.

Briggs turned to look at the man, his eyes becoming two slits. "Oh, you're pushing it, Yumby. Just tell them to put it somewhere where it can't be accidentally activated."

"Yes, sir."

"Good," Briggs started towards the door. "I'm on my way to the hangar."

Yumby sighed with relief, glad to see the back of Briggs. He was also pretty pumped about being in control. That is, he was pumped until he received the answer to his call.

"They've escaped! All the prisoners have escaped! I don't know where they are, but they're not in the cellblock. I have deployed the troops, but they could be anywhere...Man, we are so screwed."

Yumby took in a deep breath and moved to the Captain's chair. "I have accepted temporary command while Briggs goes planetside, Wiksel." An audible sigh of relief could be heard from Wiksel's end. "Tell the troops to double their efforts. Over"

"Will do. Over."

"Lieutenant Yumby, should we warn Captain Briggs?" Drex asked.

Yumby looked at Drex and smiled. "Warn him about what? The situation is under control."

"This changes everything," David said. "Now we can't just sit around here wasting our time letting blood-sucking lizards hang around on our genitalia."

"For the last time, shit boy, the wretched bastard wasn't on my dick," Levits cursed from where he sat holding the poultice the native priest had given him on the bite.

"Well, you wouldn't have guessed that from what you wanted me to do," RJ said with a wicked grin. She turned her attention to Topaz. "Aren't you done yet?"

Topaz looked up from where he stood working on the apparatus that was now attached to Taleed. "This is a complicated piece of equipment, RJ. It's robotics, it takes careful thought and delicate adjustments. You can't just slam it together with rubber bands and baling wire."

"Whatever the hell those things are," RJ said with a smile.

Topaz chose to ignore her. He stood back and looked at the boy. "Try it now."

Taleed moved his elbow, and the robotic hand grabbed the rock he'd been reaching for. His eyes lit up. "I am whole. Look Haldeed, look! I have hands." He experimentally tossed the rock, and it hit Topaz right between the eyes.

"Hey!" Topaz shouted, rubbing the wounded area. He turned to RJ and smiled. "Now that's freaking gratitude for you."

"Oh!" Taleed said his features becoming a mask of apology. "I am so sorry, Old One. It's just that my excitement is far greater than is my aim."

"Don't worry about it, son. I say that every morning when I go to the bathroom," Topaz said wiping an imaginary tear from his eye. "So isn't anybody going to say it?" he demanded.

"You are a genius." RJ walked over and kissed him on the check. "Aren't we all very impressed at how clever and resourceful Topaz is?" She started clapping, and the rest joined in. Topaz bowed less than graciously.

"However!" RJ said holding up her hand and stopping the applause.

"However?" Topaz asked with a mock pout.

"Yes. However, we don't have time to celebrate. David's right. The call from the station does change everything. Stratton, Bradley and the others are expected back on the station. If they don't show up there soon, they will be under suspicion, if they aren't already, and we miss a valuable opportunity to gain access to the station. One I don't think we can afford to waste." She looked thoughtful for a moment, then nodded her head as if to answer a question that no one had asked.

"Give me a minute," she said and then turned and walked away into the brush.

They watched as she left.

"I hope this means she finally has a plan," David said.

"Or at the very least that she's going to make one," Topaz said nodding. "It's rather unnerving to have a leader who suddenly stops leading"

David nodded his head in agreement.

"Hey! Look, Haldeed! I think I've got it this time," Taleed said as he threw another rock. This time the rock hit Haldeed between the eyes

Haldeed slung his hands around angrily, *You are either a very bad shot or a very good one.*

"I...I'm sorry. I wasn't throwing the rock at you, I was throwing it to you," Taleed insisted.

Perhaps you should try throwing something softer than a rock, Haldeed suggested rubbing his head.

"Yes, maybe I should," Taleed said and went in search of something to throw.

Bradley caught Stratton's attention and shrugged towards an area behind one of the skiffs. Bradley left and was followed a few seconds later by Stratton. They stopped in a grove of small trees about fifty feet behind their own skiff.

Bradley looked back in the direction of the group, then back at her. "I'm not sure I'm exactly comfortable with that lot making decisions that affect us all," he said.

Stratton nodded. "I know what you mean. We have the only viable ship, and I would think that would at least buy us one vote. We're being left completely out of the loop."

"Do you trust her?" Bradley asked.

"RJ?" Stratton asked.

"Yes, RJ. Who else?" Bradley said a little impatient.

"I trust her to get us all killed if it serves her purpose. I think we, unlike her own people, are in the unfortunate position of being expendable to her. I trust her not to kill us or double cross us, but I don't trust her not to get us killed," Stratton said. "She's a freak with feelings, that in itself makes her the scariest thing I've ever seen, but then there's the..."

"Disorganization, the obvious insanity," Bradley supplied.

"Yeah, those," Stratton said with a laugh. "Decker's getting better, but he certainly isn't ready for open combat, and I can't even guess at what she's got going on in her head. What she's going to order us to do."

"Have you noticed how her right arm jerks all over the place? What's up with that? Is that some sort of nervous twitch?"

"No, I read about it in a briefing. It's some defect caused by a flaw in her genetic engineering," Stratton said. "From the way she acts, I don't think it's the only one.

"We could sneak back to the skiff. We might be able to get Jackson inside and get the hatch closed before they figured out what we were doing," Bradley said.

"That's a risk I don't think we can intelligently take," Stratton said in disbelief. "These people aren't exactly the kind of people you want to catch you in a double-cross. I doubt we could even get past them. Have you watched Poley? The one they call her brother. In spite of what she said, I'm guessing he's some sort of freak, too. I imagine that he kills completely without conscience. He appears to be watching everything at once, and yet he rarely speaks, and his features hardly change. No, I don't like it, but I'm thinking we're going to have to go along with whatever plan she comes up with. Unless you just want to blow our brains out right here."

"Now that's good, clear thinking."

They both practically jumped out of their skin as RJ seemed to fold out of the plants behind them. "She's absolutely right, Bradley. We don't like to be double-crossed, and if I even think that something you're doing or are likely to do is going to cause me or one of my crew to be injured or even that it may endanger our mission, I'll kill you without conscience. That's just the sort of girl I am. You know—flawed and defective." She turned and started back towards camp, then turned around. "Well, come on. I've got my plan."

They nodded and started after her. When Stratton came up even with RJ the woman draped her arm over Stratton's shoulder, causing Stratton to jump. "By the way—just for the record—Poley is a robot with AI, not a freak." She turned her head and looked right into Stratton's eyes. "Oh, and here's something else. I don't *like* being called a freak. I can handle being called disorganized, insane, even flawed. But don't you ever call me a freak again. Understand?"

"I…I'm sorry," Stratton said. She was glad when RJ released her and walked on ahead. She turned to look at Bradley, and she didn't have to tell him how scared she was. He could see it in her eyes. She let out a long, slow breath and then started to breathe normally.

"I am going to work very hard at never pissing her off again," Bradley said in a whisper.

Stratton whispered back. "If she wasn't intending to use us for cannon fodder before, I'm pretty sure she just changed her plans."

"And you see? I can still hear you. So please shut up," RJ yelled back at them. "Or I'll make up a cannon fodder assignment especially for you."

RJ walked back into camp and right up to the fire. They followed and sat on the ground behind the others.

"All right," RJ said with a broad smile, "I have a plan."

"Yes!" David said in an excited tone.

RJ smiled at him and then continued. "The way I see it, the battle is on two fronts—the station and the palace. So we are going to have to break into two units. We will transfer enough power from the fully powered skiff to fly the other as far as the capital. That should still give us plenty of fuel to make it to the station. Jackson, can you fly the skiff?" RJ asked.

"Yes," Jackson answered.

"Good, that makes my plan that much easier. Now here's what we're going to do…"

Chapter Sixteen

David didn't know how this had happened. RJ had taken Poley, Topaz, Levits, Stratton and Bradley with her to the station while he was stuck going with the natives, Jackson and the wounded guy to the capital. Apparently he was being left behind because he had just recovered from space sickness and couldn't go back into space right away. RJ explained that it was just as well, since those going with her were all familiar with space and spacecraft. David pointed out that he had as much experience in space as Topaz did, and RJ quickly reminded him that Topaz hadn't been sedated through most of it. Levits had quickly added that Topaz also hadn't slung shit all over everybody.

David knew the truth of why he had been chosen to stay planetside, and even though he really didn't like the whole space package, it still chapped his ass to be left behind because he was considered too sickly and too stupid to be taken on the space part of the mission.

"What's wrong?" Janad asked from where she sat beside him.

"I don't like being left behind is all. I want to be part of the team," David said.

"You *are* part of the team," Janad said taking his hand in hers. "Part of *our* team."

"You know what I mean, Janad," David said. "I wanted to go with RJ. I have always gone with RJ."

"You don't want to be with me," Janad said with a mock pout. David smiled in spite of himself. "See, that's better. We need you here with us, David. They have all the high techs; we need you more than they do."

Taleed, who was playing with his new hands nervously, looked up at David. "I only hope I can do my part," Taleed said. "What if I am no better a leader than my father?"

"You will do fine, My Prince," Janad said.

"But I...I have never talked to the populace in a mass before. What if I don't say the right thing?" Taleed asked nervously. "I don't know what to say—how to tell them that everything they believe is nothing but lies. I could ruin everything by saying the wrong thing at the wrong time."

David laughed. "Well, then perhaps this really is where I am most needed, because I know everything about talking to the masses. It has been proven that I am *not* a great leader. I am, however, a grade-A, number one bullshitter. I'll teach you a few things, help you know what to say, and how and when to say it—but you have to promise me one thing."

"What's that?" Taleed asked anxiously.

"That you never let the fact that people will listen and follow you let you lead them where you know in your heart they should not go," David said.

"I promise." Taleed said with a sigh.

That is a possible solution to one of my problems, but there can be no easy solution to the other. They tell me to overthrow my father—as if it is nothing. I am to take what is his and make it mine, and then what of him? He is a proud man, and right now—according to what the aliens have told me—he is a very sick man, maybe even dying. How will I live with myself if I betray him, and can I really hope to take power without betraying him?

Taheed looked out the window at the ship that had landed below. He knew looking at it that it was a machine of battle. He took a deep breath and let it out.

"Ziphed, my brother," he said heavily.

"Yes, my lord," Ziphed answered. Ziphed's radiation sickness had quickly escalated so that he now had to have two younger priests to support him. They were sick, too, but with less of the gold metal around their necks, and younger—and therefore stronger—constitutions, they were not dying as fast.

"Go and meet their leader. Tell him that all of his men must come out of the ship. Bring dancers there to entertain them so that they do not become suspicious. Tell him that only he and two of his men may enter the palace. Tell them that this is our custom during the days that *Azure Lune* shines brighter than *Grande Lune*. Pretend as if all is well between us, and we still wish to trade with him…"

"But, My Lord…You said…the plague they brought, the kidnapping of the Prince."

"I said *pretend*. We must know what our enemies want. We must be prepared if they attack."

"But, My Lord, if we should try to trick the Reliance, if we try to make a show of force…"

"Ziphed, am I not a god? Look at how I have been cured of the illness while you are almost dead. Surely you would not now question the will of a god?"

"No, sire, all shall be as You have commanded." As hard as it was for him, he bowed to his King, and then with the help of the younger priests he left the throne room.

"Toulan!" the King called. The head of the King's army ran to his side.

"Are all the King's Guard in the palace?" Taheed asked.

"As many as could be brought back, and also as many war-ready veterans as we could gather from the surrounding villages, just as you commanded, My Lord," he said.

"Then alert the guard. Do you remember your instructions?"

"I do, and I will carry them out upon your command."

The King took a deep breath. "Then all that remains, my friends, is for fate to find us." He stood up and moved to embrace his manservant Yashi. He patted him hard on the back with his stumps. "Today our fate is no longer in the hands of the priests. Today, my noble brothers, our fate is our own. And tomorrow when the sun rises, no matter what our fate, this will be a new world."

David didn't like the information that was coming from the receiver. He liked it when they had one plan, and that plan didn't change. He hated it when you had a perfectly good, feasible plan, and then someone screwed it up, and you had to come up with a whole new plan. He especially hated it when it fell to him to make that new plan.

"Apparently he took a troop of fifty elites including three GSH's and a fully loaded battlecruiser," RJ was saying.

"How do you know?" Jackson asked.

"We passed each other. They were leaving the station; we are going to the station. The Captain made contact with Stratton, told her exactly what he planned to do and basically pumped Stratton for information about the planet and the culture. She managed to give him enough information so that he wouldn't find her answers suspect, but I think it's safe to say that she didn't tell him anything that's actually going to help him," RJ answered. "This changes everything, David. You could be walking into open combat in the streets—maybe even a blood bath. After all, Briggs has no idea that the natives are restless. I can't tell you what to do because I'll have my hands full here, and I won't know what the hell is going on there. If you want to abort the mission, then do it. It won't affect us up here."

David knew that RJ didn't want him to abort. It was an option. If she had wanted him to abandon the mission she would have said so outright. He looked at Taleed. "It's your kingdom—your palace. What do you want to do?"

Taleed didn't even take a second to think about it. "I want to remove the Reliance from my palace and my planet. How dare they send an armed guard to address my father for crimes he has not committed against them, when their crimes against my people are as numerous as the stars!"

"That's your answer, RJ," David said. "We're going in."

"Be careful and use your head. Keep your ship out of range of the battlecruiser. You may need to make a quick retreat…" Just then a magnetic pulse cut their transmission.

"You just worry about your own ass," David mumbled.

"GSH—that means like RJ, right?" Janad said. David nodded silently as he walked over to the weapons cabinet and started rifling through its contents.

"Then they can't be killed?" Janad asked.

"Oh, they can be killed," David said. He pulled a rocket launcher from the cabinet and smiled triumphantly. "Just takes a little more firepower." He tossed laser sidearms to Haldeed, Janad and Jessit. "These are easy." David held his own in his hand where they could see it. "You just click off the safety here, aim and pull the trigger. No! No! No!" he screamed at Janad who was starting to take the safety off. "You don't take the safety off until you are ready to fire, and you make damn sure that no part of yourself or any member of your unit is in front of you when you fire, because if you do..."

"We know what they do," Janad said. "We will be careful." She looked at Jessit. "It doesn't look like it is as much fun as a spear."

Jessit nodded. "Or even a really big rock."

The King looked at the three men who stood before them. Two of them were huge men, who were obviously no strangers to combat. Their leader, however, was a small, balding, ugly little man whose pompous air of importance did nothing but make Taheed even angrier.

"So you see," he was saying, "we want to trade with you in good faith. Trading has served all of our people for many generations, and there is no reason that should stop now. I want you to know that we forgive you for the attack on our station. Since your people obviously do not want to join us in our holy war, we will no longer be trading you for your people. Only those goods in which we have always traded."

The King laughed loudly for several minutes until the Reliance man started to laugh as well, no doubt thinking Taheed a foolish primitive who needed to be humored. Taheed stopped laughing suddenly and glared down at the Reliance goon until he, too, stopped laughing and looked nervously around. Then the King took the chains from around his throat and hurled them at the man's feet.

The man reached down and picked up the chains. When he noticed the weightlessness of them he stared at the King in amazement. He must have noticed then for the first time that Taheed was not as badly afflicted as the priests he had seen.

Taheed watched as the man's face seemed to fall like bread that has risen too long in the sun.

"You think we are foolish, don't you, Captain? Foolish people with foolish beliefs. Ignorant and backwards—and of course you are right. But nothing cures ignorance as fast as treachery."

Taheed nodded his head, and the Chief guard sounded the war siren. In almost the same instant the Chief guard slung his spear into the back of the Reliance chief. The man looked at Taheed in disbelief and then fell forward. His face made a sick, crunching noise when it hit the hard metal floor of the throne room.

His guards acted quickly, throwing their spears into the two huge Reliance men. As the spears bounced off the men, doing them no harm that Taheed could see, they acted just as quickly, opening fire on the King's guards—who fell like flies. With the guards out of the way, one of the huge Reliance men picked Taheed up by the collar of his shirt and the belt of his loincloth like he weighed nothing and tossed him with force into the huge window. Taheed's head hit hard, and the pain was immediate. The blood from his wounds left a stripe as he oozed quickly down the window onto the floor. He saw Yashi crawl across the floor and grab the weapon of the fallen Reliance leader. Yashi fired and hit one of the Reliance guards as he started to grab the King once again, and he just kept firing till the huge man stumbled and then fell. The other Reliance guard grabbed Yashi, and Yashi dropped the weapon. Taheed watched in horror as the giant broke Yashi over his knee and tossed him aside as a child might discard a broken toy. Then he picked up the weapons and left. He didn't even bother to finish Taheed off, and Taheed knew what that meant—he was dying.

He dragged himself to Yashi's side and saw that he, too, was yet alive. He hugged him with his stumps. "Yashi, my friend, greater was my love for you than for any woman. I am sorry. Sorry that I let you down."

Yashi smiled, shook his head, and then he died.

Taheed held him and cried. "I failed you, Yashi, because there *were* gods—I just wasn't one of them." He watched as the large moon faded and the blue moon began to shine brightly, and he smiled. "It is your time to shine, my son. Wherever you are, it is your turn to shine."

They had landed on the outskirts of the village on a small hill. From their vantage point they could see both the palace and the Reliance ship. Taleed heard the war siren as soon as the hatch opened and told the others what it meant.

"From here we can get to the back entrance of the palace through the gardens without being seen," Taleed explained. "From there it's not far to the throne room."

"All right, then," David said with decision. "Decker, you will stay here and keep the ship ready in case we have to make a quick exit. The rest of us will go." He turned and looked with meaning at Jessit. "I only hope you know what the hell you're talking about."

Decker watched them go, knowing that the real reason he was being left behind was because he would slow them down. "A stupid spear," he cursed, as they disappeared from his sight. "Dozens of battles on three different planets with not so much as a bad scratch, and I get busted by a freaking *spear*!"

He was watching the Reliance ship below, keeping an eye out for any change. He booted up the screen and focused it on the ship to get a better view. Using the viewers, he could even make out the fighting in the village below.

The Reliance had the firepower and they were mowing the natives down. But the natives just kept coming, and the Reliance men were falling, too. Just like Stratton had said, eventually they would be over-powered. He wished he could have helped them with a little added firepower, but he barely had enough power for a quick getaway if they needed one. He certainly didn't have enough to fire the plasma cannon. Even if he had the power, it wouldn't really damage the cruiser. If he fired it into the crowd he was likely to kill more natives than Reliance personnel.

He'd gotten himself hurt early in this battle, and now all he could do was sit back and watch.

He was missing the fun, and it really sucked.

They got into the palace without a hitch. "This is the way we always sneak out," Taleed explained. "The guards at the back gate are heavy sleepers. They are gone now; no doubt in battle."

"Good for us," David said. "They'd probably try to kill me and Jackson." He put the com-link to his mouth. "Decker, we're in. Clear so far. Over."

"I read you. Good luck. Over."

"Come on, it's this way," Jessit said, starting down the hallway.

The similarities between this ship and the Argy ship they had found in the side of the mountain made David a little uncomfortable. *Was that only yesterday? No! That was this morning!* No wonder his muscles still burned. He and Janad were running on nothing but pure adrenalin now. He only hoped it would be enough.

They entered the throne room, and saw immediately that the carnage was complete.

"Father!" Taleed ran to his father's side. He lifted him with his new hands. "Father?"

"Taleed?" he said, not even having the strength to open his eyes.

"The gold is tainted," Taheed warned.

"I know this, Father."

Jackson knelt and ran the pocket medic over the King for a quick diagnosis. He stood up looked at Taleed and shook his head sadly.

Taleed started to cry, the tears streaming down his face unchecked. "I am here to take your spirit, Father."

Taheed made a sound that might have been a laugh, and blood ran out of his mouth. "You don't need my spirit, son. You have your own." His body went limp in Taleed's arms.

"Jessit! Jessit, where is it?" David said as he started to rip the cloth and furs from the ship's control console. Jackson started helping him.

Jessit looked away from his dead monarch and started to look carefully at the console, trying to remember the pictures and directions in the Great Book.

"Jackson, does any of this look familiar?" David asked in a panic.

"Man, this shit is hundreds of years old. I ain't hundreds of years old; you've got me mixed up with your crazy friend, Topaz." Jackson looked at the console, but nothing looked like a weapon to him.

"Here!" Jessit screamed. He looked at the switches and buttons before him and tried to remember. He wished there was time to go get the Great Books. Finally he just pulled the lever his brain was telling him was probably the 'on' switch. A hum and the lighting of the small screen showed that he had a good brain.

Jackson walked up to the consol rubbing his hands.

"The cruiser is powering up its weapons!" Decker's voice screamed into David's ear, "and they're pointing right at your ship."

"Can we fire yet?" David asked. Jackson looked at him and shook his head. "Damn! We're screwed." He turned to Janad. "Get them and get the hell out of here."

"But, David…"

"Just do it, Janad," David ordered. Janad took the other natives, and they made a run back out the way they had come.

"Maybe you should go, too," Jackson said. "Even if this gets online fast enough, there's no way of knowing whether it still works or not, and I'm not sure which button does what."

"I'm staying here to watch your back. That's the way we do things in the New Alliance. And just let me say, shame on you! Has the Ancestor led you astray yet?" David asked with a smile and stood at Jackson's back watching the entrances.

Decker didn't give himself a chance to think about it. If he had, he probably wouldn't have done it.

They were all in there. If the battle cruiser fired its weapon, they were all dead and wouldn't need to make any sort of a get away.

He closed the hatch, swallowed hard, lifted off and flew right at the cruiser, acting as if he were going to dive-bomb it. The computer on the cruiser did what he knew it would. He watched as the cruiser's cannon turned away from its seemingly benign target to fire on the attacking ship. He took a hit that sent him spinning. He hung on tight, hit the accelerator and slammed into the cruiser.

He didn't feel a thing.

"Damn it!" Jackson screamed as he watched the skiff explode on the surface of the ship. His tears fell freely. "Damn it, buddy. I hope you didn't do that for nothing." He centered the crosshatches on his screen on the cruiser and punched the button he hoped made the damned thing fire. The ancient palace/temple/ship lurched in the ground it had lain in for centuries as the plasma cannon fired. The blast hit the cruiser, leaving nothing but fragments and a burning hole. "Damn! Now that's a weapon!"

"Crap!!!" David screamed.

Jackson turned in time to see the thing stand up out of the rubble.

David dropped his laser and quickly pulled the rocket launcher off his back. He fumbled with the safety trying to get it off, as he backed away.

"Shoot it!" Jackson screamed. "*Shoot the fucking freak!*"

The thing was almost on David when he fired. The rocket hit the GSH square in the chest. He flew through the air and hit the window, where the rocket went off, blowing GSH all over the room. It also made a new crack in the window, but it was still intact. Messy, but intact.

"Shit!" Jackson screamed, wiping GSH from his face.

David walked over and retrieved his laser from where he had thrown it. "Come on, let's go find the others. There are still two more of those bastards down here," David said. Jackson nodded, grabbed his laser rifle and followed David.

Janad led them back the way they had come. She didn't care what David said, she had the safety off the laser. If anyone was stupid enough to stand in front of her when she fired it, then that was their own fault. They heard one loud explosion from outside. Then there was another, and the whole palace shook. They were all sure the palace had been hit. They were almost outside when they rounded a corner, and there blocking the door it stood.

It was huge—easily twice as big as the biggest man Janad had ever seen, and she didn't need anyone to tell her that this was a GSH. This was the thing that was like RJ that you needed the really big gun to kill. She fired the laser sidearm at it, hoping to at the very least slow it down.

It screamed in rage, closed the distance between them in one stride, grabbed her in one hand by her throat and lifted her off the ground. She was sure she was dead, and then the thing screamed again—this time it sounded like someone was pulling its liver out its throat. From the floor where she had dropped when released, Janad looked for the reason why, and she saw that the Prince had found something else that he could do with his new hands. He literally had the thing by the balls.

The GSH started to swing on Taleed, so Janad jumped off the floor, grabbed the thing's arm and held on. Haldeed, seeing what she had done, and that it was working, jumped on his other arm. At least for the moment, it seemed to be mostly immobilized.

"Get off it! Get off it!" David screamed, and she and Taleed and Haldeed all looked at each other.

Janad swallowed hard. "*A'trois*," she said. They both nodded. "*Un, deux, trois!*" They all let go of it each jumping and running in a different direction.

There was a loud explosion, and then the thing was flying through the air and out the door. There was a second explosion outside, and its chest seemed to explode, spreading it all over the palace garden.

David ran up to Janad and took her hand. "Come on, we still have one more of those things to kill."

She smiled and followed, sure—at least in that moment—that he could do anything he put his mind to.

Chapter Seventeen

Stratton landed the ship in the hangar. They waited for the doors to close and the green light to blink telling them that they had atmosphere again before they stepped out of the skiff.

"What happened to the rest of your crew?" the guide-on asked as he looked from Stratton to Bradley. He led them toward the decontamination chamber. They wanted to make sure that no germs or spores made it from the planet's surface into the station.

"They heard about what was happening on the ship and went AWOL," Stratton said. She winked at him—a signal that he understood. He nodded back, and Stratton continued, "That's the main reason I didn't keep in constant contact with the Station. I didn't want to have to explain where they were. While we were gathering information, I was trying to find them—and giving them a chance to come back. But…it's a big planet."

"Things here have been crazy." The guide-on stepped into decontamination with them and put on the jets. "Safe to talk in here. Captain's left, took a fully loaded cruiser with him."

"I know," Stratton said.

He looked at Bradley.

"He's one of us," Stratton said. "We know everything official because Briggs briefed me on the way in. Tell me what we don't officially know."

"Briggs left the ship because there was a prison break and he was afraid to stay here. Figured he'd be safer with the natives. Made up some cockamamie story about wanting to try to keep trade open or some such shit. He left Yumby in charge, and that little bastard is walking around with a pisser hardon you could hang a crowbar on. There's been open fighting throughout the ship ever since they spaced Harker. But I have to tell you, Lieutenant, we ain't doing so good. There are more of them, and they have the GSH's. Twenty of them in all. Oh…and this is some news they aren't releasing to the general populace. The Beta 4 humanoids they sent to Earth— you know, the ones that were supposed to help them in their war with the New Alliance?"

"Yes?" Stratton prompted.

"They just trashed the camps they were being trained in. Killed all the Reliance personnel and ran away. One can only suppose that they've gone to join the New Alliance in New Freedom seeing as that's what the little guy from the New Alliance has been telling us every hour on the hour. He takes over the viewscreens whenever he wants. Briggs is going to burn."

"If he lives," Stratton said thoughtfully. "Listen very carefully. I have brought help. Take four maintenance uniforms and put them on the skiff we just left. Make damn sure no one sees you do it, and make *damn* sure no one goes near that ship till you see four people walk out."

"Can do," he said. He looked at Bradley. "I was sorry to hear about Harker. If it's any consolation, he had a lot of friends here."

"Thanks," Bradley said.

The jets shut off, and when the green light flashed they all stepped out of the unit.

Bradley and Stratton walked out of the hanger together. "Good luck, Stratton," Bradley said.

"You, too, Bradley." She started to leave, but Bradley grabbed her arm. She looked at him.

"I'm glad he had someone like you. Someone to care about him, to love him," he said. "No one should die having never had that."

Tears wet her eyes, but she managed a smile. "I'm glad I had him, too, and I'm glad he had a friend like you…Now let's go. We have work to do."

They went in opposite directions. She went towards the bridge, and he headed for a maintenance conduit.

"You suck," Levits said in a disgusted tone as he looked at RJ.

"Excuse me?" RJ said.

"You even look good in coveralls," he said with a smile.

"Be a good boy, and I'll show you how they become un-coveralls," she said.

"You guys are pushing my puke level," Topaz warned zipping up his suit. "Could you try to stay on task at least until we finish this mission?"

"Says the man who ten minutes from now will be looking for flowers in the main reactor room," Levits said.

RJ laughed as she lifted a large pack onto Poley's back.

There was a knocking on the door, apparently their signal that all was clear. They quickly left the ship. RJ led, and they all trusted that she knew where she was going.

"You there!" a booming voice said from behind them. "Turn around."

They did so slowly. "Can I help you, Corporal?" RJ asked noticing his rank on his lapel.

"I've never seen you four down here before," he said.

"We were transferred because of the riots," she answered. "We've been here all day."

"Then you know that all maintenance workers are required to submit to pop inspections until the rioting has stopped and all of the prisoners have been recaptured. I want to see your ID's, and I want you to dump the contents of that pack right now. We can't have any more of you sink-scrubbers trying to sabotage anything else," he said.

RJ put her hands in her pockets pretending to look for her ID. She looked around and noticed that he was one of only three armed guards in sight, but the three others were moving in. If she could stall him, they'd move themselves into range. She nodded towards Poley, and he started taking the pack off his back slowly.

"It's just some tools we need for working on these ships." She snapped her fingers making the guard jump. "You know, I must have put it in my pants under my coveralls," she said. "I'll just have to take these off."

"What about the rest of you guys, or do you all have as lame an excuse as the hybrid? I think we'll just run all you guys in."

RJ quickly pulled her coveralls down, and the guard saw the chain. "Ah, fuck!" he screamed and turned to run, but the chain caught him around the ankles and she pulled back, slinging his face into the floor and crushing it.

Poley slung the pack into the head of one of the others while RJ was killing the first one.

RJ spun quickly around, and her chain whipped out catching the third guard in the head and crushing her skull instantly. RJ had already wrapped her chain back around her and was pulling up her coveralls when the guide-on ran over to see what all the noise was about. He looked from the bodies to the woman with the chain, and his jaw dropped.

"We…we'll take care of the bodies. You just go," he said. He motioned, and some of the maintenance people ran over and started carting the bodies towards an air lock. When he turned back around they were gone. He looked up at the camera, sighed and then screamed. "Bar the doors! Secure the hangar. No one gets in! This is it, boys and girls! It's showtime." He picked up one of the weapons the guards had dropped and shot out the camera. "Take a look at that, shitheads!"

Stratton walked onto the bridge as if she owned it. She walked over to where Yumby was sitting in the Captain's chair and coughed loudly till he looked up and regarded her with mild annoyance.

"So, are you in charge around here now, Yumby?" Stratton asked.

"Till the Captain gets back…If he does. We haven't heard from him, and we've recorded several large explosions on the planet's surface," Yumby said.

"You know that according to the Chain of Command, as Security Chief I should be in command in a time of crisis with the Captain absent," she said.

"You weren't here. You were out on your important mission. How did that go, by the way?" he asked sarcastically.

"Not well. There is a language barrier that makes it almost impossible to learn anything of value. Therefore it's difficult to learn much from the data you've gathered—if you can get your equipment to work at all with all those damned magnetic pulses. To make things even better, three members of my away team went away, spelled A-W-O-L," she said, walking over to her own console and seeming to check things out. "But, gee! It looks like things have been going worse for you here. A prison break, large-scale rioting, dead bodies everywhere, turds floating down the hallways...."

"Here's something for you, Security Chief, sir. How does someone with a record like yours allow a huge spy ring and a conspiracy of mutiny go on unnoticed and unchecked? Roughly half the crew on this station is running completely amok. Are you going to stand here and tell me that you—you with the perfect record—didn't know what was going on right under your nose?" Yumby asked sarcastically. He nodded, and the two guards at the door moved forward and grabbed her, immediately taking her sidearm from her holster.

"Gee, Yumby. I always thought you were kind of a puppet person. Turns out you actually have a brain up there somewhere," she said. "Too bad Briggs didn't leave you in command a long time ago, because it's too freaking late now. That's the New Alliance down there on the surface of the planet blowing all hell out of Briggs and his troops. And when they're done there, they're going to come up here and blow this station to pieces."

"Then why did you come back up here, Stratton? You can't bluff me." He looked past her at the guards. "Throw her treacherous ass in the brig," Yumby ordered. "I'll enjoy seeing you spaced, Stratton."

"Not as much as I'm going to enjoy seeing you burn," Stratton spat back.

They dragged her to the brig.

"Come on, guys. Do you always want to be one of the bad guys?" Stratton asked. "Don't you just once want to be one of the good guys? Let me go. Join us and we'll take the station away from them. Make it ours."

"Shut up," the one on the right said, hitting her in the head with the heel of his hand.

Stratton was quiet. She went through the degrading full body-cavity search, and then they slung her in a cell in the brig with ten other people. They really weren't doing very well. It looked like the Elites were capturing them faster than they could break out.

Stratton took off her shirt and threw it over the camera. She had to work quickly. God, she hated this! She got down on her knees and stuck her finger down her throat, forcing herself to throw up. It wasn't a pretty sight.

"Stratton! What the hell are you doing?" one of the men in the cell with her asked.

"Quiet, Mallory," she ordered. She dug quickly through the vomit and drew out a half a dozen little round balls not much bigger than a dime.

The guard ran over to the cell. "OK, which one of you traitors covered up the camera?" He looked at her and frowned. "You, hey, Stratton? Well, you got about six seconds to take the shirt off the camera, or I blow a hole right in your pretty little head. Don't think that rank is going to save your ass down here, Stratton. Down here the only person whose rank counts is mine."

"I'm sick," she said.

He looked past her at the vomit.

"That's cute," he said making a face. "You maggots can just live with it. I'm not going to tell you again. Take the shirt off the camera."

"Now that isn't very nice," Stratton said backing away from the door. The people in the cell with her did the same.

"What are you lot up to?" he asked.

"I wanted to use you as a shield," she said with a smile.

"Shield?" he asked in confusion.

"Yeah, I wouldn't want the people across the way to get hurt." She threw one of the balls as she and the other prisoners turned their back to the door. The ball landed at the bottom of the door and exploded. The bars blew apart, sending scrap metal into the guard and slinging him against the cells on the other side of the hall. Sirens started wailing, a music the crew was starting to get way too used to.

"Come on, let's go," Stratton said to the others.

"It's no use, Stratton," Mallory said. "They just activate the GSH's and Elites, recapture us or worse. We can't win."

"Yes, we can," Stratton screamed. "Now just come on. We have to bust everyone out of here. We have to make a diversion so that someone else can take care of the GSH's." She reached down and took the com-link from the twitching, disembodied arm of the dead guard. She held it up. "Hey it still works!"

"In here," Bradley said, removing the cover from the conduit. The four walked in and he shut it back again. "This way." He led them to a huge junction where six service conduits met. About two dozen maintenance men were there waiting for them.

RJ smiled, glad to see them. She started pulling the camera looking units from the bag. "All right. Now half of you will go with Poley, and half will go with Topaz. This is what you're going to do..."

Stratton had used the explosives to blow the main gate. After overpowering and killing the guards posted there, they were sitting in the brig's main control room, systematically deactivating every lock on every cell in the brig.

Soon all the prisoners were out again, but this time they had a specific purpose and informed leadership. This time they would do something more than just cause a little trouble.

"Are you sure that this damn thing is not going to effect us?" Levits asked for the third time as they walked down the hall.

"Of course I'm sure," RJ said. "I wouldn't be messing with it if I wasn't completely sure."

"There are guards posted outside the front door," Bradley said. Just then, the sirens started blaring, signaling that Stratton had successfully accomplished her part, and that they were running a little behind.

They stopped at the door to the bridge, and Bradley showed the work order.

"I'll need to see your IDs" he said.

Bradley pulled his out and showed it. Then the guards looked expectantly at Levits and RJ, and they handed him the IDs they had just taken from two of the other maintenance people.

When they scanned through as being clean, the doors opened, and they walked in.

"What the hell are you doing here?" Yumby demanded.

"Moving the emergency switch as ordered by Briggs, sir," Bradley said.

"I'm in the middle of yet another prison break!" Yumby screamed. "Whole damn place is falling to pieces, and you're moving a freaking button!"

"Just following orders, sir," Bradley explained.

"Damn! Well I guess it won't be any real problem. You need all that stuff?" Yumby asked, looking in disbelief at the two large toolboxes and the armload of equipment..

"It's more complicated than you would think," Bradley explained.

"Well, just do it and get it over with then," Yumby ordered. "If Briggs gets back alive, we wouldn't want him to have yet another thing to bitch about."

RJ smiled and she and Bradley went to work as Levits, trying to act like he was handing them tools, watched their backs.

"Can you believe it, Drex? They're actually moving the damn button! We have to threaten to blow them out of the sky to get them to fix the hole in the side of the ship, toilets backed up everywhere and food services completely non-operational, but the *button* they're going to fix. Right now, no less!" Yumby said.

Fifteen minutes later, when they were still working on it, Yumby asked impatiently, "How long can it take to move a freaking button?"

"It's tied into emergency systems, sir," Bradley explained. "As such, you have to override a lot of safety features."

Yumby walked a little away and started pacing. It didn't seem to Bradley that he was doing too much to solve any of the problems on the station. Mostly he was just walking around trying to look important.

Bradley smiled. *He looks like a freaking idiot. Pompous ass. He's so ignorant you could tell him anything. He doesn't know how anything works, so he doesn't know that a switch could be moved in less than five minutes, and he certainly can't tell that we are planting an ancient alien weapon on the bridge of his ship.*

Ten minutes later Yumby said, "Aren't you finished yet? I have a commanding officer in a possible firefight on the surface of a third-class planet, mass class riots all over my station, and a huge hole in my transport bay to deal with. I'm really getting a little tired of having to step over one of you every three seconds."

RJ finished the last splice on a fiber optic, looked at Bradley and smiled. She brushed her hands off on her coveralls and stood up.

She raised her com-link to her mouth. "Poley?"

"Yes?" he answered.

"Have you finished yet?" RJ asked.

"Yes, we have finished," he answered.

RJ lowered her arm. She took a pair of headphones from her pocket, put them on her head and clicked them on. She turned, looked at Yumby and smiled. "It's ready to go, want to try it?" Not waiting for his answer, she punched the button they had just installed.

"No, don't!" Yumby screamed. "Hey! It doesn't work."

"Yes, it does," RJ said. "It just doesn't work on you." She jumped through the air and landed a well-placed kick to the bridge of his nose.

As he rolled for cover behind the Captain's Chair, Levits pulled the laser from inside his coveralls and shot one of the guards who was standing at the door. RJ ran forward growling, grabbed the other guard by the arm holding his rifle and slammed him—rifle and all—into the wall. As he fell dead to the floor, RJ grabbed the front of her coveralls and ripped them off in one motion. She pulled her chain from her body, looked at Drex, checked his emotions, and then killed him by slapping the chain into his head.

She turned and looked at the others.

"Who else wants to die for the Reliance?" RJ asked quickly. The remaining members of the room were silent, and a quick scan told her that none of them were likely to become aggressive. "What? No takers?"

Bradley had pulled his weapon from where he'd hidden it in his toolbox, but he didn't get a chance to use it. He sort of wished she'd let him kill Yumby. It would have been the next best thing to killing Briggs.

RJ raised her wrist-com to her mouth again. "Stratton, come and take control of the bridge."

"I'm on my way," Stratton answered.

RJ looked at Levits and smiled. "So, are you staying here, or coming with me?"

"Why I'm coming with you, of course, dear," Levits said.

Without the GSH's to contend with, the rebels were able to take complete control of the station in less than six hours. They were now loading the last of the motionless GSH's into a convenient airlock.

"I still don't get it," Levits said. "How come it's affecting the GSH's and not us?"

"Because they're hearing is superior to that of normal humans. I simply moved the frequency to a level no human could detect. That's why I have to have a sonic disrupter," RJ answered.

"It looks like a simple set of radio headphones," Levits said.

"It is," RJ said with a smile.

"But GSH's have no emotions. They aren't afraid of anything," Levits said. "What could they be dreaming?"

"See, that was what I thought until something occurred to me. GSH's have been programmed to serve the Reliance; they have been programmed for loyalty to the Reliance. So they do have a fear. A fear of failing to please the Reliance, a fear of appearing to be less than devoted," RJ said.

They had loaded the last of the GSH's into the air lock. They closed it and walked away. Bradley opened the air lock and watched as the GSH's floated off into space. Soon their terror would end.

"We'll leave the weapon here," RJ said to Stratton. "Who knows? You just might need it again some day. The New Alliance will trade with the natives for the items they need. I trust the two of you to deal with them and with our people honestly."

"How will we get supplies from Earth here or from here to Earth?" Stratton asked.

"Do I have to figure everything out?" RJ asked with a smile. "I'm a woman, not a computer. I don't know…Commandeer the *Kryptonite* and use it to fly things back and forth. You're already connected to Mickey and to Marge. You set up a teleport station in New Freedom and you trade goods."

"How are we going to avoid being shot out of the sky by the Reliance?" Stratton asked.

"Get really good pilots," RJ looked at them and smiled. "Listen, you're smart people. You started this on your own. We couldn't have done any of this if you hadn't already had the ball rolling. I have faith in you. I'm sure you can figure something out. I have more important things to do. Aliens to see, planets to undo."

She started walking.

"Wait a minute, RJ," Stratton said following her. "We need help to set things up here."

"You need help, but you don't need *our* help," RJ said, she just kept walking. "As it is, the Reliance might decide to come and knock you out of the sky. I doubt it, though. Worthless planet only has a few things worth taking, and now has a violently aggressive native population that managed to blow up a fully loaded battle-cruiser and has learned to hate them.

"Add to that a damaged station full of dissidents with no real place to go and with enough fire power to destroy several battleships before they could take it out. Nah, I don't think they're likely to bother you. But me and my crew—we're trophies. If they could put our heads on plates, they could break the back of the New Alliance. Or, at least, they think they could. If we stayed here they'd send an armada out here and blast everything to pieces just to get at us. They wouldn't care about casualties; they wouldn't care about losses. So…when they figure out what's happened here, it will be better for you if we're not here."

"You can do this," Topaz added. They had reached the skiff that was their destination. Topaz hugged Stratton and then Bradley. He turned to Stratton. "I'm only sorry that we didn't have sex at least once."

She laughed. "Ah, me, too."

"Just get on the damned ship, ya old perv," Levits said, giving him a playful shove. Levits got in and started suiting up.

RJ turned at the hatch, looked at them and smiled. "Good luck. I have to tell you—it isn't easy being a legend."

They watched in silence as the hatch closed.

"So, do you think we are legends now?" Bradley asked Stratton as they walked away from the hanger.

Stratton laughed. "To who? Do you really believe that in fifty years anyone is going to remember anything except that RJ, a seven-hundred-year-old man, and a robot AI stepped in here and stomped the Reliance to pieces? You, me, Levits, David—even the Prince—we're all just people. We can't compete." She looked around her there didn't seem to be any part of the station that didn't at least look like a disaster area. "Come on, let's get to work. We have to figure this mess out."

Chapter Eighteen

David looked out the window of the throne room at the city below. He had been surprised at how fast the debris of the battle had been cleaned away. How quickly things had been returned to—if not normal—at least something cleaner and more organized.

He doubted that anything seemed at all normal to the people who lived here, and it was a sure bet things would never be the same again.

Janad walked up behind him and wrapped her arms around his waist.

"They aren't coming back for me, you know," David said.

"Yes, I know," Janad answered. She had known that two weeks ago when a ship had come to get Jackson, and the pilot had been surprised to see David still here. He had offered to take David to the Station. David had insisted on waiting for RJ.

"I can't say that I am not happy that they didn't come for you," Janad said in a whisper.

"Why did she leave me, Janad? Why?" David asked, his torment apparent in the tone of his voice.

"Maybe because she knew how much you are needed here. How much help you can give Taleed, teaching him to be a good king. How much help you can be dealing with the New Alliance." Janad held him tighter. "Maybe she knew how much I wanted you here with me."

David took hold of her hands looking down at them. He didn't turn around; he didn't want her to see the tears in his eyes.

"I'm glad to be with you, too, Janad. I'm even glad to be here. I like it here; I like your people. This place could be

home for me. More a home than Earth has become.
Only…Why did she leave me? Why did she leave me without
even saying goodbye?"

"Because she knows you, David. She knows you could
never say goodbye to her. No matter how much you might
have wanted to stay here, you would not have been able to
watch her go. She wanted you to be happy, and she wants
to be happy, and I don't think either of you can do that if
you're together. Yet neither of you can say goodbye. So
she just left."

David smiled and looked up at the sky. "I will miss them."

"And they will miss you."

RJ lay in their bed on the ship, her head on Levits' chest. She
couldn't sleep.

"You're thinking about him again, aren't you?" Levits asked
gently.

"I know it was the right thing to do. That doesn't make it
easy," RJ said. "I'm wondering if he'll ever understand why I
did it."

"I'm not sure I understand why you did it," Levits said,
running his hand over her hair.

"Truthfully, because I couldn't forgive him, Levits. I tried,
but I just couldn't. I couldn't, and I know that he knew that I
couldn't." She gently untangled herself from him, got up,
walked to the porthole and looked out at the vastness of hyperspace. "He reminded me of my pain, and I was his constant reminder, too. Neither he nor I deserved to live in the
hell we had created, and neither of us knew how to stop it.
This was the only way."

Levits got up, bringing the blanket with him and walked
over to her wrapping them both in it although he knew she
wasn't cold. "He'll miss you."

She leaned her head back into his chest. "And I will miss
him."

Taleed handed his handwritten proclamation to the priest. It was sloppy and damn near unreadable, but the priest took it and smiled.

"I have written that letter in my own hand," Taleed said. "And it bears the seal of the King. That would be me. Let runners take the decree throughout the land. I have written all that has come to pass, what is to be done with the tainted gold, and how the Priests are to behave in their office. Knowledge will no longer be treated as an evil. The Great Books shall be copied, and everyone who desires may read them. No longer will the King force women to serve him to give him abundant children that the land cannot support.

"Birth control techniques will be taught to all the people, and it shall be seen as their civic duty that they do not bring children to the world that they cannot feed. We will tend to our land and make it prosper, so that together these two things will ensure that never again will one of our people have to make war against another. Our warriors will train, and we will remain strong, but we shall do so not to fight amongst ourselves but to stay everready to fight the evil of the Reliance. An evil that The Ancestor warned us about and that corrupt priests ignored for personal gain, almost causing the destruction of our world and our people."

He looked down at the priest and smiled. "There is more in the letter, but those are the high points."

"My Lord…What about the holy breeding program? What will become of us if we turn so completely from our old ways?"

"We shall evolve as we were meant to evolve," Taleed said with a laugh. "Now do as I have told you, or I will have your head cut off."

The priest jumped to his feet from where he had been kneeling. "I was just kidding," Taleed laughed out as the priest quickly departed. He looked at Haldeed and smiled. "I really was just kidding, Haldeed."

It wasn't very funny, Haldeed signed.

Jessit walked in, wearing the clothing of the High Priest.

"My King," he said scratching his head. "I was wondering."

"Yes, Jessit?" Taleed asked.

"What is our religion now? I mean...I understand why you want the priests to continue their duties. They must or the generators will die. I understand why you have left them as leaders of the community; there must be an order to things, but...What is it that we now *believe*? Who are our gods?"

"I don't know," Taleed said with a laugh. "Do we need any?"

"Oh, yes, I think we do. We need something that the people can believe in. Something safe, or they will make up something horrible," Jessit said.

"You're the High Priest. You make something up and tell me what you decide," Taleed said. "Now go away before I have your head cut off."

"What?" Jessit asked in shock.

Taleed laughed. "It's just a joke."

"Well, it isn't very funny," Jessit said leaving.

Haldeed gave Taleed an *I told you so* look, and the young King shrugged. He sat back in his throne, put his feet up, picked up a glass of wine and took a drink, spilling half of it on his shirt. He didn't care. He could spill a gallon of wine at a time, and the little he got into his mouth would still taste sweeter if he held the glass in his own hand.

He smiled broadly at his friend. "Ah now, Haldeed, this is indeed a great adventure."

Selina Rosen's Autobiography

Selina Rosen lives in rural Arkansas with her partner of ten years, and assorted animal and plant life. Besides writing, she enjoys (heavy) sword fighting, fencing, building things from trash, gardening, and making smug people feel small. She also enjoys drinking and singing really dirty songs.

Selina has been writing almost every day of her life since she was twelve. She has tried to quit on occasion without success, and hopes that some day "they" will come up with a twelve-step program for writers to help them with their addiction.

Her short fiction has appeared in several issues of *Marion Zimmer Bradley's Fantasy Magazine*, and anthologies such as *Such A Pretty Face*, *Sword and Sorceress 16*, and *Personal Demons* to name a few.

Other Meisha Merlin titles include *Queen of Denial*, and the first book in this series (oh...you didn't know there was a first book? Now things are starting to make sense!)...*Chains of Freedom*.

She and a few other masochists own and run Yard Dog Press, which would explain why YDP carries so many of her titles, including... *The Bubba Chronicles* (a collection of her short fiction both horror and sci-fi), *The Host Series*, *Fire and Ice*, and a sci-fi/police procedural/horror novella entitled *The Boat Man*.

She has also edited two anthologies, *Stories That Won't Make Your Parents Hurl* (children's horror), and *Bubbas of the Apocalypse* a shared universe anthology of her own creation... be afraid—be very afraid!

She publishes installments of her science fiction novel-in-progress, *Torque City Blues*, on a monthly basis at the Yard Dog website. She also posts new "rants" on the website fairly often, because as she says you can't work in this business and not stay pissed off!

www.YardDogPress.com

CHAINS OF FREEDOM

Selina Rosen

ISBN 1-892065-42-8
$16.00

"Let me tell you the short details about Selina Rosen. She's a creative soul, a builder in wood and stone and words…knows farm life, knows how to build a room, or a plot…can cope with goats and chickens, or neophyte writers. Out of this absolute wealth of diverse experience come truly outrageous ideas and a way of looking at the universe with [in some books] humor and [in other books] attitude with a capital A.

"You want a friend who'll show up with help and a truck when others are "busy that weekend", you've got Selina Rosen. That honesty shows up in the characters she writes. She's one in a million."

—C. J. Cherryh, (As posted on her web site.)

ISBN 1-892065-06-1
$12.00

"If there's such a thing as blue-collar sf, this is it. No spiffy interstellar SUVs here-Rosen's characters horse the futuristic equivalent of dented vintage Ford S-10s around the stars. With plenty of action, violence, foolin' around, and a generous tongue planted just a touch firmly in cheek, *Queen of Denial* takes some old and honored tropes of science fiction, and turns them into the kind of bawdy full-bodied entertainment western literature's furnished since long before Shakespeare."—Ed Bryant

An excerpt from chapter one of

Recycled,

the secquel to Selina Rosen's
Queen of Denial. **(May 2003)**

"But Drew said…" Stasha started.

"We can't always do what Drewcila Qwah says, Stasha. She does not have the best interests of the kingdom at heart," Zarco said. "She is self serving and mercenary!"

"It's true, no one knows the queen's short comings any better than I. Drewcila worries about nothing quite as much as her own best interests, and having a good time. But sire, let us not forget that what serves Qwah-Co ultimately serves the kingdom. She would never do anything that might cut into her profit margins. *What's good for Qwah-Co…* I'm afraid I have to agree with the queen in this matter," Facto said.

"Do you hear yourself, Facto? What you are saying? She is suggesting that we open up trade with the Lockhedes. They threaten to make war with us unless we help them set up a salvaging operation of their own and make trade agreements. They threaten us, and she wants to give them exactly what they want, to give in to their demands, and you think this is a good and sane notion!"

"Because it's what we want, too. Everything Drewcila has said is true," Stasha said in a small if convicted voice. "It's a chance for a real and lasting peace. A chance to finally unite the planet. What would better serve our people than this? Drewcila says that by making them economically stable they will have no reason to start another war. That by doing business with them we can gain control over them."

"Drewcila says! Drewcila says!" Zarco jumped out of his chair slinging his arms around and started pacing the room. "I can't believe you, any of you! These are the *Lockhedes* we're talking about! They are the ancient enemy of our people! Their brutality in war is known throughout the galaxy. They have killed, tortured, maimed, and mutilated countless thousands of our people, and now you want to make them economically stable. You think that if they are economically stable they won't make war, and I tell you that if we help to make them rich they will buy bigger weapons and come after us to wipe us out entirely. They don't want peace. They want to take over the planet and slaughter us." He glared down at Stasha. "Do I have to remind you that one the people they kidnapped and tortured was your own dear sister? That those butchers surgically removed a part of her brain making her basically dead to us? Turning her from our noble queen into a beer swilling, toilet mouthed, scavenging whore!"

"Oh that's a little harsh. I don't think my sister's a whore, Zarc..."

This seemed to make the king even madder. Wordlessly, Facto watched him rant on. When he got like this, and he did often these days, there was no talking to him.

He muttered and cursed on and on until finally he ended with, "...they took my wife, and they turned her into Drewcila Qwah!" and slammed his ass into his throne very unmajestically.

Come check out our web site for details on these Meisha Merlin authors!

Kevin J. Anderson

Robert Asprin

Robin Wayne Bailey

Edo van Belkom

Janet Berliner

Storm Constantine

John F. Conn

Diane Duane

Sylvia Engdahl

Rain Graves

Jim Grimsley

George Guthridge

Keith Hartman

Beth Hilgartner

P. C. Hodgell

Tanya Huff

Janet Kagan

Caitlin R. Kiernan

Lee Killough

George R. R. Martin

Lee Martindale

Jack McDevitt

Mark McLaughlin

Sharon Lee & Steve Miller

James A. Moore

John Morressy

Adam Niswander

Andre Norton

Jody Lynn Nye

Selina Rosen

Kristine Kathryn Rusch

Pamela Sargent

Michael Scott

William Mark Simmons

S. P. Somtow

Allen Steele

Mark Tiedeman

Freda Warrington

David Niall Wilson

www.MeishaMerlin.com